PENGUIN BOOKS

Lionheart

Stewart Binns began his professional life as an academic. He then pursued several adventures, including that of a school-teacher, specializing in history, before becoming an award-winning documentary-maker and latterly an author. His television credits include the 'In-Colour' genre of historical documentaries, notably the BAFTA and Grierson winner *Britain at War in Colour* and the Peabody winner *The Second World War in Colour*.

He also launched *Trans World Sport* in 1987, *Futbol Mundial* in 1993, the International Olympic Committee *Camera of Record* in 1994 and the Olympic Television Archive Bureau in 1996.

Currently chief executive and co-founder, with his wife, Lucy, of the independent production and distribution company Big Ape Media International, Stewart has in recent years continued to specialize in historical documentaries, including a series on the Korean War, the history of Indo-China and a major study of modern Japan.

His previous novels *Conquest*, *Crusade* and *Anarchy* were published to great acclaim.

Stewart's passion is English history, especially its origins and folklore. His home is in Somerset, where he lives with his wife and twin boys, Charlie and Jack.

www.stewartbinns.com

D0262585

Lionheart

STEWART BINNS

PENGUIN BOOKS

PENGUIN BOOKS

Published by the Penguin Group
Penguin Books Ltd, 80 Strand, London WC2R ORL, England
Penguin Group (USA) Inc., 375 Hudson Street, New York, New York 10014, USA
Penguin Group (Canada), 90 Eglinton Avenue East, Suite 700, Toronto, Ontario, Canada M4P 2Y3
(a division of Pearson Penguin Canada Inc.)
Penguin Ireland, 25 St Stephen's Green, Dublin 2, Ireland (a division of Penguin Books Ltd)
Penguin Group (Australia), 707 Collins Street, Melbourne, Victoria 3008,
Australia (a division of Pearson Australia Group Pty Ltd)
Penguin Books India Pvt Ltd, 11 Community Centre,
Panchsheel Park, New Delhi – 110 017, India
Penguin Group (NZ), 67 Apollo Drive, Rosedale, Auckland 0632, New Zealand
(a division of Pearson New Zealand Ltd)
Penguin Books (South Africa) (Pty) Ltd, Block D, Rosebank Office Park, 181 Jan Smuts Avenue,
Parktown North, Gauteng 2193, South Africa

Penguin Books Ltd, Registered Offices: 80 Strand, London WC2R ORL, England

www.penguin.com

First published 2013

1

Copyright © Stewart Binns, 2013

Typeset in 12.5/14.75pt Garamond MT Std by Palimpsest Book Production Ltd,
Falkirk, Stirlingshire
Printed in England by Clays Ltd, St Ives plc

ISBN: 978–1–405–91360–7

www.greenpenguin.co.uk

To all those who love history

Contents

Introduction

Towards the end of the reign of Henry II, the Plantagenet Empire stretched across a huge swathe of north-west Europe. The Scots had declared their fealty to Westminster, and Ireland and Wales both acknowledged the English King as their liege lord. Across the Channel, all French domains – save those of the King of the Franks, in Paris, and the Count of Toulouse – were part of a vast realm that stretched from the north of Scotland to the Pyrenees.

Like his father before him, and his Norman predecessors before that, Henry was all-powerful, especially when allied with his remarkable wife, Eleanor of Aquitaine. Fortunately, their lineage included sufficient sprinklings of the blood of their diverse subjects, including the English, to keep any adversaries at bay. However, Henry and Eleanor produced eight offspring who were so formidable they were soon called the 'Devil's Brood'. They included two future queens and two kings, but the most remarkable of all was the sixth child, Richard, Duke of Aquitaine, who would be called 'Lionheart' before the age of twenty – and fifteen years before he would become King of England.

His physical presence, his domineering personality and his remarkable military prowess – not only as a general of armies but also in hand-to-hand combat – made him a legend in his own lifetime. His struggles during the Third

Crusade against the Sultan Saladin (himself one of the most revered men in Muslim history) soon became one of the most compelling stories of the Middle Ages.

But there was more to Richard's lineage than he realized. When he became King of England on 6 July 1189, there were two men with him who had been charged with protecting the young King and guiding his future. One of them was a knight of the realm, chosen for his martial skills and personal integrity, and the other was a monk, a wise man of letters, who carried vital clues about Richard's past – evidence that would shape his future and that of England. This is their story.

1. Old Man

When I first saw the old man, it was as if I was looking at an apparition, a venerated image held in my memory since childhood.

As a boy, I had been told the stories about England's ancient heroes many times: the great King Harold and his mighty housecarls, who fought to the death at Senlac Ridge in a valiant attempt to defeat the Conqueror's Norman army; the gallant defenders of the Siege of Ely, the last of the brave souls who had defied Norman rule; and the most courageous of them all, Hereward of Bourne, the leader of England's final rebellion, about whom people still spoke with hushed reverence.

These men of legend wore their hair and beards long, carried the round shields of Saxon tradition and went into battle wielding their fearsome battleaxes. But they were from another time, a distant memory. Senlac Ridge had happened over a hundred years ago, and even though there were a few old men alive who claimed that their grandfathers could remember Hereward and the early days of the Conquest, no one really believed them.

Now everyone trimmed their hair and beards like our Norman masters. We wore Norman clothes, with their elaborate embroidery and rich colours, and we carried Norman weapons and armour. To all intents and purposes, we *were* Normans – except in our hearts, which still coursed with English blood.

But the old man in front of me did not resemble a Norman. Apart from his age – he must have been well into his seventies – he was the epitome of the English heroes of the past. Of a winter's eve, when I had sat by the fire and listened to my father tell me tales of Old England and enjoyed the ancient ballads sung to me by my mother, in my imagination I had conjured images of formidable warriors just like the man I now faced.

He was tall and broad-shouldered, with a prodigious mane of silver-grey hair flowing down the back of his heavy cloak. His hoary beard fell in gentle waves and came to rest on his chest. His weapons and armour, unmistakeably Old English, shone with a lustre born of diligent care. With eyes that were clear and sharp and skin that, although wrinkled and weathered, glowed with ruddy health, he was the living embodiment of a little boy's fantasy of heroes long gone.

But he was a contemporary lord and, by the look of the heavy seal on his ring and the ermine trim to his cloak, an earl of the realm. As far as I knew, all our lords were Normans. How was it possible for a man to be a Norman earl and yet appear to be the embodiment of England's past?

It was September 1176. I had been summoned to Wolvesey Castle in Winchester by the royal warrant of the man I served, Henry Plantagenet, King Henry II. I was part of the King's retinue at Westminster and commanded a squadron of his cavalry. I had been dubbed a knight of the realm, which, as an Englishman, was as high as I could hope to rise in the military hierarchy of the Norman army.

I was twenty-five years old and needed only to complete another eight to ten years' service before having sufficient savings to buy a small estate and live out my days in relative comfort. I would have needed a wife, of course, and I had already begun to cast my eye over suitable young ladies within London's merchant families.

Again, I was hindered by my kith and kin. The ladies of the court were almost all from Norman families and, in the main, beyond the reach of a lowly Englishman like me, no matter how eligible I may have thought I was. However, many of London's merchants were Englishmen who had managed to make their wealth by cosseting the Norman elite. So, one of their daughters was the finest bride a young buck of my modest lineage could hope for.

Life's course seemed fixed for me; I had done well, especially for an Englishman, and, as often as I could, I remembered to tell myself to count my blessings. But a life with a secure future is not necessarily a contented one. I often yearned for more, but what 'more' might be was never clear to me. When the yearnings became stronger, I made them go away by convincing myself that everyone wanted more in their lives – money, women, adventure, fame – and that it was childish to crave unattainable rewards.

Although I could make the hankerings disappear for a while, they would always come back, especially during the long cold winters in our meagre barracks in Westminster. Being a professional soldier appeared to offer a life of adventure and reward, but it was usually monotonous and dreary. Apart from occasional skirmishes against the Welsh princes, when we would reinforce the King's garrisons at Glastonbury and Gloucester, we spent most of our time providing the King's bodyguard and enduring the endless tedium of court ceremonials.

I had led my squadron on two of the King's forays against raiders in the Scottish borders, but the actions had been brief and routine. One had brought but a brief glimpse of the enemy – and, even then, only of their rear ends as they fled into the Cheviots to skulk in their hilltop lairs – and the other had been no more than a hunting expedition, as we ran down and despatched a fleeing band of brigands who were too frightened to stand and fight.

But I had been involved in one serious encounter, one that had won me my knight's pennon and bloodied me in the forbidding truths of war.

It happened in 1171, shortly after I had been given command of my own conroi of cavalry. They were a motley assembly: a few reliable Anglo-Normans; half a dozen trustworthy Englishmen; and a dubious selection of Welsh, Bretons and Angevins, whose only loyalty was to the purse on offer. We had been sent by King Henry to join a small force led by Raymond FitzGerald, a powerful warlord from Pembroke and second-in-command to Richard de Clare, Second Earl of Pembroke, known to everyone as 'Strongbow'.

De Clare and FitzGerald were made of stern stuff. The offspring of marriage settlements between Norman lords who had invaded South Wales and the daughters of Welsh princes whose domains had been surrendered, they had been raised on the lawless fringes of the Norman Empire.

FitzGerald was the grandson of Nest, daughter of Rhys ap Tewdwr, who had been described as the 'Helen of Wales'. Her beauty had led her into the bed of Henry Beauclerc, King Henry's grandfather. Nothing daunted FitzGerald, and when Strongbow asked him to lead an expedition to Ireland – to begin the conquest of the island on behalf of the King – he took only 10 knights and 100 men, including my conroi of 25 cavalry.

We landed at Baginbun Head on the Hook Peninsula, near Waterford, where we were besieged in our hastily fortified camp by a combined force of Irishmen and Ostmen. Facing an army at least 3,000 strong, we were vastly outnumbered. But when FitzGerald saw their chaotic and ill-disciplined approach, he devised a cunning ploy.

We had rounded up a large herd of cattle shortly after our landing and enclosed them in our compound. I was ordered to set them loose and use my horsemen to drive them headlong into the oncoming enemy ranks. The terrified cattle careened into the enemy like a battering ram, bowling over the front ranks like skittles and scattering most of the rest. FitzGerald then led his infantry in a charge, and they proceeded to cut down the hapless remnants in large numbers.

I then pursued those fleeing the scene; we killed dozens and rounded up many more. Some we ran down on horseback, but when our mounts became exhausted we dismounted and scoured the countryside on foot, inflicting more slaughter. It was the worst bloodletting I had been involved in.

It was one-sided and brutal, and I lost all sense of danger. As night drew in, many of my men receded into the gloom and, save for a few, I became detached from the rest of the conroi. When I checked who was with me, I felt suddenly alarmed that none seemed reliable. My English and Norman colleagues were nowhere to be seen, and I appeared to have only a small contingent of Angevins and Bretons. I became concerned; I had made the fundamental mistake of acting without thinking of the consequences. Then, out of the darkness, a dozen or more Ostmen were upon us in an instant. Instead of coming to my side as a disciplined unit, and despite my orders not to do so, my men scattered in every direction. Fortunately, most of the Ostmen followed them, sensing blood. Even so, I was left with four adversaries, all seething with anger from the mauling they had been given earlier.

I acted without hesitation; my training and discipline took over, and I launched myself at them rather than wait for their assault. For the first time, I realized how effective my years of training had been. I could move with more fluid speed than my adversaries could muster, and my blows were more accurate and powerful. I cut them down without mercy, and although I suffered a few gashes, mostly absorbed by my armour – and one heavy blow to the side of my helmet, which made me reel a little – within a few moments all four men were at my feet, their blood mingling in pools.

There is nothing like fresh blood. It is both disgusting – after all, it signifies pain and death – and captivating, the essence of our lives, like the best of wine. I stared at the ever-increasing flow from the now lifeless bodies and thought about the sons, husbands and fathers I had just killed. All their deeds and memories were now seeping into the ground like water spilled from a pail.

The bodies did not move, nor did they breathe; I was surrounded by the gloom of dusk and the silence of death. I had lost all trace of my men and thought better of stumbling into any more of the enemy, so I found a small gulley to hide in for the night. I did not sleep at first – my heart pumped from the day's ferment, and my mind was full of thoughts about the drama of the encounter – but eventually I fell into a fitful sleep.

My slumber was full of vivid dreams, the most powerful of which would recur for the rest of my life. It was fanciful, of course, but it seemed so real.

I was standing with the legends of England's past. It was not clear where we were, but they were all there: the mighty Alfred, King Harold, Hereward of Bourne and many others, all formed into a small, final redoubt of kings, earls and knights. We were on a hill and all around us was an enemy army so large it appeared to be a sea of men and horses. I was behind our legendary leaders, who were taking the brunt of the attack, but suddenly the noble Hereward demanded the attention of King Alfred and pointed to our rear. With a look of alarm, Alfred called to me: *Sir Ranulf, look to the rear, hold your position, all England depends on you!*

At that point I turned, to be confronted, no more than twenty yards away, by a huge wave of mounted knights. They were a wall of horses and men, armour, shields and swords – a wall so high, I could not see anything behind it. I looked to my left and right and, to my horror, suddenly seemed to be alone. I turned back towards my leaders, who were still there, but their forms were now indistinct, ghostly, as if they were disappearing. But not so

7

the enemy wall. Its men were now within striking distance; I could feel the breath of the huge destriers on my face.

Swords were raised and lances were couched above me. But my response was far from gallant; I lowered my sword, fell to my knees and waited for the blows. However, just when they should have landed, I woke from my fantasy with a jolt of terror and felt the cold sweat of fear all over my body.

It took me many minutes in the dank early morning, in that remote place in Ireland, to regain my composure. I became a warrior that day, and also a man. I discovered what I could do and realized the price that I would always have to pay.

With the return of daylight, I was soon able to find my horse and my men. By midday I had rejoined FitzGerald's army, where I was treated as a hero.

In hindsight, our actions had been vicious and cruel, but at the time the morality of our actions was not a consideration. Our training as soldiers had become paramount and we had done what we were required to do. The result was that over a thousand of our enemy were either killed or captured. Strongbow returned with a larger army a year later, and King Henry arrived at Waterford with a large fleet shortly afterwards – the first English king to set foot in Ireland. The Irish kings submitted to him in Dublin; the English lordship of Ireland had begun.

I was rewarded for my part in the initial victory at Waterford with my knight's pennon and a personal tribute from the King.

So, I had done my share of fighting and had killed a few wretched souls in battle. But unlike some of my comrades, it was not an activity that I approached mindlessly. It seemed to me that war was a part of our lives and that soldiers had to fight to keep their kingdom safe and maintain its discipline. Thus it was a means to an end, not an end in itself. Nevertheless, as I had chosen the life of a warrior, I had to excel in my profession in order to survive, and that is what I had always striven to do.

Then, when the direction of my life seemed set and my future predictably clear, came my intriguing summons to Winchester. Did it offer the opportunity for new adventures? I hoped so. I knew I was one of the most highly regarded of the King's men; my status as commander of a conroi of cavalry attested to that, as did my elevation as a knight. Had I been chosen for a special mission, or just as a mundane messenger for a matter of trivia in the royal household? I feared it would be the latter – except that the old man before me did not appear to be the kind of individual to engage in court trivia.

There had been little prospect of adventure when I was a boy. My father was the local priest of a small community called Heysham on the northern coast, close to Lancaster. His church was an Old Saxon chapel – one of the few built in stone in the entire area – which looked out to sea from atop a rocky headland. He was very proud of his parish and its long history stretching back to the early days of our Christian faith.

He told me that we had Norse blood on both sides of his family and made sure that I was fluent in the Danish languages spoken in the hills to the north and east and across the Western Sea, in Ireland. My mother came from the lands beyond the Great Sands to the north, from a place called Keswick, in the Cumbrian hills, and she was equally proud of her Celtic roots. Hers was a mixed community of Celts and Anglo-Danes, but she was un-equivocally a Celt. Her native language was very different from English and Danish; like my father, she made sure that I was fluent in it.

The rule in the house was simple: when we were together, we spoke English; when I was alone with my father, we spoke Danish; and when I was with my mother, it was always Celtic. It was a good grounding in languages, which my father embellished by giving me a strong grasp of Latin and, of course, fluency with the guttural tones of our Norman lords. Latin was difficult, but Norman was less so because, as my father often pointed out, it was based on the language of the Normans' Viking ancestors, who hailed from the same lands as my Danish forefathers.

We saw Normans only rarely. Twice a year our lord, Henry de Lacy, Lord of Bowland and Baron of Ponte-fract, would send his steward to collect our taxes. The de Lacys were to be treated with caution. Their domain extended across the entire north-west of the country and as far east as the great keep at Pontefract. Three of the de Lacys had fought with the Conqueror at Senlac Ridge, and the present family had lost none of its forebears' renowned ferocity. There was a large garrison of their men at Lancaster, whose main job was to patrol the old road to the north, all the way to Carlisle. The family also kept a small force at Preston and another one at Clitheroe.

Over the years, as my father and I made our monthly visits to the burgh of Lancaster so that he could attend meetings of the local clergy, I had watched the many foreign masons build the new stone castle at Lancaster. Slowly, but relentlessly, it loomed over us like the monstrous edifice of giants, built to remind everyone that what had happened to our land in the distant past – and the result of those events – was an everlasting reality.

My father had told me many times about the devastation of the north by the Conqueror, as he punished the local populace for their rebellion of 1069. Tens of thousands were killed and the farms laid waste. For three generations the lands north of Chester and the Humber were abandoned, the fields becoming a wilderness. Only within my lifetime were people rebuilding the villages and ploughing the ground again. Lancaster was one of the many places that were beginning to flourish in the uneasy truce between Norman and Englishman.

Almost no one believed that the Normans would ever relinquish control of our lives, but that did not prevent us from cherishing our English language and folk memories. As a boy, I had feared our Norman masters and thought of them as a different breed. But after several years of serving with them and for them, I had come to realize that they were not very different from us at all.

Most importantly, we English knew that our King, the formidable Henry Plantagenet, although a Norman in words and deeds, also carried enough English blood to make him as much 'one of us' as he was a Norman. His mother, the Empress Matilda, who had styled herself 'Lady of the English', was a direct descendant of the ancient Cerdician kings of England and Wessex, tracing her lineage all the way back to Alfred the Great. That simple fact of genealogy was so important to us; despite its daunting Norman facade, it made our blood a living part of the inheritance of our kingdom.

We also took great comfort in the fact that King Henry ruled an empire far bigger than either England or Normandy, making us all feel part of a mighty dominion of many peoples, languages and traditions, a vast realm of which we could all be proud. Not only that, but after several generations, our Norman rulers had come to adopt many of our customs and all could now speak English. There were so many of us, and so few of them, that they had no choice; our mother tongue had become the customary language, while the Normans kept to their own idiom among themselves and at court. Even so, Latin was always the language of government, both secular and spiritual.

My father knew that a good education afforded me one of the few routes to any kind of future. The Church, especially one of the great northern monasteries, was the objective he set for me. He worked tirelessly to make sure I had the intellectual gifts and personal discipline to succeed – so that when it came time for me to be subjected to the rigours of examination by the all-powerful abbot and his inquisitors, I would be ready.

Now, in the Great Hall at Wolvesey, I faced a similarly intimidating encounter.

'I am Harold of Hereford, Earl of Huntingdon.'

When the dignified old man spoke to me, he reminded me of my father (especially when he used to mimic the austere tones of the Abbot of Rievaulx, an imposing man typical of his Norman kind). The Earl spoke in English, without any hint of a Norman accent, confirming my assumption that I was in the presence of a man of my own kin.

'My Lord, I am Ranulf of Lancaster, in the service of our King, Henry Plantagenet.'

He looked at me with an intensity that was disconcerting. He did not speak for what seemed like an age. I wondered whether I was supposed to bring a message or say something else. It was not that being in nerve-racking circumstances was a new experience for me. The King and his earls often bellowed in my direction, and even directly at me. It was part of the life of an officer in the King's retinue; I had become accustomed to it.

I was one of only three Englishmen to have been accepted into the elite bodyguard, an accolade my father was both shocked and dubious to hear about. He had long accepted that a path in the service of our spiritual Lord was not one I would follow, but my submission to our temporal lord, King Henry, was difficult for him to accept. He had little time for men of violence, especially for those in the pay of our Norman rulers.

But the life of a warrior had become an inevitability for me. Even as a young boy, it was obvious I was stronger than other boys of my age. I could outrun them, throw further than they could, and I was able to wrestle the toughest of them to the ground. I was not the biggest boy in the area, although bigger than most, but I could intimidate anyone. It was not that I was fearless, but I enjoyed physical challenges, especially those involving the thrill of victory. Wrestling matches and children's trials of strength soon developed into military training with the men of the area and, by the age of fourteen, I was a fully accepted member of the local fyrd.

I was soon nominated to train with Lord de Lacy's

garrison at Pontefract and in less than two years had been accepted into the King's elite bodyguard. Life since then had been good. I was taller than most men, strong of arm and – so I was told by several female acquaintances, admittedly some more discerning than others – was handsome 'in a craggy sort of way'. My Celtic heritage gave me dark-brown hair, but the English blood in me gave me eyes the colour of honey and meant that every summer my tresses were bleached fair by the sun.

I tried not to be vain, but if I ever got the chance to look at myself in a lady's mirror or in still water, I was content with what I saw. More importantly, I never seemed to have trouble finding female companions – a mighty godsend to a professional soldier far from home.

After what seemed like an eternity, the old warrior spoke again.

'Your record in service to your King is to your credit, Sir Ranulf. Where sits your ambition?'

It was an unexpectedly direct question; I was thrown a little by it, and also by his piercing gaze.

'To continue to serve England, my King and my Lord.'

'That is a predictable but trite answer, young man. What about your *real* ambition?'

I was nonplussed. I had not expected questions like these, and I realized I was not properly prepared for the encounter. The Earl raised his hand and glanced at the two sergeants standing either side of him. They immediately bowed to him and took their leave. The Earl then walked over to the hearth and sat by the fire. I noticed that he appeared sprightly enough, but that he had a distinct limp and his face showed the hint of a wince of pain with every step. He sat down heavily and was suddenly less austere as he relaxed in front of the glowing embers. He stared into the flickering light almost absent-mindedly.

There was another pause.

'Join me by the fire.'

I remained standing, feeling sure the invitation did not extend to informality. I was wrong.

'Sit, boy!'

The stern look had returned to his face. But as I sat opposite him, he produced the beginnings of a grin.

'Don't be in awe of me; I am a lad from the English provinces, just like you. My men have gone, so we can speak openly.'

I had heard the name 'Earl of Huntingdon' and had assumed that the old man was one of our many Norman masters. But 'Harold of Hereford' meant nothing to me, except that it was clearly an English name. I sat down hesitantly, not having any idea what the next question would be – or, indeed, why I had been summoned to Winchester in the first place.

Wolvesey was an imposing place. The largest royal palace outside Westminster, it sat next to the mighty cathedral, the only two buildings that had survived the great fire of twenty-five years earlier, during the civil war between King Stephen and the Empress Matilda. We were alone in a hall so large that in the encroaching gloom of the afternoon I could not see the doorway at the end. There was an eerie silence, save for the distant jangling of activity in the kitchens and the hiss and crackle of the fire.

'Where are you from?'

I told the Earl my story, as confidently as I could.

Gradually the relaxed setting put me at ease, and I finished with something of a flourish as I described my pride in being selected to serve the King.

'You have done well. I am told you are a fine soldier, the most highly regarded Englishman in the King's guard.'

'My Lord Earl, that is not the highest of accolades. There are only three of us in the King's retinue—'

'Do not be too modest. The King's Constable holds you in the highest regard.'

He stared at me again, but this time more gently, almost benignly.

'I had a stroke of great good fortune as a young knight, but I also had my future forged by tragedy and hardship. Are you prepared to face the same, should an opportunity come your way?'

I realized immediately that there was a challenge in the offing. I began to feel my heart race a little as the Earl continued.

'I am looking for a special man, one who can carry a burden for me. The load is exceptional and it involves many years of devotion and almost certainly much sacrifice. Are you ready to be examined to determine whether you are that man?'

I had no idea what to say. A brave man would have said 'yes' immediately; perhaps a wise man would have said that his answer depended on the nature of the challenge. I knew it was unwise to vacillate, so I gulped hard and chose the former option.

'Yes, my Lord.'

'A brave answer, Sir Ranulf, but possibly an imprudent

one. You and I will soon find out whether your choice was wise.'

The Earl looked up to King Henry's huge war banner above the fireplace. Emblazoned with England's two lions rampant, quartered with the fleur-de-lis of his French ancestors, it was meant to be a war banner that all in his realm could follow.

'I have one more question for you. I understand you have Celtic, Danish and English blood. Yet you serve a Norman king. How does that sit with your heritage?'

'It sits comfortably, my Lord. The King carries English blood as well. He rules this land justly; that is all a man can ask for.'

He smiled broadly.

'Very good, young knight. A fine answer.'

I felt a shiver of anticipation and not a little apprehension. What was this burden I was going to be asked to carry?

I had no fear about facing an examination of my worthiness, but I wondered why my heritage was important. I was intrigued and excited. Was this my chance to play a part in the future of England? If it was, nothing on earth would prevent me from grasping it.

With a little difficulty, the Earl pushed himself up from the large carved-oak chair. I jumped to attention as he stretched to his full height.

'There will be times when you will regret accepting this challenge. After I leave this room, the examination will begin. It will take several weeks; at the end of it, we will both know whether you are the man I seek. Many men have accepted my challenge. All have failed.'

He turned and began to walk away into the shadows of the Great Hall, the flicker of the fire dancing on the back of his long, dark cloak. After a few strides he spoke again.

'In a few minutes, a knight called Máedóc will come for you. You will be under his command for the duration of the tests. He is Irish, from Limerick, formerly champion to the warlord Dermot O'Brien. When his lord was blinded by his cousin, Donal the Great, King of Thomond, he sided with the Anglo-Normans. Don't cross him; you will regret it.'

Then he stopped and turned his head towards me before speaking for the last time.

'Good fortune, Ranulf of Lancaster.'

After the echo of the Earl's heavy footsteps had waned, the hall became silent once more. I turned to stare into the fire. Its embers had died to a faint glow and I felt a sudden shiver.

Winter was coming . . . and so was my test.

2. Ordeal

I heard the great oak door at the end of the hall open again, but it was not Máedóc, merely two stewards who had come to tend the fire. They looked at me curiously as they went about their chores. Were they looking at me as if I was a beast bound for the slaughterhouse? Others had gone before me; did they know what trials awaited me?

My anxious musings were soon ended by the sound of four pairs of heavy footsteps reverberating around the walls. A quartet of formidable warriors appeared. Their leader, a very large man with the mien of a cathedral gargoyle, spoke in Gaelic, most of which I understood.

'I am Máedóc. My men are Óengus, Fáelán and Mochán. From now on, you will do everything we say without hesitation. Remove your weapons and armour.'

As a trained soldier, I wavered. It was a mistake. A mailled glove hit me in the side of the face and I was sent sprawling across the floor. A heavy kick to my midriff followed, with two more landing in rapid succession. My weapons were confiscated and my armour ripped from me. Several more blows arrived, rendering me semi-conscious, and I was dragged along the stone floor of the hall, my limp body making a wave in the straw as we went.

I was thrown into a small, pitch-black cell, given a piece of stale bread and a jug of water and left for what seemed like an eternity.

I lost all track of time; I had no point of reference and no way of recording day or night. The cold and hunger were difficult to deal with, but they were nothing compared to the horror of the confined space, and the total lack of light and human contact.

My mind raced; more than once I panicked and began to shout and scream. There was no response, and that made matters even more unbearable. The fact that I had been told it was a 'test' did not make any difference after a while. My imagination created countless terrifying outcomes.

Relief came on what I later discovered was the fourth morning. The door to the cell suddenly opened and the darkness was transformed by what seemed like the midday sun, but in fact was only a candle.

There was a vague shape behind the light. It thrust a bowl of soup and another jug of fresh water in my direction. Then a voice emanated from the silhouette. It was a Gaelic voice, but with a tone far gentler than Máedóc's.

'If the examination is too much for you, you are free to go; you have a little time to decide.'

The shadowy figure then left and the cell door slammed shut behind the departing apparition. My instincts cried out to me, imploring me to shout, 'Enough!', 'Let me go!' Fortunately, my instinct to eat was stronger than my fear and I devoured the soup and the water, but too quickly; my stomach rebelled, punishing me with agonizing cramps and, only moments later, violent vomiting.

So horrendous was the pain, by the time the door

opened once more – an hour or so later – and the mellow voice sought my response, I could hardly speak.

'If you end the challenge now, you will be carried from here and given good care until you recover. There will be no shame attached to your decision.'

Had I been more in control of my senses and emotions, I may have accepted the sweet encroachments and capitulated to the rigours of my ordeal there and then. But there was something about the sudden warmth of the offer to concede that reminded me that, no matter how arduous, this was no more than a test, merely an examination of my courage and resolve. The thought ignited a spark of defiance in me and I managed to spit out a response.

'Do your worst, I'm not finished yet!'

I regretted my boldness immediately as, once again, the door slammed shut and I was left in the bitterly cold darkness. I must have fallen asleep – for how long I was not sure – but by the time I was next fully awake I was being bound hand and foot and pulled from my tiny cell. Máedóc then hoisted me on to his broad shoulders and carried me up the narrow stairs to the castle battlements. I felt like a child being effortlessly carried by his father, except there was nothing paternal about Máedóc's intentions. My head banged repeatedly against the stone wall of the narrow stairwell. When we reached the top, he just threw me on to the floor of the ramparts like a rag doll.

'Can you swim?' he bellowed at me.

Being certain that my answer would lead to unfortunate consequences, I hesitated and again paid the price as several kicks to my midriff ensued.

'Can you swim?' he yelled, even more vociferously.

My reply in the affirmative came quickly, but reluctantly.

My legs were unbound and Máedóc, in a single easy movement, lifted me up and hurled me from the castle walls. I prayed that Wolvesey's moat awaited me at the end of my interminable plummet downwards. It did, thank God, but I hit the water awkwardly and my breath was shocked out of me. The water was pitch black and icy cold, and I lost all sense of direction. It was a dilemma that was only resolved when I felt the weeds at the bottom of the moat wrap themselves around my legs.

My foot touched the bottom of the moat and I tried to push myself upwards, only to feel myself beginning to sink into thick mud. I was fighting for air as the freezing water paralysed my chest and made my head feel as if it was held in a blacksmith's vice.

Trying not to panic, I took a moment to compose myself. I knew not to use my other foot as a lever, as that would also become trapped. Summoning what strength I had left, I managed to prise my foot from the mire that held it by using my arms and upper body to push against the water. Once free, I kicked for the surface. I saw a bright light and used it as a beacon. When I broke the surface, my childhood by the sea came to my aid; I knew to turn on to my back and use my legs to propel me to the bank. Two of Máedóc's men were waiting for me and Óengus grabbed my wrists and dragged me out of the water. He was the one with the mild voice. Once again, he spoke to me reassuringly.

'The first part is over. You will have a day to recover.'

This time he was as good as his word. The rope around my wrists was cut and I was led away to a comfortable room in the building that housed Wolvesey's garrison. Although the door was locked behind me, there was wholesome food and a pitcher of beer on the table, and the bed looked clean and comfortable.

I took care to eat cautiously this time and enjoyed what felt like one of the best meals I had ever eaten. Sleep came quickly and was long-lasting.

I woke just before dawn the next morning. My brief respite had been a great comfort, but I knew it would only herald more hardship to come.

My weapons and armour were returned to me and I was told to prepare as if for battle. I was then escorted to the castle stables. Máedóc and his men, already mounted on horseback, were waiting for me. As usual, he barked his instructions.

'Óengus and I will ride in front, Fáelán and Mochán will bring up the rear. You will be in between us and will match our pace. If you fall, or fail to keep up with us, you will be punished.'

Then, without a moment's delay, he kicked on.

I was used to forced marches – they were part of our training – but none had ever been as demanding as this one. The first hour was at a reasonable pace, and I felt comfortable. But it was only a placid beginning. We were soon up on the Downs of Hampshire, where Máedóc began to vary the pace. He chose the steepest of hills to climb and led me through streams and ditches. By midday, when he stopped to rest the horses, I was exhausted. But unlike the horses, which were able to enjoy fodder and water, I was denied any comforts and had to stand rather than sit.

Máedóc, relaxing with a leg of chicken in one hand and a flask of wine in the other, took the opportunity to goad me.

'You seem a bit skinny to be a king's bodyguard. In Ireland, men like you guard nuns and monks.'

I chose not to respond, which led him to throw his chicken leg at me. It bounced off my forehead, producing hoots of delight from his men. Mochán then walked over to me and told me to pick up the chicken remnant. Again, I did not respond, which led Mochán to aim a fist in my direction.

I was ready for him. During my morning's exertions I had decided that, although I would succumb to the tests, I was not prepared to submit to physical abuse. I blocked his blow with my forearm and landed a solid punch of my own, before twisting his arm against his elbow joint and locking it behind his back. I then pushed him to the ground.

Máedóc smirked at me, but I was determined to make my point.

'I am prepared to endure whatever has been prepared for me to examine my suitability for the task that awaits me. But if I am struck, I will strike back.'

Máedóc's condescending smirk changed into a pitiless stare. He got to his feet and strode towards me, holding me in an unblinking gaze. He was half a head taller than I was. As he neared me, he bent his head slightly to look me in the eye.

'Brave words, Englishman, but foolish ones. Mochán told you to pick up the chicken leg I so generously offered you. Do as you're told, boy.'

I stiffened my resolve. 'You pick it up; I believe it belongs to you.'

He did not answer. I knew a blow was coming, so I braced myself. But the retribution did not come as I thought it would. Although he resumed his leering expression, he put his arm around my shoulders in a mock sign of affection. It was a disconcerting experience. I felt I was in the grip of a huge bear, its arm weighing down on me like the bough of a large tree. He leaned on me, urging me to step towards his men, all of whom had adopted the same ominous sneer.

'I like you; you are strong. Few men ever cross me. You must know that, but you did it anyway. I like that.'

His flattery was a feint. The arm that rested on my shoulders slowly tightened its grasp until I was ensnared in a headlock. His grip was so powerful I was unable to break free. I reached for my sword but his men grabbed my arms, rendering me helpless. They closed in on me, surrounding me, squawking like monkeys.

'I am going to reward your bravery. I would normally let Mochán punish you for your impertinence, but I'm going to spare you that and give you a little treat. You're going to be given a little exercise in the fresh air. It will do you good. You see how kind we are to you, even though you've behaved so badly?'

He let go of my head and began to walk away, leaving his men to goad me with taunts and insults. The blood rushed back into my ears and my eyes began to focus again. Then there was an appalling pain as I was cata-pulted backwards by an almighty blow to my temple. I did not see it coming, nor do I remember hitting the ground, but when my head cleared I realized that I had been pole-axed by Máedóc's fist.

Mochán was looming over me, grinning inanely, chicken drumstick in hand.

'Are you sure you don't want a little bit of chicken?'

He forced it into my mouth; I was too weak to resist. He pressed my cheeks, encouraging me to chew, his stupid grin becoming a contorted snarl of anger.

'You would be wise never to speak to Máedóc like that again. He has killed men for far less.'

Anger started to rise in me again, but I realized that, for the time being, I had to submit. My hands were bound again and, with the aid of a long piece of rope, I was attached to the pommel of the saddle of Máedóc's steed.

For the next three hours I was put through hell. My arms soon felt like they had been dislocated at my shoulders, and I lost my footing several times. This left me helpless, to be dragged along the ground like a dead carcass. By the end of it I was unconscious, only coming round in my bed much later that night.

The first sensation I felt was warm water on my feet and sharp pains as the liquid seeped into deep lacerations on my soles and lower legs.

'Lie still.'

The words, delivered warmly, came from a monk who was sitting on the side of my bed. He was a slight man in his early thirties with olive skin and hair that was almost raven black, but with contrasting piercing grey-green eyes.

He had the look of a scholar and the soft hands of a monastic scribe.

I was in considerable pain and exhausted, but summoned sufficient energy to speak, if only with difficulty.

'Who are you?'

'I am Father Alun; the Earl is my patron and is helping me prepare to join the chapter at York. He has recommended me to Roger de Pont L'Évêque, Archbishop of York.'

'So, what is your role in these tests? Do you read over me when I'm dead?'

'Yes, I'm afraid that Máedóc's methods are severe, too severe. You are only the second one to have made it this far. Sadly, the other knight died a few days later in an accident during weapons training. My role is to assess your ability in languages, your suitability to be at ease in the presence of noblemen and your ability to conduct intelligent conversation with them.'

I managed to raise myself on to my side and could see the pitiful state of my legs, which looked as if they had been flayed from the knees downwards. My elbows were also raw, and the front of my torso burned with the pain of countless laccrations.

'I'm afraid my ability to behave in the presence of noblemen is soon likely to be an irrelevance. Unless the rest of the tests can be done from horseback, I doubt that I will be able to continue.'

'I agree. I asked Máedóc for a week to help you recover, but unfortunately he would only give you until tomorrow morning. I have sent for the Earl of Huntingdon, but he's in Salisbury and will not be back for three days.'

'Does he know how these tests are being conducted?'

'No, I'm sure not. Máedóc was recommended by King Henry, who recruited him in Ireland. The Earl wants the tests to be demanding, but I'm sure Máedóc is taking them too far.'

'Well, the man is a killer; I can see it in his eyes. And he means to kill me. As soon as I can get on a horse, I am leaving for Westminster.'

'I will help you as much as I can, but I can't protect you from Máedóc until the Earl returns.'

'I understand, but do what you can to heal my legs. Where are my weapons and armour?'

'His men have them; I won't be able to get them for you.'

'Where is my horse?'

'With the rest of the garrison horses. But Máedóc has given instructions that it is only to be released to him.'

'Do you know what the next part of the tests involves?'

'Yes, weapons.'

'Very well, let's see what tomorrow brings. By the way, do you have any idea what it is I am being tested for?'

'I am sorry, Sir Ranulf, the Earl has not told me. But I do know that he cares passionately about England, as do I. Now that he is very old, he chose me to help him, an honour I accepted without hesitation.'

'Why you? And why did you accept so readily?'

'England is in my blood, as it is in yours. We have come a long way since the dark days of the Conquest. I want that progress to continue.'

'Father, your response poses more questions than it gives answers.'

'I can tell you just one more thing. The Earl told me that his mission needs two special men. One of them must be wise without equal, the other must be brave beyond any other. I know I am not the brave one. But so far, it looks like you may just be the man the Earl is looking for. Let's hope that together we can live up to his expectations.'

The pain in my legs kept me awake for most of the night, which gave me the chance to contemplate how I was going to extricate myself from the dire circumstances in which I had found myself. By the morning I had made no real plan, but I had reached the conclusion that I would have to fight my way out of my predicament.

Father Alun was at my side when Máedóc and his men burst into my room. He had bound my feet tightly but it was still almost impossible for me to walk, and then only with searing pain.

Máedóc scowled at the young monk.

'What are you doing here?'

'Sir Ranulf is not able to continue the tests.'

The towering Irishman turned his withering glare towards me.

'Then you have failed the tests.'

'So be it. If I may trouble you for my weapons and my horse, I will be on my way back to Westminster.'

'I thought you were a weak-willed little twat as soon as I saw you.'

I chose to ignore the insult and limped past him. As I reached the door, Máedóc's men blocked the way. I paused, but they did not step aside.

Father Alun admonished them.

'Let Sir Ranulf go, his challenge is over. He is free to leave.'

Máedóc rounded on the monk and struck him across the face with the back of his hand.

'No one gives orders to my men, except me.'

With blood spewing from his mouth and splattering the floor, Father Alun landed on the ground with a heavy thump. Máedóc's men still blocked the doorway. With a leer on his face, Mochán glanced down at the monk. As he did so, I seized the opportunity to pull his seax from his belt and thrust it hard under his chin. He froze, as did his two companions.

I looked Mochán in the eye.

'Walk backwards through the door and tell your two friends to step aside.'

I saw Mochán's eyes turn towards Máedóc, who must have nodded his assent, because he began to move through the doorway as I had asked. It was excruciating for me to walk, and I stumbled several times. But I made sure to keep the blade firmly embedded in the soft skin of Mochán's throat. Then I saw my hostage's expression change and heard Father Alun caution me with a gurgled cry that he managed to spit from his blood-filled mouth.

'*Sir Ranulf!*'

I knew what the warning meant and quickly swayed to one side. As I did so, Máedóc's sword passed within a hair's breadth of my ribs and impaled Mochán through his belly. Without uttering a sound, he fell backwards and landed in a heap on the floor. Máedóc, shocked at realizing that he had killed his companion, let go of his weapon, which remained deeply embedded in Mochán's stomach.

I seized my moment and sank my seax into the lumbering Celt's throat until it exited at the other side. The giant man stood motionless for several moments as blood gushed from his neck like a stream of piss and ran down the wall next to him. Unable to say anything, he just stared at me incredulously. Eventually, his eyes lost all ability to focus; he took one faltering step forwards and fell over like a massive oak tree succumbing to the woodsman. The spew of his blood tracked his fall, leaving an arc of crimson on the wall and a rapidly growing puddle under his head.

Óengus and Fáelán looked at one another. They both drew their swords.

Father Alun, despite his prone position and the blood pouring from his mouth, was quick to remind them that killing me would also require them to kill him. And should they do so, the Earl would be certain to hunt them down without mercy. The monk had made a crucial intervention for, with only a seax in my hand and almost no agility at my disposal, my prospects were miserable.

The two Irishmen quickly realized the realities of their situation. They took one look at their stricken companions and sheathed their swords. Moments later, with neither a glance nor a word in my direction, they were gone.

I thanked the good monk profusely before the pain and exertion got the better of me and I fell to my knees.

3. Ghosts of Bosham Manor

The next morning, despite Father Alun's exhortations, I was on my horse and making slow progress towards London and the comforts of the garrison physicians at Westminster. Sitting was one of the few positions that was relatively painless; as long as I kept my horse at a steady pace, my progress was not too uncomfortable.

When I reached Farnham, I decided to rest with the monks at Waverley Abbey. It sits in an idyllic position by the River Wey and was an ideal place for me to recuperate and reflect on my recent misfortune.

It was early on the morning of the fourth day at Waverley when my life changed irrevocably. I was feeling much better. My feet and legs were still raw but, with the judicious use of a couple of sticks, they could bear my weight with only moderate discomfort. I was using the abbey cloisters to attempt some exercise while several Cistercian brothers, looking resplendent in their pristine white habits and black scapulars, were sitting in devout prayer and contemplation.

All was quiet, save for the gentle clack of my sticks and the soft shuffle of my bandaged feet – until, that is, heavy footsteps made a purposeful approach from behind me. With a wince of sudden pain, I made a slow turn just as my visitor spoke in his loud and distinctive voice.

'Ranulf of Lancaster, is that you?'

The unmistakeable voice belonged to the last man I wanted to see: the Earl of Huntingdon, the instigator of the torture I had been subjected to in Winchester. Scurrying in his wake were Abbot Henry, the head of the Waverley community, Father Alun and a sergeant-at-arms with a small retinue of men. It looked like a posse seeking my arrest, but I was in no position to resist.

Rather than looking stern, the Earl smiled warmly as he neared.

'I am so relieved that you appear to be recovering. What a dreadful ordeal you were put through. Please accept my apologies.'

Despite the warmth of the Earl's greeting and his expression of regret, I was still wary of his motives.

'My Lord, I accepted the challenge in good faith. But you left me at the mercy of a madman.'

'I know, Father Alun has told me. I am very sorry. I wanted the challenge to be stern, but not an opportunity for brutality. We have tracked down Máedóc's two accomplices. They are simple souls, but they will spend a year in Winchester's dungeons before they are shipped back to Ireland in chains. They admitted that Máedóc was a malevolent soul, and they also explained that he wanted the opportunity for himself. He was determined to make sure that no one came through the ordeal until, eventually, he planned to offer himself for the role.'

'Did he know what the opportunity was, my Lord?'

'No, but he assumed it would be lucrative in some way.'

'If I may ask, sire, is it a challenge where success will be rewarded?'

'It may be, but there is no guarantee of that. More

importantly though, it will add greatly to the vigour of a man's soul.'

'Then, my Lord, I am sorry I failed the examination.'

'But you did not fail, Sir Ranulf. I want to offer you the role that so many have striven for.'

'My Lord, I withdrew – Father Alun will attest to that.'

'I know, but you withdrew from a test that could not have been passed. More importantly, you stood up to a thug and put an end to a reign of terror carried out in my name. For that I am eternally grateful.'

'Sire, given my recent experience, I'm afraid I am not able to accept the challenge until I know what it involves.'

'Under the circumstances, that is reasonable. However, I will need some time to explain what the task is. Father Alun will help me with this, because he has a particular interest in ensuring that whoever carries this responsibility is the right man. Not only that, but should you choose to undertake the responsibility, he will be your companion and wise counsel for its duration.'

'I understand, my Lord.'

'You must also understand this: if, after hearing what the task involves, you choose not to accept the calling, you must never repeat any of the information you are given. Never. Not to anyone. Do you understand?'

'I do, sire.'

'Do you follow a code of knightly chivalry?'

'I do, my Lord, the Mos Militum, the code of the English heroes during the Great Crusade.'

'That is good to know. Then I need your solemn oath as a knight of the realm that what you hear from me and Father Alun will be known only by you.'

'You have my word, Earl Harold.'

'I have an estate at Bosham. I think you will enjoy the surroundings. Many years ago, the land was held by Godwin, Earl of Wessex, the father of King Harold. Godwin is buried in the chapel there, as is the little daughter of King Cnut, who was drowned in Bosham Creek. So you see, I have leased the manor for nostalgic reasons. I thought that the old kings of England would appreciate knowing that the home of the Godwins was back in English hands.'

I was impressed and captivated. The Earl was clearly a man of great repute within the Norman elite and yet he had leased the estate of Harold Godwinson, the Earl of Wessex and England's last English king, just for nostalgia's sake.

'Father Alun and my men will stay with you until you are fit and well. When you are, come and join me in Bosham and we can talk about what I'm sure will be an adventure that will fascinate and excite you.'

'Thank you, sire.'

Over the ensuing days, Father Alun refused to divulge anything he knew about what lay ahead, his own personal interest in it, or even anything about himself or his background. He was an engaging and knowledgeable conversationalist and helped Abbot Henry's monks at Waverley during my recuperation. But any talk of the assignment that I was to be offered was strictly forbidden.

All Father Alun would say was that Earl Harold was a wise and kind man, and that he would tell me everything I needed to know when we got to Bosham.

*

35

By the time we reached Bosham in late October 1176, I was fit and well and eager to know what more lay beyond the tantalizing morsels of information I had been given so far.

Bosham reminded me of my home in Heysham. It sat on high ground, from where an ancient chapel looked out to the many rivers and creeks that led to the sea a few miles to the south. A small cluster of thatched cottages circled the old church which, like my father's chapel, was built of stone and was said to be centuries old. Bosham was in the old Earldom of the South Saxons, not far from Chichester, an important burgh I had visited before, with its gleaming Norman cathedral and imposing castle. But Bosham was like the England of old – quiet and peaceful, with none of the pretentious scale of the new Norman burghs.

There seemed to be water everywhere, making the high ground of the village almost an island amidst the myriad creeks and mudflats. Numerous fishing boats were in the harbour and many more were pulled up on dry land all around us. Small boatyards were making and repairing vessels of assorted sizes, and there were the many buildings of the other artisans who thrived in a community that had lived cheek by jowl with the sea for centuries: chandlers, fishmongers, rope-makers, basket-makers, lightermen, watermen and trawl-makers. These were all trades I had known well as a boy.

The hall belonging to the manor sat behind the church, in its own enclosure about a hundred yards away. A modest hall, with a few smaller buildings nestling close beside it, it was far removed from a royal palace, but comfortable enough for a man of some stature.

The Earl of Huntingdon was certainly a man of stature. Despite his great age, he strode out to meet us when we arrived, offered a warm welcome and ushered us inside his hall, where food and wine had been prepared.

After the courtesies and the food had been dispensed with, the Earl cleared the hall and asked Father Alun and myself to join him by the fire.

'I am delighted that you seem to have made a complete recovery, Sir Ranulf.'

'Thank you, my Lord.'

'I think it is time to describe what I would like you to do for me and – this is very important – for England. But first, let me repeat, I will now tell you things that must remain a confidence between the three of us. Do you concur?'

'I do, my Lord. I gave you my word at Waverley Abbey. The oath of a knight does not need to be given twice.'

It was an impertinence to speak so bluntly to an earl of the realm, but I had come to suspect that the role I was going to be offered was not one for a man of timid demeanour.

'Well said, Sir Ranulf, I am duly admonished.'

In standing my ground, I had made an important point.

The Earl smiled warmly.

'First of all, let me briefly tell you about me. I am the grandson of the mighty Hereward of Bourne. My mother, Estrith, was one of his twin daughters. She was with him at the Siege of Ely and was reunited with him, many years later.'

I was in awe, my jaw dropped and my eyes opened wide.

'So, he did survive Ely after all. Many people say he did, but there are so many stories. My Lord Earl, it is a privilege to meet a man descended from such a noble family. Did you meet Hereward?'

'Yes, in a way. When I was a small child my mother and I stayed with him at his mountaintop home in the Peloponnese, in the empire of the Byzantines. But alas, I have no memory of it. When I was old enough, I attempted to make my own way in the world. It was not easy to live in the shadow of such an illustrious grandfather, but I used him as an inspiration rather than an obstacle. With more than my fair share of good fortune, I managed to make a modest mark of my own.

'I was made Earl of Huntingdon by Henry Beauclerc, grandfather of the present King, and took personal command of the Empress Matilda's forces during her struggles for the English throne against her cousin, Stephen of Blois. After the war, I became guardian to Empress Matilda's children and acted as confidant to her firstborn, our liege King Henry, through the difficult days of his succession to King Stephen. Since Matilda's death ten years ago, I have kept a close eye on the King, who – I hope – continues to regard me as a somewhat ancient but wise godfather.'

I felt myself gulp. I was in the presence of a remarkable man who had been at the centre of the affairs of England for the last thirty-five years. The Earl sensed that I was somewhat overawed. Like a caring father, he rested his hand on my shoulder and smiled at me sympathetically before resuming his story.

'Although Matilda, known to those close to her as

Maud, is no longer with us, her pedigree and that of England live on. Now I must come to the nub of the matter.'

I cast a glance at Father Alun and saw a smile forming on his face. I began to feel my heart beat faster; all I wanted to do was ask more and more questions. But I realized that I was only just at the beginning of what could be an astonishing journey for me, and so I forced myself to hold my tongue and listen.

'Empress Matilda and I fought all our lives to ensure that her son, Henry Plantagenet, would succeed to the throne that she was never quite able to grasp. Thankfully, that came to pass and King Henry now unites us all — English and Norman, all the Celtic peoples of our islands, and many other peoples from south of Normandy, all the way to the Pyrenees. He has ruled his great Plantagenet Empire wisely and fairly. And through his mother's English royal blood, he has ensured that every Englishman can look upon him as one of their own.'

The Earl's eyes began to moisten and his voice cracked with emotion. He slowly hauled himself up from his chair, walked away from the fire and paused before continuing.

'But the King won't live for ever. He is now in his mid-forties and is beginning to lose the vigour he once had. His sons are very troublesome to him, and I fear that the peace we have enjoyed throughout the Empire under his rule may not survive his death.'

Three years earlier, three of Henry's sons had campaigned against him. I was not involved in the rebellion, because I had been assigned to the King's personal bodyguard at Westminster — and most of the fighting took place in Normandy and the surrounding provinces — but it had been a time of great anxiety when many thought the Empire would disintegrate. Even though the King prevailed, and his sons were reconciled to him, many said it was only a matter of time before the issue would come to the fore once more.

'As you know, the King has kept Queen Eleanor under house arrest these last two years and I fear for her and for the future of the realm. She is a formidable woman with many admirers; the King would be wise not to continue to see her as an enemy, lest she becomes one he cannot control.'

'My Lord, I have seen her at court many times. She is, indeed, daunting and very beautiful. I hear she is currently held at Sarum Castle.'

'She is, but she is well treated. She has a huge entourage, all of whom are free to come and go, and she is constantly entertained by the troubadours and poets from the Court of Love she kept at Poitiers.'

I had heard much about the Queen's court at Poitiers. Every knight in Europe talked about its code of chivalry and how the young knights swore oaths of undying loyalty and love to their fair maidens. At Poitiers, the most esteemed knights were not just the ones who were brave in battle, but also those who could compose and sing ballads expressing their eternal love for their ladies.

'As you know, Prince Henry is heir to the throne. But he is only interested in prancing at tournaments and cavorting with girls, he is not the man to follow his father in controlling an empire half the size of Europe.'

'But, my Lord, is he not already crowned and anointed as our sovereign?'

'He is, but he is the Young King only in name. He can't be our true King while his father lives, and certainly not while he acts like a juvenile.'

'But, sire, he's only twenty-one years old. There will be plenty of time for him to become a mature leader.'

'I disagree. If you are a crowned king, even while your father lives, you should act like one.'

Although kindly in demeanour and as old as Methuselah, the Earl took on the unmistakeably fierce look of a seasoned warrior.

'We need a king who has the courage to lead his men in battle, not a mannequin in the fancy dress of the tournament.'

There had been a flash of anger on the Earl's face. But it soon subsided, to be replaced by his usual sagacious warmth.

'But there is a man of valour . . . and one day he will be the King we need.'

I looked at Father Alun again. He nodded his approval with a benign smile. The Earl returned to his seat by the fire and threw more logs into its heart.

'I feel the cold these days. When I was younger, no amount of cold bothered me, but now I have to look after myself like a newborn baby, heavily swaddled and kept close to the fire!'

He sat back in his chair and stared at the roaring fire, which crackled and spat with energy.

'The young man in question is like this fire. He burns with ambition and courage. His mother, Queen Eleanor, is wary of my interest and has kept me at arm's length, but I've watched him grow from a distance. He

41

is prodigious. Still only nineteen, but he's been leading his army in Aquitaine for three years and they already call him "Lionheart". He's tall like all his kin, with hair the golden red of a lion's coat and a beard the dark tinge of the beast's mane.'

I had heard the name 'Lionheart' before. His reputation was already known among my fellow knights. He was Richard, Duke of Aquitaine, King Henry's third son and, after the early death of his elder brother, William, was now second in line to the throne.

'Sire, I have heard of this man. But I believe he spends all his time in his dukedom, many miles from England.'

'You are correct. That is part of the problem that must be solved. Duke Richard was born at Beaumont Palace, in Oxford, but has spent very little time in England. He does not speak our language and, from what I hear, thinks our precious land is a dismal, godforsaken place off the coast of civilized Europe. He thrives in Aquitaine, where he loves the warmth, the wine and the women. He likes to fight and relishes its lawlessness and the challenge of the many formidable adversaries he finds there.'

I was now perplexed. If the task was to persuade the Duke of the value of his English pedigree, it appeared that the Earl needed a sophisticated diplomat rather than a soldier.

'My Lord, are you suggesting that I can play a role in the life of the Duke?'

'I am.'

The Earl was quick to see my furrowed brow.

'Don't be concerned, there is logic to my plan. But it does require some guesswork on my part and, I admit, for providence to play a role. However, there are several precedents for fate playing a major part in my family's history.'

He paused to stare at me keenly.

'It will also involve a leap of faith on your part, but I will leave that to your judgement. If you accept this commission, you will do me and England a great service. This young Duke has the world at his feet. He has good men around him, but they are not men who can help him understand and appreciate his English pedigree, a lineage that is far more important than he realizes. For that, he needs you and Alun.'

With an earnest intensity, Father Alun then spoke for the first time.

'I have made my leap of faith. For me there could not be a more important calling in life.'

I looked at the priest. I could see the passion in his eyes and felt humbled that these two men should think me worthy to be an accomplice in their quest. Alun had saved my life, and I knew him to be a true and kindly man. If my role was to lend the strength of my arm to the wisdom that he would bring to this intriguing mission, then I would not only be a fool to turn down such a unique challenge, but also disloyal to England and to my people.

A spark flew from the fire at that point, breaking my concentration. Realizing that I had been listening so intently that I had not moved for several minutes, I adjusted my position in my chair. My backside had become numb and I winced slightly as the blood flowed back and made my buttocks prickle.

'Some more wine, Sir Ranulf? I think you need a little respite for a moment.'

Father Alun leaned across and poured another goblet of the Earl's excellent dark-red wine.

'It is from a small estate I have in Aquitaine. You will like it there. In the winter it is not unlike here, but the autumns are mild and the springs and summers are like heaven on earth.'

'So, I am to travel to Aquitaine?'

'Yes, all is ready. Our ship is at harbour only yards from here, and I took the liberty of having your things sent down from your garrison at Westminster. We can sail on the next tide.'

'So, you will accompany us, my Lord?'

'Yes, I have to prepare the ground; young Richard has no inkling of my proposal yet.'

'Sire, with the greatest respect, I don't either. The last thing you said was that I would need to make a leap of faith.'

'Quite so. I am growing to like you, Ranulf of Lancaster; you have a good sense of humour, and you're not afraid to speak your mind. Have some more wine.'

Both he and Alun laughed heartily as my goblet was filled once more. It seemed that they had made up my mind for me and that I had accepted the mysterious role. I chose not to demur; I liked my two companions as much as they seemed to like me, and I was spellbound by the prospects that lay ahead. What was more, Bosham was full of so many ghosts from England's past. So, how could I refuse?

Earl Harold held out his hand, as did Father Alun. I shook them vigorously.

'Aquitaine is a long way from here. We will have many opportunities to talk more on the journey.'

My mission had begun. A powerful energy began to course through my veins. Even though all logic suggested that the young Duke might well dismiss Earl Harold's proposition out of hand – or, indeed, that the young warrior might have feet of clay and not be the man his reputation portrayed – the mission offered me a once-in-a-lifetime opportunity.

Not only did the Earl's commission bring the prospect of adventures in new and exotic lands, but it also offered the opportunity to be part of his attempt to manoeuvre Duke Richard in a direction that would be to England's great benefit. I knew not how – but for the time being that mattered little.

Countless others before me, including Earl Harold, had put themselves at the mercy of an unknown destiny for England's cause. Now it was my turn.

4. Aquitaine

We took ship on the next day's tide. The Earl had gathered an awesome quintet of warriors who would share our journey, but at that stage I knew them not at all. Our crossing of the Channel was uneventful and we made landfall at Saint-Valery-sur-Somme, from where, poignantly, the Conqueror had set sail in 1066. Horses were waiting for us, organized by Godric, a man who would become a lifelong companion.

We moved south rapidly, passing Abbeville, Rouen, Le Mans, Tours and Poitiers, before turning west towards Saintes in the Charente, where we hoped to make contact with Duke Richard.

I had been to Normandy only once before, and then only briefly – to Rouen, to escort the King back to Westminster – so our journey was fascinating for me. Just as Normandy was very different from England, the further south we travelled the more the people, their buildings and their languages changed. The local inhabitants were shorter and sturdier, with darker complexions, the further south and west we travelled, and their buildings became more rustic. Only in Normandy and its neighbouring provinces did we see towering castles and cathedrals; further south, the churches were more modest, the fortresses less imposing.

The people of Angers and Poitiers spoke in tongues that were similar to one another but very unlike Norman, while around Saintes the local language changed yet again to something much gentler in tone, but unlike anything I had heard before.

During our journey, the Earl travelled with all the ease of a man half his age and spent much of the time talking about the stability of the huge Plantagenet Empire and the threats from its many enemies, especially the King of France. I listened carefully, realizing how little I knew about the complex issues King Henry had to deal with every day.

I also got to know the warriors the Earl had assigned to our task. Godric was their leader – a short, broad-shouldered man with hair the colour of hay. He was an intelligent but stern taskmaster and followed the rules of military discipline rigidly. His men were Penda, Leax and the brothers Modig and Rodor. Penda had been named after the old pagan King of Mercia. He was a big, softly spoken man, with the dark look of the Celt about him. Leax was an imp of a man – small, thin, with boundless energy – who never stopped talking and kept us all amused with his quick wit and sense of fun. Modig and Rodor could easily have been twins; they said very little and had the brooding presence of English warriors of old. Their long blond locks reached well below their shoulders, and their heavy beards almost completely obscured their features.

Keeping strict formation, the quintet rode behind us. Godric took the lead; behind him, in pairs, came Penda and Leax, followed by Modig and Rodor.

Father Alun was at pains to point out that Earl Harold had trained our men-at-arms to the exemplary standards of King Harold's fabled housecarls of the past and that they were the finest of soldiers – men you would happily go into battle with. When he reminded me that they were my men to command, I realized that, sooner or later, I would have to prove myself to them.

They carried the traditional battleaxe and circular shield of the English housecarl. Their shields all had the same three-colour design: gules, sable and gold. I was curious to know what they represented. Father Alun was happy to oblige with at least part of the answer.

'Earl Harold is very fond of those colours. They were Hereward's colours during the English revolt of 1069 and have been carried by the family ever since.'

I sensed there was more, and asked what the colours signified.

'That is a good question. It is an important part of our story, and one which Earl Harold entrusted to me at the start of our mission . . .'

He paused and seemed to consider whether to continue. I waited, content in the knowledge that my journey with my new companion was only just beginning, and trusting that he would tell me what I needed to know. Even so, I was not prepared for Father Alun's next question.

'Have you heard tell of an amulet known as the Talisman of Truth?'

I confessed I had not.

'The talisman is a primeval piece of amber. It contains the image of the Devil and his familiars, but Satan is trapped by a slash of crimson, thought to be the blood of Christ. It is a symbol of five abiding truths that have brought insight to kings and emperors from the beginning of time: the need for discipline, to control the darkness within us; the importance of humility, to know that only

God can work miracles; the value of courage, to overcome our fears and anxieties; the purpose of sacrifice, to forfeit ourselves for God and for one another; and the power of wisdom. To understand the talisman itself is to understand all other mysteries and how not to fear them.

'The amulet's provenance is obscure, but it was carried by Hereward and his wife, Torfida, throughout their lives. Hereward well understood the amulet's significance, and he took its colours as his own. The gold is the amber of the stone, the sable is the black image of the Devil and his imprisoned familiars, and the gules is the blood of Christ.'

I felt like a boy listening to a magical story; I had to wipe the tears from my eyes. The amulet described by Father Alun was a tangible link with England's history and one of its legendary heroes. I could not suppress a burning question.

'But where is the talisman now?'

'It has found a guardian who will look after it – one of many over countless generations – until its truths are needed again.'

'Are you its next keeper?'

'No, that man is yet to be found.'

I decided not to press Alun further. The puzzle was still a mystery to me, but more pieces were gradually falling into place, each more intriguing than the last.

As we moved further south, the air became milder. Clouds heavy with rain from the Western Sea rolled over us almost every day. Occasionally, the wind veered round and brought cold air from the east, much like an English winter. The dark days of November and

December rendered our surroundings grey and flat, but it was easy to imagine how different it would be in the spring and summer, especially amidst the countless rows of vines and fruit trees. They were dismal and bare now but would be verdant and full of promise in just a few months' time.

Saintes was brimming with pilgrims when we arrived. Every inch of the nave of the great Church of St Eutropius was covered by a sea of humanity. They had travelled from the distant corners of Europe to make their way, ponderously but faithfully, to the shrine of St James the Great, in Galicia, and they still had months of travel ahead of them. The nave was more like a marketplace than a church. Traders sold their wares, buskers performed, and even the harlots were allowed to flourish. The monks kept a watchful eye – especially over the privies, which were a source of much stench and not a few arguments as the queues grew from early morning.

Sadly for our mission, Duke Richard was nowhere to be found in Saintes, nor was he in its vicinity. A week earlier he had left for Bordeaux with his army. Having pacified large areas of the Limousin and Angoulême, it was now his intention to bring to heel Gascony and Navarre, the land of the Basques.

Duke Richard's reputation preceded him. We heard reports that he was ruthless with any recalcitrant lord who refused to submit to him. It was said that if a siege was necessary, his strategy was an unrelenting attack by missiles and fire, supplemented by a scorched-earth policy to induce starvation and a final, brutal assault on the walls of the castle or city.

When victory or submission had been achieved, as was invariably the case, he was harsh with those who opposed him. But he was magnanimous with the garrison which had fought him and generous with local inhabitants, often insisting that their lord pay them a handsome sum as part of the peace settlement. There was little wonder that the sobriquet 'Lionheart' was so widely attached to his name.

When Father Alun told me that we would be travelling as far south as the towering Pyrenees, I was curious, especially after he offered me a quote from a new *Guide for Pilgrims*, which had just been made available for wealthy travellers. It could be read – by those who had sufficient Latin – at the great monasteries along the Way of St James, from as far away as Paris, Geneva and Turin.

The Gascons are gossipy, licentious and poorly dressed. They eat and drink too much, but not at a table, rather they squat around a fire and share the same cup. When they sleep they share the same rotting straw, master and mistress, servants and all. The Basques and Navarrese are much like the Gascons, only worse! They all eat out of one big pot like pigs at a trough and when they speak they sound like dogs barking. They warm themselves in front of the fire by lifting their kilts and are not afraid to display their genitals for all to see. They treat their women like mules and fornicate with animals. In fact, so jealous can they be of their favourite mares and mules, they have been known to fit them with chastity belts.

I was amused by this account; indeed, it reminded me of our English prejudices about the Scots.

*

When we finally caught up with Duke Richard's army outside the walls of Bordeaux, it presented a disconcerting impression. Led by a motley group of lords and knights from many parts of King Henry's empire, it was largely composed of Brabançon mercenaries from the Low Countries and the bordering German principalities. Fierce and ill-disciplined, and clearly only interested in the spoils of war, they were the antithesis of the professional soldiers I had trained and fought with. By the look of them, there was no doubting their ability to fight; what was more questionable was their loyalty to anything other than their own self-interest. Indeed, they were the kind of men towards whom it would be unwise to turn one's back — unless provided with adequate protection from comrades who could be relied upon.

Large, gnarled, unkempt, scarred, fearsome and formidable were just some of the words that sat well with them. They carried a range of weapons and armour, both conventional and unusual, but all designed to inflict maximum harm on an opponent. They wielded swords of varying designs and lengths, axes, clubs and maces and a multitude of spears, javelins and lances, some longer than a man.

Many of them were sappers and siege engineers, skilled in designing and building a range of ballista, all vital to the successful execution of siege warfare. The archers and arbalests formed separate elite forces, each of which was dedicated to a peculiar fusion of deadly accuracy aligned with brute strength. The two groups of bowmen did not mix — in fact, each was contemptuous of the other. But their two contrasting trajectories, used in parallel in battle – one slower but toweringly high, the other flatter but speedier – made a crushing impact on an enemy.

I counted a force of around seven hundred men. It was not a huge army, but clearly an efficient one.

The Earl sat high in his saddle as he surveyed the scene. The army had made camp, but it was a disorganized muster of tents. Horses were picketed in small groups, and field kitchens were scattered everywhere. Latrines were notable by their absence, the River Garonne seemingly offering the only sanitation. Earl Harold glanced at Father Alun, then surveyed the surroundings with a look of contempt.

'What a buggers' muddle! It is to be hoped they are only besieging small garrisons of burghers and merchants. In open battle in the field, this rabble would be cut to pieces.'

The Earl was right. As individuals or in small groups, these were formidable men, but together, they were an army in name only.

We rode right up to Duke Richard's tent unchallenged and were only asked to name ourselves after we had dismounted and were within ten paces of his standard, which was flying stiffly in the westerly breeze. Godric spoke to the Duke's standard-bearer in Norman.

'Tell your lord that he has guests.'

'And who might they be?' was the curt reply.

'An Earl of England and his men.'

The man pulled back the canvas door of the tent with a flourish and disappeared inside. He had not saluted Earl Harold, nor had he proffered a courtesy of any sort. The Earl looked down at the ground, clearly unimpressed. The rest of us shuffled uneasily, embarrassed that our ageing lord had been unacknowledged and left standing outside the Duke's tent.

It seemed like an age passed before a dishevelled knight emerged from the tent. He looked flustered and had hardly finished adjusting his armour and clothing. He blinked in the bright light and bowed to Earl Harold.

'My Lord, Duke Richard asks if you will join him in his tent. He is on campaign, sire, so begs forgiveness for our frugal appearance.'

Earl Harold stepped forward and beckoned to Father Alun and myself to follow him.

'Worry not, Sir Knight, in my lifetime I've seen the inside of enough campaign tents to house a multitude of armies.'

Duke Richard's tent was, despite the caveat, remarkably luxurious. Although the interior was dark and musty, the walls were richly decorated with embroideries, and thick oriental carpets covered the floor. Incense hung in the air, together with the odour of attar of roses and perfumed candles. It was more like a lady's boudoir – and a lady of dubious repute at that – than a general's campaign tent.

The sounds of splashing water, female laughter and male merriment wafted from behind a curtain at the back of the tent. The Duke was obviously entertaining young women, even though the hour had barely passed midday. Once again, the Earl looked displeased.

When the Duke finally emerged from behind the curtain, only a chemise covered his nakedness. His hair was wet and matted and he had the unsteady gait and slurred speech of a man who had consumed more than his fair share of alcohol. Despite his tousled state, he was the epitome of his much-lauded reputation. He had the golden hair of a lion, his beard a little darker with a tinge of auburn, and his eyes, although a little bleary from drinking, were a distinctive emerald green. He stood prodigiously tall with a lean, muscular frame and broad shoulders. He was strong and lithe, the envy of any man and an object of desire for any woman.

'Welcome to my tent, Earl of England. Your name, sir ?'

'I am Harold of Hereford, Earl of Huntingdon, formerly commander of the armies of your grandmother, the Empress Matilda.'

'Well, well, we are . . .' and he swayed a little, appearing to forget what he was trying to say before slurring, '. . . honoured.'

The Earl said nothing, he just breathed deeply, trying to remain calm.

The Duke shook his head, in an attempt to clarify his thoughts. He squinted at Earl Harold and then pointed at him in a sudden gesture of recognition.

'I have heard of you.' He started to snigger and staggered a little. 'Yes, of course, is it not true that you did more for my grandmother than organize her army? Were you not her tup, cuckolding my grandfather for years?'

I looked at Father Alun, astonished at what I had just heard. The Earl stiffened, and he took another deep breath.

'You are impudent; you should show the Empress more respect.'

The Duke started to laugh heartily.

'Forgive me, Earl Harold, I have had a little wine with

my breakfast. Will you not join me? I am washing the earthiness from some Bordeaux girls in my chamber; they will be more than acceptable when the stink is gone from them.'

The Earl did not answer; he just turned and headed out of the tent.

As he passed the Duke's equerry, he bellowed at him, 'Tell your lord that I will come back when he's sober.'

We found lodgings in Bordeaux that night. Earl Harold did not join us for dinner, preferring his own company, weighed down by a sombre mood born of anger and sadness.

Later that evening, over a cup of the highly regarded local wine, I asked Father Alun about the accusation Duke Richard had made.

'The story is well known at court, but the Earl has never spoken about it. Matilda was a beautiful and remarkable woman – the daughter of a king, the wife of an emperor and later a count, and then the mother of a king – there are many stories about her, good and bad. Who knows which are true?'

'What do you think?'

'I think that as our mission unfolds many things will be revealed to us.'

'Another evasive answer, Father Alun, another test of my patience.'

'The Earl will soon leave us and return to his home. He will go there to die. It is important to him to know that we will carry out our mission in the way that he hopes.'

'I would be much more likely to carry out my mission

successfully if I knew exactly what it was and if I knew all the background to it. I am hearing more and more stories: legendary families, England's sacred cause, mysterious amulets. And now I hear that the Earl was Empress Matilda's lover! You treat me like a child. Why can't I know the truth of it all?'

Father Alun smiled at me benignly.

'All in due course, my friend, all in due course. Until young Richard can be persuaded of the Earl's proposal, some things must remain unsaid. Have another cup of this excellent wine. There is no finer grape in the world than the ones produced in this region.'

Although I was frustrated, I realized that Alun was protecting not only the confidences of Earl Harold but also, it seemed, vital information about Duke Richard's lineage and England's history. I let matters lie.

Alun was right; the wine was good. We had several more cups and my impatience subsided, to be replaced by a drunken stupor that lasted until very early the next morning.

I awoke to the sensation of my shoulders being shaken.

'Wake up, Sir Ranulf, wake up!'

It was too dark to recognize who was shaking me until he held a candle in front of his face. It was Godric.

'Godric! What do you want? It's the middle of the night—'

'Not quite, Sir Ranulf, but it is very early, the cock hasn't crowed yet. The Earl is up and dressed, he wants us ready to ride in ten minutes.'

'Why?'

'I don't know, sir, he didn't say.'

I threw some water on my face and got my weapons and armour ready as quickly as I could. When I arrived at the stables, the Earl and Father Alun were already in their saddles, and Godric and his men were in the process of mounting. The Earl had a lantern in his hand, which he held high to light our way. I looked towards the east, where there was no hint of dawn. Nothing stirred in Bordeaux; it felt like the middle of the night.

'I should have warned you about drinking with Father Alun. He has hollow legs, and always has a clear head the next day.'

The Earl laughed as he kicked on. Jumping on to my horse, which did little to improve the painful consequences of my night of indulgence, I called after him.

'May I ask where we are going, my Lord?'

'We are going to teach the Duke some manners.'

I looked at Father Alun.

'Is he serious?'

'Oh yes, he's serious!'

We were soon at Duke Richard's camp and rode through the perimeter of his picket lines unchallenged. Earl Harold beckoned to us to dismount about fifty yards from the Duke's tent, where we left our horses with Modig.

The Earl extinguished his lantern, drew his sword and marched onwards with purposeful strides. We approached our quarry's tent from the rear, and the Earl signalled to Godric to take Rodor and deal with the two men guarding the entrance. Shortly afterwards, and following some muffled blows, two limp shapes, gagged and bound hand and foot, were dragged towards us and deposited in a heap at our feet. The Earl then relit his lantern from the guards' brazier before whispering to Godric and his men to stand guard.

With Father Alun and myself in his wake, Earl Harold marched into Duke Richard's tent.

There was now a less sweet but equally pungent aroma inside the tent, a heady mix of sour alcohol and stale bodies, the aura of which was of no benefit to my fragile condition. A large butt stood to one side, still full of water for bathing, but its contents now more closely resembled a greasy broth than fresh water. There were two prone knights next to the butt, each entwined with a female companion. All began to stir. The two girls began to shriek as the knights got to their feet and made a grab for their swords. Earl Harold kicked one in his midriff with a ferocious blow and hit the second one on the back of the head with the pommel of his sword.

Without hesitation, the Earl then threw back the curtain to the Duke's chamber and strode in. All was still inside. A pert female backside was partly exposed beneath several layers of rugs and bedding. It moved a little, but only to emit an audible fart. Earl Harold grimaced, his contemptuous countenance only made more scornful by the young woman's prosaic bodily functions.

Duke Richard's outline was difficult to discern, but eventually a slight movement next to the girl revealed his presence. He pushed the young woman, a tiny creature not much older than a child, to one side and sat upright. He rubbed his eyes, his vision blurred by the bright lantern.

'Who is in my tent? Show yourself.'

Earl Harold answered with an austere tone I had not heard before.

'It is the Earl of Huntingdon.'

'What do you want at this ungodly hour?'

The Earl turned to Father Alun.

'Get the girl out. Give her a shilling and send her on her way.'

The Duke was not best pleased that his plaything was being sent away.

'I haven't finished with her. She's got the body of a snake and the temperament of a whore.'

'That's because she *is* a whore!'

With a heavy thump to her backside, the Earl lent his boot to her momentum as she rushed towards the entrance of the tent. Despite his nakedness, Duke Richard immediately moved towards us threateningly. I steadied myself, ready to make sure he did not lay hands on Earl Harold, but there was no need. The Earl took a huge swipe with the back of his gauntlet and caught Duke Richard across the side of the face, sending him sprawling to the floor.

Before the stricken man could move, Earl Harold was above him. He placed a boot on the Duke's throat and held the point of his sword under his chin. The two knights behind us had stirred by now and were looking for their weapons, but a gesture from Duke Richard told them to stay their hands.

Earl Harold looked at the young man at his feet with a flash of anger that I had rarely seen from anyone.

'I don't mind you drinking and whoring – we've all done plenty of that in our time – but I'm here to tell you about two things that are unforgivable.'

The Duke, embarrassed and angry, tried to respond in kind.

'Who are you to tell me anything?'

'I am your great-uncle – in name, at least. I was "uncle" to your father and his brothers, and I was your grandmother's most trusted friend. She was very fond of you and was particularly keen that your future be safeguarded. She entrusted me with your safety when you came of age. Now that you are marauding around Aquitaine with an army, I think it is time. Your father, King Henry, agrees and has given me his blessing.'

The Duke's anger subsided, but not his discomfort.

'Let me get up; you have made your point.'

The Earl removed his foot from Duke Richard's throat and threw a pile of discarded clothes at him.

'Get dressed and we'll talk.' Earl Harold then barked an order at me. 'Tell Godric to rouse the Duke's stewards; he needs some breakfast.'

The idea of breakfast seemed odd – not only to my delicate stomach, but also because it still seemed like the middle of the night.

Twenty minutes later, the tent had been put back into reasonable order and the stewards were serving food and fresh beer. The Earl had found himself a chair and seemed more relaxed. I looked at him closely. The disdainful demeanour had gone, and he looked more exhausted than scornful. I suddenly remembered his age. What he had just done was remarkable: he had chastised a man who was half a foot taller than him and a quarter of his age. My respect for him grew even more.

The Duke had dismissed several knights who, somewhat belatedly, had rushed to his aid. He had made himself look presentable and now sat down next to Earl Harold.

The young man took several swigs of beer and fiddled with his jaw, which was obviously sore from the blow Earl Harold had inflicted on him. He then spat a mixture of blood and beer into a cuspidor at his feet.

'Did you reprimand my father like this when he was a boy?'

'No, I would never strike a child like that – only a grown man who was acting like one!'

The Duke took another quaff of beer and smiled humbly.

'So, "Uncle", I suppose I am well and truly struck down, body and soul.'

'Yes, but you will recover quickly.'

'You said there were two things I had done that were unforgivable?'

'I did. Let me address them. First of all, you insulted the Empress Matilda. Apart from being your grandmother and largely responsible for your father becoming King, thus securing your inheritance, she was one of the finest women in Europe. You were only a boy when she died, but she was brave, kind and dignified; she loved her family, her kith and kin in Normandy and England, and believed passionately in the future of your father's empire.'

'I know, and I am sorry. I was drunk and surprised by your sudden appearance. But the rumours about you and my grandmother, you must admit, have been gossiped about for years.'

'That is as it may be, but rumours are what they are. And they don't justify you speaking of them to all and sundry. Your grandmother and I were very close for many years, right up to the end of her life. That's all that anybody needs to know.'

'I agree, please accept my apologies.'

'Now, the second thing: the state of your army. It's a shambles—'

'How so, Earl Harold? They fight like Trojans and have overwhelmed every fortress we've challenged.'

'—as evidenced by our ability to reach your own chamber in the middle of the night, almost unopposed. Good siege engineers and a rabble of mercenaries do not an army make. If we had been cut-throats, you would be dead now.'

'I grant you that I should be more conscious of my own security. But when it comes to a fight, my men can overcome anything sent against them.'

'I don't doubt that they are seasoned soldiers, good in a skirmish – and especially in a brawl – but a pitched battle between armies requires a lot more than men who are good at killing.'

The Duke looked perplexed.

'You are young,' observed the Earl. 'How many major battles have you fought in?'

Duke Richard did not answer; it was obvious that his fighting had been restricted to sieges and small encounters.

'Wars are won by tactics, logistics and planning; only after those things have been taken care of is it time to fight. Then, discipline becomes the key. Men who can fight as an individual or in small groups need discipline if they are going to fight in large numbers. Only right at the climax of a battle, when it is man against man, does the ability to fight become important. Up to that point, rigid discipline is vital. An army of good men, without the discipline to take orders and act in unison, can be run off the field in a few minutes of panic.'

The Duke listened intently to Earl Harold's lecture on generalship.

'Are the deficiencies in my army easily remedied?'

'Yes, but it will take time. The mighty army of King Harold of England and that of your great-great-grandfather, King William, the Conqueror of the English, were a lifetime in the making. But you have time; you're still only a young man. One day, when you rule this mighty Plantagenet Empire, you will need an army that can defeat anything that opposes it. You start from a strong base; you are already recognized for the strength of your resolve and for your chivalry. Your mother taught you well. But if you want to lead a powerful army one day, you should start the preparations now.'

'Will you help me with that?'

'Of course, but only for a short time. I am old now and I have a home to return to, where I want to see out my days in peace. But I will leave you with these men; they have all the skills and wisdom you need.'

'Then you had better make the formal introductions.'

'This is Father Alun, one of the cleverest men in England. He knows everything you need to know about the history of the peoples of your realm.'

'But, Earl Harold, a scribe of history, how can he help me build an army?'

'Because without the wisdom of the past, you cannot understand the present. And nor can you shape the future.'

Father Alun stepped forward, bowed slightly and offered the Duke his hand. Duke Richard grasped it, a little hesitantly, clearly not convinced that he needed a learned monk in his entourage. Even so, he was polite in his response.

'Welcome to Aquitaine, Father Alun.'

'And this is Ranulf of Lancaster, hand-picked by me from the elite officers of your father's garrison at Westminster. He is an exemplary knight and the finest of soldiers.'

I bowed to the Duke and held out my hand. He grasped it warmly.

'Sir Ranulf, that is a glowing introduction. Welcome to the army of Aquitaine.'

'Earl Harold is very kind; I hope I can do justice to his praise.'

The rest of the dark winter of 1176 was spent watching the ageing Earl Harold and the young Duke Richard become closer and closer. They hunted together and spent countless hours talking. Richard was fascinated by the stories he heard, especially about England's civil war, when the Empress Matilda's army was led by Earl Harold, as she tried to claim the throne from her cousin, Stephen.

Father Alun and I shared in many of these conversations and we soon developed a strong bond with the young Duke.

Eventually, as the New Year approached, Richard decided it was time to move south to confront his intractable lords in Gascony and beyond. That was a journey too far for Earl Harold, especially in the depths of winter. His campaigning days were over and it was time for him to return to his home to the east of Bordeaux. When he was preparing to leave, I asked him where his home was.

'It is many miles to the east of here, high up above the River Lot. It sits at the top of a crag above the river and has wonderful views down the valley. It is called St Cirq Lapopie and it is as pretty as its name suggests.' He looked to the east, with a hint of tears in his eyes. 'It is a special place. I will be buried there; perhaps you will come and see my grave when your adventure with Richard is over. I would like to know the outcome of his life. Perhaps you can sit by my grave and recount it to me; I may even be able to hear you above the fires of Hell.'

'I would be happy to, my Lord, but I doubt that Hell awaits you after such a noble life.'

'Sadly, young Ranulf, you only know the half of it. When you learn more, you may have the same misgivings that I have about my eternal destiny.'

He smiled sagely, and I responded with as much admiration in my expression as I could muster. As he was in a reflective mood, I took the opportunity to prod him again about my mission.

'My Lord, I realize that I am expected to help the Duke build his army and prepare for the day when he is King. But I suspect there is more to my mission than that.'

'There is, but it is only detail, and Father Alun carries all that in his head.'

'How will I know when my task is complete?'

'You will know. Just remember why you were chosen, and keep in mind all the things from your past that you believe in. Those are things that will guide you. It is your life that will unfold as well as the Duke's. You are helping shape his destiny, but also your own. When you know more about my family from Father Alun, you will under-stand. Eventually, you will become part of my family's journey and we will be proud to have you.'

'Earl Harold, I relish the opportunity to help England's cause and that of your family.'

'Good, because they are one and the same thing. Young Richard has little regard for the English part of his father's vast realm, so it is important that you and Father Alun help him understand what England means to us and why its future is so important.'

The next day was a poignant one for all of us. For several days, the warmer air from the west had been replaced by a much cooler wind from the east. The ground had turned cold, and ponds and lakes had frozen. As the morning wore on, the icy easterly wind subsided and a stillness set-tled over us. But it was only a temporary tranquillity; heavy dark-grey clouds filled the sky over the sea to the west, and by mid-morning heavy snow began to fall.

The stillness became an eerie silence as the snow cov-ered everything like a death shroud. Everyone in Bordeaux stayed in their homes, and the men of Duke Richard's army huddled in their tents. Braziers were lit beyond the awnings and their flaps pulled back to encourage heat to circulate inside.

In the midst of this ghostly scene, I saw Earl Harold busying himself. He was preparing his mount and packing his belongings on to two bay sumpters. I called to Father Alun and walked over to the Earl.

'My Lord, would it not be wise to wait until the snow stops?'

'I appreciate your thoughtfulness, but I like the snow, it brings back fond memories.'

'Of what, may I ask?'

He did not answer, but a look of nostalgia spread across his face. Father Alun answered for him by whispering in my ear.

'Have you heard the story of how, during her war with King Stephen, Duke Richard's grandmother, the Empress Matilda, escaped from Oxford Castle in the middle of the night when a brave knight led her through the snow to safety?'

'Indeed I have. Every child in England has been told that story.'

'Well, that knight was Earl Harold.'

I smiled, but I was not surprised to hear this latest revelation because, by now, I had realized how extraordinary the old warrior was. However, I remained concerned about his welfare.

'Sire, I hope you don't intend travelling alone. Take Godric and a couple of the men with you.'

'I don't need a nursemaid, young man. I've travelled the length and breadth of this empire many times.'

'But, sire, if I may say so, you were younger then.'

He smirked at me, before turning away to give the girth of his saddle one last tug. He then called for a mounting block, thanked Godric and his men and seated himself for his long journey.

'Father Alun, offer Sir Ranulf wise counsel; he will need it. Sir Ranulf, take good care of our future King; he will need you. I have said goodbye to the Duke. The bargain is struck. You will join his entourage as a knight of Aquitaine and, like Godric and his men, will carry my grandfather's colours.'

He then kicked his horse on and, without a second glance, rode off towards the east and the old bridge over the Garonne.

As his form became smaller and smaller in the distance, he soon became no more than a receding silhouette against the white background. Snow covered his shoulders like a shawl of fur, but he never bowed his head against the inclement conditions. He was too proud for that.

I wondered whether he had tears in his eyes. He had completed the final task of his long life; his adventure would soon be over.

But mine was just beginning. I turned to Father Alun.

'Don't you think it strange that Earl Harold is so certain that the Duke will be King one day? After all, his brother Henry is not yet thirty and is already anointed as his father's successor.'

'I know, I've often thought about that. However, the old man has an uncanny habit of being right about things. I've come to trust his judgement and accept his predictions without reservation.'

I turned back to stare into the distance. The silhouette had disappeared from sight. I wondered if I would ever see the Earl again.

5. Grand Quintet

Although the time Duke Richard had spent with Earl Harold had had a mollifying effect on the young man's demeanour, he remained tempestuous and volatile. The day after the old Earl had left, Father Alun and I were summoned to see the Duke.

Warm air had returned to Bordeaux and the snow had melted, but not so the harshness of the Duke's tongue.

'Gentlemen, I have accepted the offer from Earl Harold that you join my retinue. But you must understand that I will not accept the Earl's recommendations about you at face value. Like everyone else in my service, you will have to prove yourselves.'

I readily accepted the Duke's pragmatic position.

'Of course, my Lord; you are right to require that our actions speak for themselves.'

'My senior captains will soon return from their homes to begin our campaign in the south. When they do, you and your men will each be assigned to a captain. From that moment onwards, I expect total loyalty to him and to me. Is that clear?'

'Yes, sire.'

Father Alun nodded his agreement also.

We both left the meeting with the same feeling: the Duke was well named. And we had been asked to hold this particular lion by its tail!

*

Three days later, on 6 January 1177, the Duke's loyal henchmen returned from their estates. I had never seen such formidable men before. Not many men could stand as equals in the presence of Duke Richard, but the men of this quintet could. They each had their own entourage of four or five knights and a conroi of cavalry bedecked in their personalized armour and colours, which added to their spectacular arrival.

There was a cacophony of greetings and bellows of delight as the column rode into camp. This was the core of Richard's army – a far more formidable group than his Brabançon mercenaries – which made me wonder what would have happened had they been with the Duke when Earl Harold raided his tent.

The first of them was from the Artois, Baldwin of Bethune. A man about the same age as Duke Richard, he sat tall in his saddle, his long mane of auburn hair and his bushy beard making him look ten years older. He spoke with the strong accent of a man of his region, a tongue much influenced by the languages of the Low Countries.

Robert Thornham was a little older, perhaps twenty-five; the son of a middle-ranking Anglo-Norman father, he had come to prominence as a knight while competing in tournaments. A dark-haired, powerful man, adept with sword and lance, he had been noticed by Duke Richard at the age of nineteen when he had taken one of Normandy's most formidable champions clean out of his saddle at a tournament in Rouen. He had been with the Duke ever since.

Both Baldwin and Robert had soon been recognized in

the ballads of the third member of the quintet, Jean de Nesle. De Nesle had such distinctive hair, the colour of dry flax, that he was known to everyone as 'Blondel'. Not only was he one of the great troubadours of his age, but he was also a prodigious warrior, just as capable of striking an enemy a mortal blow with his mace as he was of smiting a lady with his beguiling lyrics.

Then there was a man from Provence known only as 'Mercadier', who was very dark skinned with jet-black hair. He spoke with an accent strongly influenced by the language of his region (which, I was told, was mainly spoken in Barcelona and the lands south and east of the Pyrenees). In his late twenties, he had the aura of a man to be avoided. Straight away, it was obvious the Duke would want him as an ally in battle, not as an adversary.

The oldest of the five was perhaps three or four years older than me. Although no more than thirty, he had already established himself as the epitome of the chivalrous knight. The name William Marshal had already been in circulation in Europe for several years; it was a name I had heard mentioned many times with a hushed reverence. And now here he was, larger than life, standing before me.

Famously, when his father, John the Marshal, Keeper of the Horse for the old King Henry, was fighting for the Empress Matilda in her war against King Stephen, young William was taken as a hostage by Stephen. When John the Marshal refused to relinquish Newbury Castle to the King, Stephen threatened to tie the boy on to a trebuchet and launch him over the walls and into the castle's keep. His father then responded with the riposte, repeated over many a camp fire, 'Do your worst, I still have the hammer and the anvil to forge more and better sons!'

The King was at first furious at the response and ordered that the five-year-old boy be sent to his death as a human missile. But when the boy showed no signs of fear and just looked at the King defiantly, he relented and ordered his release. Thus, the legend of William Marshal was born.

Another story had become legend, even though it had happened only a few years earlier. It was said that while campaigning for King Henry, William Marshal had been badly wounded in the thigh and that the gash was big enough to accommodate a man's fist. Lying as a prisoner in the dungeon of his captor, Guy of Lusignan, infection and a slow, painful death was almost inevitable. But such was the impression the young knight had made on the ladies of the household, they secreted bandages and ointment in a loaf of stale bread and had them sent to his cell. He made a full recovery before being ransomed by Eleanor of Aquitaine.

Perhaps a couple of inches taller than six feet, he had a red mane not unlike Duke Richard's, but he was much broader and had the handsome but rugged face of a man who had enjoyed many a fierce skirmish. His noble prowess had brought him to the attention of Duke Richard's mother, the redoubtable Eleanor, who had made him one of her courtiers and, it was rumoured, one of her lovers. He also caught the eye of her husband, King Henry, who took him into his service. Eleanor had entered him into endless tournaments, all of which he had won, and Henry had made him a captain in his guard and entrusted him with campaigns and the putting down of revolts. He was given lands in the north of England and in Wales. And thus, through his physical and martial prowess, he had been elevated from minor nobleman to one of England's most powerful landowners.

Later that night, Father Alun and I were invited to dine with the Duke and his five loyal lieutenants. As I had five loyal men of my own, I decided to dub my men the 'Little Quintet' and Duke Richard's men the 'Grand Quintet'. Not usually overawed by the company of lords and knights, I should not have been anxious, but I knew that this group of men and their Duke were not only among the most remarkable in Europe, but that our future depended on them accepting Alun and me into their circle. I also knew that, one day, we would have to gain their acceptance as equals. I feared not at all for Alun, whose wisdom and intellect were a match for anyone, but I was a knight and would have to earn my right to stand with them as a soldier.

The Duke did not prepare the ground well when he introduced us.

'My friends, let me introduce Sir Ranulf, a knight from Lancaster, which I am told is in the far north of my father's empire. He is sent to guard me by my grandmother, the Empress Matilda, although why it has taken so long for him to arrive is a mystery – after all, she has been dead for ten years!'

There was great laughter at my expense and I faced the dilemma of whether to assert myself, or bide my time for another occasion. I looked at the Duke's trusted companions and realized that if I had any chance of earning the respect of these men, now was the time.

'My Lord, I think Earl Harold was waiting for you to acquire the maturity that would be necessary for you to embrace your future and, of course, in choosing me for the task, to find the right man to join your service.'

Duke Richard did not react angrily, but smiled a little.

'You see, Sir Ranulf is quick with his answers, like his mentor, Harold of Hereford, Earl of Huntingdon – who, before you hear it from the camp gossip, gave me a lesson in manners when he brought this knight to me.'

William Marshal's ears pricked up when he heard the name Harold of Huntingdon.

'Well, my dear Richard, if you were given a lesson by him, I would suggest you heed it. There is no finer man in the Empire.'

The Duke looked suitably meek.

'Indeed I will, William; it was delivered along with the back of his hand. I remember it well.'

The Duke then turned to Father Alun.

'And this, gentlemen, is Father Alun. I am told that he is so wise, he might be Archbishop of Canterbury one day. I think he's been sent by my grandmother to save my soul.'

Mercadier was the first to make the obvious quip.

'Really, do you want me to tell him he's too late?'

The ensuing laughter took the sting out of the Duke's barbed introductions, and we enjoyed a convivial evening of good humour. We exchanged tales of chivalrous knights and their ladies and drank abundant quantities of the strong wines of Aquitaine, for which I was acquiring a particular fondness.

*

The arrival of Duke Richard's senior commanders seemed to rouse his army. We broke camp the following day and marched at pace through the remote forests of Gascony. We followed the old Roman road, which cut through the forests along routes as straight as the flight of an arrow. The ground was as flat as a calm sea; we saw very little other than endless miles of evergreen trees, and made rapid progress.

The conroi of Duke Richard's senior lords rode in strict formation, but the Brabançon infantrymen were less disciplined, while the archers and bowmen made their way in long lines, not unlike the march of ants. The most impressive group was the siege engineers and sappers. They moved in lengthy columns of wagons drawn by oxen. The wagons were packed with the impressive tools of their trade: axes, mallets and chisels; ropes, pulleys and winches; leather, iron and timber in myriad shapes and sizes.

The whole caravan was controlled by a fascinating mix of men. Some had the brawn to fell the trees, hew the timber and manoeuvre the huge siege engines of various kinds; others had the brains to calculate trajectories and distance; a few could do both. Nothing seemed beyond their dexterity or powers of invention. They could build simple battering rams, scaling ladders or towers, or construct complex trebuchets and catapults large enough to hurl rocks as heavy as two men over 200 feet in distance. They could dig tunnels under castle walls, using men with no fear of confined spaces, or use pitch, oil and animal fats to make incendiary weapons to set fire to gates or undermine stone walls with intense heat. When mixed with sulphur or quicklime, the incendiaries could be hurled over castle walls to the great distress of anyone inside.

Their final skill was to 'scorch the earth'. If the Duke anticipated a long siege, he would order that the entire countryside around the offending fortification be stripped of anything that could be consumed or be of use to anyone inside the walls. Wells were poisoned, crops burned, livestock killed or driven off, and barns and homes razed to the ground. It was a ruthless measure, but a very effective one, which would render the local lord's domain worthless – quite apart from the devastating impact on the local peasants, who bore the brunt of it.

The Duke commanded an impressive military machine which, when unleashed, could destroy vast swathes of territory like a plague of locusts. As I watched it drive through the forests of Aquitaine, I made myself a promise that whilst in the service of the Duke, I would learn as much as I could from these artillery engineers and their weapons of vast destruction.

The Duke had assigned Alun, myself and our men to William Marshal, a decision about which I was relieved. He was clearly the first among the equals in the Grand Quintet and the one with whom I had the best chance of developing a rapport.

Impressive as the Duke's siege army was, it was not a battle army, nor was it big enough to fight wars on a grand scale. I was certain that William Marshal understood these shortcomings and I felt confident that, with his support, this was the area where I could make a significant contribution to the Duke's future.

By the middle of January we were deep in Gascony, outside the walls of the ancient settlement of Dax. The Duke chose ground for his main camp to the west of the town, about a mile away across the River Adour. It was familiar ground to him, next to the beautiful chapel of St Paul. The chapel had been built by his mother, Eleanor, on a site famed for its thermal springs, which had been used since Roman times.

He had chosen his camping ground for recreational reasons as well as for military ones. Not only did he intend to warm himself in the balmy waters, he also planned to immerse as many of the local girls as he could and frolic with them to his heart's content. He was young and virile and had an immense appetite for the fairer sex. Of course, the rest of us were not averse to cavorting with the local women – especially William Marshal – but none of us could compete with the phenomenal tally of the young Duke. Father Alun's passions were entirely cerebral – at least, as far as I could discern – and he was the only one not to indulge himself by using the warm pools for purposes other than bathing.

Few armies marauded in the depths of winter, but Richard was driven by a passion for war not unlike his ardour for nubile girls. His five lieutenants were also driven by the lure of combat, while his Brabançons had an equal fervour for geld. It was a powerful combination and one to which the stubborn lords of Gascony would soon succumb.

When Duke Richard's main camp was complete, he sent a messenger to Dax, demanding the surrender of Pierre,

Viscount of Dax, and his ally, Centulle III, Count of Bigorre, who had brought his garrison from his own fortification in Tarbes. The Duke's terms were harsh: an oath of loyalty to King Henry, a repudiation of all previous oaths and the payment of one hundred pounds of silver to the King's exchequer. Failure to comply would result in the storming of the walls of the city, the emptying of its treasury and the total destruction of the Viscount's palace. Not only that, both men would be sent to Caen in chains to throw themselves on the King's mercy.

Despite the ominous presence of the Duke's army – a force of at least 700 Brabançons, and almost 150 elite cavalry commanded by the Duke's Grand Quintet of senior lords – the two Gascon lords were defiant. Our estimates, based on knowledge derived from locals hoping to win favour with the Duke, suggested that no more than 200 men manned Dax's Roman walls. Nevertheless, the message from inside, bellowed in Euskara, the strange local tongue of the Pyrenees, was blunt: 'Take your horde back where it belongs. We will have no truck with one of the Devil's Brood!'

The final part of the response was particularly pointed and intended to infuriate the Duke. The term 'Devil's Brood' had become widely used by the enemies of King Henry to describe his offspring. It was based on an old prophecy about a devil's curse on the lineage of Henry's father, Geoffrey, the Count of Anjou. It was an insult that had been oft repeated during King Henry's many recent disputes with his sons and with his wife, Eleanor.

The Duke was languishing in the thermal springs with

a young Gascon wench when the tenacious and offensive reply was repeated to him. He flew into a rage. Damning the local girl with guilt by association, he pulled her from the water and, despite her utter embarrassment at being naked, kicked her up the arse and ordered that she be left beneath the walls of Dax. He then bellowed at the messenger.

'Tell those inconsequential Gascon lords that when I have them in my grasp I'm going to flog them in front of the gates of their city with every man, woman and child in their domain looking on!'

Not in the least perturbed by his own nakedness, with long, purposeful strides he then strode out of the pool and walked the hundred yards to his tent. The girl he had dismissed so cruelly was standing barely five yards away, pulling on her clothes and sobbing profusely. Behind her, with admonishing glowers on their faces, were William Marshal and Blondel.

They said nothing; they did not need to. Richard stopped, looked at the two men somewhat sheepishly and then turned to his steward. He reached into a pouch on the man's belt and gave the girl a piece of silver.

Then he patted her on her backside in a conciliatory gesture.

'My steward will feed you. Make sure you're ready for me when I get back.'

Richard's enforced contrition of sorts had brought the incident to a close, while the silver shilling held tightly in the girl's grasp had transformed her demeanour from tears to smiles. The Duke disappeared into his tent, hurriedly followed by his steward.

When Richard re-emerged fully dressed, wearing his gleaming armour and carrying his glistening weapons, he cut an impressive figure. His lithe athletic frame, now enhanced by his ducal finery and the regalia of battle, conjured an image of a god of war from ancient mythology.

Like Ares or Mars, he seemed all-powerful and indestructible.

6. Destruction of Dax

To see the Duke's army prepare for a siege was awe-inspiring. His woodsmen had been felling trees since dawn and his sappers and siege engineers began to assemble their devices, ready to roll them into position. Carts of stones, pots of oil and bundles of fuel for fires were made ready. The archers and bowmen chose their ground and set themselves to ensure that should any opponents on the walls of Dax have the audacity to raise their heads above the parapet, a hail of arrows would encourage them to lower them without delay.

When all the paraphernalia was ready, and the ballista and catapults had been assembled from their sets of parts, everything was rolled towards the west bank of the Adour, from where the city was well within range. Some of the trebuchets were the size of oak trees, and the scaling towers were just as tall. They moved slowly but inexorably on huge wooden wheels, making the ground tremble as they passed. It was like watching a race of giants trundle forward. Beneath them, in their shadows, were our archers and infantry, the size of mice.

All was set just before dusk, when most commanders would retire for the night. Not Duke Richard; he thought the fading light of evening was the ideal moment to launch a fusillade of fire on to the defenders of Dax.

By the time the fires were blazing and the arrows and

the various catapults had been loaded, it was fully dark. Then the Duke issued the order to launch the missiles. It suddenly became as bright as day, but with a golden glow, as the entire scene was washed with the tint of fire. Much as it looked captivating to those of us outside the walls of the city, to those inside it was the beginning of a nightmare reminiscent of the infernos of Hell.

Fire arrows embedded themselves in the timbers and thatch of the more humble of Dax's buildings. Where human flesh was the landing ground for the arrows, they did even more dreadful damage. The wounds were made much worse by the searing heat of scorching pitch.

The contents of the catapults did similar damage, but on a massive scale. Clay pots of pitch exploded on impact, spewing their flaming contents in every direction. Buildings started to burn ferociously and people ran for their lives. Many were unable to run, already consumed by the fires as buildings received direct hits, roasting everyone inside like carcasses on a spit. Some inhabitants, their clothes and hair alight, managed to escape from doors and windows, but they were only able to stagger a few feet before falling to the ground in balls of flame.

Despite the horror of the first salvo, and the screams of anguish it produced, after thirty minutes or so all became calmer within the city. Fires still raged, and we could hear frantic attempts to douse the flames, but the sounds of panic and chaos subsided; the city was well organized and its inhabitants resolute.

But the Duke was not finished.

He rode up and down the lines of siege engines and

archers, shouting, 'One more tonight, lads, then early to bed, early to rise . . . Oh, and there's a piece of silver in it for all of you!'

Huge cheers greeted the pecuniary inducement and the men set about loading another volley of incendiaries. As they did so, and our fires illuminated our positions, the defenders of the city seized the opportunity to loose hails of arrows at us. Few hit anything meaningful, but they were a nuisance and Mercadier and Robert Thornham supervised the response of our men. Our volume of arrows far outweighed the defenders' volley, and soon their archers ducked down beneath the parapets.

Dax possessed a few ballista of its own, and stones and pots of boiling oil soon began to fall on us – but not with any intensity, nor with much danger to life and limb. Our sappers and siege specialists were able to launch a second volley of fire almost unhindered. We suffered a few casualties, but the Duke had a corps of well-trained physicians skilled in the techniques of mending stricken bodies. Few armies had had such men in the past, but Christian armies had seen their value and acquired the techniques during the crusades in the Holy Land, and they had become commonplace in Europe.

The second wave of incendiaries to hit the beleaguered inhabitants of Dax had the same appalling consequences as the first, and screams and cries rang out from behind the walls the moment they hit their targets. There was very little sympathy from our side. The Duke's army was ruthless; its men had done this many times before, and there was no room in their hearts for compassion.

The Duke, now satisfied with his night's work, called a

halt to the attacks, thanked his men and rode off to eat dinner in his tent.

As I made to leave, William Marshal stopped me. He had a mischievous look on his face.

'Ranulf, how good are you and your men with a grappling iron?'

I realized immediately what was afoot. I swallowed hard; I was about to be given a dangerous mission – one it would be impossible to refuse, if I was to continue in the service of the Duke.

'As good as anyone, and better than most.' It was the only answer I could give.

'Excellent. Get a grapple from the sappers. The walls of the city are very long, the garrison is thin; their eyes won't be everywhere, and it is a dark night. Take your men with you to cover your back. I'd like a report on the situation inside the city by first light in the morning.'

I knew it was a test of my resolve and my ability, but otherwise of little value. I put myself in William Marshal and the Duke's position. They had been asked to accept me as an equal; this was one way in which I could prove myself.

I collected an iron grapple from the sappers and gathered together Godric and my men. As Modig wrapped blackened linen around the grapple to deaden its sound, Godric and I daubed our faces in mud. He then tied back his blond locks and covered them with a dark cloth.

We waited until the dead of night and crossed the Adour in a small boat, leaving Penda, Modig and Rodor on the bank to guard the boat. The city walls were only a few yards away. While Leax waited for us at the bottom,

Godric picked a spot by guessing where the sentries might stand and then hurled the grapple over the wall. It found a secure position and we sat and waited for a few minutes to be sure that no one had seen or heard it land. The defenders did not seem to be patrolling the walls so, with our hearts in our mouths, we began the ascent. I went first. It was a difficult climb and I had to stop twice and brace myself against the wall to rest my aching arms. When I reached the top, I discovered how good Godric's guesswork had been.

To my left, his back illuminated by the fires still smouldering in the city below, was a sentry about twenty yards away. He was standing motionless, peering out into the darkness. To my right, another sentry casually paced backwards and forwards, perhaps slightly further away, his eyes looking down at his feet rather than towards the enemy.

I pushed the rope into a corner to hide it, beckoned Godric to haul himself up and crouched down into the shadow of the walkway, so as not to be caught in the glare from below. Godric came up quickly and joined me in my crouching position. With sentries either side of us, it was impossible to reach a tower to find a stairway down into the city, so we had no option other than to use our rope and grapple to descend.

As Godric carefully pulled up the rope we had used for our climb, I looked out across the city to get an impression of its layout. There was plenty of movement below us. Smouldering thatch was being pulled off buildings and I could see bodies being loaded into carts. Clouds of dense smoke wafted over us from time to time, carrying the acrid smells of charred timber and immolated bodies.

As it would have been impossible to detach our rope once we were on the ground, Godric needed to stay on the wall and pull the rope up after me. Fortunately, there were piles of stones, quivers of arrows and plenty of the detritus of battle on the ramparts for him to hide behind. We anchored the rope, I pulled up the hood of my tunic and then lowered myself down quickly.

Adopting as nonchalant a pose as I could muster, I wandered around, trying to be as unremarkable as possible. I spent about fifteen minutes in the city. Most of the time, it was quiet — except in the areas where fires were being damped down. The dead had been laid in piles; I counted more than thirty, and I'm sure many more were lying injured inside the infirmaries. It was difficult to assess the number of men in the garrison but, from the size of its building, I guessed about a hundred. Assuming that the Count of Bigorre had brought a similar number, our original estimate of around two hundred defenders appeared to have been accurate.

The populace did not seem downcast or rebellious, although they were hardly overjoyed at what had happened to them. There was no sign of the noble families, nor of any of the senior captains of the garrison. I assumed they were all safely in their beds, in the palace at the heart of the city, which had its own high walls and guards.

I had seen enough, and stealthily made my way back to Godric. I had been lucky that no one had stopped me or spoken to me, but I knew there would be a limit to my good fortune. Godric saw me coming and threw down the rope. As it hit the ground in front of me, providence deserted me. One of the sentries saw Godric come out of the shadows, and he raised the alarm.

Chaos ensued. Rather than attempt the climb in full view of sentries above and defenders below, I made for the tower to my left. Godric saw my choice and headed in the same direction. He dealt with the eagle-eyed sentry who had spotted the rope by heaving him over the wall, and I dealt with another sentry on the steps of the tower. The poor boy was unlucky; I had heard his footsteps coming towards me and he ran straight on to the point of my blade.

When I reached the top of the tower, Godric was waiting. He had already secured the grapple and thrown the rope over the outside of the wall. As sentries closed in on our position, he insisted that I went first and he followed close behind. Arrows started to fly past us and at least one came very close, hitting the wall next to my face and bouncing on to my shoulder. It did not penetrate my hauberk, but the shock of the impact almost cost me my grip on the rope. Our men had seen that we had been discovered and were shooting as many arrows as they could at the top of the ramparts to try to cover our escape.

I had just reached the bottom, with Godric about ten feet above me, when the rope was cut at the top. Godric hit the ground with a thud, but was not injured. Leax was hiding nearby in the undergrowth and he shouted to us to run, just as a hail of stones and rocks came tumbling out of the sky in our direction. Fortunately, darkness was our saviour and we ran to the Adour. Deciding that if all of us were to jump into the boat, we would make too big a target, I shouted to everyone to split up and swim for it. We plunged into the freezing water almost as one, and the splash gave our attackers something to aim at.

The city walls were now full of men, and arrows cut through the air all around us. They made sounds like men spitting as they hit the water and plunged into the depths.

It was a swim of over fifty yards, but the temperature made it seem much further. I was fortunate in that I had spent many hours in the sea around my home in Heysham, but I had no idea how well the others could swim, especially in such cold water.

In fact, only Penda, the biggest of us, struggled in the last few yards, but we were able to help him reach the bank safely. Only when we had run beyond the far bank of the river did the volleys of arrows subside. As we approached the thermal springs, our run turned into a gallop. We discarded our clothes on the move and plunged into the warm waters.

We had all made it back unscathed, but we had been lucky. I thanked Godric and the men. They knew that we had all been tested and were relieved that we had come through it successfully. But, like me, they resented the risks involved for no obvious value. There were still a few hours left before dawn, so we went back to our tents to get some sleep.

I slept well; I think I deserved it.

Despite my annoyance, I reported my findings to William Marshal the next morning in a calm and collected tone. He listened intently until I had finished, then smiled approvingly.

'Well done, Ranulf; it was not an easy assignment. But

at least we have accurate information about what is happening inside the city.'

'Yes, but not much more than we had before – and involving unnecessary risks to me and my men. The assignment did not make military sense. I am happy to be tested in battle, but futile excursions like the one we carried out last night could have lost you two or more quality soldiers for no real reward.'

Marshal did not answer, but he acknowledged my caustic response by putting a hand on my shoulder and nodding approvingly.

That day saw a change of tactics from Duke Richard. From first light to dusk he ordered that volley after volley of stones and rocks be hurled at Dax. Some rounds were aimed at the tops of the walls, while others were sent high into the air with a trajectory that would see them strike the Viscount's palace and other prominent buildings. His archers and arbalests were given a routine whereby, at regular but unpredictable intervals, their arrows and quarrels were launched at the city. The archers aimed high to hit targets beyond the walls, while the arbalests concentrated on the defenders manning them.

The Duke had a huge arsenal of arrows of many different kinds in reserve. But even so, the fletchers had to work furiously to keep pace.

When the Duke was in command of his army he was meticulous in his planning and relentless in its execution. Even though his infantry and cavalry were redundant, he insisted that they all help the siege engineers, quartermasters and anybody else who needed extra hands. Even his knights would readily remove their armour and help load the ammunition carts, or trim arrow shafts for the fletchers.

Richard and his Grand Quintet were everywhere – cajoling, encouraging, scolding – while Godric and I looked on in admiration.

I turned to Godric, and noted the appreciation in his eyes.

'The Duke is impressive, is he not?'

'He is, sire. He will make a fine general one day.'

Godric was right; Richard just needed experience in major battles. And he needed to create a body of infantry as good as the cavalry of men like William Marshal and Robert Thornham. If he succeeded, the world would be at his feet.

'Do you think we can help him?'

'Yes, sire, as long as he listens to you. That foolish mission last night must have earned you some standing with the Duke. But he is wild, and that is going to be difficult to control.'

'You're right, he's well named. He's a beast, and I suspect no cage will be strong enough to hold him, but that is our mission. I am glad I have you with me.'

'And I'm glad to be here, sire, and so are the men. Without this assignment, we would be patrolling the wilds of Wales, or chasing mad Irishmen across the Bogs of Allen.'

'But now you're chasing mad Gascons?'

'Yes, but this is only the beginning; I think there will be better places than Wales and Ireland, and greater challenges than crazy Celts.'

Father Alun had joined us, unbeknownst to Godric.

'Don't be too unkind to the Celts; they have their faults,

just like the English. And remember, the Normans think we're all savages.'

'Sorry, Father Alun, it's just that I've probably seen the worst of them in battle.'

'No need to apologize. There's good and bad in all men – in fact, the Duke is a case in point. We need to find a way to bring out the best in him, without sacrificing his warrior spirit.'

He was right. But my job was to help the Duke enhance his ability as a soldier; improving his moral virtue was Father Alun's realm.

'Do you have a plan, Father?'

'Perhaps the beginning of one.'

He glanced towards the industrious young firebrand, and I saw an appraising look flash across his face.

'Are you going to tell us?'

'No, not yet; I have to send a messenger, and call in a couple of favours.'

He then walked away with a mischievous grin on his face. As usual, Father Alun had given half an answer to a question, but had posed many more.

As dusk fell, Dax's ordeal by fire resumed. The Duke ordered two murderous incendiary attacks before retiring for the night. Oblivious to the screams and mayhem within the city, he rode back to his tent with the air of a man who had had a successful day's hunting. As he passed, he called out to me.

'Sir Ranulf, join me for some food and wine.'

The Duke was wont to relax with a host of young women, and was much inclined to enjoy to excess his food and wine. His invitation was not a test like scaling the walls of Dax. It was, nevertheless, another step along the path of acceptance. And so, despite my misgivings at the prospect of matching his prodigious appetites, I had little choice but to agree.

'Thank you, sire; I would be honoured to join you.'

The evening was hardly a chore. All five of Duke Richard's lieutenants were there and at least a dozen young girls, several of whom I had not seen before. After the food was cleared away, the Duke's chosen concubine set the tone for the rest of the night by removing her chemise.

Mercadier was too drunk to be interested in girls and staggered off into the night. Blondel seemed content to woo rather than bed his girls and sang the chansons of the troubadours to two who sprawled at his feet. Baldwin of Bethune and Robert Thornham, too exhausted from the exertions of the day to tarry further with nocturnal toils, dragged themselves to their beds, which left me with a more than acceptable bevy of concubines to choose from. When it came to it, the choice was easy. She had been staring at me all evening and I at her. I was at the bottom of the pecking order among the Duke's guests, so I had been praying that none of the others would take a shine to her.

Her name was Negu, which meant 'winter'. Although she was dark of skin, with eyes as black as pitch, there was nothing else wintry about her. She was vivacious, with a fine sense of humour, and could certainly bring the fecundity of spring to my demeanour and fill my heart with the warmth of summer.

We found a discreet corner of the Duke's tent and I

enjoyed a night of passion as intense as any I had experienced before. She said she was seventeen years old and that only a few of the boys in her village had bedded her, but I suspected that she was older and had been the plaything of the well-to-do of Dax for some time. I cared not at all; she was beautiful, I had drunk my fill, and she responded to my most robust endeavours in equal measure. The cock was crowing when my cock wanted to sleep, but she was still eager for more and would not let me rest until I had satisfied her one last time.

When the Duke's stewards arrived with breakfast, I can only have had a few minutes' sleep and then had to face the communal mockery as, one by one, the Duke's men gathered to eat.

Duke Richard led the assault.

'Well, Ranulf, we didn't need the cockerel this morning, the shrieks of your girl as you tupped her were enough to wake the dead!'

Then Baldwin of Bethune chimed in.

'Was somebody keeping count? He was at it all night!'

The consensus was that I had won my pennon in the bedchamber. It was the third ordeal I had had to face since meeting Earl Harold at Wolvesey, but this one had been an ordeal by delight.

I sluiced my head with a pail of water, gave Negu a piece of silver and asked her to come to my tent at the end of the day; I had had my fill of communal fornicating. She seemed delighted – an emotion that may have been contrived, but I hoped it was genuine. I then had to face Godric and the men, who were equally scathing about my public trial in the arts of lovemaking. The most erudite jibe came from Godric.

'We heard that you unhorsed her with just one blow from your lance, then ran her through with your sword, not once, but several times, just to make sure you'd finished her off!'

Three days later, the Duke heard the dramatic news from Dax just before he was preparing to leave his tent to begin another onslaught on the city.

A breathless messenger appeared and proclaimed, starkly, 'The Sergeant of the Watch says, "Come at once to the gates of Dax." You will be very pleased, my Lord.'

When we reached the city walls, the Duke was indeed pleased. With their wives, ladies of the court and various senior knights cowering around them, the Viscount Dax and Count Bigorre were stripped to their underwear, bound hand and foot, and tied to the quayside, right outside the gates of the city.

The Duke immediately ordered that they be released. While they were being untied, the gates of Dax opened and two men marched purposefully across the bridge over the Adour. One was the captain of the garrison and the other was a civilian, one of the city's most powerful burghers.

It was the burgher who addressed the Duke, not obsequiously, but in a matter-of-fact tone.

'My Lord, I am Ademus, a son of Dax. We are humbly offering you these men, our lords, Pierre and Centulle, and throwing ourselves upon your mercy. We have suffered enough and know that resistance to your onslaught is futile. It is a grievous thing that we do, for our lord, Pierre, will never forgive us for what we do. But it is either his wrath, or yours; we choose his.'

The Duke was clearly impressed by the candour of Ademus of Dax. He jumped down from his horse and held out his gauntlet. Ademus immediately fell to his knees, grabbed the hand and kissed the Duke's ring. The captain of the garrison repeated the obeisance.

Duke Richard pulled them both to their feet and embraced them. They were mortified; having been taught to lower their eyes in the presence of a viscount, to be embraced by a royal duke was unprecedented. I looked at Father Alun, who was standing close by; he had a knowing look on his face. I nodded at him, acknowledging the same admiration for young Richard's bravura.

'Men of Dax, you have acted wisely and with great courage. This has earned you my respect and the affection of the people of Dax.'

The Duke then grabbed Viscount Pierre and Count Centulle. He made them prostrate themselves before him.

'You have nothing to fear from these two. With their families and lickspittles in tow, they will be sent to King Henry in Caen, where they will beg for forgiveness. If the King smiles on them, they may return, but only if they acknowledge that, through your actions this day, you have saved them from much greater humiliation by my hand. In the meantime, they will forfeit two-thirds of their treasuries to me. They will be allowed to keep half of the remainder to protect the future of their families, and the other half will be distributed to the good people of Dax.'

Ademus turned to the captain of the garrison with a beaming smile on his face.

'Go and make an announcement in the city. I will escort Duke Richard and his men. There will be a celebration tonight. Open the wine cellars, and tell the women to prepare a feast.'

Escorted by half a conroi of cavalry – and with their families, personal belongings and their share of the treasury hastily loaded on to carts in their wake – Pierre of Dax and Centulle of Bigorre were on the road to the north within the hour, leaving the city and its captors to enjoy a long night of celebration and revelry. The Duke was the centre of attention for the entire time. It was easy to see how he had won the accolade 'Lionheart'; he had the rare ability to strike fear into the hearts of his enemies while earning the love of his friends and allies.

Negu and I enjoyed another night of passion – this time, a more private tryst – after which she asked if she could travel with me. Her request, tempting as it was, presented me with a major dilemma.

Despite a likely dubious past, she was a gorgeous creature, who was also intelligent and vivacious. But my mission had only just begun and no matter how attractive she was, she would become a distraction that could jeopardize what lay ahead.

The next day, I sought advice from Father Alun and put his renowned wisdom to the test.

'So, what is your advice?'

'Seek permission from Sir William, but you should take her.'

I was astonished. I thought I knew what my decision should be – that it would be unwise to be sidetracked from my mission by Negu's intoxicating company – and was certain that Father Alun would confirm my judgement. I had only asked him in order to make a difficult decision easier; now his answer had made it much harder.

'I am amazed. Why do you think I should agree?'

'I like her. There is something intriguing about her – apart from her more obvious charms, of course. It is better that you have a companion you are fond of, rather than a succession of whores and opportunists. You'll be a better man for it.'

'What about you? Doesn't the same argument apply?'

'I've chosen celibacy. It suits me; the entanglements brought by women are not to my liking.'

'Alun, I thank you for your advice, and I am grateful for your wise words. But I suppose she will have to travel with the other women, who are hardly the finest examples of either beauty or virtue.'

'That is her choice. She clearly sees you as a way out of the small world that is Gascony. You can't blame her for that. She has probably had to use the assets God has given her to get this far, and most likely with some fairly unsavoury characters. Now she has found you, and – if I may say so – you're a much more attractive proposition.'

I was happy to hear the compliment, and smiled at him.

'No,' said Father Alun, 'I don't mean that you're a handsome and chivalrous knight. But you're in the service of the Lionheart, and he's a duke who may rule an empire one day! For a girl from a small village in Gascony, that's a dream come true.'

'Now I don't know what to do.'

'Take her; our allowance from Earl Harold is very generous, and we can easily afford to look after her. Besides, she may be useful if I can persuade the Duke to go where I want him to go.'

'That's the second time you've mentioned your little plan. Are you going to share it with me?'

'Not yet.'

'You may be a wise man, but you are also an infuriating one!'

'I haven't had an answer yet, but I'm hoping to take Richard to meet an old nun.'

'Why?'

'Because he'll learn things from her that will help him fulfil his destiny.'

That is all Father Alun would say. Once again, I had to be patient.

7. Captain of the Guard

Before making my final decision about Negu, I needed to ask her some questions.

'Tell me about your life before the Duke's army appeared?'

She was very hesitant and embarrassed.

'Is it important to you?'

'Yes.'

The next thing she said confirmed my admiration for her. She was not overawed, but just threw the question back at me.

'You first.'

I gave a full account of my life before arriving in Gascony, in some detail. Then it was Negu's turn. After telling of a simple childhood in Riscle, a remote village fifty miles east of Dax, where her parents toiled in the fields from dawn until dusk, her eyes began to fill with tears when she described reaching the age of thirteen.

'The priest of Aire-sur-l'Adour, a large village near to my home, was a clever man and ran classes for children in the district. Most of them were boys, but he did teach a few girls – if they were very clever, or very pretty.'

'Which category did you fall into?'

'Both, of course! Anyway, I was lucky; he taught me to read Euskara and how to speak Occitan. But there was a price to pay. I had to suck his cock every day, and a few months later he demanded that I had sex with him once a week. I think he was doing the same with the other girls, but nothing was ever said. He was very careful and made sure I didn't get pregnant.'

I could see that she was trembling as she told her story.

'Don't be ashamed; you had no choice.'

'I *did* have a choice. But I decided to keep going to his lessons; I didn't want to end up working the fields like my parents . . .' Then she hesitated and started to sob.

'It's enough,' I reassured her. 'You don't have to tell me any more.'

'I do . . . I've never told anyone before, so I have to finish. It's my confession.'

I held her in my arms, and she put her head on my shoulder.

'Ranulf, what I'm about to tell you may change everything. But please try to understand, and forgive me.'

'It's not my place to forgive you, Negu; you have done nothing wrong in my eyes—'

'Except behave like a harlot. In fact, I *am* a harlot.'

The tears cascaded down her face, and her chest heaved in great spasms of anguish.

'The truth is too awful, but I must tell you. The priest – his name was Beti, Euskara for "Peter" – was quite old. Although I hated what he did at first, after a while I began to like it. He was kind and gentle, and I became very fond of him. I made him stop doing it to the other girls and, well, I suppose we became lovers.'

She then pulled away to see my reaction.

I smiled reassuringly. 'Well, he took advantage of you and stole your innocence. One day he will pay for that – perhaps not in this life, but certainly in the eyes of God.

You had to make a choice; it was your decision. You still haven't done anything wrong.'

'Ranulf, you are so wise and kind. I thought you would be angry.'

'No, not angry; you did what you had to do. So, now you've told me. Don't be too upset. It's over. And it could have been worse – he could have been cruel to you.'

'I know, at least he wasn't cruel. But he should never have been a priest. Anyway, when I was fifteen, he managed to find me work in the palace kitchens at Dax and I didn't see him very often. I suppose he found another girl. That is where I met Raymond, the son of Viscount Pierre. I was able to catch his eye; he was handsome, and we became lovers. He took good care of me – he had other girls, but I was his favourite. He wasn't so gentle in bed with me, but he was a lot younger, and I enjoyed it even more than with Beti. So, there you have it: Negu, the whore of Dax!'

'Hardly a whore; I would wager that most of the ladies of Viscount Pierre's court will have had many more lovers than you.'

'But is it not a sin to enjoy sex so much?'

I laughed out loud.

'Only in the eyes of the Church! And they're all hypocrites. Priests like Beti know the truth of it. You're just like everyone else. All the girls I've known – rich and poor, young and old – like sex. Usually as often as possible.'

At this, her face broke into a smile.

I held her as tightly as I could to reassure her.

'So, how did you find your way into Duke Richard's tent?'

She hesitated again. But this time she looked at me mischievously, rather than with embarrassment.

'I was sent as an infiltrator into your camp. Viscount Pierre knew that his son was bedding me and asked to see me. He told me to use my charms to get myself noticed by the Duke, or one of his captains, and send information back into the city. I couldn't refuse; they would have thrown me on to the street. So, when your army approached, I left the city and waited at the thermal springs at St Paul de Dax. It wasn't difficult to get myself noticed.'

I was far from annoyed – on the contrary, I admired her fortitude. But I decided to tease her a little.

'This is quite a confession. Are there any more sins to tell me about?'

'Ranulf, I am sorry. You're angry; I suppose you're not going to take me with you now.'

I tried to keep a straight face.

'Well, not if you're going to spy on me . . .'

'I only sent one message to the Viscount, to tell him how many men and siege engines you had. But he could count those for himself. Then, when I met you, I didn't send any more—'

I kissed her fervently and stopped teasing her.

'Of course I'll take you with me. I think you're a treasure, and I'm so lucky to have found you.'

The tears started again, but this time they were tears of elation. When we made love, it was tender and passionate. I realized I was truly infatuated with her.

William Marshal readily agreed to my request for Negu to join me on our campaign, remarking that she was a cut above the rest of the girls in the baggage train. Godric bought a good horse for her, and a mule to carry her belongings. She avoided the young whores and found some companions among the older women of the camp.

Dax had been dealt with to the Duke's satisfaction, and so we moved on to Bayonne, where another viscount was brought to heel. We stopped our advance in the Cize Valley, in Lower Navarre. It was called the 'Gateway to Iberia', leading to the lands of the Duke's ally, Alfonso II, King of Aragon.

With the capitulation of the Cize Valley, in the foothills of the snow-covered Pyrenees, Aquitaine was once again under King Henry's control. Duke Richard's mission was now at an end. He paid off his Brabançons and sent them on their way back to the Low Countries. His five lieutenants also returned to their homes, leaving just the Duke's small retinue of stewards and servants, and his own conroi of personal guards.

After a few days of hunting in the mountains, he decided that he too should head north to his home in Poitiers, which we reached at the beginning of February 1177. Sadly for Richard, his mother, Eleanor, was not there. For the previous four years she had been held in Winchester, and various other English castles, at the King's pleasure, after she had connived in a plot against him by her son – and Richard's elder brother – Henry. Although she was hardly incarcerated in an oubliette, she had to stay within the confines of any castle where she was kept, and communication with the outside world was prohibited.

I had always found royal politics and intrigue a mystery.

The protagonists had so much power and wealth, but it never seemed enough; sons fought fathers, brothers fought brothers, mothers fought husbands. Even more oddly, family members who once doted on one another often became mortal enemies and then were soon reconciled to their familial bonds. So it was with the Plantagenets – the 'Devil's Brood', as they were called.

The Duke's garrison in Poitiers was very comfortable, and we made ourselves at home. But within days, we heard news that made Duke Richard's blood boil. His Brabançon mercenaries had made their way home through the Limousin, where they had caused mayhem under the leadership of William le Clerc, one of the thugs Richard used when he faced a particularly stubborn opponent.

So awful had been the killing and pillaging perpetrated by the Brabançons that the local nobles and citizenry had created a huge people's militia to put a stop to them. Under the leadership of Isambert, Abbot of St Martial, and beneath a cross brought back from Jerusalem, an 'Army of Peace' sallied forth. It caught up with the mercenaries at Malemort, near Brive, and put the entire rabble to the sword, including William le Clerc, whose body was dragged through the streets until it was no more than a bloody trail of flesh and bone.

Although the incident was over, and the wrongdoing had been punished, word had already reached the King. Much of the good work Duke Richard had done in Aquitaine had been undone in the Limousin, another part of his father's empire which he found difficult to control. Not only that: the Duke had lost the bulk of his army, most of his siege engineers and all of their materiel.

Father Alun, Godric and I thought it a blessing in disguise; we believed the Duke was well rid of his band of cut-throats. Perhaps most significantly, Duke Richard would now have to travel to Caen to face an angry King Henry, not a rendezvous anyone would relish.

The Duke went hunting for several days, presumably to find time to gather his thoughts. When he returned, he summoned Father Alun and myself to see him in the Great Hall of Eleanor's elegant palace at Poitiers. Ostensibly, he was in good humour and put on a brave face when he spoke to me.

'I have to go to see the King and do penance for the actions of le Clerc and his bully boys in the Limousin.'

'Yes, my Lord, I've heard the news. If I may say so, sire, I would not regret their passing too much. It gives you a chance to build a new army, an army of professionals, loyal to you and you alone.'

'Yes, yes, but I fear my father will put me in limbo for a while and deny me the money to create a new force. And now that my mother is under house arrest, I can't get the funds from her either.'

Father Alun was suddenly animated by what he was hearing.

'My Lord, that being so, may I make a suggestion?'

'Please do.'

'After you have knelt before your father, would you consider kneeling at the feet of another to whom it would be prudent to genuflect?'

'Who else is there? Louis of France is our sworn enemy, and Frederick Barbarossa of the Germans is hardly a close ally. That leaves Pope Alexander ... and he's no friend either, after my father's acknowledgement of his part in the death of Thomas Becket.'

'Sire, with respect to all those men, I am referring to a woman – someone who, I would humbly suggest, is at least their equal.'

I suddenly realized that Father Alun was at last using the gambit he had mentioned in Gascony.

The Duke looked perplexed.

'Is she a queen? Other than my mother, there is no woman in Europe who could be seen as equal to a pope or an emperor.'

'Except one, my Lord.'

'Name her, man!'

'Hildegard, Abbess of Rupertsberg in Bingen, on the Rhine.'

'A nun! Are you serious, Father?'

'I am, sire. She is a living saint, and the wisest creature in Europe – man or woman.'

'I've never heard of her! The Rhine is at the edge of the world. Why would I want to go there?'

'To benefit from her wisdom, my Lord.'

'Because I don't have enough of my own, I suppose?'

'Indeed, that is correct, Duke.'

On hearing Father Alun's undaunted response, I smiled inwardly.

'You're a madman, and rude to your lord.'

'Perhaps a little, sire. But my task – a role that you accepted when I was offered to you by Earl Harold – is to counsel you. That is what I am doing.'

Like a sage, Father Alun had a way with words; I could see Duke Richard's mood become more acquiescent.

'Do you fear for my soul, Father?'

'Not yet, my Lord, there is plenty of time for redemption. It is more your temporal future that concerns me.'

'So, you think I lack wisdom. And this nun is going to make me prudent?'

'Not immediately, sire, but I hope she will inspire you.'

'To do what?'

'Wisdom is about making decisions, my Lord. Hildegard will guide you towards a path that will help you discover your destiny.'

'So, she is a seer?'

'She is old and clever, like Earl Harold. He said that you are destined to be a great leader and a great king, because of your heritage and because of the gifts you have been given. But you could lose your way. Ranulf and I are here to make sure that you don't.'

'I see. Does that mean that I am to do your bidding? Because if that's what you're saying, you can go back to England.'

'No, sire, all that we ask is that you listen. Then you can make your own decisions.'

'Very well, then, I have listened. We leave for Caen in two days. I'll hear no more talk of the old nun until then.'

Father Alun did not appear to be disappointed. The first move in his gambit had prepared the ground well – by astutely playing to the Duke's considerable ego – and I was intrigued to know how and when he would make his next move.

The Lionheart then turned to me.

'Ranulf, the Captain of my personal conroi, Ademar, is almost forty years old, and I promised him that our campaign in Aquitaine would be his last. He wants to take his pension and retire. I envy him. He has a house by the sea at Les Sables d'Olonne, a young wife and a brood of children. He wants to enjoy them in peace and quiet – a privilege I suspect I will never have.'

'But you will have others, my Lord—'

'Now *you* sound like Father Alun! Anyway, I would like you to become my Captain. Will you accept?'

'I would be honoured, sire. But what of your men? I am an Englishman, and new to your service. Will they accept me?'

'They will do as you and I tell them. You have made a good impression on all of us. Do you accept or not?'

'I do, my Lord, with gratitude.'

'Good, Ademar will leave us before we travel to Caen. You had better go and see him and prepare for the hand-over. He knows about my decision.'

I could hardly contain my excitement.

After the Duke had left the hall, to go to his chambers, I bounded to the door like an excited child, leaving Father Alun in my wake. Realizing I had forgotten my manners, I stopped and turned to say goodbye. With a broad grin on his face, he waved to me to go on.

I rushed to tell Negu and the men, and that night we all ate together in celebration.

Later, as Negu and I embraced one another in private, she whispered in my ear.

'Well, I missed the man with the heart of a lion by a whisker . . . but I managed to snare his cub.'

I took her remark as a compliment – which, I am sure, was what she intended – but it did make me smile a little.

*

Ademar was gracious in the handover of his responsibilities. Two days later, we were riding north to Caen with me at the head of Duke Richard's conroi of personal guards.

I had made Godric my sergeant-at-arms and integrated my Little Quintet into the column as the first two ranks.

It was a proud moment for all of us.

Negu rode with me. It felt very grand to be marching through the mighty Plantagenet Empire at the right hand of its most famous son.

I was unashamedly proud of what I had achieved.

8. Old Nun of Rupertsberg

When we reached King Henry's palace at Caen, the warmth of spring was in the ground and the city was stirring from its winter hibernation. The markets had fresh vegetables, and people walked with a lighter step, without their heavy winter cloaks and boots.

The King's castle at Caen had been built by Richard's great-great-grandfather, William, Conqueror of the English, over a hundred years previously. It was created to be a symbol of his lordship of Normandy, just as his Great Tower in London had been built to emphasize his subjugation of the English. It was the biggest fortified place I had ever seen. Its walls were so thick, it was possible to move along them with a cart and a full team of horses. The bailey was the size of an English burgh and even though it was full of various buildings, there was still space in the middle to hold tournaments and accommodate large crowds of spectators. The tall rectangular exchequer building sat next to the donjon to its east. The numerous heavily armed guards, and the thick oak doors, were testament to the vast hoards of gold and silver locked inside.

There were immaculately turned-out men and horses everywhere. The stables, armouries, forges and storehouses were without blemish, and there was a pervasive air of discipline and organization everywhere. I was reminded of Westminster; I felt very much at home.

Negu, my men and I were accommodated in the garrison's barracks, while Richard was taken to the royal apartments in the huge square donjon that towered over the bailey and served as the King's royal palace.

Later that day, when the Lionheart went to supplicate himself before the patriarch of his pride, he asked Father Alun and me to accompany him.

When we entered the Great Hall, it was a wonder to behold, even bigger and more opulent than the King's Great Hall at Westminster. The walls were covered with tapestries and hunting trophies while, at the end of the hall, silver dishes and candleholders glistened on the King's high table. A fireplace large enough to roast an ox sat prominently in the middle of the wall, to our left, around which several ornate oak chairs were arranged for the King and those granted an audience with him.

While four houndsmen played dice against the wall, several lyam hounds, which King Henry liked to use as scent dogs when hunting, and a couple of very large Alaunt guard dogs sprawled in front of a roaring fire, hot enough to warm our faces several yards away. Servants and stewards scurried and skivvied, and members of the King's elite personal guard, at least one of whom I recognized, stood to attention at every doorway and on either side of the massive fireplace.

The King's regal chair sat at the end of a refectory table so long it seemed to merge into the horizon. Suspended above it, as a centrepiece on the wall, was the Baculus, the Norman war club of legend that had been carried to Normandy by Rollo the Viking, ancestor of all the Dukes of Normandy and Kings of England since the

Conqueror. It was now only of symbolic importance, but old men of my grandfather's generation said that King William had carried it into battle at Senlac Ridge and throughout his campaigns against the English Resistance. Some even said that the Conqueror had used the Baculus to strike down Hereward of Bourne at the end of the Siege of Ely.

Duke Richard looked ill at ease, and even more so when a commotion in the direction of the King's private chambers announced his impending arrival. The stewards hurriedly checked that all was in order in the hall, the servants made themselves scarce, the dice players pocketed their gaming cubes and even the dogs pricked up their ears.

Just as the King – the progenitor of the Devil's Brood – appeared, the Duke ushered us out and asked us to wait in the hall's antechamber. Thus we were not privy to what was said next, but the echoes of the King's invective rang long and loud. Duke Richard lent his fair share to the din, and the arguments went on for many minutes.

Suddenly, the door to the hall opened and a sergeant-at-arms gestured to us to enter. I looked at Father Alun. He was not in the slightest overawed, and signalled to me to go first. We had hardly entered the hall when King Henry bellowed at us.

'Step forward, Earl Harold's disciples, and let me see who presumes to be my son's guardians.'

As we drew near, and the light of the fire illuminated our faces, the King – who was as imposing as ever, but now in his mid-forties with his long red mane streaked with grey – recognized me.

'I had heard that the Earl of Huntingdon had chosen one of my Westminster captains as Duke Richard's counsel. I remember you; tell me your name.'

'Ranulf of Lancaster, my Lord King.'

'Yes, I dubbed you knight. The Earl has made a good choice. And you, priest, you are going to save my son's soul?'

Father Alun did not hesitate with his response.

'My Lord King, just as the safekeeping of the Duke's corporeal self is Sir Ranulf's area of expertise, mine is the well-being of his soul. But where his spirit will rest at the end of his days will be determined by his actions, not mine.'

The King looked at Father Alun sternly.

'I am told that you are a very astute man. I don't like clever men; be careful with your riddles.'

Father Alun bowed deeply. Again, he did not seem in the slightest perturbed. It was as if he was playing a game of chess against a good opponent who had just made an aggressive move.

The Duke now intervened.

'If I may interrupt, Father. You are right, the priest came to me with a formidable reputation. Indeed, he may be useful to us in offering a solution to our current impasse. If I am to be punished by being denied a domain of my own until you think I merit it, and if you will not grant me any funds to recruit a new army, he has a proposal.'

Duke Richard then nodded to Father Alun, who recognized his cue and took it without hesitating.

'Sire, I have asked your son to take a pilgrimage to

cleanse his soul, not a journey to the relics of a long-dead saint, but to a living one: Hildegard, Abbess of Rupertsberg, at Bingen on the Rhine.'

The King looked surprised.

'The Old Crow of the Rhine, who preaches to emperors and popes and teaches girls to sing? She must be dead by now!'

'On the contrary, sire, she is alive and well and perfectly capable of dispensing wisdom to popes and emperors . . . and also to kings and dukes.'

I expected the worst at that moment, but King Henry's ire was not stirred by Father Alun's sarcasm. He just smiled.

'You will go far, priest. You remind me of a certain Archbishop of Canterbury, who was also dubbed the cleverest man in England. But remember, Becket met a grisly end thanks to his sharp mind and ready insolence.'

Again, Father Alun just nodded in acknowledgement of another powerful riposte in their verbal sparring. The King then turned to his son.

'So, do you want to make this pilgrimage to see the old witch?'

'Yes, Father, I do. But I want your promise that upon my return you will let me resume my ducal sovereignty in Aquitaine with the resources to defend it properly.'

The King looked at him intently and thought for a while before answering.

'So be it. Sir Ranulf, keep a watchful eye on my son and bring him home in one piece. Priest, redeem his soul, but don't inhibit his spirit.'

The King then left amidst the same flurry that had

announced his arrival, leaving the three of us to collect our thoughts.

Duke Richard spoke first.

'Father Alun, your ridiculous suggestion about the nun suddenly became very fortuitous. The King had wanted me to take the cross and go to the Holy Land, but that is even further away than England. I am not ready for the Outremer just yet; I haven't committed anywhere near enough sins to need the redemption afforded to a crusader. So, a short excursion to the Rhine is much more appealing – and I'm out of sight and out of mind, as far as my father's concerned.'

Father Alun grinned from ear to ear.

'I will make the arrangements, my Lord.'

Wily Father Alun had been either very shrewd, or very lucky. But either way, he had got what he wanted.

So, the son of the great Plantagenet King, who was an emperor in all but name, was to venture into the domain of the mighty Frederick Barbarossa, Emperor of the Holy Roman Empire, a man sanctified by the equally impressive Pope Alexander III, God's Emperor on Earth.

Barbarossa, despite being in his fifties, was in Lombardy trying to stop his Italian princes from forging an alliance with Manuel I, the Emperor of Byzantium. Fortunately, this meant we did not need to make a detour to his imperial palace in Aachen to offer our respects.

We travelled light. The Duke had sent all but five of the twenty-five members of his conroi back to Poitiers. We avoided Paris, so as not to provoke King Louis, and travelled through Rheims, Metz and Trier, before reaching the Rhine at Bingen. Hildegard's Benedictine foundation was close to Bingen, nestling in the forests, high on the left bank of the Nahe River, where it met a dramatically sharp elbow in the Rhine. I marvelled at the rivers I had seen since leaving Westminster; they made the rivers of England seem like brooks in a hay meadow. Where the Nahe met the Rhine, the vast river was over 500 yards wide and yet it still had to journey over 250 miles to reach the sea.

Hildegard had chosen the ground at Rupertsberg because it was the resting place of the physician and alchemist St Rupertus, who had built a chapel there hundreds of years before. She hoped he would be an inspiration for her own work and had arrived thirty years ago, with eighteen other women from the nearby foundation at Disibodenberg.

Rupertsberg flourished and, in 1158, Archbishop Arnold of Mainz granted it official recognition. Five years later, it was guaranteed protection by the Emperor Barbarossa himself. Soon afterwards, both men began to seek guidance and advice from the 'Oracle of the Rhine'.

As we climbed towards the monastery, I was struck by the large number of people in the fields and vineyards and the orderly way in which they were working. They seemed properly fed and comfortable, their humble houses in neat rows and well maintained, each with its own patch of market garden. There were no monks to be seen; all the supervision was being done by nuns, impeccable in their dark-brown habits and black scapulars. Their fresh, earnest faces were framed by clean white wimples, their only ostentations being the silver crucifixes around their necks and the plain silver bands on their ring fingers, demonstrating their marriage to Christ.

The most dramatic aspect of our arrival drifted across the valley of the Rhine like a chorus of angels. I had never experienced anything like it before. I had heard plainsong every day at old King Edward's abbey at Westminster, sung by men and young boys. But this chanting was different. It was sung by women and girls but it was also a new sound, something I had never heard before, not just one layer of song but a series of them, each one rising above the other. I turned to Father Alun who, with his head thrown back and his eyes closed reverentially, was wallowing in the sounds.

'Her music?'

'Yes, isn't it marvellous? She says that when she composes, she is performing the Rituals of the Virtues, and she writes her songs in praise of God. She calls them her Symphonies, her Harmonies of Heavenly Revelation.'

'Do the nuns sing all the time?'

'The Benedictine Rule observes the Divine Office eight times each day, beginning in the dead of night at two in the morning and concluding at nine in the evening. They sing every three hours. It's like being in Heaven.'

Although I did not have the same appreciation of Hildegard's musical ambition as Father Alun, I could certainly hear the soaring harmonies. I was moved by what I heard, as was the Duke. He looked around at the simplicities of monastic existence and listened to the melodies in the air. Then he nodded at me, and smiled.

Father Alun came back down to earth and reverted to the mundane.

'My Lord Duke, let us get our men settled. Abbess Hildegard is expecting us for dinner.'

'Where do we stay?'

'Sire, you, Ranulf and Negu may stay with me in Hildegard's cloisters. But remember, the cells will be very austere. The men are excluded from the proximity of the nuns' cells and must make camp outside the monastery walls. And they need to be reminded that they must keep their pricks in their braies.'

'Does that injunction apply to me as well?'

'Of course, sire. The only passion you will find here is a love of Jesus.'

Duke Richard looked as if he had been scolded by his mother.

'Father, why do you reprove me, even before I have sinned?'

'Sire, my rebuke is based on prior experience. Your previous behaviour suggests that it might be wise to admonish you *before* you commit an inevitable indiscretion.'

'Oh, ye of little faith!'

It was good to see the Duke relaxed. The almost relentless energy that he showed during his campaigns in Aquitaine had faded. For once, he had the air of a man at peace with himself. Father Alun smiled broadly, pleased that the Duke was happy to engage in banter with him and impressed that he was able to quote from the New Testament.

The Lionheart jumped from his horse and put his arm around Father Alun's shoulders.

'The chanting of the nuns is very soothing. Let us go inside; I want to meet the woman who creates such sounds.'

When we arrived, Abbess Hildegard was sitting in the locutory, surrounded by half a dozen nuns.

She was dressed exactly as the others. Framed by a pristine white wimple, her face had the same pale countenance as the nuns who attended her, which contrasted sharply with her dark habit and the gloom of the shadowy interior. The only difference was her heavily wrinkled complexion. The single candle on the table in front of her illuminated the ravaged skin of a woman of great age – at least seventy-five, or even eighty. Her back was hunched, and she was frail to the point of being not much more than skin and bone. Her hands, one of which grasped a walking stick so tightly that her knuckles gleamed like ivory, had no flesh on them, but were just scraggy bones, traversed by bulging blue veins.

Although she had a body racked by age, she looked serene as one of the nuns read to her in Latin from an ancient tome. When she saw us arrive, she tried to get up, but Duke Richard stopped her.

The Lionheart sank to his knees at her feet.

'Abbess, we are honoured to visit you here at Rupertsberg.'

Father Alun then made the introductions.

As he did so, Hildegard smiled benignly at each of us in turn. But when it came to Negu's introduction, the Abbess called her over and put a hand on her head and stroked her hair.

'Where are you from, child?'

'I am a Basque, Reverend Mother.'

'Ah, that is why you are so dark. You are very beautiful. You must sit next to me tonight at dinner. I prefer to have girls next to me when I eat; men smell too much.'

She then turned to Duke Richard.

'Your Grace, you and your companions are very welcome in our humble home. You must be tired from your journey, and I must go to pray. Let us talk this evening.'

We withdrew, leaving the nuns to help Hildegard make her way to her cell.

Dinner that evening, although good humoured with fine conversation, was a frugal affair, a thin stew of meat and vegetables, but at least the bread was fresh and the sweet fruit beer intoxicating. Hildegard ate like a horse and swilled copious pots of beer; she belched regularly and occasionally lifted one buttock to fart loudly. The other nuns were just as uninhibited with their digestive functions.

After the food, the Abbess was helped to the locutory by a pretty young novice. Here the Duke, Father Alun, Negu and I joined her. Hildegard began drinking kirsch, and the novice poured the strong, clear liquid into small wooden bowls for us. It was a new taste for me and one that took some getting used to. However, Hildegard was well beyond the beginner's stage and quaffed it with abandon.

She insisted that Negu sit at her feet so that she could stroke her hair. 'Do you mind me stroking your lovely hair? Here, we cut our hair short and our wimples mean I can never feel the tender silk of a woman's hair.'

'Not at all, Reverend Mother; you have gentle hands.'

'Can you sing, child?'

'I don't know; I've never tried.'

'Listen to the nuns singing in the chapel now. Can you make sounds like those?'

Negu immediately produced a high-pitched note as clear as a Sanctus bell.

'I thought so; you have a clear and crisp voice, and a young throat. I knew you could sing. If you would like, I will teach you how to sing like the nuns. In every church I know, the monks sing and the nuns do the chores. Here my girls sing. It is through our singing that we express our love for one another and for Our Lord.'

Negu beamed from ear to ear.

'I would love to learn, Reverend Mother. I have never been able to do anything other than make a man happy in bed.'

'Well, that is a gift too, child, but it is always good to have another string to your bow.'

Hildegard was unlike any nun I had met before. She exhibited a generosity and a sense of mischief that was infectious. She had made Negu feel welcome and charmed her with her openness and lavish attention. She then turned her focus to the Duke, who had been sitting patiently, drinking the kirsch that the attentive novice kept pouring for him.

'We make it ourselves, you know, from our own morellos, which we also use to make our Kriek Lambic, the beer you had with dinner. Our kirsch is particularly potent, and it is good for the flatulence we get from the beer – which visitors are often relieved to know, after they've suffered for two hours listening to my girls break wind in the refectory. You see, I encourage them not to be inhibited about any of their bodily functions.'

Hildegard delivered her comical homilies in a totally matter-of-fact way, making it difficult to know whether she realized how droll she was being.

'Father Alun tells me that you are called "Lionheart". So, I wonder how I should address you?'

'As you like, Reverend Mother.'

'Good, then I shall call you Richard. And you may call me Reverend Mother. Father Alun tells me that you are seeking wisdom?'

'I am, Reverend Mother.'

'Are you sure? He also told me that you only agreed to come here because your father had a much more onerous penance for you in the Holy Land.'

'That is true.'

'Not an auspicious introduction, Richard, but at least you're honest; that's a good start.'

On Hildegard's signal, the young novice then leaned forward to fill the Duke's bowl with yet more kirsch.

'Would you like to bed her?'

'Well . . .'

He hesitated. Hildegard finished the sentence for him.

'You mean, if she was not in a nunnery and not wearing the white habit of a novice.'

'Exactly.'

'She is very pretty and may well oblige you. I rescued her from Robert, Count of Nassau, who threw her out when he found her cavorting in the stables with several of his grooms.'

With a smile on her face, the young girl interrupted the Abbess.

'All of his grooms, Reverend Mother. But I am trying to give up such base pleasures to find the more gentle love of God.'

The novice patted the Duke on the cheek, then backed away to sit at her Abbess's feet.

Hildegard put her hand on the novice's shoulder.

'You see, Richard, it is possible to control the most powerful of our feelings. Our teaching here emphasizes honesty and truth above all other things. We must be truthful about our demons, otherwise we can't learn to control them . . . But enough kirsch, and enough talk.' She suddenly gestured to the novice that she wanted to leave. 'We must go to our beds.'

After she had gone, the Duke shot questions at Father Alun like an archer in battle.

'Has she always been like this?'

'As far as I know, yes. But I think she was making a point with the young novice.'

'Astonishing! What do the Church and the Emperor make of her?'

'I am told she is the same with them. But her knowledge is beyond equal, even among the most learned men in Christendom. Some say she's a witch, but many more revere her as a living saint. Either way, no one dares threaten her or challenge her.

'She has had visions since childhood, and the Church has lost count of the number of cures and miracles that have been ascribed to her. Besides her music and poetry, she has written leading texts on theology, healing and the natural world – and in her own alphabet, which she devised so that her nuns could have their own private manuscripts. Wise men come from all over Europe to seek her advice and hear her pronouncements. She has travelled as far as Milan and Vienna, preaching against corruption in the Church and calling for reform. When they held the Synod of Trier thirty years ago, she sent a simple message: "Glance at the sun. See the moon and the stars. Gaze at the beauty of earth's greening. Now, think."

'Because it didn't include God in its litany of wonder, the assembly of the great and the good of the Church at the Synod thought it was blasphemous. But Pope Alexander raised his hand to stop them and repeated her word: *think*. He said, "Do as she asks before you speak." They did; and no one spoke. When I heard that story as a young monk, it changed the way I saw the world, and still does. She teaches us that God is everywhere, not just in Heaven. By "greening" she means nature as the pagans saw it, as in their Green Man of legend in England.'

Father Alun continued for some time. We all listened intently, including the Duke. I had never seen him so still and so quiet before.

Later that night, as Father Alun, Negu and I walked to our cells, he grasped my arm and said that what we had just talked about was important. He insisted that I remember it.

'Think back to what I said about Earl Harold's family. One day, tonight's conversation will make more sense to you, so you must remember it.'

'Another riddle for me, Father?'

'No, just another observation for the future.'

*

We spent almost three weeks at Rupertsberg. The Duke went hunting almost every day, but we spent every evening and several afternoons listening to Hildegard talking about the mysteries of life – not just on the earth we know, but elsewhere. She talked about worlds above and beneath ours, and about phenomena that were both real and surreal. She asked us provocative questions about the stars and what was in the heavens, and about good and evil and the nature of men's souls. Usually we had to seek guidance from Father Alun about what exactly she had said or meant. Sometimes he helped explain things, but on other occasions he admitted that he was as baffled as we were.

Most importantly, Duke Richard was like a man transformed. He hung on every word Hildegard uttered, especially when she talked about honour and chivalry. The turning point came when she talked about a man from the past she particularly admired.

'Have you heard of Pierre Abelard?'

The Duke knew the name because his mother, Eleanor, also worshipped the man's memory. But he confessed that he had never taken much notice when she talked about him. She had become wistful, almost tearful, when speaking of him.

'Abelard was the most important philosopher of the last hundred years, and a great influence on me. Had we been contemporaries, and had I not taken my vows to Christ, I would have gone in search of him and married him. He challenged the Church and all modern thinkers to base their views on questions and answers, on logic and thought, rather than rely on blind dogma. He was hounded for his radical views by the Church hierarchy, but young people came from the far corners of Europe to listen to him. I was one of them. I heard him speak in Paris, when I was not much more than a girl. I was so moved by what he said about the power of the human spirit, I cried all the way home to the Rhine. After that, I knew that I had to devote myself to God's greatest creation – the human imagination.'

The Duke had heard a different story about Abelard

'Did he not seduce the lady Heloise, a deed for which he was castrated?'

'Indeed, he was a human creature, weak like the rest of us. Heloise may well have been his intellectual equal, but their affair meant that she had to leave Paris and become a nun. Now, the story of their tragic love affair has become an inspiration to young knights and their ladies all over Europe. But his most important legacy is his insistence on the importance of our ability to think, as well as our ability to act.'

The ancient nun then beckoned Duke Richard to kneel before her. With her sitting slightly slouched in her chair and him kneeling upright, their eyes were level. She stared at him intently, placed her hands on either side of his head and gripped him firmly. She began to sway, with his head in her hands, and brought his head close to hers, so that their noses were almost touching.

'If you take anything from here, young Lionheart, take this thought: Your mind is much more powerful than your sword arm. That is why, when soldiers fight wars, they win land and riches. But when thinkers fight wars, they win men's minds. You can't change the world with land and wealth, but you can with men's minds.'

Hildegard's words had a profound effect on the Duke and influenced the rest of his life.

I was also moved by them. I had come so far already, but Rupertsberg seemed like only the beginning of our journey.

When Negu began to whisper in my ear on the eve of our departure from Rupertsberg, I was not surprised by what she had to say.

'Please don't be upset, but I want to stay here with Mother Hildegard and the nuns. I am so happy, and my voice is improving all the time.'

I had become very fond of Negu, but I knew that my journey was only just beginning and that she was still searching for her own identity.

'Are you sure?'

'I'm sure I want to stay, yes.'

'And to become a nun?'

'I don't know. But here, I'm a woman, respected for what I am, rather than being viewed as a body to be desired by men.'

'I hope I haven't treated you as merely a body—'

'No, of course not. You have changed my life, and I will always be grateful to you. But now I can live my life through *me*, rather than through you. Do you understand that?'

'I do . . . but I'll miss you.'

'And I'll miss you. Always. Come back here, and tell me all about your adventures with the Lionheart.'

Alun had been right about Negu; she had taught me the importance of love and companionship, and how a woman's view of the world can be so different from a man's. I had lived the life of a soldier and, other than my mother, had not treated women with much respect – and certainly not as equals. Now, at last, I understood the folly of my ways.

9. Triumph at Taillebourg

The journey back to Poitiers was uneventful, as were the next two years. The King did not honour his side of the bargain by letting Duke Richard resume his lordship of Aquitaine, but insisted that he stay in Poitiers to build a professional army and forestall the need to rely on thugs and mercenaries. I was delighted; it meant that I had the time and resources to train a body of men who could fight in any situation, and fight effectively – whether in a small-scale skirmish or siege, or in a full-scale pitched battle.

Before Rupertsberg, King Henry's broken promise would have sent the Lionheart into an apoplectic rage, but he had become much more sanguine and now devoted himself to long hours of military training and man-oeuvres.

Building a new army from nothing was a daunting but exciting challenge, especially as there would be two stern judges of our work: the Duke's five lieutenants, who had promised to review the army when we had finished its training; and the stubborn and fierce Gascons who, once again, had been troubling the King.

We sought young men who were ambitious and hun-gry: Normans for our cavalry squadrons, English archers and some infantrymen – with a sprinkling of tough Celts in the infantry – and sappers and siege engineers from Iberia and Italy. They made a good blend, welded together by rigid discipline, clear limits to indiscretions, good food and generous pay.

Hildegard of Rupertsberg died in September 1179. By then, the King had relented and sent the Duke with his new army back to Aquitaine. We were camped near a Gascon village called Nogaro, not far from Negu's village of Riscle. Our men had passed the harshest of scrutiny by the Duke's loyal friends – especially William Marshal – and had performed well in the various small encounters of that year.

Word of Hildegard's demise spread through the ecclesiastical cloisters of Europe like wildfire and prayers were said in every church, large and small. Priests prayed, bishops wrote eulogies and the Pope began the process of her beatification. In truth, they were glad to be rid of her and her radical thinking.

Richard sent a generous donation of silver to her monastery so that a large cross could be made in her honour and ordered that the army be stood down for a week so that he could go into mourning. Typically, on the last night he organized a feast which, as closely as could be arranged, was a replica of the frugal meal we had eaten on our first night at Rupertsberg. His cooks were amazed when he ordered the thinnest stew that could be made, then sent his stewards in search of a fruit beer to match the lambic of the Rhine and to find a drink similar to kirsch. The nearest match that could be found to kirsch was the local Gascon speciality, Teneraze, a much more palatable offering.

During his absence from the area, old enmities had surfaced in Gascony, as had the desire of its local lords to extricate themselves from Henry Plantagenet's sovereignty. Even more significantly, Duke Richard's old ally, Alfonso II, King of Aragon, had widened his influence to include the whole of the Iberian side of the Pyrenees and into Roussillon and Provence. Here was another king with imperial ambitions, as 'Emperor of the Pyrenees'. It was fortunate that we had spent the previous year and a half recruiting and training a new army in Poitiers; it, and the Duke, were about to be tested to the full.

The summer of 1179 had brought success upon success for the Duke. Pons, Richemont, Genzac, Marcville, Grouville and Anville all capitulated, some with token resistance and some with a fight. But our next challenge, a mighty fortress looming over the Charente, was an entirely different proposition. Taillebourg Castle stood on a high rocky outcrop on the Charente, five miles downstream from Saintes. Defended on three sides by a sheer rock face with a massively fortified fourth side, many said it was impregnable. It was just the kind of challenge the Lionheart relished – especially as it was defended by a man for whom he had a particular dislike.

Geoffrey de Rançon was a minor Gascon lord, well known for his thuggery and for being the custodian of a big belly and a small intellect. Rançon had discredited himself during the Second Great Crusade, where he had made a foolish decision while leading the army of Eleanor, Duke Richard's mother – a mistake which nearly cost the French King, Louis VII, his life. He had brought shame on the Plantagenets and was sent home in disgrace.

Although he lacked brains, he was cunning and had

managed to keep some of his lands in the south-west. He now skulked behind Taillebourg's colossal walls.

The Emperor Charlemagne had held the Muslim army back at Taillebourg, almost 400 years earlier – a fact that inspired the Duke even more. Richard deployed his entire range of ballista and catapults, which he used, together with his archers, to launch a relentless bombardment of incendiaries against the walls and into the castle's interior. He also began to lay waste to the countryside for miles around, denying the defenders any prospect of further supplies.

Then he made a move that would seal his reputation as a general of great cunning and great bravery. He called his Grand Quintet together, asked Father Alun to join us, and we sat down in his tent and dismissed his stewards. We only knew something was afoot when he began to pour the wine himself. It was a very good wine; clearly something important was about to be said.

'Gentlemen, I have looked at Taillebourg long and hard and from every angle. It is a beast – more formidable than anything we've tackled before. It will fall, but it could take weeks. And I, for one, have got better things to do with my time than wait for that fat Gascon in there to starve.'

William Marshal knew something audacious was brewing and tried to advise caution.

'Richard, you have built a fine army and your siege weapons are as good as any in the world. Don't jeopardize everything by being rash. As you said, if we wait, it will fall.'

'William, your advice is well put and well meant, but I have a plan. It is daring, but it will bring us a victory that will make everyone in Europe sit up. Not even the great Umayyad warlord, Abd-ar-Rahman I, Emir of Cordoba, could bring Taillebourg to its knees with an army of forty thousand men. But we will.'

The Duke had hooked us; we all sat expectantly, waiting for his heroic military coup.

'I need beer brewed, butts of that local spirit bought. And bring in some girls; we're going to have a feast, right under the walls of Taillebourg.'

Mercadier, not averse to speaking his mind bluntly, was the first to ridicule what seemed a farcical idea.

'Wonderful, Richard, an idea on a par with anything Alexander or Caesar could have devised.'

'Wait, listen closely.'

The Duke leaned forward and took a deep gulp of his wine; he was warming to his task.

'First, we will move up the army and camp as close to the walls as possible. They won't bombard us immediately until they work out what we're doing. That evening we will have a huge feast in the open. But the beer will be low in strength and we'll dilute the Teneraze. The girls will only be for show; there will be no fornicating. The men will be informed of the plan and be told to hide their weapons and armour. Crucially, they must be ready to fight within minutes of my signal.'

The Lionheart then turned to me directly.

'De Rançon does not know you. So you will keep two conrois of men hidden in tents close to Taillebourg's gates. They must be fully armed and ready to fight at a moment's notice.'

Robert Thornham realized what the Duke's strategy was.

'You think they'll come out and fight; they'll assume that we've been overconfident and left ourselves exposed.'

'Yes, de Rançon is not the most astute of men. But more importantly, he would love to redeem himself and restore his reputation after his catastrophe in the Holy Land. He would see this opportunity as divine intervention, given that it was my mother he disgraced in Palestine.'

Blondel asked what his mistake had involved.

'He chose exposed ground against advice, isolated the Queen's force from the rest of the Christian army and ignored repeated requests to change his mind. The Muslims attacked and his men were cut to pieces. Like a coward, he escaped, but he was stripped of his titles and sent home to Europe. The only reason he is here is because Alfonso of Aragon has given him the silver to buy estates in Aquitaine.'

It was a devious plan. For Eleanor's son to be seen to make the same mistake that de Rançon had made – and the prospect of getting the credit for humbling the Lionheart – was irresistible bait. Everyone nodded their agreement, and the plan was toasted with plentiful goblets of wine.

The Duke looked at Father Alun.

'Will you pray for our success, Father?'

'No, my Lord, I can't pray for our success in battle. But I will pray that we are all delivered from it in one piece.'

I could see Mercadier bristle at Father Alun's answer. After taking a breath, he spoke his mind.

'What's the point of having a priest with us if he won't pray for our victories?'

Father Alun stood his ground and calmly, without

rancour and without flinching, he looked Mercadier in the eye.

'My Lord, priests who pray for victories in war are both hypocritical and immoral. I am here to counsel the Duke, not to provide him, or you, with a shield on the battle-field.'

Mercadier started to rise to the provocative answer, but the Duke gestured to him to hold his tongue.

'Let us drink well tonight; tomorrow we will be sober.'

From early the next morning, Richard moved the majority of his army from its base camp nearby and pitched tents right under the walls of Taillebourg. We numbered 1,200 men, with another 600 in reserve. The siege engines were moved up a little closer and, late in the day, the cooks began to roast meat in the open. The girls appeared, min-strels started to sing, and the drink – or, at least, its poor relative – began to flow. Duke Richard and his Grand Quintet made sure they were prominent amidst the rev-elry, enjoying the feast as much as the next man.

My men and I waited in our tents, passing the time playing dice, cleaning our armour and sharpening our weapons. All the while, our activities were scrutinized with incredulity from Taillebourg's walls. At close to mid-night, a message came from the Duke to say that frantic activity had been heard behind the castle gates and to expect an attack at first light.

I organized a watch for the night and issued an order for everyone to be awake an hour before dawn. The trap was ready.

Geoffrey de Rançon took the bait at full light the next

morning. The huge gates to the city, so big that they had to be opened with a capstan, inched their way back and a wave of cavalry spilled out from inside in a crescendo of noise. Horses reared, men screamed and hooves thundered down the cobbled approach to the gates.

Our attackers assumed they were falling upon an army of heavy eyed men, the worse for wear after a night of debauchery. For a few moments, that is how it appeared. But the trap was sprung immediately. I led my men from our tents and we immediately began to unhorse our attackers with our pikes and lances. Duke Richard's men soon followed us. They had gathered their weapons and armour and now ran from their tents in large numbers. Men who had been sleeping in the open had been lying on their swords and hauberks and were soon ready for the melee.

De Rançon's men were still pouring through the gates in numbers. But when they saw that they were riding into a snare of men that significantly outnumbered them, some tried to turn back, causing mayhem in the barbican. Duke Richard saw the confusion and called on William Marshal and his other lieutenants to join him in a charge into the open gateway. I bellowed at Godric and my Little Quintet, and we joined the Lionheart in a sprint to the gates before they could be closed against us. We pulled down horses by their reins as we went and scattered men in droves as we forced a way through. Such was the awesome sight of Duke Richard and his senior knights, all of whom towered over their opponents, few stood and fought. Those who did were quickly despatched with efficient and deadly intent.

By the time we were in the interior of the barbican, we could hear the winches at work as the defenders tried to close the gates against us.

The Lionheart shouted his order.

'Sir Ranulf to the right, Lord Mercadier to the left. To the capstans!'

The order was clear. As we turned to the right, we could see four large men with muscle-bound arms straining to turn the capstan as quickly as they could. They were defended by a posse of de Rançon's garrison, who knew that if they were unable to close the gates, their day would be done. The space behind the massive gates was small and dark, too small for the effective use of swords, so Godric and the men wielded their English battleaxes, just like their Saxon ancestors. A look of fear immediately spread across the faces of our opponents. Penda and Leax formed a vanguard, with Modig and Rodor on the flanks, while Godric and I formed a second rank. We locked our shields like housecarls and advanced like a shield wall of old.

Our foes found it hard to swing their swords, and the brutal blows from our axes soon took their toll. We had to step over bloodied bodies to make progress, but we were soon within striking distance of the capstan. There was no need to assault the capstan men, as one blow from Penda's axe was enough to sever the rope to the gate, thus rendering the mechanism redundant. Realizing that their muscular arms were of little value to them without a sword to wield, the burly winchmen soon held them aloft in surrender.

I called to the Sergeant of our army, which was now

streaming through the gates of Taillebourg, to take the defenders of the barbican in hand so that we could rejoin the Duke, who was now fighting his way across the castle's bailey against stubborn resistance. Geoffrey de Rançon's portly frame was at the back of the melee, trying to form his men into a redoubt in front of the keep.

The fighting was at close quarters and vicious. Conscious of my primary responsibility to protect the Duke, I formed my men around him to make sure that his drive forward could not be outflanked. Marshal and Thornham led from the left, and Mercadier and Bethune from the right. As usual, Blondel took up his preferred position directly behind the Lionheart. Our advance was impressive; amidst a din of clashing blades and the cries of stricken men, we moved ever closer to the ground floor of the keep. The beaten-earth ground of the bailey was awash with blood, some it forming into pools before running away along the drainage gulleys in a crimson torrent.

I kept a wary eye on the Lionheart, but I need not have been concerned; he led the assault from the front, fighting in the best traditions of man-to-man combat. He swung his blade in powerful but measured arcs and used his shield perfectly to parry blows. His great height and powerful frame gave him a distinct advantage, but it was his training and technique that were most telling. It was an impressive sight, the stories of which would soon resonate across Europe.

Here was a lion rampant; I watched in awe, relieved that I was supporting his onslaught, not trying to defend against it.

De Rançon had managed to form a semi-circular

redoubt. But as soon as it was set, he had banged on the small door of the tall keep and disappeared inside. There were immediate howls from his men, and the fight soon went out of them. Like ripples on a pond the raised hands of surrender spread across the entire redoubt within moments, leaving de Rançon trapped in his keep.

Although he undoubtedly had food and water within the keep, and perhaps a few loyal bodyguards, his capitulation was only a matter of time. The Duke, covered in blood from head to toe, steam rising from him like a stallion after a gallop, his chest heaving to suck in great gulps of air, raised his sword in triumph. Our men hollered and cheered and began to chant his name, '*Lionheart, Lionheart, Lionheart* . . .' until echo upon echo rebounded off the walls of Taillebourg.

Even though he was just twenty-two years old, it was the moment that established the Duke in legend. All who witnessed it would never forget the image: with his sword proclaiming victory, the tall blood-stained hero had removed his helmet to reveal his golden-red mane. He was Achilles in front of the Gates of Troy, Alexander on the Plain of Gaugamela, Caesar at the Siege of Alesia. I shivered with emotion as I fully realized the power of the man to whom I had committed my future.

The Duke instructed that de Rançon's men be disarmed and that order be restored to the castle and its occupants. Then he asked that tables be erected in the bailey and that a real feast, with full-strength beer and potent Teneraze, be prepared to celebrate the fall of the 'impregnable' Castle of Taillebourg.

An hour or so later, with his family skulking behind

him and half a dozen knights in attendance, de Rançon emerged from his keep. He walked up to the Duke sheepishly and offered him his sword.

'My Lord Duke, I throw myself upon your mercy. Please spare my family, I beg you.'

'Your family has done me no harm; they have nothing to fear. In fact, they may join us for our feast tonight. As for you, I have a small group of unruly lords of Gascony under guard in my camp. You will join them. The food is adequate, but far from lavish; by the look of your girth, that may be a blessing. When my campaign ends, you and they will travel with me to see the King, where you can pay homage to your liege lord.'

De Rançon knew he had got off lightly, so just meekly bowed his head and walked away under guard.

Duke Richard's ruse had been a clever one – not without risk, in placing his army within range of anything hurled from Taillebourg's walls – but he had achieved what no one had ever done before and humbled the most formidable fortress in western Europe. The celebratory repast that followed that night involved no bogus revelry; the feast was truly bacchanalian, enjoyed by the citizens of Taillebourg as much as by their conquerors. With his usual panache, the Duke had made the local people beneficiaries of de Rançon's ransacked treasury and thus ensured that they had no regrets about the demise of one lord and his replacement by another.

As our army began to move on, the Duke ordered that the fortress of Taillebourg be dismantled stone by stone. We repeated the same destruction at several more castles until

Vulgrin, the Count of Angoulême, the last of Aquitaine's rebels, rode into our camp with the keys to all of his fortresses, including Angoulême and Montignac, and begged that they be spared being razed to the ground. The Lionheart accepted the keys with gratitude and spared the Count the humiliation of paying homage to King Henry. But he destroyed the castles all the same.

His mission in Aquitaine complete, the Duke stood down his army and his Grand Quintet went home to their estates. With his little coterie of Gascon aristocrats in tow, we arrived in Caen in October of 1179, only to find that the King was in Winchester. Although he made it clear that he dreaded the prospect of crossing the Channel with winter approaching and the likelihood of being buffeted by autumn gales, the Duke was energized by his success in the south and nothing would have prevented him from presenting his father with the trophies of his hunting trip. He had two counts, three viscounts, four lords of tenure and several castellan chevaliers in his bag, and he was determined to display them in front of his father and the English court.

On the journey across the Channel, I realized how limited was the Duke's English. He asked me to help him, but he struggled with it, saying that he found its mix of Celtic and Scandinavian vocabulary confusing and its pronunciation baffling – especially when compared to the harmonic vowels of his native Occitan. To his even greater consternation, when we made landfall at Fareham, England had already donned its autumnal cloak of leaden skies and cool temperatures. Within an hour of beginning our ride to Winchester, it began to rain – not just the usual drizzle of an October day, but the squall of a south-westerly storm.

Although I tried to reassure the Duke that such downpours were the exception, rather than the rule, he was not convinced.

'Why does everyone keep telling me that England is the jewel in the King's crown? I remember always being cold and wet as a child, and it appears nothing has changed!'

As if to prove his point, England then did its worst. As we climbed up on to the Downs, the driving rain turned to hailstones and cut into our faces like the lash of a whip. A miserable Lionheart said no more, just looked at me from under his sodden hood with all the contempt he held for my homeland.

Then I remembered that he had been born in England, and I chanced my arm with a quip.

'Welcome home, my Lord.'

'Don't remind me!'

Mercifully, by the time we reached Winchester, the weather and the Duke's humour had improved. Not only that: the King had prepared a welcome fit for the conquering hero. He had sent a royal squadron, complete with heralds and horns, to escort us into the burgh, the streets of which were thronged with people, mostly four deep. Usually such receptions were encouraged by generous inducements to the crowd, including gifts of food and drink, but on this occasion the warmth seemed genuine for a famous son of the realm whose exploits were already being written about by the scribes and related by the storytellers.

The King was overjoyed by his son's success and

particularly pleased that Duke Richard had brought him so many Gascon rebels to humiliate – a task he undertook with great relish. In front of a large gathering outside his Great Hall at Winchester, after berating them at length for their insolence and making each of them fall to their knees and swear an oath of allegiance to him, the King immediately sent the miscreants to Fareham to begin the long journey back to Gascony. For all of them, unless they could find a benefactor, it would be to face a life of penury, shorn of their wealth, their fortresses and their lands. These were the risks of challenging the might of the Plantagenet Empire.

For Duke Richard, the Little Quintet, Father Alun and myself, our immediate future was much more auspicious. The King had arranged for the Lionheart to undertake a grand progress across the length and breadth of the kingdom; it was a journey that we faced with considerably more enthusiasm than did the Duke. For us it was a nostalgic homecoming, for him it would be several weeks of purgatory.

His only comment when he heard the news was, 'If I have to endure England in the depths of winter, you must make sure that all our hosts provide fine wine, fresh game and game girls.'

The Duke refused to travel as far as Durham and, despite my pleading, refused to travel to my homeland of Lancaster. But he did travel to York and Chester in the north, and to all the major burghs of the south. It was a triumphant cavalcade, with rapturous greetings in every burgh and village we passed; everyone wanted to see the man called 'Lionheart'.

Our hosts, England's all-powerful earls and bishops who enjoyed significant autonomy on their island with a King who spent a major proportion of his time in Normandy, were generous with their hospitality. Each knew that their guest was a man of rare stature who might well be their King one day, and they were keen to impress him Their wine was outstanding, they provided excellent hunting, and the finest young women of their earldoms were paraded for the Duke. He was spoilt for choice and made many conquests, but one of them had such an impact on him that he began to warm to England's charms after all.

She was called Ida de Tosny, and she first caught his eye in Norwich. In truth, everyone's eye was drawn to her when she walked into the impressive Great Hall of Norwich Castle, the home of Roger Bigod, Second Earl of Norfolk.

She was visiting him at the suggestion of the King, who thought they would be a good match. Roger had just succeeded his redoubtable father as Earl and needed a wife, and Ida needed a husband. She was from the Anglo-Norman gentry, but she had lost both her parents as a child and had been made a ward of the King. However, when she reached womanhood, she became much more than Henry's ward. Petite and slim, with striking blue eyes and chestnut hair, her perfectly symmetrical figure made men gasp. More than aware of her charms, she used them to great effect. Her dresses always clung tightly to her and she walked in a sensuous, sinewy way that demanded attention. It was said that the King first seduced her when she was just fifteen and that he became infatuated with her. She had borne him a child, William, who was sent to the nuns in Lincoln to be cared for. Eventually, he tired of her and now a marriage to the Earl of Norfolk was an ideal solution for all three of them. The King would be rid of her, Ida would become the countess of one of the richest earldoms in England, and Bigod would acquire one of England's most beautiful women.

However, that expedient plan was undermined when Ida's curvaceous form glided towards the Lionheart. His eyes opened wide and he immediately got to his feet to greet her.

The Earl made the introductions.

'My Lord Duke, Ida de Tosny. Her family's domain is just to the south of Rouen, and her great-grandfather fought with the Conqueror at Senlac. She is now your father's ward.'

With his usual flamboyance, the Duke bowed deeply and kissed her hand.

'Madam, I am honoured to meet a woman of such rare beauty.'

Ida curtsied and smiled coyly. The attraction between them was apparent to everyone there, especially to Earl Roger – who must have known at that moment that his intended betrothal would either never happen, or have to wait.

As soon as he could, Father Alun took the Duke to one side.

'Sire, she has had the King's child and he intends her to marry the Earl. He will not be pleased if you upset his carefully laid plan.'

'Don't fuss, man. I'm only going to bed her. The Earl can have her when I'm done. He can hardly complain;

she's already been stretched by the King's cock, a little more from mine won't make any difference.'

There was nothing more Father Alun could say. He looked at me, but I just shrugged my shoulders; it was the only appropriate response.

Unfortunately, the Duke did not just 'bed' Ida, she accompanied him across the length and breadth of the earldoms of England! She soon acquired a lady-in-waiting and two maids, as well as an ever-growing baggage train of female paraphernalia and gifts bestowed on her by the Duke and every host we visited. The silver lining, we hoped, would appear at the end of our sojourn, when we felt sure he would leave her in England.

Not so: he deliberately avoided his father, and we crossed the Channel from Bosham before heading south to Poitiers.

When we arrived in the city, the situation worsened. We had only been there for a couple of days when Ida complained of being unwell, a malady that her mature lady-in-waiting soon diagnosed as morning sickness. The 'Nymph from Norwich', as we had begun to call her, was pregnant. Father Alun and I had both taken a dislike to Ida and felt sure that the pregnancy was designed to snare the Duke on a permanent basis. But she had been far too ambitious. Her social status was just about high enough for an earl, but not for a duke who one day might be King of the Plantagenet Empire.

As soon as the Lionheart knew that Ida was pregnant, he put her down as quickly as he had swept her up. With just one coarse exchange of words, she was gone. Instructions were given that the child would be delivered by the nuns at Poitiers, where it would stay under the Duke's guardianship, after which Ida was to return to Norwich with a generous dowry for Earl Roger.

In due course, the Duke's son was born. He was named Philip and made Lord of Cognac. The Earl of Norwich swallowed his pride, accepted the dowry and married the mercurial Ida. Whether the marriage was a happy one, I know not, but the saga of the Lionheart and the Nymph did little for the King's humour. It began a time of bad blood between him and his son that would produce very unfortunate consequences for the Devil's Brood. The King was furious with his son, but Richard avoided his father for the next two years. Even so, the wound festered and would soon become gangrenous.

10. Family at War

In December 1182, King Henry issued a unique invitation to his Christmas Court at Caen. Not only did he summon his entire family, but he invited every magnate from his Empire. His intention was transparent: he was approaching fifty years of age and he wanted to show the world that his brood was not the work of the Devil, but was a family at peace with itself within an enduring Empire that would go from strength to strength under the future rule of his three sons.

Henry's eldest son and his anointed heir, Henry the Young King, led the brood. Richard's younger brother, Geoffrey, Duke of Brittany, brought his family, as did his sister, Matilda, who came with her husband, Henry the Lion, Duke of Saxony. Over a thousand lords and knights filled Caen with a colourful medley of gonfalons and pennons, the like of which had not been seen since the crusaders gathered to march to the Holy Land. The merchants and innkeepers of the city had a windfall, as the horde cleared their shelves and cellars of anything edible or wearable; the whores made a king's ransom. Each night, as the hours passed from twilight into darkness, the festivities descended from elegant feasting into drunken debauchery and, eventually, into violent brawling. The infirmaries were overrun and even the gravediggers were called upon on more than one occasion.

In the midst of all the raucousness, the King called his three sons together in his Great Hall at Caen and, with his entire family and as many senior magnates as could squeeze into its vastness as witnesses, made them swear an oath. Not only did they have to affirm their loyalty to him and to the Empire, but also to one another.

After each had made his declaration, he knelt before his father, kissed his hand and then embraced him. Duke Richard looked imperious. When it was his turn to swear, his height and aura dominated those around him, including the King. He wore a long red cape with the golden cross of Aquitaine emblazoned above his heart. His ducal coronet glistened, its jewels catching the light, as did his lion's mane, the perfect complement to his regal bearing. Many in the hall had not seen him since he was a boy, and there were audible gasps as he rose to speak. Here was the Lionheart, already a legend. Helped by the fact that he was taller than all those around him, when he placed his hand on the ancient Bible of the cathedral of St Pierre and spoke, his voice carried to the farthest recesses of the hall.

'I, Richard, Duke of Aquitaine, Duke of Gascony, Count of Anjou, Count of Maine, Count of Nantes, do swear fealty to my father, Henry, Lord of all the domains of our Empire. I do also swear loyalty to my brothers, Henry and Geoffrey, and undertake to protect them and support them in preserving their realms and possessions, as we do as a family, in maintaining the honour and security of our Empire.'

After the oaths, the King rose and held the arms of his sons aloft amidst a rapturous reception from the assembly.

I looked around the room at the awesome gathering: Normans, Plantagenets, Bretons and many more. These were the descendants of men who had built an Empire that stretched the length of Europe and whose kinsmen had carved new realms across the Mediterranean and the Holy Land. I had mixed feelings: I was overawed by the power embodied in that room and all that it had achieved – indeed, I was now part of it – but, on the other hand, my people were one of those who had been vanquished by these mighty clans.

Sadly, the King's good intentions came to nothing. Young Henry, despite being his father's heir to the whole Empire, was jealous of his brothers' dukedoms in Brittany and Aquitaine. He wanted his own domain; Normandy or England would have assuaged him but, despite endless pleading, the King refused. Frustrated by this, he had begun to plot against his brothers and father, and sought support from the new King of France, Philip Augustus.

The Lionheart got wind of this, at Caen, three days after Christmas Day, and summoned Father Alun and myself to his chamber. He was white with anger.

'My brother is committing sedition; there could be another civil war. Send messengers to William Marshal and the others to assemble in Poitiers. Recall the army. We leave for the south immediately.'

Father Alun looked alarmed.

'My Lord, should you not tell the King?'

'I dare not; I can't be sure whether the plot is being hatched by Young Henry on his own, or whether my father is behind it. All I am certain of is that my brother is being denied Normandy and England, so he plans to usurp me in Aquitaine.'

I had rarely seen the Duke so angry. He roared like his namesake.

'My own brother is trying to take my beloved Aquitaine from me. I will rip his heart from his chest and throw it to the dogs!'

The Grand Quintet gathered in Poitiers quickly, and Richard's powerful army was mustered with commendable speed. By the end of January 1183, we marched south.

We had travelled for no more than two days when the news deteriorated. The King, who had also heard of the Young King's attempt to undermine the Lionheart in Aquitaine, sent his other son, Geoffrey, to act as mediator. Again, Henry, who must have been in despair at the behaviour of his offspring, had miscalculated. Instead of acting as peacemaker, Geoffrey immediately sided with his brother in his campaign against Duke Richard. Not only that: he had taken his army with him, which had swelled the Young King's force significantly.

News of yet another squabble in the Plantagenet Empire spread rapidly. The scorn with which it was received was made worse because it immediately followed the King's attempt at a show of unity in Caen. His dormant enemies resurfaced and he became a target of widespread derision. Chaos soon followed as the view circulated that the Devil's Brood would soon be engaged in a civil war. The Lionheart knew that he had to act quickly, not only to save his dukedom in Aquitaine, but also to save the Empire.

Geoffrey and Henry had united their armies near Limoges, where they were joined by other troublemakers including Aimar, Viscount of Limoges, William Arnald, a mercenary who commanded a large force of Gascon routiers, and Raymond le Brun, Arnald's notorious uncle. His routiers were renowned for their acts of brutality, which included the public rape and mutilation of women and the castration of men.

By the time we reached the small settlement of Aix-sur-Vienne in the Limousin, Duke Richard's mood had darkened rather than softened. The rebels had split into smaller groups and were rampaging around Aquitaine, causing as much devastation as they could. We had heard endless stories of atrocities – all, no doubt, part of his brothers' plan to lure Duke Richard into their lair.

But the Lionheart was too shrewd for that. We tracked Raymond le Brun's force of Bretons to the small settlement of Ruffec, in the Charente. They were enjoying a respite from their marauding amidst the peaceful surroundings of the vineyards and farmhouses of the area, and we caught them unawares. The locals had departed in a hurry, leaving their meagre chattels at the mercy of the rebels.

What followed was not for the faint of heart. There was no local populace to be concerned about, and no question of these men being forced to pay homage to the King; they were the dogs of war and had been unleashed by his brothers, so they would be treated like the beasts they were.

We approached le Brun's camp just before dawn. They numbered perhaps 300 men, but we were more than

2,000. The Duke deployed the contingents of the Grand Quintet to his left and right, in his usual formation. As the sun crested the hills beyond the River Tarn, he ordered the attack with a simple command.

'No quarter!'

The slaughter was short-lived but savage. Few of le Brun's men were able to get to their horses, and most were cut down trying to flee. They were unable to don their armour or wield their weapons; some were still barefoot, not having had time to find their footwear. Few survived the cull, but le Brun was one of them. When the Lionheart saw him, he leapt from his horse in a single, agile bound and set about him. Le Brun was a bear of a man with thick black hair and a beard to match. He was scarred across the forehead and left cheek and had lost most of his teeth. He had managed to find his sword and shield and, for a while, was able to parry the Duke's blows. But their power and ferocity were too much for him, and he soon fell to his knees and begged for mercy.

'Lord Richard, spare—'

But before his foe could finish his plea, the Lionheart plunged his sword through his Adam's apple and deep into his chest. For a moment the stricken man stared upwards in horror, until his life ebbed away. The Duke, without hesitation or remorse, simply placed his foot on le Brun's chest and pulled out his bloodied blade. He then turned to Mercadier.

'Execute any prisoners. Tie their hands and throw them into the Tarn like abandoned whelps.'

I watched the orders being carried out with regret, preferring that even these men should meet a quicker death.

But the Duke's blood was up, and nothing would have inclined him to leniency. Father Alun tried to reason with him, citing Abbess Hildegard frequently, but the look of anger on the Lionheart's face soon made him realize that he was beyond reason.

After the bloodletting, Duke Richard announced a typically audacious plan. He sent the Grand Quintet and the major part of his own army in different directions to crush whatever opposition they could find and ordered me to select an elite force of four conrois to accompany him to Limoges. He intended to ride straight into his brothers' lair and confront them face-to-face.

We took spare mounts and rode for two days and two nights, only stopping to rest and feed the horses. When we reached Gorre, a dozen miles to the west of Limoges, it was the middle of our third morning in the saddle. The men were exhausted and few were in a fit state to fight. Not so the Lionheart – especially after he saw with his own eyes the crimes that were being committed.

Aimar, Viscount of Limoges, sat to one side on his black destrier as William Arnald's mercenaries defiled the small settlement. The local priest had been hanged, his naked body swinging from the cross at the top of his church, and the ground was littered with the mutilated corpses of the local men and children. The women were nowhere to be seen, but the anguished screams coming from inside the small thatched church were testament to their fate.

The Lionheart did not issue any orders, nor pause in any way. He rode straight into the middle of the carnage and began to waylay the perpetrators. He was like a whirl-wind, scattering men before him like ninepins. Godric and I, with our men in close support, tried to cover his back, but he did not need us. The routiers started to run when they saw the ferocity of the Lionheart's assault. It soon became a rout, as men fell over one another to get away. As they fled, many could be heard calling out the Duke's name in an awed tone.

William Arnald, one of the most feared men in the Empire, was one of the few not to be intimidated. The Duke summoned his cavalry to pursue the fleeing merce-naries, again issuing the command, 'No quarter!' and then he confronted Arnald. A heavy-built Burgundian who had spent his life as a cut-throat for hire, he would have put the fear of God into all but a handful of men. But Duke Richard was such a man. He did not hesitate. Not even when Arnald shouted his blood-curdling threats.

'You are but the runt of a litter of cubs of that fat father of yours. If he is your father, of course. I hear that your mother will bed anything, man or beast. Let me send you home to them cut and diced, ready for the pot!'

I gestured to Godric to have the men stay close as the two warriors' swords clashed. The Duke had been in a fury since news of his brothers' treachery reached him, but the insult to his mother inflamed him even more. He swung at Arnald like a man possessed – so much so that I feared that, against a man of such experience, his ferocity might be ill judged. At first, the contest was even; Arnald smiled as he parried blow after blow, hoping that the Lionheart's strength would wane. He goaded him, in an attempt to provoke even more bursts of tiring aggression.

'Is that the best you can do, boy? My junior knights offer a greater threat than that.'

I glanced at Godric and saw that he had the same concerns: before long, we might have to step in and protect the Duke from the retaliation that would surely soon come. Then the inevitable happened; one of the Duke's swings lacked conviction, and Arnald sensed the fatigue. He launched his own furious attack. The Duke started to go backwards and stumbled to the ground, giving the Burgundian brigand the chance he needed. He thrust the tip of his sword at the Lionheart's midriff; for a moment, it looked like the younger man was done for, but he managed to deflect the blow towards his left arm. Even so, the point of the sword sliced into the maille of his hauberk just above the elbow and blood immediately gushed from the wound.

Most men would have begged for mercy at that point, but Duke Richard rolled away and regained his feet. It was as if he had been jolted by a butt of water; instead of being cowed by the blow, he fought back with even greater savagery than before. Despite the blood that was running down his arm, he managed to gird his shield and hurl himself into another attack.

Arnald suddenly appeared to look anxious. He had not expected the Duke to get up from such a severe and painful blow. Perhaps he now began to accept the truth of the Lionheart's almost mythical reputation. It was his turn to retreat. As he did so, the Lionheart's blows became stronger and Arnald's defensive posture slumped lower and lower. Eventually, the older man could parry no more and Duke Richard ran him through just below his right collarbone.

Arnald fell to his knees; his arm went limp, and his sword fell to the ground with a dull thud. The only thing keeping him upright was his shield, which anchored him to the ground as he leaned on it. As all those who looked on waited for words of contrition or an act of submission from the wounded mercenary, the Lionheart stole the moment. With an almighty swipe of his sword, which began with his forearm resting under his chin, he all but decapitated Arnald with one blow. Blood spurted into the air and washed over the Duke like water splashed from a puddle in a road. The Burgundian, his head attached to his body by only a small remnant of his neck and tilted at an inhuman angle, fell forward in a heap. A crimson pool seeped beneath him as his lifeless eyes, now turned almost in the opposite direction to the one God intended, stared upwards towards Heaven. It was a vain hope; there would be no place for him there.

Now sated, the Duke also fell to the ground, the loss of blood from his own wound taking its toll. On my signal Modig and Rodor helped the Duke to his feet, and Father Alun rushed forward to tend to his wound. He wanted the Duke to rest and take off his hauberk to have the deep gash bandaged properly. But the Lionheart refused, insisting that he only need roll up the sleeve of his maille so that a temporary binding could be applied.

'I'll rest when we've put down all my brothers' hounds.'

The executions of the survivors did not take long. The Duke did not want to admonish them or gloat; he just wanted them dead. Some were drowned, a few were decapitated; none were spared, despite their pleas for mercy.

Unfortunately, Viscount Aimar had managed to make an escape and had ridden back to skulk behind the walls of Limoges. But the city was far from being a stronghold. The Duke had destroyed its stone ramparts in the rebellion of 1181, and its only bulwarks were earth banks and wooden palisades. Even so, we had no option but to send for the rest of the army before attempting a siege. Father Alun was relieved; the delay would mean that the Duke's injury could be treated properly, and he could try to prevent any infection.

Three weeks later, all was ready for an attack on Limoges. The Lionheart had mustered his men and materiel with his usual aplomb. He was a master of strategy, and his attention to tactical detail was astonishing. He was as adept in the skills of his specialist archers, arbalests and cavalrymen as the best of them, and he knew every nuance of the mechanics of his siege engines. He was as brave as any he commanded; they all knew that had he been of low birth, his prowess, although unlikely to have made him their King, would certainly have rendered him their General.

Both his brothers were inside its flimsy walls, as was Viscount Aimar. The Duke was intent on killing all three. His arm was far from healed, but he could not be dissuaded from issuing a challenge to engage each of them in a trial of combat when the city fell.

Perhaps fortuitously, the King arrived on the eve of the attack. He brought a large army of his own and immediately called a council of war.

When everyone was gathered, including the Duke and

his Grand Quintet and the King's senior commanders, Henry rose to make a speech. It was ill conceived and provocative, and the ending incensed the Duke almost to the point he had reached before the slaying of the mercenaries.

'This bickering between my sons has to end. But as they have shown no willingness to resolve their differences themselves, I will have to do it for them. Richard, you will withdraw your army by a day's march so that I can enter Limoges and talk to Henry and Geoffrey.'

The Duke's ruddy complexion turned puce with anger, and he started to get to his feet. William Marshal grabbed his sleeve and tugged at him to sit down. The King stared at his son. It was like a confrontation between an old stag and a young buck. The Lionheart pulled his sleeve from Marshal's grasp and began to bellow at his father.

'Your sons are committing treason; they have reneged on the oath they took in Caen, and yet you expect me to withdraw. Are you mad?'

Fearing a familial brawl there and then, I walked into his line of sight, standing between Richard and his father. I turned to address the King.

'Sire, Duke Richard will need time to organize his men and find a new camp. May we discuss this later, when our plans are finalized?'

William Marshal and Baldwin of Bethune used my surprise intervention to almost grapple the Lionheart away from a confrontation with his father, and we hastily retreated out of the King's earshot. The Duke pulled away from the protective embrace of his friends and paced up and down in a rage.

'The King is the King, Henry is his anointed heir, Geoffrey has Brittany and I keep order in the most troublesome domain in the Empire. Yet Henry wants more! He's a limp-dicked coward who fights with thugs and murderers. But my father never renounces him. Why does he always defend him?'

We stood and listened; it was the wisest option.

'I've had enough. No more oaths, no more concessions! When this is over, we travel to England. I will release my mother from those draughty English castles where my father keeps her out of harm's way, and we'll rule this Empire together.'

After a few minutes to let his friend's anger subside, William Marshal offered some words of wisdom.

'Tell the King that you will withdraw and go hunting, so that he can talk to your brothers. But since they have allied themselves with mercenaries who can't be trusted, your army will stay where it is under my command.'

It was sound advice, but the Duke was reluctant.

'I know what will happen: when I return, there will have been a rapprochement between them and I will be asked to swear another meaningless oath of loyalty. Well, I won't be deceived again. I am staying here and will storm Limoges, whether my father likes it or not.'

Father Alun then intervened.

'My Lord, remember what the Abbess said about using your mind rather than your sword.'

'Be quiet, priest!'

After blurting his rebuke, the Duke began to walk away. But Blondel, who sang much more often than he spoke, called after him.

'Listen to the priest. It will cost you nothing to let events take their course. We will still be here with your army. Your father is no fool, he knows what Henry is up to; let's see what transpires over the next few days. Robert and Baldwin will go hunting with you. Drink some wine; take some girls with you.'

The Duke thought for a while before turning to Father Alun.

'What is your advice? Should I take my leave?'

Father Alun smiled.

'I think so, my Lord. You can use the time to reflect on your sins. God always looks kindly on a penitent.'

The Duke relented and spent the next week hunting in the forests of the Limousin, one of the finest places in the Empire for game. Meanwhile, the King went backwards and forwards to the city to negotiate with his sons. He had not been happy that the Duke had refused to move his army. But he had no choice other than to accept his son's stubbornness, as Richard's answer was delivered to the King long after he had left for the chase.

William Marshal and Father Alun had been right to persuade the Duke to bide his time. The King failed to persuade Young Henry to back down, and an impasse developed. But the stalemate only applied to the Limousin. When word spread that Young Henry was defying his father, the chaos in the Empire spread.

More of the Plantagenet's dormant enemies reared their heads. Philip, King of France, mobilized his army in support of Henry and Geoffrey, as did Hugh, Duke of Burgundy, and Raymond, Count of Toulouse. The Empire was on the brink of collapse from within, and the foment was being brewed by its own ruling family, the Devil's Brood.

For the first time in his long and illustrious reign, Henry Plantagenet was unable to impose himself on his vast realm. He was too old, and his sons were too powerful.

He knew it, they knew it, and so did the great and the good of the Empire.

11. Westminster Beckons

Richard returned from his hunt relieved to discover that his father had now been convinced of Young Henry's duplicity. But the King still demanded that Richard must not attack his brother.

Sometime later, the Duke told me the details of their conversation, beginning with his father's words to his increasingly impatient son.

'Henry is digging a deeper and deeper midden for himself, soon he will be up to his neck in shit.'

'That's as may be, Father, but in the meantime, our enemies are massing. Your authority is being undermined.'

'My "authority" can survive a little longer. I don't want the future of this Plantagenet Empire to be decided by a fight between my sons!'

'But the fight has already begun and you're in the middle of the brawl.'

'That's why it must not end in a decisive outcome, one way or the other. When he's older, I am going to give your little brother John the lordship of Ireland. Henry can retain Normandy, Geoffrey can keep Brittany, and you can have everything to the south.'

'What about England?'

'I know, I don't have enough sons . . . perhaps I will give it to your mother.'

At that moment, Duke Richard realized that the King

had no real strategy for his succession and was afraid of making a decision that might tear apart his precious Empire.

The imperial impasse lasted through the lengthening days of spring and into the summer of 1183. At his father's request, Richard campaigned far and wide as we put down revolts and saw off challengers to his father's rule. The Duke was as ruthless in this campaign as he had been earlier in the year and earned a deserved reputation for wanton cruelty to add to his other more noble distinctions. He still had a regard for the innocent victims of conflict, but in dealing with enemies to his dukedom, or to the Plantagenet Empire, he was without mercy. The insult and betrayal he had suffered at Caen had left an open sore that would not go away.

Father Alun tried to calm the savage beast, but to no avail.

The dire circumstances of the Plantagenet family feud were only relieved by an unexpected event. Young Henry became short of funds and in the dead of night started making clandestine forays beyond Limoges to pillage local monasteries and churches. He stole plate, crosses and candlesticks to pay his mercenaries.

The locals said that a curse had been placed on him for his sins. Whatever the cause, a few days later he was struck by severe vomiting and diarrhoea, a condition that worsened rapidly. He was smuggled out of Limoges and taken south to the monks at Martel, three days' ride from the city. The monks could do nothing and it was soon clear to his followers that he was dying. He was confessed and given the last rite of extreme unction. In penitence for his war against his father, he prostrated himself naked on the floor of the monastery's chapel and begged for forgiveness. As he lay dying, he asked to be reconciled to his father, but the King, fearing a ruse, refused to see him. He died four days later, clasping a ring his father had sent him as a gesture of absolution. The King, heartbroken when he heard the news, said, 'He cost me much, but I wish he had lived to cost me more.'

Although he had become his brother's bitter enemy, the Lionheart was also saddened when he heard the news at our camp near Cahors. He dismissed the King's messenger who had brought the news and left his tent to stand by the River Lot nearby.

I watched him as he stared across the wide, deep waters and into the hills of the domain he loved so much. He must have been reflecting that the future that so many had predicted for him had come to pass. With Young Henry's sudden death, the Lionheart would be the next King of England and ruler of the mighty Plantagenet Empire.

When he returned to the tent, he asked me to take him to see Father Alun. He had a surprising question for him.

'When you were introduced to me by Harold, Earl of Huntingdon, he said that he was returning to his estate in the Lot. Do you know where it is?'

'I do, my Lord. It is not far from here, less than a day's ride.'

'Good, then let's go. How old will he be now?'

'In his mid-eighties, sire.'

'Perhaps he's still alive. If he is, I want to talk to him about England.'

'But, sire, you know that when you cross the Lot to the

east, you are in the domain of Raymond, Count of Toulouse?'

'Of course! But he won't mind if we pay our respects to one of his subjects.'

Two days later, as we rode along the banks of the Lot with its tall limestone crags looming over us, I had mixed feelings. I was pleased to think that we might meet Earl Harold again, but concerned that we were more likely only to find his grave.

St Cirq Lapopie was an enthralling place. With the river several hundred feet below, the Earl's home stood on an outcrop of rock, facing north towards England. A small community of peasant houses nestled around his hall, and in the hinterland huge swathes of forest stretched as far as the eye could see. On the northern bank of the Lot, the terrain was much flatter and a wide expanse of vines, crops and livestock thrived. The sun shone and the air was sultry, refreshed by cool breezes from the river. As soon as I saw it, I realized why Earl Harold was so fond of it; it was a little enclave of Heaven on earth.

Everyone we passed seemed well fed and happy. Adults and children alike waved as we ascended the steep slope to the Earl's hall; they were not in the slightest alarmed by a long column of armed men led by a duke.

As we approached, we were greeted by Gretchen and Ursula, the children of Eadmer, Earl Harold's loyal companion throughout his many adventures. He had died several years earlier, but his children and grandchildren were a charming little brood of blue-eyed Anglo-Saxons deep in the forests of the Lot.

When we arrived in the courtyard, Harold's steward was waiting for us. He bowed deeply to greet the Duke.

'Welcome to St Cirq Lapopie, my Lord Duke. We are expecting you.'

'How did you know we were coming, steward?'

'We have carrier pigeons down in the valley. The Earl is devoted to them; they were very useful to him many years ago, when your grandmother stayed here, in my father's time.'

The Lionheart looked shocked to hear that the Empress Matilda had visited St Cirq Lapopie. I turned to Father Alun, who just smiled knowingly.

Then, in his usual agile way, the Duke leapt from his horse.

'Where is the old boy? I must tell him my news.'

'Sire, he is waiting for you; he's sitting over there, looking out over the river. But, my Lord, he's very frail and soon we will need to get him back to his chamber.'

Father Alun and I followed the Duke as he went to sit next to the figure slumped in his chair at the edge of St Cirq Lapopie's sheer cliffs. He was shaded from the sun by a wide canopy. Although it was very warm, he was wrapped in a heavy woollen blanket. He was, indeed, frail. He had lost a lot of weight since we saw him last, and his head was tilted to one side, resting on his right shoulder. His eyes were watery and bloodshot, and his face was pale and deeply creased by age. He was only a shadow of the man I had first met in Winchester.

His speech was a little slurred and his voice thin. It had lost the authority it once had, but it was still audible.

'So, you have brought me some news.'

'I have. You were right, I am the new heir apparent. Young Henry is dead.'

Not without some difficulty, the old Earl lifted his head slightly. He looked very sad.

'I have heard about the squabbles within the family. Nothing changes in life, young Richard. I am sorry to hear that your brother is dead. I trust it was not by your hand?'

'No, he died of the flux. Mind you, I would have been sorely tempted to end his days had I been given the chance.'

'I see. It appears my good friends, Ranulf and Father Alun, have still not helped you acquire any wisdom.'

Earl Harold cast a glance in our direction before raising his voice as much as his years would allow. He tried to summon some anger in his tone.

'Brothers do not kill brothers!'

'They might if they had brothers like mine. Now I have another one to contend with. Little John is a man now, and my father has to find a domain for him.'

The Earl paused, to gather some breath.

'But you will be King soon; then you will be the guardian of the Plantagenet dynasty. You must unite the family, not tear it apart.'

'Yes, yes, but I'm not King yet. For now, that's my father's job.'

The Earl's face softened and he attempted a smile, perhaps realizing that he had neither the time nor the tools to get involved in the affairs of the Plantagenets.

'I am glad that you have come to see me, Richard. My days are almost at an end; knowing that you will soon be our King means that I can die in peace.'

'Your steward told me that my grandmother visited here.'

'She did, many times; she was very happy at St Cirq Lapopie.'

'Will you tell me about you and her?'

'She was beautiful and brave, the epitome of all that is good in both the Norman dynasty and that of England. I was honoured to know her, and privileged to spend so many happy times with her here. She loved England and the Empire and would be very proud to see you now – especially in this precious place. Father Alun will tell you more when you are King. I will be long gone by then. He will also tell you more about England, and why it is so precious to all of us.'

As if he were administering a blessing, the old Earl stretched out his hand and gestured to Father Alun and myself to move closer.

'We are all children of England; we all carry its precious blood. Remember that.'

His eyes filled with tears and his head sank even lower on to his shoulder. His steward, who had been hovering close by, stepped forward and summoned a couple of assistants.

'My Lords, the Earl must rest now. Perhaps you can have a little more time with him after dinner.'

As his retainers began to lift Harold from his chair, the Lionheart grasped his hand and knelt at his feet.

'I have heard many stories about how you helped my grandmother in the war against Stephen, and throughout the rest of her life . . .' He paused to kiss the Earl's ring. 'Thank you.'

Earl Harold, tears now running down his pale, wrinkled cheeks, placed one hand on the Lionheart's golden-red mane and the other against his face. A sudden ember of the strong and determined Harold of old blazed in his eyes and lit his face.

'You must love England, as England will come to love you.'

Then, as he was carried away, the sharp look subsided and the Earl's melancholy expression returned.

We stayed at St Cirq Lapopie only until the next afternoon. None of us wanted to linger as Earl Harold entered the last few days of his life. He had said what he needed to say, so we left him to depart in peace.

The death of Young Henry brought a brief period of calm to the Empire. King Philip took his army back to Paris, and Hugh of Burgundy and Raymond of Toulouse returned home. We were then able to deal with Aquitaine's rebels with relative ease and all submitted to the King, albeit with their usual duplicity.

The King punished his wayward son Geoffrey by denying him access to any of his castles in Brittany, and the young man had to rely on the hospitality of his friends until his father's anger subsided. All remained calm until the Christmas of 1183, when the King summoned his family to Caen once more.

The gathering would lead to yet another squabble between the Devil's Brood.

Henry wanted a domain for his fourth and youngest son, John, who had just reached the knightly age of eighteen. Once again, he expected Richard to make way. As the

Lionheart was now heir apparent to the entire Plantagenet Empire, the King wanted him to surrender the dukedom of Aquitaine to John in exchange for John's oath of loyalty to him as his future liege.

The Duke hardly knew his youngest brother; John was disliked at court, and was said to be both spiteful and petulant. He was shorter and darker than the other Plantagenets and lacked both the presence and personality of the Lionheart. All in all, there was nothing appealing to Richard about his brother, and he had nothing to gain from agreeing to his father's request.

Father Alun and I travelled to Caen with the Duke, but neither of us was privy to what was said when he met his father. However, when Richard returned from the meeting, he asked Father Alun to help him compose a letter to the King.

'I bit my tongue when the King made his preposterous suggestion. I asked for time to think about it, then embraced my brother and left. Now, I'm going to respond in a formal letter. Abbess Hildegard would be proud of me.'

Father Alun smiled broadly.

'Indeed, I believe she would, sire. Well done.'

It took some hours to craft the letter as the Duke wanted it, but eventually it was composed.

Dearest Father,

I understand your desire to give our beloved brother a great and powerful domain to mark his passage into manhood. Aquitaine is such a realm. However, for the past eight years I have fought countless battles, extinguished the reserves of so many treasuries, and received too many wounds in keeping Aquitaine within your Empire to relinquish it now.

Even if I were already King and too occupied elsewhere to oversee the Duchy myself, I would not entrust it to a young man like John – untried in battle, unproven in governance.

He should be happy with the lordship of Ireland. The Celts are not as intransigent as the lords of Aquitaine.

So, at the cost of incurring your wrath, I must tell you that I reject your proposition. I will return to Poitiers to await your response.

Your Devoted Son,
Richard

The Duke did not wait to witness the inevitable anger of his father; we left for Poitiers early the next morning. No doubt the King's reaction was apoplectic, but we did not hear from him for several months.

Nor did we hear anything from either of Duke Richard's younger brothers.

We spent most of 1184 training the army, relaxing on hunting expeditions or enjoying life at court in Poitiers. The Duke and Father Alun spent many hours discussing the diverse subjects raised by Abbess Hildegard, and the respect they held for one another grew.

The Grand Quintet made an appearance in June, which became a time of great revelry. They also brought some news.

Apparently, the King had been trying to negotiate a marriage for Richard – either by cementing an alliance with a daughter of the Emperor Barbarossa, or by confirming his long-standing betrothal to Alyse, the sister of

Philip Augustus, King of France. Both notions had little chance of success. The Emperor's daughter was a sickly child with no chance of producing children, while it was well known that when Alyse was under the King's guardianship at Caen, as a girl, he had been unable to resist seducing her. As far as the Lionheart was concerned, diplomatic marriages were one thing, but marrying one of his own father's conquests was completely out of the question.

The King then turned to what he thought would be a gambit that Richard would be unable to defend. Although it had much potential risk, and he did it reluctantly, he decided to release his wife from her confinement in England.

For the first time in eleven years, Eleanor of Aquitaine – the most powerful woman in Europe, and its most beautiful – was on the loose.

12. Return of the Duchess

The King's gambit was the work of a master of chess. In May 1185, Queen Eleanor arrived in Normandy and the King immediately sent a message to Richard at Poitiers, asking him to travel to Caen once again to greet his mother and escort her back to Aquitaine. Once there, she would be reinvested as Duchess of Aquitaine.

It was a brilliant move.

Such was the esteem the Lionheart had for his mother, he ordered that we leave for Normandy the next day. In addition, he readily agreed to step aside and acknowledge Eleanor as Duchess of her domain. Richard's agreement initially appeared to be a capitulation but was, in fact, far from it. He was his mother's heir in Aquitaine, which significantly strengthened his claim. And he was also his father's heir to the Empire. Even more importantly, his prodigiously capable mother was now free to become his most important ally.

Neither John nor Geoffrey was happy with their father's elegant solution to the Aquitaine game. But there was little they could do to challenge the outcome. Among those who were inclined to manoeuvre against the Plantagenets and support rebellious offspring, Geoffrey did not command the respect that Young Henry had mustered and John was too young. With the King and his formidable wife allied in a pragmatic truce focused on Richard, a triumvirate had been created that was far too powerful to be challenged, even by Philip of France.

Richard's position was strengthened even further during the following year. In August 1186, as was his wont, Geoffrey was competing in a chivalrous tournament in Paris. In a vicious encounter with a very tenacious and skilful knight from Saxony, he was thrown from his horse. Ominously, his right ankle remained caught in its stirrup. The horse was badly injured and, enraged by its pain, charged around the tiltyard, rearing and kicking, until it trampled Geoffrey to death beneath its hooves. The physicians did all they could to save him, but his injuries were too severe; his chest was crushed and he had deep wounds to his head.

The King was heartbroken. He had lost three sons – one in infancy, and now two more in their prime. Many said that the family was being punished for its sins and that the Devil's Brood was now receiving the retribution that it deserved.

Life in Poitiers was very different after the arrival of Eleanor. The 'Court of Love' that she had created before her incarceration by the King returned. The routine we had enjoyed under the Lionheart – one of severe military training, frequent hunting and various forms of debauchery – was replaced by music and poetry, debate and learning, chivalry and manners. When Duke Richard needed to escape from the high morality of his mother's court, he had to go in search of one or all of the Grand Quintet for baser amusements.

Although the Duchess – a title she held in her own right and much preferred to the title of Queen, which came courtesy of her husband – was closer to seventy years of age than sixty, there was no doubting her radiant beauty, nor her intellect and cunning. She was slim and shapely and walked like a woman half her age. She still had all her own teeth, all of which were unblemished and neatly aligned, giving her smile a wonderful symmetry; her face had few wrinkles and although her chestnut hair had become pure white, it shone with a healthy glow.

For a woman to be called both the most beautiful in Europe and its most powerful was a remarkable dual accolade. She was a patron of troubadours, poets and artists and a strong advocate of chivalry. She surrounded herself with handsome men and nubile women and encouraged them to let nature take its course, indulging their instincts. Rumours about her morality abounded and there were many tales of her numerous infidelities and sexual peccadilloes – most, no doubt, apocryphal.

Her exploits during the Second Great Crusade had added an almost supernatural allure to her reputation. She had taken the cross after hearing Bernard of Clairvaux's famous clarion call, and insisted on taking personal command of her own domain as Duchess of Aquitaine. She recruited large numbers of ladies-in-waiting, who became known as her 'Amazons'. She was fêted in Constantinople as 'Penthesilea, Queen of the Amazons', and she enthralled the Byzantines with her beauty and courage. Although the Crusade was largely a failure, her heroic journey to Jerusalem and back, usually dressed in armour, and her survival through mountains, deserts, shipwrecks and battles became fabled.

Like the Empress Matilda and her confidant, Earl

Harold, the one overriding passion of Eleanor's life was the preservation of the Plantagenet dynasty through her sons.

And her favourite son by some distance was Richard.

The early days of 1187 were a period of relative calm in the Empire, but as spring blossomed a thorny issue that had been pricking the King for many years became a much bigger issue.

Despite being under his care for twenty-five years, and at one time his concubine, Henry had still not found a husband for Alyse, the sister of Philip, King of France. The King had promised several times that she would be married to Duke Richard, but it had never happened. Philip wanted her back, or he wanted her wed; at the very least, he wanted her estates and castles in the borders between France and Normandy returned to him. Henry refused to return Alyse, fearing that Philip would use her to forge an alliance with someone else.

The powers of King Philip Augustus were waxing, while King Henry's were waning, and both were aware of the changes in the other's prowess. The French King calculated that the time was right to challenge the Plantagenets head on. And so, in the summer of 1187, two huge armies gathered near Châteauroux.

Towards the end of June, on a vast expanse of the flat, featureless farmland of Berry, all the lords and knights who could be mustered from the realms of Henry and Philip faced one another. At their sides were their allies from lands far and wide and thousands of bowmen, infantry and sappers, both regular soldiers and mercenaries, who made up the bulk of the two armies.

Most of the knights assembled had fought one another in tournaments many times, where the spilling of blood was commonplace, serious injuries were frequent and death part of the price they were prepared to pay for their sport. But what was in prospect on that inauspicious day was the mass slaughter of a major battle.

All was prepared. The din of men, armour and horses subsided and a menacing calm descended on the chosen field of battle. Pennons and gonfalons fluttered in the breeze, horses snorted, some peed or defecated on the ground. A few men did the same, or vomited where they stood.

I had been in many fights, some particularly vicious, but these were two mighty armies of huge proportions. I shifted uneasily in my saddle and took deep breaths to try to calm my racing heart.

Richard commanded the left flank, his brother John took the right and their father the middle. The Grand Quintet's men supported Richard's force, and I took command of Richard's personal conrois. By the morning of 23 June 1187, all was ready for the mighty encounter to commence.

It was hard to count how many men faced one another that day. My estimate was at least 10,000 on each side. I had never seen so many men, let alone fought a battle amidst such numbers.

We were perhaps within an hour of the battle commencing when Father Alun rode up to our lines escorted by two men-at-arms. He carried a vellum scroll in his hand that would not only change the course of the day, but would also change our lives for ever.

Aware that a major battle between the two most powerful men in Europe was looming, he had travelled to Clairvaux in Champagne, the home of the Cistercian monk St Bernard of Clairvaux, whose passion for war had been focused on a world many miles from Europe, on a war driven not by the wants of men, but by the wishes of Christ himself.

St Bernard had been the main instigator of the Second Crusade of 1147 and one of the earliest supporters of the Knights Templar. Although he had been dead for over thirty years, his influence was still pervasive, and the great abbey of Clairvaux was still the spiritual focus of the crusader spirit in the Outremer.

It was well known that Christian control of the Holy Places was under threat and that Jerusalem itself was in danger, but the news that Father Alun carried was much more alarming. The Muslim leader, Salah al-Din Yusuf, known to the Christians as the Sultan Saladin, had issued a Jihad – a call to Holy War – in the spring and had been amassing a huge army ever since. The words of the Jihad had reached Rome and had sent a shiver down the spine of all who heard them, in every monastery and church in Christendom where they had been read:

Fight and slay the infidels wherever you find them.
Seize them, beleaguer them and lie in wait for them with every weapon of war.

Saladin's reputation had spread far and wide in Europe. He was a man who had risen to rule the entire Levant by dint of his generalship and his code of chivalry, based on the Muslim knightly tradition of Futuwwa. He was much admired and widely imitated.

Although the Christian principalities in the Holy Land were powerful, and they had built imposing fortifications during the three generations they had been there, they lived a long way from western Christendom and were surrounded by millions of devoted Muslims. The Christians sometimes had the support of the Orthodox Christians of the Byzantine Empire to their north, but that was not always guaranteed. Their main bulwark was provided by the military orders of fighting monks, the Knights Templar and the Knights Hospitaller. They were redoubtable warriors, well funded and resourced from their properties and patrons in Europe, but they were jealous of one another and prone to competing rather than uniting in a common cause.

The figurehead for the Christian Outremer was the King of Jerusalem. In the past, these leaders had been warriors of great renown, but ten years earlier, the widowed Sybilla, Princess of Jerusalem, whose son had died, needed to produce a new heir to the kingdom. After much intrigue and haggling, a young French nobleman, Guy of Lusignan, was chosen and summoned from France. Sadly, he was not of the same calibre as the indomitable crusaders of the past. Since his arrival as King of Jerusalem, he had made several catastrophic mistakes in trying to meet Saladin's growing threat.

When the Lionheart heard the detail of the situation in the Holy Land and read the contents of Father Alun's scroll, he immediately sent a messenger to his father and brother. Within a few minutes, King Henry had called a council of war of his senior commanders and invited his opponent on the other side of the field of battle, Philip of France, to join him and the Plantagenets and to bring his senior nobles with him.

Campaign chairs were brought on to the killing ground between the two armies. With the massed ranks looking on, the most powerful men in Europe gathered to hear the contents of Father Alun's missive.

At King Henry's invitation, and without any sense of trepidation, Father Alun rose to describe the current situation in the Holy Land. There was not a murmur from his immediate audience, nor from the two armies on the periphery. When he gave the details of Saladin's army and its gains, there were looks of horror all round. For almost a hundred years, the Holy Places had been under Christian hegemony, which now seemed to be under severe threat.

Then Father Alun unfurled his scroll. In a clear voice that echoed out to both armies he prefaced the statement with his own introduction.

'Pope Alexander has decreed that plenary indulgences for all sins of this earth will be granted to all who rise to the challenge in Palestine and take the cross in defence of Christianity. All debts will be suspended, and all who answer the call will be exempt from taxes levied to pay for the expedition.'

A gasp of astonishment spread through the ranks as Father Alun spoke. Then he raised his hand to demand silence and, like an archbishop in his pulpit, held out the vellum epistle. He had the entire audience in his thrall:

kings and dukes, lords and knights, soldiers and camp followers.

'The Pope has decreed that the revered words of St Bernard of Clairvaux of many years ago be read again in every place of Christian worship in the world. With all humility, I read it to you all now and pray that you . . .' He paused and stared pointedly at both King Henry and his opponent, King Philip, '. . . heed its impassioned message.'

He then read St Bernard's letter.

Oh mighty soldier, oh man of war, at last you have a cause for which you can fight without endangering your soul; a cause in which to win is glorious and for which to die is but to gain. Are you a shrewd merchant, quick to see the profits of this world? If you are, I can offer you a bargain which you cannot afford to miss. Take the sign of the cross. At once, you will have indulgence for all the sins which you confess with a contrite heart. The cross is cheap and if you wear it with humility you will find that you have obtained the Kingdom of Heaven.

As Father Alun finished, there was a stunned silence for several moments. He then rolled up the vellum and walked over to Henry, his King. He fell to his knees, bowed his head and handed the scroll to his liege. Henry took the vellum and looked over to King Philip.

The French King was already on his feet; he walked over to Henry and offered to embrace him. The gesture was immediately reciprocated, and the two men hugged each other warmly. A powerful wave of cheers rolled across the open ground as both armies greeted with elation the rapprochement between the two monarchs. The embrace between the two kings spread among the opposing commanders like a contagion, and there were hugs of goodwill en masse.

The Duke called me over.

'It looks like today's fight is over. But I fear there are bigger battles to come – battles that will be fought a long way from these shores.'

In the most remarkable of circumstances, by the middle of the next day the two armies were preparing to leave.

There had been celebratory feasting overnight and, at a brief but effective negotiation over breakfast, the Plantagenets and the French had agreed a truce. It would last until, at the very least, the threat to the Holy Places had been overcome.

Later that day, the Lionheart summoned Father Alun and myself to his tent. We were to join him and his Grand Quintet to hear his plans for the future.

'I am clear about what I should now do. I intend to take the cross, and I would like all of you to join me. But I am also clear that if the Christian armies are to be successful against this Sultan, we need to unite all the armies of Europe. My father is now too old to go to Palestine, so it will be my responsibility. A deal needs to be struck with the Emperor Frederick Barbarossa. But first, it is vital that I build on this truce with Philip Augustus and win his confidence so that we can act in unison.'

I was in awe as I listened to the Lionheart.

He had matured considerably; he was now the heir

apparent to a vast empire and had taken on the mantle appropriately.

Father Alun nodded sagely as the Duke spoke. He knew that the Lionheart's destiny would not only be determined by his lordship of the Plantagenet Empire, but also by his leadership of the mission to save the Holy Land from the Sultan Saladin and his Muslim hordes.

13. Taking the Cross

Following the remarkable events on the plains of Château-roux, where a battleground became a scene of harmony and goodwill, we travelled to the court of Philip Augustus in Paris to begin the planning of the next Great Crusade.

Philip and the Lionheart warmed to one another, to the point of genuine friendship. Although he was ten years younger than Duke Richard, Philip was an instinctive soldier, strong-willed and clever. Not as tall, nor as imposing as the Duke, he was powerfully built and athletic, with strong features and long wavy black tresses that framed his face like a wimple.

The two men spent the warm days of July 1187 hunting and feasting. Philip showed Richard his plans to add to the magnificence of the cathedral of Notre Dame and to pave the streets of Paris and strengthen its walls. The armies shared military training techniques and ideas in preparation for the challenge that we knew was coming in Palestine. It was a challenge that became much more pressing towards the end of the month.

We were all having breakfast in King Philip's great hall in Paris when Father Alun brought in a young Templar knight who had been found exhausted by the altar of a small monastery on the road from Toulon. Both looked ashen-faced, the knight bedraggled and thin, his crimson pectoral cross almost obliterated by the dirt on his surplice. He had refused any care from the monks at the monastery, insisting that he must reach Paris as soon as possible. The King's stewards brought him a chair and gave him food and drink, but he was in no fit state to relay the news he had carried. Instead, in his clear authoritative tone, Father Alun told his story.

'My Lords, on the morning of 4th July, a great calamity was inflicted on us all. First of all, you will be horrified to hear that when the Sultan Saladin issued his Jihad in the spring, the Christian armies in the Holy Land, added together, could only muster 1,800 knights and 8,000 infantry to meet the challenge.'

There was a look of horror on the faces of all at the table. We all knew then that there had been a catastrophe.

'Saladin has been building his army for years and can call on a force of over 50,000 men. He took Tiberias on the shore of the Sea of Galilee, eighty miles north of Jerusalem, on 1st July, killing many and holding hostage the Countess Eschiva, wife of Count Raymond – who was with the King, in Jerusalem. Despite long and bitter arguments about the wisdom of going to the aid of the embattled Countess, Guy of Lusignan, King of Jerusalem, took the fateful decision to sally forth from the city and confront Saladin. He got only as far as a dry open plain five miles to the west of Tiberias, beneath pillars of rock known as the Horns of Hattin, from where Our Lord delivered his Sermon on the Mount. The heat was overwhelming and they were unable to find water for the men or the horses.'

Some heads in the room had already dropped; experienced soldiers, they knew what was coming.

'Saladin set fire to the parched scrub of the plain,

sending thick smoke into the Christian ranks. A makeshift camp was made and the army spent a fearful night deprived of water and proper sleep. When daylight came, they saw that they had been completely surrounded by the Muslim host. Even though the army carried the True Cross, held aloft by the Bishop of Acre, they knew that their position was almost hopeless. Saladin waited for the sun to reach its blistering zenith before attacking.

'The Christian army fought for its life, knowing that no quarter would be given and that the future of Jerusalem depended on their bravery. Few survived the battle. Those who did – especially the Templars and Hospitallers, who the Muslims fear and despise – were beheaded in mass executions. Despite a courageous final redoubt around the True Cross, Guy of Lusignan, King of Jerusalem, and Gerard of Ridefort, Master of the Templars, were captured and taken prisoner. Raynald of Châtillon was executed by Saladin in person for his previous crimes of cruelty. The Bishop of Acre was killed and the True Cross was defiled. It was tied upside down on a cart pulled by donkeys and sent back to Jerusalem.

'Raymond, Lord of Tiberias, and Balian of Ibelin escaped – Raymond to his castle at Tripoli, and Balian to Jerusalem – to begin the process of defending the city. It is said that when he reached the city, he found only twelve knights to add to the two who had escaped the battle with him.'

There was a silent disbelief in the room. Father Alun paused for several moments before delivering the final, shocking piece of information.

'There are almost no knights left in Palestine to defend

the remaining citadels. Jerusalem only has its walls to protect it. This noble knight here before you, who fought at Hattin and has travelled to Paris with the news, says that every acre of the Holy Land will be under Saladin's heel by Christmas.'

Philip Augustus ordered that the Templar knight be cared for by the monks of Paris and immediately sent heralds around his French realm to order a gathering of all the magnates of France. Richard did the same for Aquitaine and sent word to his father in Caen.

Within a month, a new tax had been agreed, the Saladin Tithe, to pay for a new Crusade. Word also arrived from Aachen that the Emperor Barbarossa would take the cross and join the Crusade.

News from the Levant continued along its inevitable path. Beirut and Sidon fell; Saladin then moved south, taking Caesarea, Arsuf and Jaffa. Ascalon capitulated, leaving the ring around Jerusalem complete. The holiest place of them all was now at the Sultan's mercy. Previously an open city under Muslim rule, after slaughtering its inhabitants the Christians had closed it to Muslims for the last ninety years. The world waited for Saladin to exact his revenge.

When the end came, it was a different story. The Muslim attack began on 26 September 1187. It was said that Saladin's army was so numerous that the dust from their marching obscured the midday sun and that the hail of Muslim arrows was so dense that not even a finger could be raised above the city's walls without being hit.

Balian of Ibelin, who had escaped from Hattin, had taken charge of the defence of the city. A fine and chivalrous soldier, he had given the population hope; to bolster its manpower, he had made knights of merchants, artisans, old men and young boys. After several days of fighting, Jerusalem's walls began to crumble under the relentless barrage from Saladin's siege engines. When it was clear that the city could hold out no longer, Balian rode out himself to plead for the innocents within its walls. Saladin, recognizing a fellow man of honour, put to one side the crimes previously committed in Jerusalem by the Christians and agreed to the city's surrender. On 1 October 1187, the Christian population of Jerusalem began to leave the city and head for the coast.

The next day, Saladin marched his army into the holiest city in the world. Many of his emirs and clerics begged him to destroy the Holy Sepulchre and to defile the site of Calvary, but he refused, ordering only that the doors to the Sepulchre be locked.

Three days later, he ordered that they be opened again and that Christians be allowed to enter if they wished to. He also issued invitations to Jews to return to the city, in the hope that it would become the free city it had been before.

The only act of retribution he allowed was the removal of the gold cross from the top of the Dome of the Rock. This was sent as a gift to the Grand Caliph of Baghdad, who had it embedded in the steps of the city's mosque, so that the faithful could walk on it on their way to prayers. By the end of 1187, only the citadels in the coastal cities of Tyre, Tripoli and Antioch were still in the hands of Latin princes.

None of this chivalrous generosity of spirit made much

difference in Europe, where the mood was one of outrage and vengeance. Stirred up by Rome and every priest in his pulpit, the Church preached that soldiers of Christ must take up arms to slaughter the Muslims.

By contrast, as Father Alun pointed out, when Muhi al-Din, the Grand Caliph of Baghdad, gave the first Muslim sermon in Jerusalem in three generations, he said: 'Beware, lest Satan make you imagine that this victory was due to your sharp swords, your fleet steeds and your fearlessness in battle. No, by Allah! Victory cometh not from the Mighty, but from the Wise.'

It was reminiscent of what the Abbess Hildegard had said in Rupertsberg, and we all remembered it well – especially the Lionheart. Duke Richard took the cross in Tours, in the autumn of 1187, in the new cathedral that was rising above the old one. His father was horrified to hear the news. With old age looming, he faced the prospect of his heir leaving for the Holy Land, just at the time when he would be needed to bring stability to the Plantagenet Empire.

While the Saladin Tithes were being collected and we prepared our armies for the Third Great Crusade, we spent the next year dealing with new squabbles in the south, especially with Raymond, Count of Toulouse.

All the while, the Lionheart's martial skills improved and his generalship matured. He remained an unpredictable mix of ruthlessness and generosity, and his temperament continued to be volatile. But he was learning to unleash his anger only in extreme circumstances. Alun's calming influence grew all the time, and he was often able to bring the Duke back from the brink.

Count Raymond repeatedly asked King Philip for aid and, occasionally, the goodwill we had built up with Philip Augustus became strained. There was much posturing, threats were made by both sides, and there were small-scale skirmishes. But the situation in the Holy Land stopped the pot from boiling over, and our friendship with the King of the Franks survived.

The issue of Richard's intended marriage to Alyse, Philip's sister, and the settlement of her disputed lands in Berry and the Vexin, still churned away beneath the surface, and Philip would not let it rest. Old King Henry tried to interfere, sometimes as peacemaker, sometimes as agent provocateur. But either way, he invariably made matters worse.

The once great master of the chess game of European politics was losing his cunning. He had sent Queen Eleanor back to England, where her movements were restricted and she was closely watched. His suspicions about her loyalty and her intentions towards him had surfaced once again.

King Henry spent the Christmas of 1188 in Saumur. Few of his magnates responded to his invitation to join him. They knew that the future was in the hands of the young Lionheart and the even younger Philip Augustus. The King had become a broken man, unable to cope with the waning of his powers and the growing influence of Richard and Philip.

The bickering went on into 1189. Finally, at Easter, a papal legate, John of Anagni, arrived to organize a peace negotiation. It was held near La Ferté-Bernard, in Maine, twenty-five miles north-east of Le Mans, and was arbitrated by a council of wise men. John of Anagni was joined by the archbishops of Rheims, Bourges, Rouen and Canterbury. The Pope's intention was to man the council with enough ecclesiastical muscle to make even kings take notice and, possibly, to make them behave themselves. All three protagonists brought personal bodyguards who were heavily armed; the atmosphere was tense.

After we had made camp, the Lionheart called us together. As always, he was very clear with his instructions.

'Father Alun, I want you at my right elbow at all times. Ranulf, stay close, my father is bitter and unpredictable and King Philip has lost patience with both of us over Princess Alyse. But you both need to know this: I have already come to an agreement with Philip Augustus. I will marry Alyse and acknowledge her rights in the disputed estates; King Henry will acknowledge me as his heir; and my brother John will take the cross and accompany me to the Holy Land.'

The Lionheart had a self-satisfied look on his face. Not so Father Alun, who was exasperated.

'Sire, I wish you would consult me before agreeing to things like that.'

'Why, it solves all the problems!'

'No, sire, it does not. If anything, it's likely to make matters much worse.'

The Lionheart looked perplexed, and his anger began to flare.

'Explain yourself!'

'My Lord, first of all, it gives King Philip exactly what he wants, something you and your father have denied him for years. And secondly, your father will not even discuss it. We'll be back where we started.'

'But I get what I want, which is for the King to confirm me as his successor.'

Father Alun smiled benignly at his liege, as if he were a tutor pointing out the obvious to a not very clever pupil.

'But, my Lord, the succession is yours by right anyway. The King's confirmation doesn't add anything to your claim!'

The Lionheart stared at Father Alun with a stunned expression on his face. The priest was right, of course, and the Duke had just realized it.

'Very well, I concede. That's why I want you at my elbow today.'

In the course of the negotiations, Father Alun was proved right.

While the Lionheart sat impassively, King Philip outlined the three points that he had secretly agreed with Duke Richard. King Henry listened politely until all the points had been made, then sat for a moment before fixing his gaze on the learned men of God to his left. He roared a torrent of abuse at them, at Philip and at Richard.

It ended with a closing tirade.

'So you can take that back to the Pope in Rome and tell him to shove it up his holy arse!'

He then turned to his son and spoke to him in a hushed tone, but one laden with bile.

'As for you, if you ever do another deal that insults your father with this little Capetian upstart from Paris, try to make your treachery a little less obvious!'

With that, King Henry pushed back his chair and stormed out of the gathering with his retinue scurrying in his wake.

Father Alun's prediction had been accurate; Richard had been embarrassed by his father in front of the man he needed as an ally for the Crusade.

The boiling anger we had witnessed several times before in Richard began to rise. The next morning, the Duke bade farewell to the clerics and thanked them for their patience and understanding. He made his apologies to King Philip and then, before we had gone no more than five paces from Philip's tent, he issued his orders.

'We ride to Le Mans; I am going to make my father listen to me for a change.'

I felt compelled to advise him how dangerous such a plan might be.

'Sire, we have only one conroi; Le Mans is heavily fortified. We would be like a mouse nibbling at a bear.'

'Then send for the army! We ride within the hour.'

I did as I was bid and sent a messenger to Poitiers to mobilize the army and ride north. I considered pointing out to the Lionheart that the army was in training for Palestine, not for another Plantagenet squabble.

But I thought better of it.

All through the spring of 1189, we harassed the King across Maine and Normandy. He was not prepared to fight his son, nor to concede to him – even though he had only a single conroi of bodyguards. When our army finally arrived from the south, the Duke began to attack the King's strongholds in the hope that it would force him to fight. We took Tours at the beginning of July, which gave us effective control of the whole of Maine and Normandy, and Philip Augustus joined us shortly afterwards to add to the pressure on the King.

Henry was at his ancestral home at Chinon; his condition had worsened, as had his prospects. He was unable to find any supporters who would come to his aid, all of whom realized that the Plantagenet Empire had reached a watershed in its history.

Eventually, we received a message that the King would meet us at Ballon to discuss terms. Ballon was nearby, only half a day's ride north of Le Mans. Duke Richard and King Philip prepared for a gathering to settle – at least for the duration of the impending crusade – the ancient feud between the Capetians and the Plantagenets.

The King had chosen Ballon deliberately. It was only a small settlement. The local lord had a hall no bigger than a modest barn, and Henry wanted to be well away from prying eyes – especially from the high and mighty archbishops of his realm, the men he had insulted at La Ferté-Bernard in January.

Hugh of Ballon, an ageing but proud knight who had fought in the Second Great Crusade, and his villagers were in awe of the circumstances. Two kings and a duke who would soon be a king descended on them with all their regal paraphernalia, retainers and military escorts. Hugh had provided food and refreshments, which must have exhausted his stores for the entire year, and gave up his modest hall for the gathering.

When King Henry came in, he was in a sorry state. He needed help to walk and looked like half the man he had been in his prime. His eyes were sunken and the once notorious fire that smouldered in them had gone out.

Even though I was in the service of the Lionheart, I found what came to pass very sad. Duke Richard and King Philip had drawn up a set of draconian requests designed to humiliate the old King and strip him of his power. Father Alun had been unable to persuade them to be less harsh; they were in no mood to compromise. It was like watching an ageing stag being driven out from a mob of deer, facing a forlorn death deep in the forest.

Although it was a fait accompli rather than a negotiation, Father Alun was cast as mediator. The pained expression on his face was plain to see as he presided over the coup de grâce. There was no haggling; King Henry agreed to everything that was asked of him. Within less than an hour, Father Alun stood and announced the details of the concord, which the scribes immediately began to commit to vellum.

Let it be known that on this day, 4 July 1189, in the County of Maine, that our Lord, Henry Plantagenet, King of England, Duke of Normandy, Count of Anjou, Count of Maine, Count of Nantes, Lord of Ireland, has agreed with his son, Richard Plantagenet, Duke of Aquitaine, Duke of Gascony, and his friend, Philip Augustus Capet, King of the Franks, the following terms:

1. He will pay to the King of the Franks the sum of 20,000 marks.
2. In all things he will submit to the judgement of the King of the Franks.
3. The Princess Alyse will be handed to a guardian nominated by Duke Richard and that when he returns from the Holy Land he will take her hand in marriage.
4. The loyal subjects of King Henry, both here and in England, will swear their allegiance to Duke Richard.
5. The date for the muster for the new Great Crusade to the Holy Land will take place at the Abbey of Vézelay in Burgundy, where St Bernard of Clairvaux launched the Second Great Crusade, and is set for Lent in the year of Our Lord 1190.

Finally, it is acknowledged that should King Henry fail to abide by these terms, all his lords and subjects are to transfer their allegiance to Duke Richard and King Philip.

With the Lord as our witness, so be it.

There were several moments of stunned silence. The look on the face of Hugh of Ballon said it all. His small village had not only been visited by the three most powerful men in western Europe, but he had also witnessed two turning points in history. First, he had seen the humiliation of a man who had ruled the Plantagenet Empire with an iron fist for thirty-five years and the passing of that mantle to a new ruler. And second, he had heard the declaration of the launch of a third Great Crusade to the Holy Land.

King Henry, hunched and in pain, struggled to his feet. As he did so, the Lionheart approached him to receive the

Kiss of Peace. The King gave the kiss, but with obvious detestation. When their cheeks met, the old warrior, in a thin, frail voice, whispered in his son's ear.

'God grant that I may not die until I have my revenge on you.'

Richard ignored the bile and helped the stewards take his father outside, where a litter stood waiting to take him back to Chinon.

Two days later, Henry was dead, a passing that had been made yet more melancholy by the news that his youngest son, John, had also deserted him.

England and the Plantagenet Empire would have a new King.

14. Ricardus Rex

The autumn of 1189 became one long regal procession for the Lionheart. His first act was to release his mother from the incarceration which his father had imposed on her; this was a hugely popular move. He rewarded his Grand Quintet with lands and titles, and made a particular point of rewarding those who had stayed loyal to his father until the end. He was heard to remark, 'If they stay loyal to me, like they were to him, then I will have nothing to fear.'

He was deliberate and calculating in trying to create a good impression. He smiled and waved wherever he went – gestures that were reciprocated with warmth and goodwill. He released King Henry's enemies from captivity, restored lands and titles to those who had had them unfairly removed, and assured those who had been cowed by the King that they would not suffer the same fate under his own rule.

To my joy, I was granted five carucates of land in the valley of the Lune near to my beloved Lancaster; Godric was made a captain of the guard, and each of the Little Quintet was promoted to sergeant. Father Alun was perhaps the greatest beneficiary; he was made Abbot of Rievaulx, a Cistercian foundation near Helmsley in Northumbria. The Abbey provided him with an income and a home to go to after his service to the Lionheart. But more importantly, it was close to his roots, the significance of which would only emerge later in our journey together.

The Duke was girded with the ducal sword as Duke of Normandy at Rouen amidst great pomp and ceremony. Soon afterwards, we sailed from Barfleur for England where, on Sunday 13 September 1189, our liege was crowned King of England at Westminster Abbey. As the sun beamed down like a day in high summer, we travelled to Westminster Abbey from St Paul's, passing thousands of ecstatic well-wishers cheering their new warrior King. With my men to my rear, I rode escort just behind the King and, as an Englishman, felt very proud to do so. He was a Plantagenet of Norman blood, but he also carried our blood and thus he was greeted as one of us.

Many said he resembled King Harold, who had fought so bravely to withstand both the Norwegians and the Normans in 1066. Every building flew the new King's gonfalon – three golden lions passant on a gules shield. When the crowd saw Queen Eleanor next to her son, looking resplendent in a pure white linen kirtle and a glorious fur mantle of alternating white miniver and brown sable, they cheered even more loudly. Although she was approaching seventy years of age, in their eyes she was still the beautiful queen they had welcomed to England all those years ago and who had since been so badly treated by her husband, a King they were all glad to be rid of.

The ceremony was held before a gathering of the entire hierarchy of England, and was attended by guests from all the Celtic domains. The abbey was a tapestry of colour, with regalia of every hue and kind; coronets, armour and weapons gleamed, and pungent incense filled the air.

Wearing only plain braies and a white cotton chemise open to his waist, the Lionheart was anointed by Baldwin, Archbishop of Canterbury, with holy chrism from the Gold Ampulla, on his hands, chest and head. Monks then stepped forward to dress him for the crowning in his corselet and robes of cloth of gold, with gleaming regalia of sword, sceptre and orb.

As the echoes of the Te Deum rang around the towering vaults of the abbey built by his ancestor St Edward the Confessor, before the Normans arrived in England, the Lionheart startled everyone. In an unprecedented move, and with the audacity that defined him, he picked up the crown and held it aloft before handing it to the Archbishop so that Baldwin could place it on his head. Shocked at first, the assembly suddenly burst into spontaneous applause. Instead of being horrified that the heir to their kingdom should be so bold, they adored his bravura.

Because it had been locked in the treasury at Westminster since Henry II's coronation thirty-five years before, few people had ever seen St Edward's Royal Crown. Said to include jewels from the crown of Alfred the Great, I was within ten feet of the throne and could see the crown in all its glory. A heavy, solid-gold band lined with red velvet and an ermine ruff, it had alternating decorations of crosses and fleur-de-lis. The band and crosses were encrusted with pearls, sapphires, rubies and emeralds; it was an extraordinarily beautiful object to behold.

Led by the Grand Quintet behind the new King, and flanked by every earl and bishop in the realm, a great roar of approval echoed around the nave. England had a new monarch, Richard the Lionheart, descendant of both the houses of Wessex and of Normandy, a man of Saxon, Plantagenet, Viking and Celtic descent. He was a warrior king behind whom all could unite, in every corner of the Empire. I thought of Earl Harold and of the Empress Matilda. How proud they would have been to see this day.

The coronation banquet was organized by Eleanor, now the Dowager Queen of the realm. A thousand guests were invited and the nave of the great cathedral was cleared to seat them. Four oxen were roasted and three dozen hogs; the serving tables sagged under the weight of meat, game, fowl and fish. Fresh fruit was brought from as far south as the Mediterranean, some varieties of which had never been seen in London. It took the potters of burghs far and wide two months to make the dishes and pitchers for the feast. Wine was brought from Bordeaux on a fleet of specially commissioned ships. The chroniclers later wrote that the steps of Westminster Abbey were awash with torrents of wine. This was not true; hardly a drop was spilled, because it was too good to waste.

Sadly, one community did not enjoy the coronation. Hostility towards Jews had surfaced because of the mood of outrage at the loss of Jerusalem. Although the Jews were not involved in the wars in the Holy Land, as 'non-believers' people associated them with Muslims and they bore the stigma of the nation who had turned on Jesus. When several Jewish leaders came to Westminster to offer gifts to the new King, the crowd outside denied them entry and turned on them, killing several and wounding many more. The rioting spread to the walled burgh of London and eventually to other burghs around the country. Richard asked me to lead his conrois into London to quell the trouble and we arrested several troublemakers, all of whom Richard ordered to be hanged as soon as the festivities were over.

But we could not protect the Jews of York, where they were slaughtered in their hundreds. A few managed to find refuge in York Castle, but when they realized their position was hopeless, there was a mass suicide, leaving only a handful of survivors. Their besiegers then made them an offer, saying that if they came out and promised to convert to Christianity, they would be spared. The hapless inmates accepted the offer. But when they emerged, the crowd turned on them and kicked and beat them to death.

When the Lionheart heard the story, he was livid. He despatched a messenger to the Castellan of York, demanding that the perpetrators be punished. Within a week, he had appointed Geoffrey, one of his father's illegitimate sons, as the new Archbishop of York, ably supported by Otto of Gisors, a good soldier, as the new Earl of York. His instructions to them were clear.

'I want peace in Northumbria. You will enforce it. If you fail, you will answer at the end of my sword.'

Over the coming weeks, the new King made many similar appointments: bishops, abbots and priors, as well as earls, barons, sheriffs and knights. His father had left many appointments vacant so that he could collect the revenues from their tithes and taxes for his own exchequer.

The Lionheart gave all his appointees the same command, 'I want peace in my realm,' followed by the same punitive threat, 'or you will feel the point of my sword.'

Shrewdly, the Lionheart wanted to secure the peace in the Celtic parts of his realm before his commitment to the Holy Land began. So, after the festivities in London, which continued for three days, we travelled to the scenes of my forays into Wales when I served King Richard's father fifteen years previously.

With no concern for his own personal safety, in late September the Lionheart took only the Little Quintet and a single conroi of men and journeyed into what was known as the 'Lair of the Welsh Dragons', Mathrafal, the castle of the Prince of Powys, to meet him and the other Welsh princes. No English monarch had ever entered Mathrafal in peace, nor with so few men. The Welsh were impressed, both by the new King's reputation and by his demeanour.

He was a model of diplomacy and charm; he gave gifts and spoke of goodwill and friendship. By the end of his visit, the Welsh lords gave solemn assurances to keep the peace in their lands while the King was away. Indeed, several young knights agreed to take the cross and join the expedition. It was a strange experience for me; these Celts were noted for their ferocity and intransigence, especially towards the English, but the Lionheart had drawn their sting and soothed their savage hearts.

I was immensely proud to be at the Lionheart's side. I was reminded of stories that my father used to tell me of exploits of years ago: of King Harold when he was Earl of Wessex, when he rode into Wales to challenge the fierce Celtic princes with just the housecarls of his personal hearthtroop; or of Hereward, Thegn of Bourne, and his band of followers; or of King Arthur challenging the Danelaw. They were childish thoughts of hero worship, but very real all the same.

With four knights of Powys keen to take the cross, distinctive in their deep-red Celtic leines and carrying their massive shields and long pikes, we traversed almost the entire breadth of the domain, to reach Canterbury. There we welcomed William, King of the Scots, also called 'Lion' for his powerful build and red hair. As he had charmed the Welsh dragons, so the Lionheart charmed the Scottish lion. After much horse trading, brokered by Abbot Alun, he framed the agreement in which, in exchange for 10,000 marks, King Richard agreed to return Berwick and Roxburgh to the Scots, which his father had forced them to surrender, and acknowledged Scotland's independence from Westminster.

The Lionheart knew it was a momentous agreement, so he had the arrangement widely heralded and enshrined as the 'Quitclaim of Canterbury', written in Abbot Alun's own hand in his impeccable blackletter script and sent to be stored with the King's Pipe Rolls at Winchester. Abbot Alun said it was his greatest achievement.

It caused consternation among the English earls, who were astonished that their King had relinquished sovereignty to a land that their fathers and grandfathers had fought so hard to seize. But it was greeted with euphoria north of the border, where Richard's reputation knew no bounds. And there was the rub; as Abbot Alun was quick to point out, in less than a month, the Lionheart had won over two nations which had been implacable enemies of England for centuries.

The new King was also generous to his brother, John.

Although not entirely altruistic, as he needed his sibling's loyalty while he was away, he plied him with new titles and granted him the lordships of six English counties, including Dorset, Somerset, Devon and Cornwall, and approved his marriage to Isabel of Gloucester, whose inheritance included Bristol, Glamorgan and Newport. In a symbolism that was not lost on a grateful brother, the lands he gave John were almost an exact match to the realm held by his grandmother, the Empress Matilda, in her civil war against Stephen of Blois in the 1140s.

In just four months, the Lionheart had transformed the hierarchy in England and brought a calm sense of goodwill that had not been felt in living memory. And he had appeased and charmed our Celtic cousins in a way that had not been experienced before.

On the road to Dover, getting ready for our departure to Normandy, Abbot Alun remarked on Richard's achievements to me.

'Our young lion is no longer the ferocious beast; he has the sagacity of a ruler twice his age. Hildegard would be proud of him.'

Over the next few months, Richard also proved to be a master of military preparation and quartermastering. He decided to sail the materiel for his army to the Mediterranean, rather than carry it on a baggage train, and began the process of commissioning the ships and the men to sail them. The Cinque Ports alone had to provide thirty ships. Henry of Cornhill, one of London's sheriffs and a fanatic for detail, was made responsible for building the navy and recruiting its crew. He offered

2d a day for sailors and 4d for steersmen. He also took charge of finding the materiel for the voyage. The task was immense: 2,000 horses, 200 farriers, 400 grooms and 50,000 horseshoes from the ironworks in the Forest of Dean.

Arrows and quarrels came in long convoys of carts from all over England. Carpenters, shipwrights and cordwainers, as well as blacksmiths, weaponsmiths and armourers, had to be recruited. Feeding the army was one of the biggest challenges. Every large house in the realm had to train new kitchen staff so that its cooks could be enlisted. Their utensils had to be commissioned, providing a windfall for every cutler, tinker, tinsmith and pewterer in the Empire. They flocked to Smithfield, just beyond London's walls, where Henry of Cornhill was assembling his arsenal and storehouses.

Salt in huge barrels and sacks of herbs and spices were brought from the warehouses by the Thames, and the infirmarers prepared their pennyroyal potions and other remedies to ward off the putrid fever and bloody flux that had devastated previous crusades. Siege engineers from Aquitaine arrived with their tools: grappling hooks, winches, pulleys and ropes, and their sulphur and lime for their notorious incendiaries. Nothing like it had ever been seen in London before, and crowds flocked through the postern at Aldersgate to gawp at the preparations, which stretched as far as the eye could see.

By March 1190, the third leader of the Great Crusade, the Holy Roman Emperor, Frederick Barbarossa, was already on his way down the Danube. Kings Richard and Philip, not wanting the German legend to steal all the glory, set the date of departure of their armies for 24 June.

In the meantime, we travelled south, to the Pyrenees, so that the King could make a point to Raymond, Count of Toulouse, who was the only major Latin prince not to take the cross. There was no doubting what the Count's intentions would be once we had left for the Holy Land, so the King wanted to exert his authority and remind the Count of the consequences of any infringements into Plantagenet territory while he was away.

The excursion was an overt demonstration of pomp and power. We journeyed with a body of men sufficient to reflect the scale of the Plantagenet Empire and a courtly retinue appropriately resplendent in their regalia and finery. Behaving impeccably and smiling profusely, we went from lord to lord. The King enjoyed their hospitality and in return dispensed expensive gifts or parcels of new land, and arbitrated over disputes. It was all very civilized on the surface, but each of our hosts knew the King's real, if unspoken, purpose: While I am away fighting for Christ's holy realm in Palestine, remember who your temporal master is here in Aquitaine, especially if the Count of Toulouse comes to woo you.

There was just one unsavoury incident. Bernard IV, Lord of Bigorre, a minor Gascon fiefdom in the Pyrenees, was a notorious warlord in an area noted for recalcitrant rulers and endemic lawlessness. We had crossed swords with his family before, a dozen years earlier, when the young Lionheart was dealing with the rebellion in Aquitaine against his father.

Numerous plaintiffs complained to the King about the

Lord of Bigorre's behaviour. Not only was he filling his treasury by stealing the precious possessions of pilgrims on their way to Santiago de Compostela, but he was also humiliating, beating, torturing and murdering them if they tried to resist his thieving. The King despised bullies and was intent on teaching this one a lesson.

When we approached his fortification at Bagnères, he was nowhere to be found. His family and garrison were also gone, and his treasury was bare. But it was not difficult to track him down. The townsfolk of Bagnères, who had suffered his cruelty for many years, were only too willing to reveal to us that their lord had sent his family to Bayonne with his treasury and half his garrison. However, he had taken the rest of his men and hidden in the high Pyrenean forests at the headwaters of the Adour River.

The King organized a small troop of light cavalry and with that gleam in his eye that always signalled his love of the chase, we rode up the valley of the Adour in deadly earnest.

Only three hours later, we saw the smoke from Bigorre's camp. There were perhaps fifteen of them, a posse of cut-throats posing as a local militia. We numbered six knights, their men-at-arms and one of our elite conrois of cavalry. It was hardly a contest. Within moments of the Gascons seeing the Lionheart's standard at the head of our galloping column, they scattered into the trees like startled sheep.

Bernard of Bigorre attempted to do the same, but his considerable girth made that impossible. His groom had also deserted him, and his horse was nowhere to be seen. He did have one companion, a sobbing young girl –

perhaps fourteen or fifteen years old – who, judging by her peasant clothing, was his current plaything.

The Lionheart dismounted with his usual athleticism and strode towards the Gascon. Even though the rotund lord had drawn his sword, the King kept his in its scabbard, knowing that he did not need a weapon; his presence was enough to make his opponent buckle. The girl continued to sob, but the King walked over to her, turning his back on the fat Gascon, and held out his hand. Reluctant at first, she was won over by the Lionheart's warm smile. He led her to Godric and asked him to give her some food and water.

As soon as the King turned back to face his quarry and fixed him with an awesome stare, Bernard of Bigorre threw down his sword and fell to his knees. He grovelled at the Lionheart's feet, attempting to kiss his boots. The King had nothing but contempt for him. He leaned down to pick up the man's sword, which he used to poke him under the chin, making him get to his feet.

The Gascon continued to plead for mercy. Like all tyrants, once stripped of the means to intimidate, he was a quivering wreck. He wept and wailed, but the King said nothing, his jaw set resolutely. He gestured to a sergeant, who brought a rope. With the help of two men-at-arms, the sergeant tied a noose and secured it to a nearby tree.

Bernard of Bigorre was hanged for his crimes moments later. The King turned away from the scene before the executed man had stopped writhing in his death throes, and gave Godric an order.

'Strip him of his armour and weapons and have them sent to his family in Bayonne. Give the girl some silver and an escort to Bagnères. Send my proclamation with her that this corpse is to rot where it hangs; anyone who cuts it down will suffer a similar fate.'

The Lionheart had a clearly defined threshold in his mind regarding behaviour he would not tolerate. The Lord of Bigorre had crossed that line and paid the price.

We then crossed the mountains to meet with King Alfonso II, the Lionheart's old ally. Alfonso had formed a new alliance with Sancho VI, King of Navarre, which further extended Plantagenet influence into Iberia. More significantly, for all of us and for England, Sancho had a daughter who would make the alliance between England and the kingdoms of Iberia much more agreeable and permanent.

The King met her for the first time in Pamplona, at the banquet given in his honour by Sancho at the Palace Real de Olite. When she walked into the hall for the feast, the Lionheart was transfixed, as were we all. She was twenty years old and stunningly beautiful. She looked like a pure Basque of her homeland; in fact, she bore a striking resemblance to the lovely Negu I had met in Gascony. She had the same dusky complexion, strong features and flowing black locks formed into a fashionable chignon held with a clasp of gold. Tied with a dark-blue tasselled silk cord, she wore a stunning ice-blue kirtle, which hugged her voluptuous figure to intoxicating effect.

She was called Bérengère, a charming name that suited her perfectly. King Richard's fascination for the princess seemed to be reciprocated by her, and her father's beaming smile also seemed to lend approval; the King of the mighty Plantagenet Empire was a fine catch for his little kingdom.

However, I was immediately concerned because of the solemn undertaking that the King had given to Philip Augustus that he would marry his sister Alyse. But Abbot Alun was able to put my mind at rest with some dramatic news, which had been revealed to him by Queen Eleanor when she was released. Not only had King Henry seduced Alyse as a girl, but she had borne him a child, a boy now approaching adulthood, who had been brought up in Blois by her sister Alix, Countess of Blois. The Lionheart had not yet told Philip Augustus, but he would do so when challenged about the promise to marry his sister.

The King was in a hurry to return across the Pyrenees to make the Crusade rendezvous at Vézelay. And so, once again, Abbot Alun's diplomacy and legal skills were put to good use and a marriage settlement was quickly agreed for the two to marry. It had been a whirlwind betrothal, and Abbot Alun was convinced that the King had already bedded the princess by the time we left, but nothing was ever said.

Richard was irrepressible. He had inherited the most powerful Empire in Europe, had found a wife with whom he could extend his influence into Iberia and with whom he could produce an heir who would add Latin blood to England's pedigree, and he was about to embark on an expedition to save the heart and soul of Christianity.

Just as the King was invigorated, so I was content. I had shared so much already with the Lionheart and I knew there were great adventures to come, but I was still curious about the things I did not know.

As we rode up the Valley of the Rhône, I asked Alun once again about the background to the mission we were undertaking at Earl Harold's behest.

'Alun, is the time now right for me to know of the things that lie behind our journey?'

Alun adjusted his position in the saddle and took a couple of deep breaths.

'Ranulf, let me tell you what you need to know. First, you must know about my personal commitment to Richard's cause and that of England.'

Alun then turned to look me directly in the face. I sensed that what he was about to tell me was something deeply cherished, about which he rarely spoke.

'My father was called Bryn, a sergeant in the service of the Bishop of Durham. He was born in the early 1130s, in Hexham, high in the Pennines. He married a local Durham girl of Anglo-Norse origins called Alditha, and I was born in 1155. I was blessed with a gift for learning and by the age of seven I was being taught by the monks of the cathedral. My father died when I was a boy, but his ancestry was very unusual. Before he died he told me about our heritage.'

I discerned the faintest of smiles begin to soften his face before he took another deep breath and continued.

'Bryn's father, Afan, and mother, Carys, both had ancient Celtic names. They were among the last survivors of an old tribe of Celts called the Gul, a final remnant of the peoples who lived in the north from before the time of the Romans. Carys was born sometime before 1120, the daughter of Awel, a princess of the Gul, whose father was Owain Rheged, the last Druid King of the Gul. Her name means "Gentle Breeze", and she was apparently very beautiful.'

'So, you are of royal Celtic blood?'

'Yes, but that's only half the story. Although Awel was never married to him, Carys' father was a man of great importance in our history . . .'

He paused, and I sensed that he was reaching the crux of the story. I readied myself for what he was about to reveal.

'So, to my great-grandfather; he had sought the remote realm of the Gul on a small estate called Ashgyll, near Alston, high in Northumbria. It was said he chose it because it was the remotest place in England. He lived to a great age after a life full of intrigue, heroism and sadness. Awel comforted him in his last years, and Owain Rheged and the Gul protected him when his few retainers died. Carys, my grandmother, was his only child.'

'What was his name?'

'Edgar the Atheling, prince of Old England.'

It took a moment for the significance of Alun's words to sink in. But then I realized how profound they were.

'But that means you are the true English heir to the throne?'

'Well, yes. But that's now unimportant, because the Lionheart carries enough Cerdician blood to suit us all. That's why I'm here – to protect the heritage that I carry in my veins. Earl Harold carries the same heritage, and so do you.'

I wanted to ask countless questions, but Alun was in

full flow with information I had yearned to hear for so long.

'In the late 1120s, the great scribe William of Malmesbury travelled to Ashgyll with an apprentice, Roger of Caen. When they returned to Malmesbury, the young monk committed the Atheling's story to vellum and stored it in their famous library. A few years later, when our mentor, Earl Harold, was in the service of the Empress Matilda, he met Roger of Caen, then Prior of Salisbury. The Prior had guarded the precious story of the Atheling's life, a document he entrusted to Harold's safekeeping.'

'It must tell a story that no one has ever heard. It is something I would give a fortune to read.'

'You should; and perhaps one day you will. But all that is for another day.'

I smiled to myself, content for now. My decision to accept Earl Harold's commission had been a good one, and it was now entering a new phase with our journey to the Holy Land. I had learned to be patient – I had been so for a dozen years – and had now been rewarded with the amazing revelation of Alun's personal commitment to the mission.

I knew there were more revelations to come, but I had learned to trust Alun's judgement about when it was wise for me to know what I needed to know; so far, it had been infallible.

15. Excalibur

Before the rendezvous at Vézelay, we travelled to La Rochelle to meet the armada of crusaders that had left England. When we arrived, almost a hundred ships were at anchor in the port. There had been mayhem in the town, as the English and Norman sailors and artisans had overwhelmed the taverns and whorehouses. Their disappointment in not finding enough mead, beer or women turned to anger, which soon boiled over into rioting and looting. Women were raped, including the daughter of the Castellan.

The King's fury knew no bounds. He ordered that twenty men be executed on the harbour wall and 200 flogged. When it was pointed out that it was difficult to know who the guilty ones were, his answer was blunt.

'Like the Romans, decimate them. One man in ten is to be flogged; after the flogging, one in ten of those is to be hanged.'

He knew how many men were in his fleet and had already done the arithmetic. After the punishments, he stood on the battlements of the keep that towered over the harbour and spoke to the assembled fleet.

'Listen carefully to my words, for woe betide anyone who does not. Any man who kills another will be bound to his body. If at sea, he will be thrown overboard with the body, and if on land, into a pit. Any man who rapes a woman shall suffer emasculation by her hand. Any man who uses blasphemous or abusive language will be fined one ounce of silver for each offence and any act of theft will be punished by tarring and feathering and being put ashore at the next landfall.'

The King stared out over his huge flotilla; there was silence from the men, punctuated only by the cries of seagulls and the lapping of waves. The men knew he meant what he said. When he turned away, the silence continued for several moments before the men returned to their duties.

To my astonishment and the King's, despite his threats, the same chaos happened when the fleet anchored on the Tagus in Lisbon, and again in Marseilles. The same punishments were meted out on both occasions and the decimation was doubled, then trebled. But the effects were only temporary.

As the Lionheart said later, in a moment of reflection, 'They are the scum of the earth; let's pray that they treat Saladin with the same contempt as they treat me.'

After our rendezvous at Vézelay, the main army and that of Philip Augustus marched south to Marseilles. The Grand Quintet had joined us, making a combined force of 1,500 knights and 10,000 men. Armies of that size were rarely seen. Only when we reached the open plain of the Lower Rhône valley could the end of the column be seen from the front, and only then if viewed from high ground.

In our vanguard was Walter of Coutances, Archbishop of Rouen, who carried aloft the Holy Host in a golden pyx. Behind him came small contingents of new recruits to the ranks of the 'Soldiers of Christ' in their distinctive cappa robes: there were the Knights Templar with their crimson crosses, the Teutonic Knights with their black crosses, and the Knights Hospitaller with their white, eight-pointed Amalfi crosses.

Each contingent had its own colours on their shields, but it had been decided that all the gonfalons and pennons would bear the crimson cross of the Crusade. As a consequence, we painted the broad valley with a long snaking ribbon of white, splashed with blood red. Previous Crusades had cost many lives. As I watched the vivid column pass, I wondered how much of the symbolic blood on display would be real by the time we returned.

At Marseilles, a Genoese fleet carried us to Sicily in several convoys, but instead of the island being merely a staging post on our journey to the Holy Land, it became much more. We made landfall at Messina at the end of September and entered the city with all the panoply befitting the arrival of kings.

The Sicilian King, Tancred of Lecce, was hardly a foreigner to the Normans among us. A descendant of the Normans who had ruled southern Italy for 120 years after its foundation under Roger the Great, he governed a land noted for its diverse population of Greeks, Muslims, Jews and Christians, who had all lived side by side without malice for years. But Tancred was a new King, said by most to be a usurper and not all that popular. A small hedgehog of a man, with no obvious redeeming features, he was no more than the illegitimate cousin of the previous King.

Infuriatingly, on only our second night there, we were

awoken in the early hours by trouble on the streets of Messina. There were just too many crusaders, too taken by drink and too amorous for their own good. Fights had broken out with King Tancred's militia and had spread to the local population. Some of the army had begun to intimidate the local Jews and Muslims, who had retaliated, causing more bloodshed.

Tancred was furious and summoned Richard and Philip to demand an end to the fighting and recompense for the damage. It was a difficult meeting. With the sounds of looting and burning only yards away, I stood at the Lion-heart's shoulder as Philip and Tancred bickered about who was to blame and how the fighting should be stopped.

After half an hour, King Richard's patience was exhausted. He had taken a dislike to Tancred, who he thought was an uncouth bully. He got up from his chair and marched towards the door. As he did so, he calmly issued his orders to me.

'Tell Godric to send your men to Mercadier and the others with instructions to wake their men. Muster my personal conrois. We will take control of the city and occupy Tancred's citadel.'

All those years of training to build a new army, which had begun when his Brabançon mercenaries went on the rampage in the Limousin, in 1177, then paid off. The King's conrois were in their billets and sober when I roused them. When the Grand Quintet and their men arrived, we swept through Messina. We arrested those who surrendered, but cut down any who did not, regardless of whether they were Sicilians or members of our own army.

By dawn, the city was calm. We disarmed King Tancred's personal garrison and locked them in their barracks.

Then the Lionheart marched back into Tancred's hall, where he still sat with Philip. They were calmly eating a breakfast of fresh bread, cold cuts and beer.

'Join us, Richard. I see you have been busy.'

The Lionheart did not respond, nor did he sit; he just took some bread from the table and quaffed a pot of beer.

Tancred continued in a supercilious tone.

'As my guest, it's not very polite to maraud through the streets of my city, arresting my men and assaulting my garrison.'

Philip then intervened.

'Our view was that we should let them fight it out; it gets rid of troublemakers.'

The two men had obviously struck some sort of deal, but Richard was not in the slightest concerned. He took another swig of beer and a piece of bread, then left with only a brief comment.

'At the moment, the objective of every Christian ought to be to fight Saladin, not one another. When you two realize that, I'll release the arrested men and unlock the barracks.'

The impasse lasted for several weeks. Richard spent the time constructing a wooden palisade close to Tancred's main palace, in Palermo, as his quarters. He thought Tancred a fool, but was furious that Philip had not helped him bring the city to order. He took the view that this kind of issue of command needed to be resolved in Sicily rather than in Palestine. When he discovered that Philip had been promised ships by Tancred and was planning to take his smaller army of 2,000 men to the Holy Land on his own, he was even more annoyed.

The stalemate became even more intractable. Tancred's mood of apparent indifference changed. His considerable pride had been wounded and he became more and more angry that King Richard maintained an iron grip on his city and his garrison and refused to relinquish his hold.

Then news arrived that changed the situation significantly. It was carried by the personal herald of the Holy Roman Emperor, Frederick Barbarossa, and what he had to say mortified us all.

The army of the Emperor, a mighty host over 70,000 strong, passed into the Byzantine Empire at the end of 1189. They were warned in advance by Queen Sybilla of Jerusalem that the Byzantine Emperor, Isaac Angelus, had entered into a secret pact with the Sultan Saladin. They therefore avoided Constantinople and the Golden Horn, but the Byzantine Emperor did all he could to impede the crusaders' progress by laying waste all around them. Even so, despite his seventy years, Barbarossa's inspirational leadership and the army's discipline got them across the rugged terrain of Anatolia in the depths of winter. They withstood constant harassment by the Seljuk Turks, including a major pitched battle at Iconium against Qilich Arslan's army. They finally arrived in Armenia in the spring of 1190, from where, as a chivalrous gesture, Barbarossa wrote a formal letter of warning to his adversary.

Now that you have profaned the Holy Land, over which we, by the authority of the Eternal King, bear rule, we will proceed to restore the land you have seized! You shall learn the might of our victorious eagles and shall experience the anger of Germany: the youth of the Danube, who know not how to flee, the towering Bavarian, the cunning Swabian, the fiery Burgundian, the nimble mountaineers of the Alps. My own right hand, which you think enfeebled by old age, can still wield the sword that will bring the triumph of God's cause.

Also an honourable knight, the Sultan Saladin sent Barbarossa a reply.

If you count Christians, my Arabs are many times more numerous. Between us and those who aid us, there is no impediment. With us are the Bedouin, the Artuqid Turcomans, even our peasants, who will fight bravely against those who invade our country and exterminate them. We will meet you with the power of God. And when we have victory over you, we shall take your lands with God's good pleasure.

Chivalrous warnings given and returned, Barbarossa began to move his army through the Cilician Gates. The herald gave a graphic account of what happened next.

'On 10th June of this year, we came to a river called the Saleph. It was a hot day; my Emperor was in full armour, but he still sat high in his saddle in the middle of the river, his great red beard cascading down his chest as he barked orders at his men. Suddenly, his horse, hit on the leg by a log floating down the river, stumbled, throwing my Emperor into the water. It was not very deep, but the shock of the cold water was great and he either suffered an apoplexy or his heart gave out. We got him to the bank in seconds and pulled off his armour, but he was already dead . . .'

The herald paused; there were tears streaming down his face.

'My Lords, it took me many weeks to find you, but I have to tell you that most of our army has turned back and returned to the Empire to wait for the election of a new Emperor. Only Barbarossa's son, Frederick, Duke of Swabia, has made it to Antioch with a much smaller army, about five thousand men in total.'

The Lionheart thanked the herald and told him to rest in Messina before making haste to Antioch, where he should tell Duke Frederick that Plantagenet and French armies would reinforce him as soon as possible. The German herald had brought chastening news, but it did not deter the Lionheart; in fact, he seemed more invigorated than ever. He called his Grand Quintet together and sent for Abbot Alun.

He came straight to the point.

'We must sail for the Holy Land before winter has us in its grip.'

William Marshal was the first to respond.

'None of us is a sailor, but even I know that the gales of autumn are just as dangerous as the storms of winter. It is almost November; we can't sail until early spring next year.'

'Then we will go overland. The fleet can follow.'

I made the next interjection.

'Sire, with the loss of the Germans, our supplies are even more important. We must be cautious.'

The Lionheart looked around the room. No one supported his proposal.

'But the Christians are hanging on by the skin of their teeth in Antioch. And now they have five thousand hungry Germans to feed.' He turned to Abbot Alun, and implored him, 'Alun, we must do something!'

'We can pray, my King.'

The Lionheart seethed with impatience, but he knew we were right.

'Then send for Bérengère. I'll be married and sire an heir.'

'We can pray for that too.'

Alun's ready quip eased the Lionheart's mood. The King continued in a more reflective vein.

'Perhaps that would be wise, given that Barbarossa's army has gone home and I may die by Saladin's hand and never return to England.'

Knowing that there would be a long winter ahead, Richard released his prisoners and unlocked the garrison; all remained calm in Sicily. Just before Christmas, the Lionheart called us together once more.

'I have decided that the most sensible way to get the army to the Holy Land would be to employ Tancred's existing ships and use his boatyard to build more. He has powerful triremes, equipped with Greek fire, and men who know how to use it. But I don't want to pay for them. What do you suggest?'

Mercadier answered immediately.

'Conquer the island, imprison Tancred and take his ships.'

'I've thought about that, but Alun has some interesting information for you.'

Alun stood and spoke in his now familiar paternal tone.

'Tancred is King here because of the Pope's intervention and he will not tolerate us interfering in a realm so close to Rome. The throne should have gone to Lady Constance, the aunt of the old King, when he died without an heir. But she is married to Henry, a German prince of the Holy Roman imperial house, and the Pope does not want a German to rule here at the southern end of the Italian peninsula when he has more than enough Germans in the north to worry about. So he and the local Norman lords found Tancred and manoeuvred him on to the throne.'

Alun then looked at the King in his scholarly way, before issuing a warning.

'Sire, the last thing you want is to be excommunicated before you even get to the Holy Land.'

'So, what's the answer?'

Alun was now in his element; a mischievous smile spread across his face.

'Your sword, my Lord.'

'What about it?'

'It is a fine piece of craftsmanship, is it not?'

'Of course, it was made in Toledo, the home of the world's finest swords, by Master Zahib, the city's most famous craftsman, who died a long time ago. It was given to me by my good friend, Alfonso of Aragon; it is very old.'

'You know, of course, the story of King Arthur and his sword, Excalibur?'

'I do, indeed. I was made to read Geoffrey of Monmouth's *History of the Kings of Britain* in Latin until I was sick of it! What are you plotting?'

'Well, Tancred has been asking me about King Arthur; he's fascinated by the story and is reading the *Romances* of Chrétien de Troyes, one of which tells of Arthur and Excalibur.'

'And?'

'Well, sire, let us tell him that your sword is Excalibur, passed to you at your coronation from all the kings of England back into the mists of time. If he could own Excalibur, he would give you his entire island in exchange.'

We all looked at Abbot Alun with expressions of amazement. Blondel led the questions.

'For an Abbot, you're typically devious, but unusually astute. Also, on this occasion, a bit naive. Do you really think he would believe it? And, if he did, isn't there something very immoral about this, coming from you, who is supposed to be the keeper of the King's conscience?'

'Well, two things in reply, my dear Blondel. First, I have no doubt he would believe it; he's stupid and he's vain, an unfortunate combination for him, but fortuitous for us. As for the morality of the ruse, I would say this: Excalibur is a myth, so any sword could be called Excalibur, especially one as fine as this, with its jewelled pommel and beautiful workmanship. And if the King of England calls it Excalibur, then that's its name. Besides that, Tancred is an odious little toad whose only gift seems to be an ability to spit wads of phlegm into his cuspidor. He is not worthy of any moral veracity – neither the King's nor mine!'

We all looked at Alun in admiration. He was as clever as a fox, and a silver-tongued fox at that.

The Lionheart pondered for a while before speaking.

'I'm very fond of that sword, or should I say "Excalibur"? But if it will buy us the use of Tancred's war galleys, then let's make use of it. I think Abbot Alun is right; the man is an upstart little bastard, he'll believe it's Excalibur and he'll crow about it across the Mediterranean. Alun, as it's your fiendish scheme, you can handle the negotiation.'

Blondel picked up his lute and broke into song. The stewards served some of Sicily's rich wine, and we celebrated Alun's wicked scheme. As we were drinking, Alun turned to me with a broad grin on his face.

'Do you know who sponsored Geoffrey of Monmouth to write the story of Arthur?'

I answered honestly; I had no idea.

'Robert, Earl of Gloucester, the bastard son of Henry I, the Lionheart's great-uncle, who fought with Earl Harold in the Empress Matilda's civil war against Stephen of Blois. Earl Robert heard the story of Arthur from the Welsh bards and asked Monmouth to write it down for posterity. Small world, is it not?'

When I was first introduced to Alun, when he was just 'Father' Alun, I was told he would be Archbishop of Canterbury one day. I had realized many times how astute that prediction was; this was another such occasion.

Alun's devious plan worked perfectly.

Tancred was beside himself when offered Excalibur. Alun presented the offer with great aplomb and persuaded the Sicilian King to loan his entire fleet to the Crusade for a whole year. He opened his shipyards to the Lionheart to commission more ships, and also threw in a handsome geld: a hundred gold bezants and a chest of silver denarii, all of which were secured for a single sword.

The good Abbot's next task was to deal with the thorny issue of the Lionheart's betrothal to Princess Alyse With Bérengère's arrival imminent, the problem had to be resolved quickly.

Abbot Alun's first move was to include provision for Philip's army in the new fleet that had been hired, for which the French King had little choice but to be grateful. He then called a discreet meeting just for Philip and Richard. He did not give me a full account of what transpired, just the detail of the vital moment.

When the encounter reached boiling point and Philip was about to fly into a rage, the wily Alun produced a beautifully scrolled letter from an admiring nephew to a famous uncle. It was from 'William', Alyse's bastard son sired by Richard's father, Henry Plantagenet. Now almost a man, he was writing from Blois, asking his uncle if he might join his service in Paris as a knight.

I can only imagine the look on Philip's face. He had known about Henry's seduction of Alyse, but the news about William was of a different order altogether. Not only was William his nephew, but the boy was Richard's half-brother; a marriage between the Lionheart and Alyse was now out of the question.

Alun did, of course, promise to be extremely circumspect about the letter. He also had another palliative to soothe Philip: he offered him 10,000 pounds of silver to ease the disappointment.

Alun had amazed us all yet again.

A few days later, as the Lionheart and the Grand Quintet relaxed over several flagons of wine, Robert Thornham asked Alun when he had received the letter from young William.

His reply was equally astonishing.

'I didn't, the letter is undated; William wrote it before we left. I brought it with me. I thought it might be useful.'

So, by February 1191, all was well in Sicily. Tancred could caress his Excalibur, and show it off to his friends, and Richard and Philip's passage to the Holy Land was secure.

16. Fauvel

The beautiful Bérengère arrived in Palermo at the end of March. The excitement surrounding her landfall was multiplied when it was known who her mentor for the journey had been.

When the Lionheart sent word to Poitiers in the autumn that Bérengère should be despatched to Sicily, none other than Queen Eleanor herself had undertaken to escort the young princess. Despite her great age, and having suffered the travails of bearing ten children during her lifetime, she had crossed the Pyrenees with winter nigh, crossed back again and then, in the depths of winter, traversed the Alps. She took only a small retinue of cavalry and a light baggage train and made the entire journey without a single complaint – except to bemoan the slow pace of her escort. Hannibal the Great would have been proud of her; on the other hand, it was anybody's guess what Bérengère made of her mother-in-law to be.

A great feast was held to greet the Lionheart's intended bride. Philip Augustus did not attend – perhaps out of pique, or perhaps out of diplomacy – for he was already at the harbour at Messina preparing to sail for Antioch. Queen Eleanor did not dally either; within three days, she was making her way back to Aquitaine. For some old campaigners among the Lionheart's senior commanders, there was a sigh of relief, as rumours had circulated that she intended to join the Crusade. The stories that surrounded her participation in the Second Crusade of 1145 were legion and caused unease. It was said that she had led a brigade of Amazons, but that the presence of women had cursed the entire venture – especially because their leader was the mother of the Devil's Brood. Some even said that she was the Devil's succubus and that she had entered the dreams and drained the potency of the crusaders, as well as diminishing the powers of her husband, King Henry.

As the Lionheart bade his mother farewell, he faced another dilemma. It was Lent, not a time appropriate for weddings. Not only that: his fleet was ready to sail. Dozens more ships had been arriving in Sicily throughout the winter to add to his own formidable fleet. The ports could not cope, and it was time to leave. Richard decided to resolve the dilemma by taking Bérengère with him.

Later, with his fiancée snuggled in his lap, he declared his intentions to us over dinner.

'We will be married in Jerusalem, by the new Patriarch. I shall appoint him.' He then turned to Alun. 'A job for you, perhaps, to preside over the holiest place in Christendom?'

'I think not, sire, I'd rather preside over the holiest place in England, at Canterbury, where I can keep my eye on you.'

In early April, the weather was fair and the fleet was ready to depart. On the eve of the embarkation, we all attended a feast as guests of King Tancred in his fine hall at Palermo.

With Excalibur hanging on the wall above him in pride of place, a bizarre guest appeared.

The heavy oak doors to the hall suddenly opened, followed by a cold gust of wind. As two guards rushed to close the doors, the silhouette of a reedy outline appeared in the doorway. The guards moved towards the figure, but it stared at them with piercing green eyes and a steely resolve; they hesitated. He announced himself as Joachim of Fiore, a renowned mystic from Calabria. He carried a staff that was little more than the spindly branch of a tree, wore neither crucifix nor sandals, and was dressed in rags. He was at least sixty years of age, and was all but bald, with a long scrawny grey beard that was home to the residue of all the meals he had eaten for the last month.

The Lionheart, uninterested, turned away; he fixed his gaze on the beautiful Bérengère. But Tancred ushered the man in and said it would be wise to listen to him. The old ascetic raised his hand to demand silence in the hall and approached the high table.

He spoke like an orator.

'I will address the one they call "Lionheart".'

The King turned, annoyed at being interrupted.

'I am Lionheart.'

'You are famous before your time, young King. Are you worthy of the fame?'

The King, disarmed by the old man's showmanship, smiled.

'I doubt it, old man; the Abbot Alun here tells me that none of us can know if we are worthy until we stand before God on Judgement Day.'

'Your Abbot is a wise man, be sure to listen to him.'

'Do you have wisdom for me and my friends?'

'I do; it would be prudent to listen to me, as you listen to your Abbot . . .'

Holding his audience with his wild eyes, he paused and looked around the hall.

'First, you must repent your sins, for where you are going is no place for sinners.'

'But we are going to the Holy Land; is that not the best place for sinners to repent?'

The mystic raised his voice and filled the hall with a roar.

'The Holy Land is not holy any more; it is in the hands of the infidel!'

He looked to the heavens and closed his eyes.

'I have been searching to know the future for all of us. I have found the hidden truth in the Book of Revelation. We are approaching the Third Age of the Spirit, a time of love and joy. But before that we must destroy the sixth of the Seven Great Persecutors of the Holy Faith. Herod and Muhammad and the others have passed; the Sultan Saladin is the sixth.'

He then pointed his staff directly at the King.

'You, the one called "Lionheart", must annihilate him!'

He paused again and moved the staff closer to the King.

'Cast him into the fires of Hell!'

I could see that King Richard was transfixed by what was being said. But not so Abbot Alun, who had a look of disdain on his face. The Lionheart leaned forward in his chair.

'But if I kill Saladin, what of the Seventh Persecutor?'

'He will come; he will be the Anti-Christ. He is born

already and is now fifteen years old and lives in Rome. One day he will be elected Pope, before he reveals himself as Satan! Beelzebub! Lord of the Flies!'

The old man fell to his knees, as if in prayer.

'But he will rule only for three years until we rise up to challenge him. For now, Saladin is Satan's emissary. He defiles the Holy Places, but God has chosen you to cast him out.'

He then stood and raised his staff over the Lionheart's head; his voice growled even more.

'Your arrival in the Holy Land is vital. Go there quickly; God is calling you. He will give you victory over His enemies and will exalt your name beyond all the princes of the earth!'

There was a stunned silence in the room. Moved by what he had heard, King Richard was ashen-faced. Bérengère looked dumbstruck, in awe of what lay ahead for her betrothed. Tancred offered the mystic food and drink but he refused, and turned and left.

After a few minutes, the volume in the hall rose slowly and the guests continued with their feast. The Lionheart turned to Abbot Alun.

'What do you make of him?'

'A fine performance, sire.'

'Of course, man . . . but what about the things he said?'

'A fine speech, my Lord, but the Book of Revelation can be read a hundred ways. When you meet the Sultan Saladin, I would rely much more on your sword and your siege engines, rather than on divine intervention.'

'You sound more like Marshal and Mercadier than one of God's abbots!'

'Sire, I would listen to them much more closely than to Joachim of Fiore when it comes to the tactics of the battlefield.'

Although the Lionheart listened carefully to what Alun said, I could sense that the old preacher's words had had a profound effect on him.

They had also given Bérengère much food for thought. Later, as we sat and reflected on the evening, she spoke to me in the very stilted Occitan that Queen Eleanor had taught her on their journey from Navarre.

'Ranulf, how dangerous is our mission against Saladin?'

'Very challenging, ma'am; as you know from your Muslim neighbours to the south, in Iberia, they are very resourceful and very proud. Now that they have retaken Jerusalem, they will not give it up easily.'

'Richard tells me that you were chosen to be his guardian by his grandmother.'

'Not exactly his guardian, ma'am, more his adviser.'

'He says that you are a great knight.'

'Ma'am, I am not the kind of knight that you may know – a nobleman who fights in tournaments – I am a professional soldier, who fights for a living. I was granted my pennon for my services to King Richard's father.'

'What do you think of what the old man said?'

'I don't know; I try not to become too involved with the Church and its teachings. But there are lots of seers and mystics who think they know the future. Some say we'll be damned, some say we'll be saved. They can't all be right. I tend to agree with Abbot Alun; the battle with Saladin will be decided by mortal men, not by God.'

She then paid me a compliment – flattery that came

with a burden which only added to the one I already carried.

'You must be very brave to have been chosen to be at the right hand of the Lionheart. For the sake of us all, please protect him in the Holy Land.'

We sailed through the Straits of Messina and headed east on 10 April 1191. In addition to the 50 or so ships which had already sailed with King Philip, I counted 219 ships in total. The Lionheart had taken command of all the other crusaders who had arrived in Sicily in the summer, and now led a force which I calculated at over 20,000, including almost 3,000 knights.

Commanded by Mercadier, Robert Thornham, Blondel and Baldwin of Bethune, he put Bérengère, his treasury and half his personal conroi in four heavily armed dromons in the vanguard. Bérengère was accompanied by Joan, Dowager Queen of Sicily, who was not only the Lionheart's younger sister, but also the widow of William II, Tancred's predecessor as King of Sicily. The rest of the fleet was arranged in a massive pyramid-shaped flotilla behind the leading dromons. We took the port point, while William Marshal led the starboard flank. As we sailed past Cape Spartivento and into the open sea, the Lionheart stood at the prow of our ship. Wearing his gleaming helmet and flowing red cape, he could easily have been the Doge of Venice aboard his Bucentaur progressing along the Canalosso of Venice.

From our position, our flotilla looked like an enormous flight of geese heading south for the winter, its maroon lateen sails billowing in the wind like the puffed-up breasts of preening seabirds. It was a stirring sight.

Our vanguard's captain used his lodestone every hour to check our course; we kept a formation that was so tight, it was possible to shout from one ship to another. At night, each vessel's captain lit a wax candle to identify its position. Our fleet resembled a sea of stars as the candlelight flickered against the black depths of the Mediterranean. I found the sounds of the sea enthralling as it tossed us backwards and forwards, straining our sails and stretching our ropes. Our timbers creaked as if they were crying out in pain; huge beams of oak twisted and were squeezed like young saplings.

We made good progress, but on the eve of Easter Day we were caught by a fierce storm that had us clamouring for anything to which we could lash ourselves. When the maelstrom abated, our formation was no more; the fleet had been flung far and wide. Several days passed before the majority of the scattered flock found one another. But the four 'mother hens' were missing, along with their precious passengers and cargo.

We anchored off Crete for minor repairs then set sail again, making landfall at Rhodes, but there was still no sign of the four dromons of our vanguard. The Lionheart was beside himself with anxiety about Bérengère. He decided to send out scouts in fast coastal trading galleys to try to locate the missing dromons.

Eventually, the scouts returned with good news and bad. Blondel's dromon, which carried the Lionheart's treasury, had been shipwrecked on Cyprus, where he had fought valiantly against the Cypriot garrison before being overwhelmed. Many had been killed, the gold and silver in the treasury plundered, Blondel imprisoned and a large ransom placed on his head. Fortunately, the three remaining ships had managed to stand off the coast, but they were stranded in uncomfortable conditions.

The scouts then proceeded to brief the Lionheart about Cyprus and its lord. The island, a vital Mediterranean staging post between Europe, the Levant and North Africa, had always been rich in food and wine and was one of the most desirable realms in the Mediterranean. Several years earlier, Isaac, a junior member of the family of the Comneni Emperors of Byzantium and a nephew of Manuel Comnenus, had arrived on the island with fake credentials from Constantinople purporting to be the new governor. Slowly but surely, he had managed, step by devious step, to assume control of the island. As soon as he felt himself to be unassailable, he took the title of 'Emperor', donned the purple garb of his imperious ancestors and added all the names and paraphernalia of the glories of Byzantium.

To be servants in his palace, he took young boys and made them eunuchs. He adopted the fabled Manticore as his emblem, gave members of his family Byzantine titles like 'Nobilissimus of the Empire', and appointed a 'Grand Domestic' to be commander of his army. Not only had Isaac tricked his way into power, but he ruled his Cypriot subjects with great cruelty. Summary executions were routine, as was torture of all kinds; he collected his taxes ruthlessly, and showed no compassion to anyone too poor or too ill to pay.

The Lionheart was not only distressed about the plight

of Bérengère, but he was livid that a preposterous little despot, who pretended he wore the Purple of Constantinople, should have the audacity to ransom his loyal Blondel. He ordered William Marshal to take command of the fleet and to follow on, then gave me his usual clear and precise orders.

'Two conrois – the best men – bring your sergeants, and commission two of the fastest galleys. We sail for Cyprus in the morning.'

Rhodes was almost 300 miles from Cyprus, but we were downwind of a strong westerly and we made excellent progress. We soon found our three stricken galleys at anchor off the Cypriot coast. Bérengère, Joan and their ladies-in-waiting were distressed at being marooned amidst a ship's company of men. Mercadier, Baldwin and Robert were embarrassed and angry at being rendered helpless, but they had made the right decision in waiting for help.

The Lionheart immediately took control and ordered an assault on the island. Mercadier and Robert were more than happy to get on to dry land, but Baldwin advised caution.

'The Emperor is just beyond the beach with a large force. They have built a crude palisade of timber, but it gives them cover; it would be a suicide attack.'

Predictably, the Lionheart's temper rose.

'First of all, he's not an emperor – he's not even a prince. Get your armour on, man!'

Within minutes, with my Little Quintet in close support, King Richard, in full armour, was lowering himself down the yardarm and wading across the shallow water to the beach. The waves were strong and several times washed right over our heads. More than once, one of us fell over and, weighed down by our weapons and maille hauberks, had to be helped to our feet.

Mercadier led the King's elite conrois behind us, while Baldwin and Robert formed small squadrons of archers and arbalests to our flanks. As soon as the Lionheart made dry ground, he charged up the beach like a Viking Berserker. Despite the 50lbs of armour and weapons he carried, such was his athleticism and energy, it was difficult to keep pace with him. By the time we reached the top of the beach and the Cypriot defences were in sight, the missiles from our archers began to plummet into their positions with devastating effect. The crossbow was the Lionheart's favourite weapon, and our men could use it with great accuracy; its quarrels could go straight through a man and his maille hauberk at fifty yards.

Without even turning to ensure that we were in close support, our King hurled himself at the makeshift Cypriot defences, fashioned from hurdles, wooden boards and upturned carts. Godric and I managed to position ourselves to his left and right, while the quartet of Modig, Rodor, Penda and Leax tucked in behind us. We had fought at close quarters with the Lionheart before and had as much confidence in him as he had in us. The Cypriots, men from Isaac's personal garrison, were well trained, some having been recruited from Constantinople, but they were no match for the ferocity of our tried and tested techniques. There was soon an arc of space around us, as the Lionheart's blows sent men to the floor beneath his feet. He strode over body after body, most of them mortally wounded from the cuts and thrusts of his blade. We protected his flanks and had soon opened a wedge in the Cypriot wall through which the rest of our men poured.

To fight in the presence of the Lionheart was a remarkable experience. Only the most accomplished of warriors could keep pace with him – and I flatter myself that I was one of them. He wielded his sword as if it had no weight to it, elegantly wafting it through the air with lethal speed. His actions had an instinctive choreography about them; they looked like well-rehearsed techniques from the training ground, but they were not. All were improvised in the heat of battle. Such were his height and strength that he had a physical advantage over most men, but it was his speed and dexterity that set him apart.

But even that was not the whole of it. The Lionheart's essence was his indomitable spirit. He knew no fear, and his opponents could see that in his eyes; they were beaten before they had a chance to strike a blow.

Within minutes, the whole of the Cypriot line had started to flee. With almost reckless bravery against overwhelming odds, the Lionheart had established a bridgehead where none seemed possible. As we all took some air and gathered ourselves, we looked around and realized that about 150 men had scattered a force at least four times that number, simply because of the Lionheart's remarkable daring. I looked at Mercadier, who was standing close by. We smiled at one another in acknowledgement of yet another example of the Lionheart's remorseless spirit.

But he was not resting on his laurels. On a nearby hill, mounted on a striking, white-maned palomino stallion the colour of pale honey, an ostentatiously dressed figure surveyed the scene.

'Ranulf, get some horses, it's him, the Emperor of Minion. After him!'

We found some Cypriot horses that had been scattered down the beach during our assault and we were soon in pursuit of our quarry. Accompanied by half a dozen knights, the Emperor Isaac bolted as soon as he saw us ride towards him. When we reached the top of the hill, the Lionheart put his hand up to halt our gallop. Isaac's knights had made good ground on their steeds, but his stallion had travelled over a hundred yards more. The King looked on in admiration.

'Look at it go! That stallion is so graceful, so quick. When I bring that pup to heel, his horse will be mine, or I'll kiss the Devil's arse.'

Perhaps for the first time that day, the Lionheart looked around. Some of his main fleet could be seen in the distance.

'Let's bring Princess Bérengère and Queen Joan ashore and get them comfortable. We'll need to land our destriers and get them used to the ground, so that we can conquer this little prick of an island.'

Cyprus was far more than a 'little prick'. But to the King, Isaac and his island were an irritation he did not need – especially when news arrived later that Philip had arrived safely in the Holy Land. The report about Philip emboldened the Lionheart even further.

'Ranulf, who's the best scout?'

'Leax, sire – he's excellent.'

'Good, send Penda with him. I need to know where this Isaac is, and where he has stored my geld.'

It took Penda and Leax only three days to find Isaac and his stronghold. Leax, by far the most talkative of any of us, gave his report lucidly and without hesitation.

'My Lord King, Emperor Isaac has gone to ground in a stone keep called Kolossi, about ten miles to the west of the city of Limassol. The castle guards the approach to the city and also protects Episkopi Bay, about two miles to its south-west. The bailey is quite small and is protected by a deep ditch and wooden barricade. The barricade is well made and there is only one gate and bridge. I would estimate the defenders may number around four hundred, perhaps a few more. It looks like the civilians have left and gone to Limassol. We found several talkative locals, who have no affection for their Greek ruler. One of them had lived on Sicily and spoke Norman. He said that there were some catapults in Kolossi, but none of any scale, and that he was sure the prisoners and the treasure had been taken there after the shipwreck.'

'An excellent report, Leax, well done. Ranulf, send a message to Isaac. Tell him that if he releases Blondel and the others and returns my bullion, I will spare his men and put him on a ship with safe passage to Constantinople. If he does not yield, no mercy will be shown to him or his men.'

A short and blunt reply came back immediately from Kolossi: 'Tell your Lord that emperors do not yield to kings.'

It did little for the Lionheart's humour; his response was also uncompromising.

'I want incendiaries. We'll burn down the walls and pour through them like a fast-running tide. There will be no quarter!'

It took the King's sappers and siege engineers a day and a half to prepare the pitch, oil and sulphur to attack the walls of Kolossi. When they were ready, we drew up our knights and conrois of cavalry in formation, poised to charge through the breaches we were going to burn into the bailey's walls.

The siege tactics were simple: the Lionheart ordered that the fire be directed at three points at the base of the wooden walls, where it would ignite the timbers, and at the heavy wooden gates at the end of the single bridge that gave ingress to the castle.

The summer heat of Cyprus was beginning to encroach, and the ground and everything above it was parched. Within three hours of the assault beginning, Kolossi's walls were ablaze. We stood off, sweltering in our saddles, waiting for the signal to attack. It was fortunate that our war horses, the Norman destriers of legend, were battle-hardened by countless tournaments and military campaigns. The Lionheart's decision to transport them by sea was an unprecedented move. Now, after weeks on the water, including several embarkations and disembarkations, these beasts, raised in cool northern climes, were about to be asked to charge through flame and smoke in the heat of a Mediterranean summer. We need not have been concerned; the horses were as keen to attack as we were. They stomped, neighed and pulled;

they were like the Lionheart himself, eager to take flight and go to war.

The King scoured the flames and smoke, looking for holes in the walls that would allow us to assault the castle's bailey. The main gates were much more substantial than the walls and withstood the flames far longer, but eventually one part of the walls, about three yards wide, was burned down to waist level.

The Lionheart looked at me.

I nodded, as confidently as I could. But I knew that, once again, the beast I had by the tail was about to drag me into another fight to the death.

Within seconds, I was next to the King as we plunged into the castle's ditch and up the other side. With the arrows and quarrels from our archers trying to keep the defenders at bay, we jumped through the flames into a bailey which was bristling with men and weapons. The Lionheart's horse was hit the moment we entered the open space. The defenders had created a cordon of lances, bows and swords, and we rode into a bombardment of missiles. Godric took an arrow through his arm and Rodor was hit in the thigh by a lance that glanced off his shield and embedded itself into his flesh.

I jumped from my horse and made sure Modig took care of Godric and Rodor. Leax and Penda gathered around me and we placed ourselves at the Lionheart's shoulder as he waded into the defenders. I was anxious that we had stuck our heads into a cauldron, and I turned in the hope of finding our men flooding in behind us. To my immense relief, led by Mercadier on his huge black destrier, our conrois were flooding through the smoke and flames to support us. The King had not hesitated and, with his shield held high, was raining blows on to the wall of defenders.

But we faced troops who were determined not to yield. Four, in particular, attacked the Lionheart with venom and managed to force him backwards. For once, in hand-to-hand fighting, his safety was under real threat. 'Varangians!' shouted Mercadier as he ran one through with his lance. Isaac must have recruited the legendary mercenaries from Constantinople, where they had served the Byzantine Emperor for generations. Distinctive in their dark-blue capes and with their long hair and beards, these Norse and English warriors had a fearsome reputation – especially for the use of their formidable battleaxes.

In a moment of terror, I watched as King Richard had his sword knocked from his hand. One of the Varangians had got between me and the Lionheart, and I was too far away to help, as were Mercadier and my men. Fortunately, the King always carried a small pugio on his belt for emergencies like this. With lightning speed, he was able to draw it, duck under the arc of his assailant's axe and plunge it into his belly. Mercadier had brought the Lionheart a horse, and he was able to get into the saddle and continue his onslaught.

However, I remained isolated. The two Varangians I faced were at least half a head taller than I was, and the blows from their axes hit my shield like blacksmiths' hammers. I had no choice but to retreat under the onslaught. I looked for Penda and Leax; both were on the ground. Penda was moving, but in great distress from a wound to his shoulder that was discharging blood profusely. Leax was motionless, but with no sign of a wound. I was forced back against the walls of the bailey, which put an end to any further retreat. My prospects were not good.

The Varangian to my right launched his axe towards my helmet but, inadvertently, he gave me a chance. His blow was too close to the wall and instead of splitting my skull asunder, it cleaved deep into the timber of the wall. In the moment it took for him to pull it free, I was able to lunge under his shield and thrust my sword deep into his midriff. His eyes opened wide in horror and pain as he fell on to me, his bulk protecting me from his comrade's blows. Then, with all the strength I could muster, I used the Varangian's body as a battering ram to force myself away from the wall. My sudden movement unsteadied the second Norseman, who tripped over a body behind him and landed on the floor with his comrade on top of him. He was at my mercy and I despatched him before he had a chance to free himself.

By the time I found the Lionheart, the battle was all but over. Defenders were streaming out of the door at the bottom of the keep, followed by Blondel and the other prisoners. Our men were already carrying out the plundered treasure and laying it before the King's Chancellor to be checked against his inventory.

At the end of the flow of people came Isaac, the self-styled Emperor of Cyprus. He had been stripped to his underwear and was being prodded at the end of a sword by his own guards, who had finally had enough of his cruel regime and had turned on him. The Lionheart ordered that he be put in chains. But the hapless man wailed that, as a boy, he had been held hostage in chains for several years and he thus had a hatred of iron. The King smiled benignly at him and spoke softly.

'I'm so sorry, my Lord Emperor, I will resolve your anguish for you.' He turned to his steward and commanded, 'Tell the blacksmiths to make chains from the silver he stole from me.'

Godric and the men were taken to the infirmary to have their wounds treated. Their injuries were serious but none were a threat to life, nor to their future on the campaign, as long as they stayed clear of infection. Leax was the least seriously hurt; he had suffered a blow to the head from a shield, which had knocked him unconscious for a minute or two. The rest of us hoped it would also knock some sense into him.

Two days later, resplendent in his gleaming silver chains, Isaac, the 'Emperor of Cyprus', was put on to a ship. He was to be incarcerated on the coast of Palestine, in the forbidding Hospitaller Castle of Margat. His two daughters, Theodora and Anna, were put into the care of the Lionheart's sister, Joan. The King also acquired Isaac's horse, the palomino he had admired so much from a distance. It was an amazing creature, which he christened 'Fauvel' because of its remarkable honey colour. William Marshal thought it a cross between a pure white Arab stallion and a bay Norman mare; it was an observation that led the King to speculate, with his usual mischievous humour, about his own value at stud.

'I wonder what would happen the other way round. I must conduct a trial when in the Holy Land to see what this fine Plantagenet stallion would produce if coupled with a sleek Arab mare!'

The Lionheart ordered that final preparations for the crossing to the Holy Land be made. Our destination was close, less than a hundred miles to our east, across waters that were usually kind to sailors. But before we left, the King had one more task to perform.

Conscious that he was about to face a redoubtable enemy and his mighty host in battle, he needed to marry Bérengère before we left and, hopefully, impregnate her with his heir. Abbot Alun was summoned to prepare the nuptials. As always, he had something profound to say.

'Sire, this is the land of Aphrodite, the Lady of Cyprus, the Greek goddess of love and of pleasure. It is also the home of Adonis, their god of desire; he is like our Wodewose, a symbol of fertility and nature. There could not be a better place to marry Bérengère.'

'Where do you get all this knowledge from, my dear Alun?'

'I read books, my Lord; you should try it.'

'No thank you; you do the reading, I'll do the fighting.'

The wedding ceremony was conducted by Alun and assisted by the Orthodox clergy of the island, who came to pay homage to their fellow-Christian King. It was held just before dusk in an early Christian shrine, the Chapel of St George, in Limassol Castle on 12 May 1191. Far removed from the scale and grandeur of Westminster or Rouen, on a balmy evening in the enchanting Mediterranean, it was, nevertheless, a charming and romantic occasion. Bérengère looked radiant and the Lionheart looked ... well, like the Lionheart: he was every inch a king among men.

After the marriage, Bérengère of Navarre was crowned Queen, Duchess and Countess of her domains by John, Bishop of Évreux, thus uniting realms that spread from the west coast of Ireland and the Hebrides of Scotland to the middle of the Iberian Peninsula.

Queen Joan acted as matron of honour and, even though they must have felt much anguish about the demise of their odious father, Isaac's daughters, Anna and Theodora, who had been made ladies-in-waiting to Bérengère, added yet more glamour to the proceedings. They were both very striking creatures with their raven hair and olive skin.

Anna, in particular, caught my eye. She was perhaps seventeen or eighteen, about two years younger than her sister, and very attractive. I kept reminding myself that she was the daughter of an 'Emperor' – at least, in name – and beyond my expectations as a catch. All the same, I could not keep my eyes off her.

And I was unable to for the next several days.

Just before our departure for the Holy Land, three ships appeared on the horizon to the east. When they docked, off strode the once King of Jerusalem, Guy of Lusignan, the former nemesis of William Marshal and the man blamed for the catastrophe of the Battle of Hattin. He had been imprisoned by the Sultan Saladin for a year after his capture and had lost his strongest claim to the throne of Jerusalem when his wife, Sybilla, the true heir to the kingdom, had died a year later. He had brought his ships and knights to lend his allegiance to the Lionheart, but was complaining vociferously that Philip Augustus, King of the Franks, had sided with his rival, Conrad of Montferrat, Marquis of Tyre.

Having left behind the politics of his Plantagenet Empire, the last thing the King wanted was to be drawn into the squabbles of the Latin Princes. But, as Alun and William Marshal pointed out to him, he would be wise to accept all supplicants and welcome them to his bosom. Lusignan was thus showered with gifts, given 2,000 silver marks to re-equip his men, and his knights were taken on to the King's payroll. Although generous, the Lionheart could afford it. He had already entered into negotiations with the Knights Templar to sell all tithes and revenues on the island of Cyprus for 100,000 bezants, with 40,000 payable immediately. This was a vast sum, even by the standards of kings and ransoms, and was reminiscent of the Danegelds of yesteryear.

Lusignan brought news from the Holy Land to which the King, attended by his senior commanders, listened intently. It was a remarkable story not known in Europe. In an attempt to redeem himself after his release from Saladin's clutches – a release only permitted when he promised not to take up arms against the Sultan – Lusignan immediately broke his promise and raised a new army. He then committed himself to a challenge which seemed to have even more potential for catastrophe than Hattin.

'I knew the chances were slim, but we had to do something to prevent Saladin from capturing the entire Holy Land. The Muslims had taken the citadel of Acre, a formidable fortress, but I knew it well and thought that if we could preoccupy Saladin there we would deflect him from besieging the other Christian enclaves, such as Tyre and Antioch. So, I decided to besiege the besieger. I began two years ago and threw everything we had at the city. For most of the knights, it was a fight for their homeland; many are grandsons of the First Crusaders and know no other home. Although we did not take the city, I built a timber motte on Toron, a hill with its back to the sea close to the citadel, from where I could continue to attack it with our ballista. I dug a double defensive trench on the landward side for protection, and to keep open a route to the sea for reinforcements and supplies.'

Glances of admiration were exchanged between the Lionheart and his men as Lusignan continued his account.

'The plan worked; Saladin arrived to try to relieve the citadel about a year ago. We've held him at bay ever since. I paid the Pisans and Genoese a king's ransom to send men and supplies; they have delivered both regularly, and to good effect, and our route to the sea remains open. We occasionally venture out and attempt to scale the walls of the citadel, but most of the fighting takes place in our trenches when Saladin sends in his infantry. The clashes are bloodthirsty and at very close quarters. At times, we have had to eat our own horses, and our morale has been very low. But we survive. We are kept going by the thought that it is just as dire, or even worse, for the Muslims inside the citadel—'

The King interrupted.

'But what of Philip Augustus and his men? It must have made a difference when he arrived.'

'It did; the balance is now tipped in our favour. But we need your army to finally clinch it.'

My Little Quintet had been restored to me in good health. With Blondel in fine voice, leading the singing, we sailed from the port of Famagusta on 5 June 1191. The great fleet that had sailed in such symmetry from Sicily was reformed, and on an even grander scale than before. Shrill trumpets rang out, pipes and crumhorns wailed and drums resounded across the water as the galleys, each with its crimson cross flying from its mast, headed east.

This time, the Lionheart's galley was in the vanguard with the entire flotilla fanned out behind him. He stood on the ship's prow with Bérengère at his side; they looked like the perfect regal couple, the progenitors of a dynasty even more powerful than the Plantagenets, Normans and Cerdicians that had gone before them.

I wondered about the child we all hoped she was carrying. Would he inherit not only the colossal Plantagenet Empire of his father and the noble Iberian realms of his mother, but also a new Latin domain in Palestine, even greater than the conquests of the First Crusade?

17. Siege of Acre

Our mighty armada made landfall close to the Hospitaller fortress at Margat, a huge bulwark overlooking the sea, and the site of the incarceration of Isaac of Cyprus. When Anna and Theodora saw it, they begged to be put ashore so that they could visit him. The Lionheart refused – even when Bérengère and Queen Joan intervened on behalf of the princesses – despite the fact that boats had been put ashore to bring fresh meat and fruit on board.

Acre was much further south. After hugging the parched and dusty coastline, we got our first glimpse of the city on 8 June. We disembarked the fleet during the whole of that night and the next day. We could see Saladin's scouts in the distance; they would soon know the immense scale of the Christian army.

I was in the Holy Land, the place I had heard so much about from my father in his stories of the English contingent under the command of Edgar the Atheling, in the service of Robert, Duke of Normandy: the Siege of Antioch, the Battle of Dorylaeum, the Fall of Jerusalem. It was just as I had imagined in my mind's eye. I was moved by setting foot in Palestine, and when I looked at Abbot Alun I saw there were tears in his eyes.

There was much jubilation when the army had completed its tasks. The King ordered that butts of beer be brewed and meat roasted to celebrate. As the men enjoyed themselves, the King asked Alun and myself to walk with him to look at Acre's defences.

'Impressive, are they not?'

'Indeed, sire; Acre will be a tough nut to crack, even for an army as formidable as ours.'

The city was defended on three sides by the sea. But even on the seaward side, towering walls rose from the rocks to create an almost impregnable obstacle. A double wall protected the landward side, with eight large towers offering numerous shooting positions for missiles. We could see light from the braziers of the Muslim defenders flickering against the setting sun over the Mediterranean. It had been another blisteringly hot day, a stark fact that led Alun to reflect on the plight of those inside the walls.

'Women and children, old men, thousands of restless troops, with less and less food, rationed water, stone walls that reflect heat like a blacksmith's furnace. They've been besieged for two years with no prospect of relief. This is an enemy worthy of our journey, sire.'

The King placed his arm on the man who had now become his close friend.

'I agree, but I will soon bring them respite.'

'Do you remember, my Lord, what Hildegard said in Rupertsberg, in her message to the Synod of Trier?'

'I'm going to surprise you, but I do. I have learned much over the years. As she said, we should look around us and count our blessings. Most importantly, having reflected on the world and our place within it, we should think before we act and always take decisions carefully.'

The Lionheart was pleased with himself and smiled at

us both. He then reached out and included me in his embrace before turning to stare out to sea.

'We face as great a challenge here in the Holy Land as any men have ever faced. Our enemy is a great general and, I am told, a fine man. His army is a match for any. Our Christian forces will be riven by jealousy and intrigue. Lusignan is already at odds with Montferrat, and I heard today that Philip Augustus is offering my knights three bezants to fight for him. And all of this is before the Germans arrive! Marshal and the others will always support me, but I want you two to know I would like you to be at my side at all times. I am easily seduced by fanciful words like those of Joachim of Fiore. I need you to remind me of the more considered words of Hildegard.'

The three of us began to walk back towards the camp, at the edge of which we passed two of our heavily bearded Bretons guarding the perimeter. They snapped to attention as we passed. Typically, the Lionheart paused to talk to the two men, encouraging them to stay alert as Alun and I walked on. We were soon met by Mercadier, Godric and the Little Quintet, who were on their way to join the drinking.

The air was cooling rapidly; it had become a characteristically beautiful Mediterranean evening, with a cloudless sky bristling with countless stars, one of which shot across the horizon like a burning arrow.

Suddenly, the harsh reality of the cruel world we had arrived in breached the peace. One of the perimeter guards came staggering towards us; it was barely possible to tell that he was the same man we had seen only moments earlier. His face was obliterated by the blood that spewed from his neck; his beard was crimson, drenched by the torrent that he was trying to spit from his mouth. He had been sliced from ear to ear; he could not speak, nor could he gesture. Both hands were clasped to his throat as he tried in vain to stem the ebbing tide of the last few seconds of his life. He took only two more swaying steps before collapsing into the dirt.

'Assassins!' shouted Mercadier.

The other guard was nowhere to be seen, but the Lionheart was about fifteen paces from us. He had drawn his pugio and was peering into the darkness.

Godric bellowed, '*There!*'

Three cloaked black shadows seemed to glide towards the King. They moved quickly but without a sound; only their silhouetted outlines were visible in the moonlight. We all raced towards the Lionheart as the three shadows closed to within a few paces of him.

As they did so, an arrow cut through the air from Rodor, who had assumed a kneeling position to our right. The arrow struck the trailing shadow with such force that the victim's torso twisted sideways as he recoiled from the impact. He fell to the ground and, without uttering a sound, squirmed in agony.

The two leading attackers reached the King together. The first had the thrust of his knife parried by the Lionheart's powerful forearm as he plunged his pugio deep into the man's midriff. Again, there was no cry from the stricken man, only the dull thud of his body hitting the ground. The final intruder leapt over his fallen comrade, his dagger already making its strike, aiming for the throat of the King. But as he flung himself forwards, the blade fell short. The two clashed heads as they fell in a heap. The King was unconscious before he hit the ground, but his would-be killer was only stunned and held on to his dagger as he rolled away from his fallen victim.

Just as we reached the scene, the killer got to his haunches, steadied himself and raised his weapon to strike at the prostrate body in front of him. In the same moment, Alun grasped the end of the man's trailing cloak and pulled with all his might. This caught him off balance, and he toppled backwards. Although he jumped to his feet again with the alacrity of an acrobat, Alun's instinctive action had bought a vital few seconds. Before the hooded shadow could strike again, the figure was confronted by an arc of pointed lances. The cornered man backed away as Mercadier and my men closed in. In desperation, he flung himself at Mercadier, who thrust his sword into his chest almost to its hilt.

The man was motionless for a second, before he sagged in that limbo between life and death, then fell to the ground. The King's momentarily still form began to rouse itself and he started to get up, aided by Godric and myself. Mercadier put his foot on the dead man's chest to ease out his sword, and then spat on him.

'These three look like Assassins. Their owners rip out their tongues when they are boys so they have no future, other than under the protection of their sadistic masters. They feed them well, give them women and hire them out to the highest bidder. The next fiend could be a yellow-skinned bowman from the east who can skewer a man from two hundred paces, or perhaps a coward with a serpent in a basket, who crawls into camp on his belly like the creature he carries.'

The King, shaken and woolly-headed, asked the obvious question.

'Sent by whom?'

'Not by Saladin; it's not his way. My geld would be on that snake, Philip.'

The Lionheart looked dumbfounded.

'We're supposed to be allies!'

'I don't think he'll ever forgive you for not marrying Alyse. Besides that, he wants to take the glory here and claim the Holy Land for the Franks.'

'But I like him.'

'You're going to have to learn to like him less. As long as he rules in Paris and you rule in Caen, you will always be enemies.'

We all learned a salutary lesson that night. Within moments of the King asking me and Alun to stay close to him in the months ahead, the significance of those words had been made all too obvious.

Alun had saved the life of the Lionheart, something he never forgot.

Saladin had entrusted his bravest and most resourceful commander – the Atabeg, Baha al-Din Qaragush – with the defence of Acre, and his garrison was full of quality troops. He sent out elite butescarls who slipped into the harbour to sabotage Christian ships; they would risk the depths of the water in the middle of the night with a sack of silver strapped to their backs to pay the soldiers. They also used small dhows to run the Christian blockade of the harbour to try to get food and ammunition into the city.

Qaragush used homing pigeons to carry messages to Saladin, and hurled missiles and incendiaries at his Christian besiegers at all hours using a range of improvised ballista. He sent skirmishers out from his walls, sometimes in the glare of the middle of the day, to wreak havoc in the Christian camp. Even though they were almost always suicide missions, they kept coming.

As the hot days of June passed, Qaragush's position worsened. Not only had the Lionheart's troops tightened the noose around the Muslim lines of supply and increased the frequency and scale of projectiles raining down on them, but more Latin troops were arriving all the time.

Henry of Champagne, the grandson of Queen Eleanor from her first marriage to the King of France, arrived with 1,000 knights and 10,000 infantry. He was also accompanied by several dignitaries, including Hubert Walter, Bishop of Salisbury, who brought a gold dish from Glastonbury, which he claimed was the Holy Grail mentioned in the *Romances* of Chrétien de Troyes, a book from which every troubadour in Europe was quoting.

Large contingents of Danes, Frisians, Flems and North Saxons appeared, as did new recruits for the Hospitallers and the Templars. And finally, at the end of June, the 5,000 survivors of the huge army that had left Germany with the Emperor Barbarossa arrived under the command of Leopold V, Duke of Austria.

Our mighty Christian army of the Third Great Crusade against the infidel was complete. I tried to count our numbers, but it was almost impossible; the pennons were so numerous they merged into a sea of colour and extended as far as the eye could see. Mercadier guessed that we numbered 50,000; William Marshal said closer to 75,000 if we included all the non-combatants. Most significantly, we had over 12,000 knights, each with at least one of the heavy destriers the Muslim faris feared so much.

But Saladin's army was also being reinforced. Saladin had renewed his call for Jihad and sent messengers to every corner of the Muslim world. One of the messengers had been captured and the King had the message he carried read out to him.

> The Latins have spared no effort and withheld not a dinar. Now their mightiest kings are here. We must cast off our lethargy; all believers who have blood in their veins must answer this call. As long as the seas bring reinforcements to the enemy our country will continue to bring suffering to our land and our hearts will bleed. I call on the honour of all Muslims, the pride of the believers, the zeal of the faithful!

The Lionheart was moved by the Sultan's rallying cry and immediately sent an emissary to ask for a meeting with him, accompanied only by interpreters. But the request was politely refused with a thoughtful comment.

> It is not customary for kings to meet, unless they have previously laid the foundations of a treaty. For, after they have spoken together and given one another gifts, it is

not seemly for them to return to making war on one another.

The King was impressed by the message.

'I like this man; he is a worthy opponent.'

Saladin's impassioned plea to the Muslim diaspora was soon answered. Devout warriors armed to the teeth came in droves. To the east, they came from Mesopotamia and from beyond the Tigris, as far away as India. To the west, they came from Muslim Spain – European crusaders, but for the Muslim cause. And from North Africa, they came from the furthest reaches of the Sahara, from Mauretania and the Kingdom of Mali, the realms of the Black Men.

Everyone in our camp saw the battles to come as the final Holy War between Christians and Muslims, lending credence to what Joachim of Fiore had said in Sicily. Even Alun, who had dismissed Joachim's prophecies as pure theatre, admitted that the outcome could shape the future for generations to come. He spent long hours in prayer, and even persuaded the Lionheart to join him on occasion.

After Saladin's rejection of his offer to meet, King Richard threw himself into the capture of Acre like a man possessed. He ordered the construction of two dozen ballista and three large canopies that he christened 'moles'. They would allow his sappers to dig under Acre's massive walls. While his catapults and archers bombarded the defenders, his 'moles' were wheeled into position. Made from heavy timbers and covered with hides soaked in vinegar to counteract Greek fire, they provided cover for the sappers to dig into the soft ground beneath the foundations of the walls. They worked night and day. When they opened a large enough space beneath the stones, they supported their work with wooden props until they had created a chasm large enough to undermine the wall above.

After an immense effort, one of the holes was ready. On the morning of 5 July, the King ordered the army to stand by. The sappers packed kindling and logs around their props and drenched everything in oil before igniting their handiwork. The timbers burned for over an hour before groans and cracks heralded the imminent collapse of a large section of Acre's walls. When it came, a thunderous roar and a cloud of choking dust signalled the vital breakthrough. We all waited for the King's order to attack, but it never came. The dust settled and an eerie silence replaced the deafening noise. A warm wind from the sea caressed our faces; men stood or sat on their mounts in quiet contemplation; pennons snapped in the breeze. I looked at the Lionheart; he was staring intently at the slowly dispersing cloud of debris where the wall had been. As if on cue, a figure appeared bathed in the glow of the morning sun behind us.

In a loud voice that echoed across the ranks of our army, he spoke in perfect Norman French.

'I am Baha al-Din Qaragush, Atabeg of Acre. I will parlay with the King, the one called "Lionheart".'

Without any bodyguards, the Atabeg of Acre then stepped over the ruins of his city's walls and began to stride towards us. The Lionheart immediately jumped from his horse and went to greet him. The Muslim leader bowed deeply to the King, who returned the compliment with a short bow of his own.

Atabeg Qaragush was given a seat in the Lionheart's tent where, with Philip Augustus, Henry of Champagne and the Duke of Austria in attendance, the King dictated his terms.

'All Christian captives held by the Sultan Saladin must be released unharmed. A geld of 200,000 bezants is to be paid by the Sultan. Two thousand Muslim soldiers will be taken into my captivity. One hundred of the noblest citizens of the city, including you, my Lord, will be held as hostage. Finally, the True Cross is to be returned to us. All of the above must happen before the next new moon.'

The Atabeg blanched at the severity of the terms, as did everyone present. Qaragush stood and took a deep breath.

'You are called "Lionheart". But your heart is not that of a beast, but of stone!'

'Those are our terms.'

The forlorn man looked around the tent appealingly, hoping for sympathy. He saw only unyielding faces, except for Abbot Alun's. Disconcerted by the harshness of the demands, he turned his eyes downwards.

'Your terms are agreed. But remember this, noble Christian kings, although you may not think so, Muslims and Christians worship the same God. I hope He forgives you for what you do today.'

The next day, the King ordered the army to form up on either side of the road out of Acre as a guard of honour for its surrendering garrison and citizens. Despite the months of hardship, they streamed out with dignity; their weapons, armour and clothing were immaculate, and their heads were held high. In all, 2,700 members of the garrison were immediately taken into captivity, while the civilians began their long trek to the safety of Saladin's camp.

We thronged into Acre amidst scenes of jubilation; it was the most secure bridgehead we could have hoped for in Palestine. The Lionheart, Bérengère and Queen Joan occupied the royal chambers in the citadel, while King Philip took charge of the Templars' Palace in the northeast corner of the city.

That evening, Blondel unpacked his lute and sang the chansons of victory, including the 'Ballad of Robyn of Hode', said to be about Hereward of Bourne and his family, which was one of my favourites and hugely popular with the army. It was a memorable evening, one that lasted long into the night, with some revellers still celebrating at sunrise. Sadly, in the days ahead, there would be less cause for celebration.

Despite several visits by the Lionheart's envoys to Saladin's camp to demand the release of his prisoners, the payment of the gold and the return of the Holy Cross, none of these undertakings was fulfilled by the deadline of the next new moon. The King was furious and summoned Alun and myself to the Palace. When we arrived, he was pacing the room, with the Grand Quintet gathered around him and looking pensive.

'I thought he was a man of honour!'

As usual, there was reluctance to challenge the King when his ire was rising, but William Marshal tried to soothe him.

'The sum of 200,000 is a lot of gold; he has probably

had to ask the Grand Caliph of Damascus for most of it. Also, if the rumours are true, the Holy Cross has been embedded in the steps of the mosque of the city, and the Caliph will need to give his permission for it to be removed.'

'Damn it, William, I think he's testing my mettle. I'll tell him I'll execute the prisoners if he doesn't deliver on the terms within a week.'

Alun immediately intervened.

'Sire, remember, Saladin was not privy to the terms and can only have heard of them after we had entered the city. He's probably furious that Qaragush agreed to them and that he's been presented with a fait accompli.'

'That's as may be, Alun, but a fait accompli is what it is. He *must* deliver.'

'I agree, but think carefully; if you threaten to kill the prisoners and he calls your bluff, you will have no choice but to carry out your threat.'

'I understand that; that's why he must know it's not a bluff.'

With that ominous thought, the Lionheart brushed aside all further entreaties, threw his goblet of wine into the empty fireplace and left the room.

I looked at Abbot Alun, who was as sombre as I had seen him.

'Let's pray that Saladin can raise the money and find the Holy Rood.'

Two days later, Alun persuaded the King to send one final demand to Saladin. But when no answer came back, he summoned me to see him. When I arrived in his quarters, he was standing in the window, looking out to sea. He did not turn round, and spoke in an unusually subdued voice.

'Have the prisoners rounded up and tied together. They are to be taken on to the flat plain between our army and Saladin's, close enough so that the Sultan can see what's happening, and lined up in rows of a hundred men. Choose a squadron of sergeants as executioners, men who have the stomach for it; I want the Muslims beheaded a hundred at a time. See to it.'

I stood rooted to the spot. I knew instantly that I had to refuse, but did not know how to.

The King turned to stare at me.

'Well?'

'Sire, you must relieve me of this task; I can't obey your order.'

The volcanic response did not happen as I felt sure it would; he just spoke in the same calm voice.

'Very well, send for Mercadier.'

When I left the Lionheart's quarters, I was shaking with anxiety. I knew I had done the right thing. But at what price?

I sought out Abbot Alun, but he was nowhere to be found.

Two hours later, led by Mercadier and accompanied by several conrois of the King's bodyguard, men of my own command, a long line of Muslim troops snaked its way on to the flat, fertile ground to our east. As they did so, William Marshal came into my chamber. He looked at me uncompromisingly.

'You are relieved of your command and all your responsibilities to the King, here and at home. You may retain your status as a knight of the realm and your lands in England, to which you must return forthwith. You may take your men with you.' He then turned and left, but as he reached the doorway, he added, 'I'm sorry.'

My fate was inevitable as soon as I refused to accept the King's order. I tried to convince myself that I had done the right thing, which I knew to be true, but living with my virtue was not going to be easy. I found the Little Quintet and told them what had happened. For them, good pay, a secure future and the acclaim of being a crusader was at an end. They were kind enough to say that they respected my decision, but it was as big a body blow for them as it was for me. When I found Abbot Alun, he was standing on the walls of Acre looking eastwards. His head was bowed in prayer.

The executions had begun; they could be seen in the distance. Lines of men, 100 abreast in almost 30 rows, were all kneeling in their immaculate dark-blue qaba tunics, waiting stoically for the executioner's blade. One hundred Christian sergeants struck in unison, rendering the kneeling figures into distorted shapes on the ground. Heads rolled away, some with their pink silk turbans still attached; blood spilled on to the ground. It would have had a dance-like symmetry had all the strikes been clean, but some heads had to be hacked off with several blows, making the spectacle even more horrific.

The city was quiet and there was a stillness in the air; the birds seemed not to sing, the crickets not to chirp. We were too far away to hear the swish of the blades, but it was as if we could.

Alun looked up.

'I'm sorry to hear your news. You did a noble thing, my friend. I'm only sorry our King does not possess the same nobility. When do you leave?'

'This evening. We need to get past the Muslim lines before morning.'

'Where will you go?'

'North, I think. I want to go home overland and see Constantinople and Venice. If the Germans can make it, then so can I. I might even go and see Negu in Rupertsberg, to see if she has become a nun.'

'May I come with you? I cannot stay after this.'

'But what of your promise to Earl Harold?'

'I've done all I can. I have accepted that the Lionheart has a temper and is ruthless. But this is too much.'

'Very well, we are leaving by the North Gate at dusk. There will be just seven of us; we will travel light, and quickly.'

About an hour before dusk, as we were preparing our horses, Alun appeared. He was out of breath – not a state in which he was often seen.

'The princesses, Anna and Theodora, have heard of our departure. They have begged the King to let them accompany us to Margat to see their father.'

'That's out of the question; it's over a hundred and fifty miles away, across the Muslim lines.'

'The King has given them a galley and a conroi of men.'

'Then what happens after Margat?'

'The galley and the men must return. We can continue our journey.'

'And the princesses?'

'It is of little concern to the King. Once they reach

Margat, they become responsible for themselves, or they throw themselves on the mercy of the Hospitallers.'

Although I did not relish the responsibility of protecting two princesses, Margat Castle was only a mile or so from the sea. And the journey by sea in the galley supplied by the King was far less perilous than the prospect of the journey overland through Muslim territory. Besides which, the princesses were both very beautiful – especially Anna, who had captivated me on Cyprus.

'When do we sail?'

'Tomorrow morning, at dawn. We have been given a good captain and the weather is set fair.'

18. Margat

By mid-morning the next day, we were making rapid progress along the coast of Palestine. The princesses had come on board bleary-eyed and sullen, with only a handmaiden each, a modest chest of belongings and a small casket of silver. I felt sorry for them; only a few weeks ago, they were princesses of a beautiful island realm, surrounded by all the trappings of wealth and without a care in the world. Now, all but alone, they had voluntarily relinquished the lifeline of a place at the court of Queen Bérengère to go to a father imprisoned in a remote Hospitaller enclave, in the midst of a relentless enemy.

The galley put us ashore in a small horseshoe-shaped sandy bay. The King's conroi escorted us to the barbican of Margat, before it returned to board the ship and sail back to Acre. It was strange to be in a small group of eleven after so many months in the company of an army of thousands, especially as we appeared to be so small beneath the colossal walls of Margat.

It was a forbidding sight, a towering edifice of black rock, high on a hill, looming over a countryside dotted only with small farms and hamlets. The land was patterned with olive groves and vineyards, as it had been for centuries, but was now dominated by this new Christian sentinel. Amidst the sweltering heat of summer, the castle's only redeeming feature was its cool interior.

Otherwise, it was an austere place with none of the trappings of a regal palace. The Hospitallers lived spartan lives; even Gerard, the Castellan of Margat, a tall and gaunt Burgundian, lived frugally, with only two chairs and a prayer desk in a room without decorations or luxuries of any kind, except the Bible that sat on the desk.

Margat was home to over 1,000 men: almost 400 knights and their attendants, plus other non-combatants. The Hospitallers presented a menacing image in their long black cappas, especially when in large groups early in the mornings, with their hoods up against the cool of the dawn air. In the half-light, with their soft leather shoes making no sound on the castle's sett stones, they looked like spectres of long-dead knights killed in battle centuries before.

Anna and Theodora's father was free to move around the castle's rooms and bailey, but not beyond its walls. He had just one steward to attend to him and lived in a chamber as austere as the knights' quarters. When he greeted us, he looked weary and despondent, but he was thrilled to see his daughters.

As the princesses went inside Margat's keep to enjoy their reunion, I sat with Alun and Godric and the rest of the Little Quintet to explain our route to the north. Godric had reservations about the journey.

'Sire, the Hospitallers only guard the road to the north for about a hundred miles from here; after that, we would be at the mercy of the Muslims. Then we have to cross Anatolia, which is the domain of the Seljuk Turks. None of us has ever been there, and they say the conditions are treacherous – even without the Turks.'

I could sense the apprehension emanating from all five of them, but tried to convince them.

'The only other way is by boat. But the King has all the vessels in use for the Crusade.'

'But, sire, we could use a small boat and keep close to the shore.'

'Let me think about it.'

I believed firmly in my preference to travel overland. But my men had a point, and their views were worthy of some thought. For me, the challenge of crossing Anatolia, like the legendary figures of the First Great Crusade, was very appealing. I was in two minds and sought Alun's advice. As usual, he had wise words for me.

'You should travel the route you want to travel. Our future – both yours and mine – has changed and no longer lies in the Holy Land. It rests in England, and I am content to follow your lead home.'

My quandary about how to make our way home to England was made starker only an hour or so later, when the two princesses and their father hurried across Margat's bailey to see me. With his daughters either side of him, Isaac Comnenus, the deposed Emperor of Cyprus, began to plead with me; he spoke not like the haughty lord we had known on his island, but like a distraught father.

'Sir Knight, I believe you are called Ranulf of Lancaster?'

'I am, sire.'

'I beg a noble service of you. My daughters must reach Constantinople. As you know, I am of the Comneni family, a family that has produced Byzantine emperors for the last hundred and fifty years. The princesses have no future as ladies-in-waiting to an English queen; they must go home to their ancestral family. Please take them. These Hospitallers will not venture beyond the Holy Land; you are our only hope.'

'But, sire, safe passage would be by sea. I intend to go overland, across Anatolia.'

'I know they would be safer by sea, but your preference to travel overland gives me an opportunity to help my girls in a way that I didn't think would be possible. Many years ago, I was the Byzantine Governor of Isauria; my palace was in Tarsus. We were invaded by the Cilicians, who overran the city and imprisoned me in chains for many years. But before I was captured, I hid part of my treasury in a secret chamber in the walls of the Church of St Paul of Tarsus. Now it can serve as my daughters' dowry. I have told them where the chamber is. If you get them to Tarsus, I will give you one tenth part of the geld. If you then get them and their dowry to Constantinople safely, you will be given another hundred bezants by my family. I will send word to them, you have my oath on that . . .'

Looking at me imploringly, he paused.

'Will you do it?'

'My Lord, I need to talk to my men and to Abbot Alun. With only ourselves to be concerned about, we can take our chances. But with two princesses to protect, seven men is a very small entourage. Are you sure it's not possible to recruit some Hospitallers?'

'I have asked them repeatedly, but they won't do it. They insist they're here to protect the Holy Places and the pilgrims; they won't go beyond the Cilician Gates.'

I looked at the two princesses who, like their father, were more like little peasant girls lost in a strange place than noble ladies of the court. Anna stretched out her hand and placed it on mine.

'Sir Ranulf, please help us; you are indeed our only hope.'

'I can't promise anything, ma'am. I will need the agreement of my men; let me talk to them.'

I called Alun and the Little Quintet together to discuss Isaac's proposition. When I offered them a share of the geld, Godric had no hesitation.

'If I may say so, sire, crossing Anatolia for the sake of your sense of chivalry was one thing. But for a handful of gold bezants, well, that's something else altogether.'

He looked at the others, who all nodded decisively.

'Alun?'

'The risks are considerable. Do the girls know how perilous it will be?'

'I believe they do. But regardless of that, they are desperate to get to Constantinople and to recover their dowry along the way.'

'Do *we* know how perilous it will be?'

I smiled at my learned friend. Typically, he had made a telling point. Anatolia was a vast wilderness that had been the graveyard of many travellers who had gone before us, including tens of thousands of crusaders. Even so, I would get my wish; the Cilician Gates beckoned and, beyond them, Constantinople.

Assuming that the less significant we appeared, the safer we would be, I devised a plan to disguise the importance of the princesses Anna and Theodora and to reduce our value as potential hostages. Alun would lose his insignia as an abbot and become a humble monk, I would hide my knight's pennon and spurs, and we would all pack away our weapons to become simple Christian artisans journeying home from the fallen city of Jerusalem. Anna and Theodora and their handmaidens would hide their jewellery and fine clothes and dress drably as laundresses to the noble ladies of the court.

It was a tearful departure from Margat.

The princesses were distraught to leave their father, who looked like a broken man, shorn of all the trappings of his former glory. Despite his appalling behaviour on Cyprus, he had at least found a way to offer his daughters a route home. He was worthy of some sympathy.

Our journey north was uneventful for many days, during which we moved at the sedate pace of pilgrims and drew as little attention to ourselves as possible. We avoided villages and made camp only in remote locations well away from other travellers. Having lived a life of luxury, Anna and Theodora found the privations of the journey difficult – especially sleeping amidst a group of men.

Sleeping separately would have been unwise, as it would have suggested that the women had a higher status than the men. But having them in close proximity was also a problem, as their attractions were all too obvious. As we approached Tarsus, I had no choice but to ensure my men kept any carnal thoughts at bay if we were to retrieve the princesses' geld from the ancient church of St Paul's. However, I recognized that I still had yearnings for Anna, feelings that became more difficult to suppress as time went on.

With the Seljuks in control in southern Anatolia, St Paul's had been desecrated and was in a state of ruin. Its windows and doors were open to the elements and its only occupants were bats, birds and rodents. Even though the church was deserted, it was close enough to other buildings to mean that we would have to make our sortie in the middle of the night. Unfortunately, our arrival in Tarsus coincided with a full moon, so we had to wait two nights for sufficient clouds to help hide us.

While Alun and Godric looked after the horses and the princesses' handmaidens, I posted Leax, Penda, Modig and Rodor to stand guard at the four corners of the church. Anna and I would be in charge of finding the hidden geld. Isaac had given his daughters very simple instructions.

From the door of the church, take twelve paces along the centre of the nave, then turn left and walk towards the wall. Immediately above you, you will see a roof beam entering the wall. Climb above the beam and find the stone that sits on it, hidden from view below. The mortar around the stone is sandy and not very deep. Use a dagger to hack away the mortar and loosen the stone. The stone is thinner than the others in the wall, and behind it is a space that hides the casket you seek.

I was unhappy that Anna had not thought to tell me that we would need a ladder to follow the instructions, and told her so sharply.

'I'm sorry, Ranulf . . . I just didn't think.'

I was immediately sorry for having been cross. I reminded myself how lonely and afraid she must be.

'I'll go and get one of the men to help me climb up to the beam, my Lady.'

'There's no need; I can do it.'

She held out her hand and raised her foot towards my knee.

'It's only like getting on a horse.'

As I lowered myself on to one knee, Anna climbed without any hesitation from my knee to my shoulder and placed her feet on either side of my neck. I then pushed myself up against the wall to give her enough height to grasp the beam and haul herself on to it. She took my seax and our wax lantern and, with her legs straddling the beam in a most unladylike manner, started hacking at the mortar. It took her only a few minutes to loosen the stone, but then she was unable to pull it away from the wall. Fortunately, a solution was to hand – one that meant she had to remove an item of her clothing. Even in these tense circumstances, I found the prospect tantalizing.

'Ma'am, take off the cord around your kirtle; use the seax to push the cord behind the stone and down its sides. When you have the cord in position, you should be able to use it to pull out the stone.'

'How clever of you! I see your mind is as agile as your body.'

I was enjoying the excitement of my escapade with my Cypriot princess and allowed myself a self-satisfied smile – especially when the stone started to slip along the beam. When it was clear of the wall, Anna raised the lantern and peered into the cavity.

'It's there! I can see a small wooden casket. Thanks be to God!'

After she had lowered down the casket, which was heavier than I thought, Anna pushed the stone back into position and handed me the lantern.

'Can you jump, ma'am?'

'I don't think so.'

'Don't be afraid. Jump towards me; I'll catch you.'

As she grimaced with apprehension, I could see her strong cheekbones and the dusky hue of her olive skin in the flickering light of the lantern. Then she jumped, and her kirtle – without the cord, which she had forgotten to put back around her waist – billowed up to reveal her linen loincloth. She emitted a muffled shriek as she landed in my arms. We both giggled in amusement at the involuntary exposure of her legs, emboldened by the excitement of finding the casket.

When I set her on her feet, the top of her head was tucked under my chin; I could feel her silky black hair and smell its earthy fragrance. She moved closer to me, and I could feel her breasts as she took a breath. I was sorely tempted to put my arms around her and kiss her. But we were in a vulnerable place, and the men were outside – no doubt extremely anxious for us to reappear. I leaned back to break the intimacy of the moment. She smiled warmly and pushed herself up on her toes to kiss me on the cheek.

'Thank you, Ranulf.'

'A pleasure, my Lady.'

We left the chapel as stealthily as we had arrived. Alun counted the contents of the chest: our windfall was over

300 bezants, an amount to flutter the heart of even a very rich man.

With smiles on our faces, we rode north towards the Cilician Gates.

Passage through Palestine had been the least risky part of our journey, as almost all the Muslim warriors were preoccupied with Saladin's campaign against the Lionheart. But when we reached the gorge of the Cilician Gates, we entered the heart of the domain of the Seljuk Turks. Although Muslims, they were not directly allied with Saladin's cause. Many of the local warlords made a good living, either ransoming or robbing pilgrims, and had little love for the Christians whose armies, like a plague of locusts, had devastated their countryside many times.

I decided that we would only travel at night, and rest during the day. Thankfully, we passed through the gorge without even a hint of danger. Then we wound our way upwards, on to the Anatolian plateau, where it would be easier to find a path well away from the usual trade routes.

On the tenth night out of Tarsus, we reached a heavily wooded area beyond Ereğli, the ancient staging post north of the Cilician Gates. We could see the fires of the city from our high vantage point and decided to make camp among the tall pine trees that filled the atmosphere with their distinct musk. It was the middle of August; the sun had baked our backs all day, and we were exhausted. I decided that, as we were in a remote place with good shade and fresh water, we should rest the horses and ourselves. I also had an ulterior motive: I wanted to find out if my intimate moment with Anna in the church of St

Paul, in Tarsus, could be extended into something much more meaningful. I was no longer daunted by her high-born status; I wanted her, and had decided that I would just let events unfold. Whatever followed from then on would be what it would be.

After we had found a good place to camp, we unpacked our weapons and armour. I organized a four-hour watch, divided between the six of us, before we all sat down together to eat dinner. The humour was light-hearted and we drank a strange but potent local mead that we had bought from a farmer along our route. Everyone's mood was buoyant, thanks to our boon at Tarsus. The Little Quintet would be able to live well upon their return to England, and Anna and Theodora would be able to attend the imperial court in Constantinople in a manner that was appropriate to their status.

Only Alun was subdued.

After dinner, I asked what was troubling him.

'The further away we travel from the Holy Land, the more aware I become of my failure to honour the promise I made to Earl Harold.'

'You did as much as you could, and you have been a major influence on the Lionheart. But he is now well over thirty years of age, and unlikely to change any further.'

'But that's not the point, Ranulf; I made a promise to be his mentor. In some ways, after what he did at Acre, he needs me even more. Besides which, Earl Harold and I both have a very personal interest in his future and that of England.'

'I remember; you hinted at that when you revealed the truth of your lineage. Isn't it time for me to hear the full details of Harold's story?'

'Yes, it is; you've been very patient. It is a long story. Let's spend tomorrow morning by the lake, before it gets too hot, and I'll tell you everything you need to know. After I've done that, I think I must go back to the Holy Land.'

'But you can't go back on your own—'

'I will have to accept the risks. I took the decision to leave, and I will have to live with the consequences of going back.'

'We'll come back with you. At least let us accompany you into Christian territory.'

'No, you cannot, Ranulf. Your responsibility is to the princesses; you have to get them safely to Constantinople.'

Alun was right, of course. But I knew he would be in grave danger if he made the journey alone. I watched him walk away. I felt sorry for him – especially as my banishment from the King's retinue meant that I would no longer be able to help him with the Lionheart's cause.

The euphoria of earlier had evaporated, and I decided to walk down to the lake beyond our camp. It was a clear moonlit night and still wonderfully warm. I found a large tree at the edge of the lake, sat at the base of its trunk and looked out over the silvery veneer. Within moments, I was soundly asleep.

My next sensation was heavenly. I could feel the heat of a body next to mine; it was a naked body, and it was female. Then I heard Anna whispering in my ear.

'I wanted you so much in Tarsus, and I know you wanted me. It was not a good time then, but now it's perfect. No one will disturb us here.'

Although I was by then fully aroused and desperate to ravish her, I managed a word of caution.

'Are you sure? I am but a knight, and a disgraced one at that.'

'You are far more than a knight in my eyes.'

She was so encouraging, and our coupling was prolonged and deeply satisfying. Anna's body was lissom and powerful; her skin became ever more lustrous through her snakelike exertions, until it was covered in a warm dew.

We bathed in the lake to cool down before resuming our passions, something we repeated once more before fatigue got the better of us.

My watch was due to begin at dawn, so I helped Anna put on her kirtle and walked with her back to camp. She embraced me and I was reluctant to let her go before she snuggled down next to her sister. By the time I relieved Modig on watch, I was exhausted and just wanted to sleep – an inexcusable sin.

At least I could savour what had just transpired and fantasize about the kind of future Anna and I could have together. Perhaps her imperial Comneni family would find me a governorship in a beautiful and peaceful part of the Empire; perhaps I would be offered command of a Byzantine theme, or a senior position in the Varangian Guard.

Sweet musings melded into real dreams. Within moments, I was fast asleep.

19. Passion and Purgatory

I was suddenly woken by anguished female screams, desperate male shouts, the shrill clash of weapons, and a dreadful realization: I had fallen asleep on my watch.

I jumped to my feet, put on my helmet and drew my sword. As I did so, an arrow cut through the air and hit me just above my left eye. Luckily, it caught the rim of my helmet; even so, it was a powerful blow and I started to lose consciousness. But not before I saw a shadowy shape to my left and felt the searing pain of a blade of steel splitting open my hauberk and cutting into my stomach.

Then there was nothing; for how long, I know not. When I regained a vague consciousness sometime later, I could hear nothing other than the typical sounds of a hot day in the forests of Anatolia. My head throbbed, I could feel blood on my face and, as I lifted my helmet, I found a very painful gash on my forehead. The arrow had made a dent in the edge of my helmet deep enough to cleave the metal, allowing the tip of the arrow to cut into me. Even so, the helmet had saved my life.

The wound to my midriff was much worse. The shattered rings of my hauberk were a dark red, as were my leggings down to my knees. I was lying in a pool of blood, but most of it had dried, which I hoped meant I had stopped bleeding. However, I knew that if I started to move, the bleeding would almost certainly start again.

Nevertheless, I had no choice; not only was I desperate to find the others, but I was also driven by the terrible thought that whatever their fate might have been, I was responsible.

I could breathe well enough, had no blood in my mouth and had not pissed any, so I prayed that the blade had not torn into my innards. I managed to get to my feet and staggered unsteadily to the camp. I could feel the bleeding start again, but it was the least of my concerns. The sun was high; it was midday, and very hot. I saw nothing at first – no horses, no signs of the camp – but then I tripped. To my horror, the obstacle I had fallen over was Rodor.

His lifeless face, covered in the dirt of the ground, was pointed towards me at a contorted angle, his eyes gawping, frozen in pain. He had several arrows protruding from his back, his sword was still sheathed and his shield was nowhere to be seen. Then I saw Modig a few feet away; he had suffered a similar fate, but his eyes were at rest. Although I could feel every movement open my wound even wider, I turned to peer into the trees for the others.

At first, I could find no trace of them, but then I saw the bottom of a shoe protruding from the side of a tree trunk. It was Godric, and close by were Penda and Leax. All three had been hacked to pieces. I turned away, unable to dwell on the scene. The anguish I felt in my heart was now far greater than the pain of my wounds, and I sank to the ground in despair. I was holding my stomach with my left hand; it was covered in fresh blood. I needed to take off my hauberk to try to dress the wound, but there was no sign of Anna, Theodora and Alun, which was a much greater priority.

I could see marks in the dirt nearby, which looked like the impressions of someone being dragged along the ground; I hauled myself up to follow the spoor. After about twenty yards, I came across a sight even more horrifying than the ones I had already seen.

In a torture by crucifixion, Alun had been stripped naked and tied to a tree by two of its branches. He had been emasculated and his eyes had been gouged out. He was covered in blood and his head was lolling to one side. I was certain he must be dead. But as I cried out his name, there was a slight movement of his head. By the time I limped over to him, he was spitting blood from his mouth and beginning to speak.

'They were Armenians, not Muslims, and they had Kipchak bows and Phrygian caps. They must have been mercenaries on their way to the Holy Land. Perhaps it was a chance encounter; perhaps someone saw something, but they've taken everything, including the women.'

I cut him down as carefully as I could, but his lukewarm body convulsed in spasms of searing pain. I gently lowered him to the ground and supported his head against the trunk of the tree.

'I'm so sorry, I didn't hear them coming; I fell asleep on my watch.'

'Don't be sorry, they came from behind us. You would not have seen or heard them. We were all awake, but they were among us before anyone saw anything. They slaughtered the men before they could draw their weapons.'

'Did they harm the girls?'

'No, but they took them. I'm so sorry. I know you and Anna had become lovers, I saw you come back to the camp with her just before dawn.'

'I must try to find them.'

'They have been gone for at least three hours, and they took our horses and everything worth stealing. They will be miles away by now. I can hear that you are in pain, Ranulf. Are you injured?'

'Yes, I am dazed from an arrow that smashed my helmet. And I have a stomach wound.'

'They must have stumbled across you as they were leaving. Let me help you get your hauberk off.'

'No, let's try to make you comfortable.'

Alun shivered even more profusely and winced in pain.

'There's no point, my maker awaits me; the meeting will be soon.'

My friend suddenly grasped my hand tightly and pulled me towards him.

'There is something I must tell you before I die . . . and something I must give you.'

Alun adjusted his position and took a couple of deep breaths. His breathing was shallow and all colour had left his face. His head turned, as if searching with his absent eyes for the direction of my face; he grabbed my arm in a desperate, pitiful gesture. The faintest of smiles creased his face before another tremor of pain took it away. He took another breath and started to speak.

'First, you must make me a promise.'

'Of course.'

'You must go back to Richard and find a way to reconcile yourself with him.'

'But he banished me.'

'I didn't suggest it would be easy, but you must find a way. You're a resourceful man and an excellent soldier – find a way, please!'

Without hesitating, I agreed; I had no choice.

'I will try. You have my word.'

Alun's head suddenly fell to one side. He was in a dreadful state; his eye sockets were deep caverns of flesh, from which rivulets of fresh blood still oozed. I desperately wanted to rouse him to hear his story, but knew it was kinder to let him fade away peacefully. I felt my own wound, which was still stabbing me sharply; my head still throbbed, and my vision was less and less focused. I was losing too much blood.

Alun suddenly moved his head and spoke in a thin, laboured voice.

'Is there any water nearby?'

'There's water at the lake, but there's nothing to carry it in.'

'Drag me there; I can help you with my legs.'

'You're in no condition to be dragged anywhere.'

'It doesn't matter. I'm a dead man; I just need a few more minutes to finish my story.'

I summoned all my strength. With my hands under Alun's armpits, I started to pull him down the hill towards the lake. It must have been an excruciating journey for him, but he withstood it without complaint. My own agonies were almost unbearable, but they were as nothing compared to what he must have endured.

When we reached the lake, we both collapsed to the ground and recovered our breath for several minutes.

Then Alun rolled over and submerged his whole head under the water to drink deeply. The impact of the cold water on his eyes must have seared deep into his brain, but he just shook his head like a dog and asked me to lean him against a nearby rock. He also asked me to rob the body of one of the men so that he could wear their braies to hide the horrors of his mutilation. When he was as ready as his condition allowed, he continued.

'I haven't got much time; my life is slipping away quickly. Can you lift me up a little more?'

We were both exhausted, but the one saving grace was the warmth of the Anatolian sun. Had we been cold, Alun would have long since expired. I pulled Alun higher against the rock.

He adjusted his position by lifting himself on his hands and took a long, deep breath.

'Ranulf, would you sit closer to me and hold my shoulders? The pain is hard to bear; I need your strength to continue.'

I was more than happy to oblige my dying friend. Even though he had no eyes with which to shed tears, his chest heaved and there were sobs in his voice. I held him as tightly as my diminished powers allowed.

'I have told you how Earl Harold was entrusted with the manuscript containing the exploits of Edgar the Atheling and his loyal brethren. Eleven years before we met at Wolvesey, Earl Harold had decided to repeat what Prince Edgar had done with William of Malmesbury and Roger of Caen. He told me he had been inspired by Edgar's story and knew it was important that his own story be recorded for posterity – not because it was the story of his life, but because of its importance for our history. Now, I am passing it on to you; it is vital that you become its guardian, because I am the only one who knows it.'

'But I am no more than a minor English knight of low birth, banished by our King.'

'You must find a way, Ranulf, for me, for Earl Harold, for those who went before him and for England.'

'I will try, my friend.'

Alun composed himself again.

'Earl Harold first met Gilbert Foliot in 1139, when he was Bishop of Gloucester. The Earl had been involved in a violent skirmish at Oxford, during which he was badly wounded. Foliot protected him and saved his life. Nearly fifty years later, the Earl sought out Foliot, who was by then Bishop of London. Foliot was a dying man, but over many days, with the help of his scribes, the story of the Earl's life was committed to vellum. It was a remarkable story, but one part of it is particularly important and something you must carry with you, for the Lionheart and for England.'

I felt Alun's hand tighten its grip on my arm as he rested his head on my shoulder; the blood from his eyes started to run down my arm. His head felt heavy and his voice was getting thinner. His end was near.

'The gossip that Earl Harold was the Empress Matilda's lover was true, of course. Their affair began at the Earl's eyrie, St Cirq Lapopie, in the most romantic of circumstances, and they remained close for the rest of their lives; that's why his home in the Lot was so special to him and is where, I'm sure, he rests in peace.'

Alun gripped my arm more tightly. I sensed a great urgency in his words.

'Listen, this is the vital truth: all three of the Empress's children were sired not by her husband, Geoffrey of Anjou, but by Earl Harold. This included Henry Plantagenet, King of England, the Lionheart's father.'

I peered at where Alun's eyes should have been; he could not see the amazement on my face, but he knew what I was thinking.

'Yes, Earl Harold is the Lionheart's grandfather. Our King has far more English blood than he realizes, blood which includes that of Hereward of Bourne, his paternal great-great-grandfather.'

Suddenly, everything about my mission made sense: why it was so important to Earl Harold and, of course, to England's legacy. I had often wondered what could have been so important to persuade such a man to devote his life to a recalcitrant duke from Aquitaine. Now I understood; it was the protection of his family's pedigree that drove him.

'Alun, I'm not certain of both lineages, but does this not mean that you and the Lionheart must be relatives?'

'Yes, but not that close. Our great-great-grandparents were brother and sister: Edgar the Atheling on my side and, on the King's side, Edgar's sister. She was Queen Margaret of Scotland, the wife of Malcolm Canmore.'

Alun's grip on my arm tightened once more.

'Now, remember these important details. Earl Harold's story was sent to Rome in the autumn of 1187 by Gilbert Foliot. It was sent into the safekeeping of his friend, Thibaud of Vermandois, Cardinal Bishop of Ostia, who deposited it in the secret vaults of the Vatican Library. He also sent a casket, which contained the manuscript of the life of Prince Edgar, *De Vita Edgar, Princeps Anglia*, and other precious items, including scrolls and letters . . .'

Alun paused for a moment.

'Foliot is now dead and so is Vermandois, but there is a relic, an amulet I have already described to you, that will give you access to the vaults of the Vatican if you want to retrieve the manuscripts. It is the fabled Talisman of Truth, which is now your responsibility, the responsibility for which you were chosen at Wolvesey.'

The weight of responsibility on my shoulders had suddenly become enormous. I was in the middle of remote Anatolia with a dying friend at my side, my comrades were dead and the new love of my life was lost to me in the hands of ruthless brigands. I felt very alone.

Alun started to feel heavier, and his head slipped further down my shoulder. I looked at his eyes and realized that he was shedding tears, but tears of blood. I nudged him a little and he responded slightly.

'The amulet is hidden in the soil below the tree where you found me. I managed to hide it without the Armenians seeing me. It was given to me by the Earl Harold, its guardian. Now you must look after it. It is called the Talisman of Truth, but it has also been called the Devil's Amulet, among other things. Guard it well.'

Alun raised his chin slightly and, with a grimace of pain, managed a final intake of breath.

'Remember what I have told you; guard the talisman well.'

Only moments later, Alun breathed no more. Blood

still trickled down his face, but its life-giving essence had gone. I laid him down by the side of the lake and sat with him for some time.

I started to feel very lethargic, but I knew that I must not succumb to the desire to sleep. I roused myself as much as I could, for had I not done so, I would have joined my friends in death. I got to my feet and lit a large fire. After a prolonged struggle, I managed to remove my hauberk. My stomach wound was deep, as I had feared. But as I was still alive, I assumed the blade had not penetrated any vital internal organs. Even so, I had to cauterize it to stop the bleeding. When the fire was hot enough, I poked my seax deep into its hot ashes and waited until it was ready to do its worst.

Without help to do the deed, I lay on my back and positioned the blade. When I let it go, it fell on to the open wound. It was the most painful thing I have ever had to endure. But I had no choice; I had to bear it, if I was to survive.

After the pain had subsided, I resisted the temptation to sleep. I lay still for over an hour until the wound had cooled, then submerged myself in the lake to cleanse my body. I stripped the leggings off one of the men and used the cloth as a bandage to dress my wound. I drank deeply from the fresh water of the lake and made some traps for fish and rabbit, before finally allowing myself to sleep.

It was a fitful, disturbed sleep; my pain and my conscience gave me no respite, and I woke suddenly in a state of remorse and panic. Fortunately, I had snared a fish in my simple trap and I roasted it on the fire and ate it like a hungry dog.

The pain in my head had lessened and my vision had cleared, so I walked to the tree where Alun had been tortured. I retrieved the relic from its roots; the amulet, tied in a small leather pouch, was just as he had described it.

Hanging from a heavy silver chain was a translucent piece of amber the size of a quail's egg. It was set in scrolls of silver, each of which was a filigree snake, so finely worked that the oval eyes and forked tongues of the serpents could be seen in detail. At first glance, apart from its size and smoothness, it seemed unremarkable. But when it was held to the light, silhouetted in the baleful yellow glow of its stone was the face of Satan, the horned beast that has haunted men from the beginning of time. Close to the hideous face, trapped in the stone, were a tiny spider and a group of small winged insects, the devil's familiars. Cutting through the stone was what Alun had said was the blood of Christ, trapping the devil in the stone. It was a streak of crimson, like a bloody Milky Way, which, at a certain angle, obscured the face of Lucifer.

When I examined the talisman, I remembered asking Alun the question prompted by Hereward of Bourne's colours when they were carried by the Little Quintet during our journey to Angers. Now I truly understood their significance. At that moment I promised myself that, should I survive my current ordeal, I would always wear Hereward's colours as my own.

Feeling that I was not worthy enough to put it around my neck, I returned the talisman to its pouch and tied it on to my belt. It made me shudder to think that I was now the guardian of this sacred object, but I knew what I had to do, and I knew who the talisman's next recipient should be. However, I had been dismissed from the service of the man who should wear it with pride; he was several hundred miles away to the south, and I was hardly in a fit state to travel.

I still had to think of a way to discover what had happened to Anna and Theodora, and to their dowry. I needed to get my wits about me and garner my resources. But first, I had to deal with my dead friends.

It took me the rest of that day to drag the bodies to a central spot and to construct some sort of tomb for them. It was a gruesome task, pulling and tugging the bloodied corpses of friends like carcasses in an abattoir. As I only had my seax and sword with which to dig, I decided to build a stone cairn around them as a memorial. The lake shore was littered with rocks, and I set about collecting them to build a final resting place for my comrades. It was a long way from their home, but there were trees and water nearby and I hoped they would think it not too unlike England.

At dusk, with a sickening discovery, one of my immediate predicaments disappeared. Even though the light was fading, there was no mistaking what I could see. About five yards from the shore, just beneath the surface of the water, three shockingly white, spread-eagled outlines drifted into view. A fourth shape lapped against the water's edge.

I knew instantly that the bodies belonged to Anna and Theodora and their handmaidens. They were naked and facing downwards, but their female contours were unmistakeable. I sank to my knees and wept uncontrollably.

Life was often cruel, but this was unbearable. And what was even worse: I was to blame.

I should have found another way to get them from Tarsus. Perhaps we should have turned back to the sea and taken a ship? But I was driven by my passion to see Constantinople. Then, I had fallen asleep on my watch. Even though the brigands had attacked from another direction, had I been more alert, I might have been able to help prevent the slaughter.

After a few minutes, I got a grip of myself and waded into the water to retrieve the bodies. Their throats had been sliced from ear to ear, and I feared they had suffered other unspeakable indignities. The bodies must have been in the water for some time; their wounds had been washed clean, their bodies were drained of blood and were beginning to stiffen.

I looked at Anna and saw that, despite the pallor of death, she looked serene; I hoped she was at peace. I tried not to think of what had happened to her at the hands of her killers, choosing to remember instead the exquisite pleasures of our night together.

Even though the gloom of night had descended, I used the moonlight to help me finish my task. I made a separate cairn for the four girls. Then, before I rested, I finished my crude mausoleum with a simple cross fashioned from broken branches lying on the ground.

20. Battle of Arsuf

When I woke before dawn the next morning, I was still distressed by what had happened. But I was also emboldened by the new responsibility I now carried. I began to trudge downhill towards the road between Ereğli and the Cilician Gates. I had no horse, no money and only the clothes I stood up in. But I had my weapons and armour – and with them, by either fair means or foul, I had all I needed to acquire a mount and a handful of silver.

Ereğli was typical of a settlement at a crossroads; it bustled with traders and travellers and people of many nationalities. It was raucous, dusty and had the fetid atmosphere of too many bodies in too small a space. Christian pilgrims were sometimes seen, but most thought it wise to avoid the city. I did the same, but from a distance I glimpsed what I wanted to find. There was a large group of Armenians in the city, sporting their Phrygian caps and Kipchak bows, just as Alun had described them. I was certain they were the ones who had massacred my friends.

I wanted revenge, but my stomach wound was still very tender. And besides, there were at least two dozen of them. My priorities lay elsewhere. All I needed was a horse and enough silver to get me back to the Christian army in Palestine. I decided to bide my time and waylay one of them. I chose a quiet spot above the city, on the road to Tarsus, and waited.

It took a while for the opportunity to arise but, eventually, one of the brigands left the city and rode towards me. It was immediately obvious that he was part of the group responsible for the slaughter, because he was riding Godric's horse. My anger rose, but I knew I had to remain calm. I used my bow to take him out of his saddle, my arrow hitting him just below his throat. He hit the ground with a thump and did not move.

As I dragged his body to the side of the road, I saw that he was still breathing, so I pulled him up and leaned him against a tree. He opened his eyes but could not speak, as his chest was filling with blood. Then, with great relish and a cruelty I could not resist, I drew his khanjar from its jewelled scabbard and slowly slit his throat. Moments later, he keeled over into a pool of his own blood and I hid his body with leaves. I had never killed a man so heartlessly, but he deserved it. His pouch contained a fistful of the princesses' silver and one gold bezant. I stole his khanjar, his lance and his quiver of arrows, before retrieving Godric's destrier and making a rapid escape.

I travelled only at night and avoided all major roads. I ate what I could kill and only occasionally bought some dried fruit or goat's milk from farms well away from settlements. It was a long and tedious journey, and one during which remorse hung over me like a shroud.

When I reached Antioch, I met a group of German knights who were escorting some maimed and sick comrades to the coast for their journey home to Europe. They told me that after the fall of Acre, there had been many changes to the crusading army. King Philip of France had returned to Europe, leaving only a small contingent of knights and sufficient money to pay them. Leopold, Duke of Austria, had also left, taking most of the Holy Roman Empire's army with him. Only Richard's Angevins and Englishmen remained to fight the Christian cause.

Leaving Bérengère and his sister, Joan, in the relative safety of Acre, Richard had marched south after his victory. Using typical tactical acumen, he hugged the coast and advanced in tight formation with his baggage train closest to the sea, his knights in the middle and his archers on the landward side to keep the Muslim bowmen at bay. He ensured that his fleet shadowed him along the coast, keeping the army supplied, and he always camped close to a plentiful supply of fresh water.

The German knights told me that even though he had lost his allies and almost all of their men, the Lionheart remained determined to liberate Jerusalem. I was not in the least surprised; I would not have expected him to do anything else.

Now that I was within the narrow strip of the Palestinian coast that was still in Christian hands, I could travel openly and with much more speed. As I moved south, I could see little other than the devastation of war. What were once villages were now ruins, some still smouldering; barns had been ravaged, crops burned, wells poisoned and every edible creature had either been eaten or killed. September had begun, but it was still hot. The land was parched; it was either hard rock or searing sand. The only comfort was the distant Mediterranean, shimmering to the west.

On the fifth day of September, I saw the rear of the Christian army on the horizon. It manifested itself as a huge column of dust, like an approaching sandstorm. But I knew what it was, because I could feel the rhythm of its tread in the ground and hear the din of its men, horses and weapons drifting on the wind.

When I reached the massed ranks, I worked my way through the tightly packed units until I found William Marshal's contingent. I had decided he was my best passport back into the King's army. I also resolved that when I next saw the Lionheart I would be frank with him about my circumstances and my reasons.

Fortunately, his men-at-arms recognized me. Although they looked askance at my sudden reappearance, they let me approach their lord. Marshal also looked surprised to see me.

'Ah, the man with a conscience. What brings you back?'

'I have good reasons, my Lord.'

'The King will not take kindly to seeing you again.'

'I know, sire. I intend to keep a low profile until I can find a good time.'

'How will you do that?'

'Let me join one of your conrois as a man-at-arms?'

'Where is the Abbot Alun and your men?'

'All dead, my Lord.'

'I'm sorry to hear that. But how?'

'In Cilicia, ambushed by Armenians. Isaac of Cyprus's daughters are dead as well.'

'What in God's name were you doing with them?'

'Taking them to their family, in Constantinople.'

'Through the Cilician Gates? But that's madness!'

'I know, sire, but there were compelling reasons; it's a long story. But at the end of it, in his death throes, Alun extracted a promise from me that I would finish the mission he and I were given by Earl Harold, and so I've returned to the service of the Lionheart.'

'I'll take your word for that. I respect a man with a conscience; there are too many who are driven only by greed and their sword. I'll talk to the King for you, but a battle is looming with Saladin; your reconciliation with the Lionheart will have to wait until it's over. See the Captain of my English conroi, he's a good man and will fit you in with his men. But whatever you do, stay out of the King's way.'

I spent the rest of the day, and the next, with my new colleagues, many of whom knew me. They also knew that I had been dismissed by the King, and there was a danger that word would reach him about my return. But I had been reduced to the ranks, which happened often, and most were sympathetic towards me. With a battle in the offing, I did not think the risks too great.

We were thirty miles north of the vital port of Jaffa, close to a Christian fortification called Arsuf. Jaffa was vital to an attack on Jerusalem, because it was one of the main ports from where Saladin could get reserves and supplies from Egypt. The Sultan's skirmishers had been harassing our army all the way down the coast, but word had spread around the camp that he was about to mount a full-scale attack. It was designed to stop our advance before we reached the port.

On the morning of 7 September 1191, the King's orders were despatched around the camp. I missed the thrill of being close to the King as he laid his plans, but I had a job to do, like any other cavalryman, and I had to concentrate on doing it.

We advanced as we would on any other morning, but we knew that this one would lead to a major battle. It was a typically clear day and, although only an hour after sunrise, it was already hot with a gentle breeze wafting in from the sea to assuage the heat. Our pennons and gonfalons flapped and cracked, flying proudly in every conceivable colour. The King's standard, three golden lions passant on a gules shield, which had already become such a potent image, led us from the vanguard.

With him in the van were the Knights Templar commanded by Robert de Sable. Then came four of the Grand Quintet and their conrois: Poitevins, Bretons, Angevins. Guy of Lusignan, the absent King of Jerusalem, was there with his local knights, many of whom were third-generation Palestinians.

William Marshal led our contingent, close to the back of the column, in order to stiffen our rear. With us were the Knights Hospitaller led by their Master, Garnier of Nablus, a man whose grandfather had fought with Robert Curthose and Edgar the Atheling in the First Great Crusade. Henry of Champagne commanded a corps of light cavalry, deployed to break ranks if needed, and Hugh of Burgundy led the rump of the French troops left by Philip of France.

I counted our numbers and estimated we were close to 25,000 men and 3,000 knights. Our baggage train and the men of our fleet must have been close to another 4,000. It was a mighty host, by any standards, but we were led by one of the few men who could fashion such a large number into an effective fighting force in such difficult conditions.

As wc moved down the coast, through the Forest of Arsuf, Saladin's army slowly came into view, stretched out along our left flank in huge phalanxes of alternating infantry and cavalry. They were clad even more colourfully than we were, comprising men from many different countries: Seljuks, Armenians, Mamluks, Nubians, Sudanese, Bedouin and Egyptians.

Not only did the Sultan's forces parade all the colours imaginable, but they were also men of many shapes and hues. Some had faces from the east and had the sturdy build and strange pallor of the yellow races, while others were brown men of the Arab world. There were paler ones from Anatolia, and dark-brown desert people like the Bedou. Some, like the Nubians, were very tall and as black as night.

Their weapons were just as diverse: they were equipped with bows of many designs, wielded by both mounted archers and infantry bowmen; they carried ornately patterned kilij, talwar and shamshir swords; and they held countless styles and sizes of lances, pikes, poles and javelins.

Their qaadis rode out towards us, beyond their lines, to bless their troops and blaspheme ours; their war drums and tabors beat an incessant rhythm, and the cries from their horns and the crashes from their cymbals pierced the air mercilessly. It was difficult to assess their numbers from a distance, but they seemed to be significantly greater than ours.

The two mighty armies and their now legendary leaders

were ready to engage in a pitched battle for the first time. There is always acute tension among men before a battle, but we all knew that this one was going to be a day of destiny.

Our orders came down the line every fifteen minutes. They were the same each time.

Hold your formation, don't break ranks, keep your discipline.

The Lionheart was explicit about the signal to attack: the command would come as six blasts from the trumpets, and the order would come from him and him alone.

Saladin's tactics were also clear. He launched a constant onslaught of arrows and javelins from his highly mobile cavalry, while small units of infantry made lightning raids on our flanks to try to provoke a crack in our discipline. It was not easy to be a sitting target and resist the temptation to retaliate. But our orders were clear, and we knew we had to obey them. Men fell all around us, unlucky enough to be in the path of a missile falling from the sky. Our arbalests and archers were our most potent defenders – especially the crossbow quarrels, which the Muslim faris feared above anything else.

We waited all morning for the King's signal to wheel left and attack, but it never came. By early afternoon, the heat of the day and the trauma of hours of Muslim attacks, with no response from us, were taking their toll. The Hospitallers at the rear of the column bore the greatest burden. In order to keep the Muslims at bay, their arbalests were having to load and shoot while walking backwards.

It was a game of chess. Saladin knew that an army of 25,000 disciplined men, with the sea as a bulwark to one flank, was impregnable. He had no other recourse but to use his knights to taunt, tease or terrify our human castle and make us attack him. On the other hand, the Lionheart knew that, sooner or later, he would have to commit his knights, followed by the massed ranks of the infantry, who were his pawns; it was just a matter of when to strike for the end game.

Garnier of Nablus rode at a gallop from the back of the column to reach the King's position, accompanied by two of his Hospitallers. We assumed it was to seek permission to launch an attack. When he rode back and no attack ensued, it was clear his request had been refused. Another hour passed and on we marched relentlessly. The army was at breaking point; we had lost many horses and dozens of knights, some of whom had lost their mounts and been forced to join the infantry. The horses were difficult to control. Men could drink in the saddle, but the horses could not and were thirsty and exhausted. Disquiet spread and men started to talk openly about the wisdom of the Lionheart's strategy. The only reassuring fact was that the skirmishing by Saladin's men was costing many more Muslim lives than Christian; even so, our discipline was being tested to its limit.

The front of our column had reached the citadel of Arsuf, a powerful fortification in an elevated position overlooking the sea, which only added to our defensive strength. Here the King could protect vital elements of our baggage train.

Saladin, realizing that King Richard was playing a game of arithmetic with the lives of his men, rode into the fray to encourage his skirmishers. He was accompanied by his brother, Saphadin, and both came well within range of our arbalests and archers. I looked at William Marshal, who brusquely declined the suggestion by his Captain of Archery to direct the flight of their arrows directly at the Sultan. Saladin's appearance intensified the attacks on our flanks, and he began to commit more and more men in what were almost suicidal assaults on our tightly packed column.

I looked around at the ranks of the Hospitallers. The neat lines of black mantles were awry, horses were rearing. Suddenly, a knight carrying the great black standard of the Order of Hospitallers, with its white Amalfi cross, was struck square in the chest by a Muslim javelin. He was less than three yards from Garnier of Nablus and was taken right out of his saddle. The distraught Master, without even looking towards the Lionheart's position, grabbed the fallen standard and ordered his men to charge.

We could hear the cry: '*For St George! For St George!*'

The saint had been our crusader hero ever since it was said he appeared before the Christian army at the Siege of Antioch, ninety years earlier, during the First Great Crusade.

I looked at William Marshal who, in turn, stared at Hugh of Burgundy. Both men looked perplexed, but Henry of Champagne had not hesitated and was already off in pursuit of the Hospitallers. All eyes turned to the Lionheart. He was at least 250 yards away, but we could see him standing high in his stirrups, surveying what had happened.

Moments later, he raised his sword and thrust it in the direction of Saladin. We could not hear his battle cry, but the six strident blasts from the trumpets came immediately. The wave of noise from the mass charge of his vanguard swept over us like a roll of thunder. The rest of the army wheeled left en masse and moved off to the east.

It was an exhilarating sight, a huge tide of men and horses washing over the parched earth. It took the Muslims by complete surprise. Although Master Garnier had flagrantly disobeyed an order, the Lionheart had, within moments, realized what he had to do and had grasped the initiative. It had given us a vital advantage.

After hours of pent-up anguish and anger, our cavalry careered into the Muslim ranks ferociously, our huge destriers creating mayhem. With our blades swinging freely and repeatedly, we cut down the fleeing foot soldiers as if we were reaping a harvest. The ground behind us was littered with bodies, many dead, but those still alive were first trampled by the hooves to the rear of our conrois, then were easy pickings for our infantry. Few, if any, survived.

I looked to my right, to the south, where the King was leading the charge from our vanguard. They were scything through our enemies like a squall of wind flattening tall grass. The Lionheart was at the apex of the charge, distinctive with his flowing ruddy-blond locks. High in Fauvel's stirrups, he swung his longsword on both sides of his saddle like a villein cutting hay. To my left, the Hospitallers had charged into the Muslim ranks for over 300 yards and were still pressing on. Saladin and Saphadin were gathered up by the Sultan's personal bodyguard, and were escorted to the rear. The Muslim army was in full retreat, losing hundreds of men as it fled.

I lost count of the number who fell to my sword. My heart pumped from the thrill of it, an energy that did not abate until both my horse and I came to a stop from sheer exhaustion. Ahead of me was just a wall of dust as the enemy disappeared into the hinterland; behind me, the sun was beginning to fall towards the horizon, making the Mediterranean glisten. The low sun also started to cast long shadows over the battlefield. There were bodies as far as the eye could see. A few were moving; maimed horses limped and stumbled; and one man, with his arm almost severed and blood pouring from a gash across his face, was attempting to kneel, facing east to pray. Another, badly cut across his chest, was staggering from one stricken comrade to another trying to rouse them. It was a pitiful sight.

Then I heard our trumpet horns sounding the recall; the Lionheart wanted us to form up defensively and make camp before nightfall. We collected quivers of arrows, pikes and lances and other useful weapons for our supplies, while some men took swords and daggers and signet rings as souvenirs.

We made camp around the walls of Arsuf, and there were raucous celebrations long into the night.

In the early hours, the Lionheart rode through our section of the camp to thank the men. He was effusive in his praise and generous with everyone. Behind him were carts of food and drink, which his stewards threw to the throng. Flasks of beer and leather sacks of wine, flitches of bacon, legs of lamb and roast birds of all kinds were gratefully received.

There was much banter – especially about the precipitous act by Garnier of Nablus. One burly Breton arbalest shouted out as the King passed.

'My Lord, when is Master Garnier going to be flogged for his disobedience?'

Without a moment's hesitation, the Lionheart's reply came back.

'At dawn, just after you!'

Although there was no question of Garnier being flogged, William Marshal was later at pains to point out that the King had intended to attack about thirty minutes after the Hospitallers' impulsive charge.

Importantly, the Lionheart's plan had involved a more compact cavalry thrust. His aim had been to cut right through the heart of the Muslim army and attack Saladin's central command, in the hope of confronting the Sultan face to face.

Whether the King's plan would have worked was a moot point. But when the casualty figures became known the next day, it was clear that the bulk of the Muslim army remained intact. Over 7,000 bodies were counted, including more than 30 emirs; it was a large number, but wise judges in our ranks suggested that Saladin's force still outnumbered ours by a third.

Muslim morale had been dented: their route to the sea had been cut and Saladin's reputation sullied. But the road to Jerusalem was still blocked by a huge army. And the Holy City's walls were still amongst the most steadfast in the world.

21. Return to the Colours

After the calamity of Arsuf, Saladin realized how prodigious his enemy was and adopted different tactics to thwart the Lionheart. He had already destroyed the citadel at Jaffa and immediately set about dismantling Ramla and Lydda, both on our route to Jerusalem. He also continued his policy of ridding the land of anything useful to us on our path to the Holy City and thus putting us at the mercy of the unforgiving heat and dust and dependent entirely on our own lines of supply.

We reached Jaffa on 10 September 1191, an arrival that prompted great celebration, despite our weariness. After a night of much revelry, there was more good news for the army. With one of the Holy Land's most important ports at our backs, and its ships plying us with supplies from Acre, Genoa and Pisa, the Lionheart ordered that we make camp among the olive groves so that we could rest and recuperate for some time.

The King had allowed only 'elderly' laundresses to accompany the army as camp followers on the march from Acre, so the men were starved of female company. This was an irritation he now rectified by sending ships to Acre to bring the younger camp followers south, a cause for yet more celebration – especially after he also issued a bonus to his men in gratitude for their exploits.

The Lionheart used this time to begin the rebuilding of

Jaffa's citadel and to re-equip his baggage train for the assault on Jerusalem. To the horror of the Grand Quintet and his senior commanders, he also went hunting – despite the obvious dangers, and against vociferous advice – and frequently joined patrols deep into Muslim territory.

I decided that the King's forays might give me the opportunity to be reconciled with him, and sought William Marshal's advice.

'Yes, it's possible; he's in a good mood at the moment. We're going hawking on Sunday, with Mercadier. You can join my retinue; but keep your face obscured until I break the ice.'

When Sunday came, it arrived with an autumnal wind, which blew the dry sand of the summer into clouds of dust, making hunting unpleasant and unrewarding. Undeterred, the Lionheart changed his plan and announced that we would ride to Emmaus, on the road to Jerusalem. It was a journey of over twenty miles and into the hills close to the Holy City, from where he could see the disposition of Saladin's forces. Both Marshal and Mercadier were adamant that it was too dangerous without two conrois of bodyguards. The Lionheart would not hear of it, so we rode out in a group of just twelve men.

We cantered through olive and citrus groves at a distance of about a mile from the old Roman road to Jerusalem and saw along it many groups of Saladin's men making their way back and forth. The dust was excessive, so I was able to keep the ventail of my maille coif tied across my face without attracting any attention.

By early afternoon, the Lionheart had seen all he

wanted to see. We had eaten a good lunch of cold meat and wine, in the shade of a picturesque grove of lemon trees. I thought about Alun; he would have cherished the setting and would certainly have wondered whether Christ might have relaxed amidst groves like these, perhaps even in this very one.

Marshal decided the time was right to announce my return to the fold. However, the sound of horses approaching through the grove startled us. The King's response was predictable.

'To your horses; there is game afoot!'

Not for him a cautious retreat. He leapt on to Fauvel in one bound and, as the blond stallion reared, urged us on.

'Quickly! They will be upon us before we can get up a gallop.'

Then he was gone.

By the time we caught up with him, through the trees, he had already taken one of the Muslim faris off his horse with his lance and had deflected a blow with his shield from the heavy bronze latt of another. It was difficult to know how many opponents we faced. But there were at least a couple of dozen visible through the trees, and no doubt more men we could not see. I was thankful that Mercadier, Marshal and their elite bodyguards were with us; our situation was precarious. Our foes were Turcomans, from Anatolia, brothers-in-arms to the Seljuk Turks who had fought so hard against the early crusaders and were noted for their horsemanship and ferocity.

The King seemed oblivious to the danger and made no attempt to find refuge, even when he was surrounded by adversaries. Mercadier beckoned to us to form a cordon around the Lionheart, which was easier said than done; it was as difficult to keep him within it as it was to keep the Muslims outside.

We were beginning to be overwhelmed, as more and more enemy riders burst through the trees. Marshal bellowed at us to retreat, but the King pulled Fauvel round towards the Turcomans rather than away from them. Marshal looked at me anxiously.

'Grab the King's bridle. Pull him away!'

I hesitated for a moment, knowing that the Lionheart would be furious and just as likely to strike me down as an assailant. But I knew Marshal was right; the Muslims had recognized 'Melek-Ric', as they called him, and were desperate to claim him as a prize, dead or alive.

I sheathed my sword, took a firm hold of Fauvel's bridle and yanked his head round. As I did so, a Turc to my left, fewer than ten paces away, hurled his lance directly at the King. Fortunately for the Lionheart, I managed to raise my shield just in time so that it took the blow, rather than the King's chest. However, I was not so fortunate; the lance cut through my shield and deep into my arm, just above the wrist.

The pain was excruciating, but I managed to keep hold of Fauvel's bridle. Luckily, Mercadier and his standard-bearer were close at hand and helped me pull the King away at a gallop. My left arm was of no use to me and fell limply at my side. My shield was still held around my shoulder by its leather guige, with the offending lance trailing along the ground behind me. The King, still at a gallop, saw my predicament. Leaning far out from his saddle, he cut the guige with his seax and, with an almighty tug, pulled the lance from my arm.

After three or four miles, and when we were sure we were not being pursued, the King called a halt and jumped from Fauvel. He was unharmed, but we had lost three men and had come very close to losing him.

With Mercadier and Marshal's help, the Lionheart pulled me from my horse and the three of them laid me on the ground. Marshal ordered the rest of the men to ride out and keep watch for danger. I had no feeling in my arm below the elbow. The King looked at the wound and made explicit what I feared.

'You're lucky it's your left arm, soldier; your wrist is shattered. You're going to lose your hand.' Turning to Mercadier, he instructed, 'Take the man's weapons, we need his belt as a tourniquet to stop the bleeding.'

My face was still obscured. But as the Lionheart began to twist the tourniquet, he started to untie my ventail.

'What's your name, soldier?'

Before I could answer and before my face was revealed, Marshal spoke up.

'You know this man. Stay your temper, sire, it's Ranulf of Lancaster.'

The King pulled back my mask of maille and looked at me scornfully.

'What in God's name are you doing here? I thought you would be in England by now.'

'It's a long story, sire.'

'It had better be a good one! I should have you flogged. But as you've just saved my life and you're about to lose your arm, I suppose that might be harsh.'

The Lionheart gave a final and powerful twist to the leather band around my arm. To my relief, I could see that the bleeding had stopped.

'Let's get him to the surgeons. Put him in the hands of Peter of Bologna; he will make a neat job of it.'

I had heard of Peter of Bologna. It was said that he had learned his skills from Arab physicians and their texts. He was renowned for his use of opium, hemlock and mandrake to ease the pain of surgery. But many said his painkillers were just as likely to kill you as his cutting, and that it was better to drink a flagon of wine and bite on a piece of leather. Either way, I was terrified of what was to come.

They had let my arm bleed every half an hour as we rode back to Jaffa; each time, the blood flowed like a fountain. They said it was to stop my flesh rotting. By the time we reached the camp, I had lost a lot of blood and was feeling very light-headed.

When Peter of Bologna appeared, he was far from reassuring.

'Yes, I must amputate, just above the wrist – otherwise, it will never heal. It will hurt, young man; we have no dwale, and our opium and mandrake are finished. We have only hemlock, but on its own, it will kill you. You will be held, of course, but the amputation is the easy part; it's the cauterization that hurts the most.'

'Thank you for your words of comfort. What are my chances?'

'About one in four survives my amputations – twice the average of other surgeons. The Templars and the

Hospitallers undergo it without alcohol or dwale. What is your choice?'

'I'll have as much alcohol as I can drink.'

I was given a few minutes to gulp mouthfuls of a foul but strong local brew called Araq which, for reasons all too obvious to anyone who has tasted it, means 'dog's sweat' in Arabic. Despite its flavour, it soon made my head reel. But not as much as the pain that I was about to endure.

My terrors were well founded. Despite the weight and strength of four large men, I fought like an injured bull as Peter of Bologna did his work. He cut quickly and, thankfully, his blade was sharp, but the blood spurted like a man peeing as he neared the bone. And when he brought down his butcher's cleaver to finish the job, I spat out the leather strop they had put in my mouth and howled like a wolf in a trap.

Peter of Bologna was also right about which part was the worst. I had barely taken a breath after the fall of the cleaver, when a red-hot blade burned into my stump like the fires of Hell. The pain reached into every part of my body and made me convulse like a rabid animal. My teeth ached as if every one of them had been pulled out, my head hurt as if it had been struck by a blacksmith's hammer, my guts knotted as if they were being wrung out like a tub of washing, and my chest felt as if it would burst open and spew its contents into the air. Fortunately, after a few moments, my body had had enough and I descended into oblivion.

When I awoke a few hours later, the pain was still there; it was dull rather than sharp, but no less difficult to bear.

It was a challenge to focus my eyes and get my bearings, and for the next two days I felt like I was suffering in Hell. My only comfort was the thought that it might possibly be a purgatory rather than an eternity.

The infirmarers kept pouring hot soup down my throat and, after about a week, declared that I had not got the canker and that my stump was healing well. They bathed it in salt every day, then made me sit in the sun to let it dry. I was fortunate, because most of the men around me had the smell of foul meat about them and had to have the canker maggots applied to their wounds to eat the rotting flesh. It was a humbling experience to see them die in agony; almost every day a corpse was taken away for burial in a shallow grave.

By the time the Lionheart came to see me, I was able to walk down to the sea to swim and had regained my strength. Most of the pain had gone, although I suffered sudden sharp jolts, just to remind me of what had happened. It was also odd not to have a limb that my mind still assumed was there. I would reach for things with my left hand, or try to scratch an itch, only to realize a moment later that where my hand had been was now thin air.

Accompanied by all five of the Grand Quintet, the King arrived at the infirmary with his usual charm, an aura that so endeared him to his men. He slapped them on the back as if they were old friends and asked them about their recovery and the well-being of their wives and families. Most importantly, if a man was in a bad way, or in need of financial or personal support, he would do what he could to help him, often giving the infirmarers specific orders to help in a particular way, or summoning his stewards to dispense pieces of silver.

He was particularly effusive when he came to my hammock.

'It is good to see you so well, Ranulf.'

'Thank you, sire; Peter of Bologna did a fine job, but it's not an experience I would like to repeat.'

'Nor will you. There are not many men to whom I owe my life. In fact, most of them are here now. I have reinstated you to my command, but not in a combat role; you will act as a military adviser and be close to me at all times.'

'Thank you, sire, but I like to think I can still fight.'

William Marshal then seized the chance to scold the King.

'I'm sure you'll have to, if you stay close to the King and he continues his ridiculous forays into Saladin's territory.'

The Lionheart ignored the barb.

'I don't doubt you will be able to fight, but not as effectively. I don't want to lose you, so you will not command a conroi but will help me with tactics and organization. I will send my best cordwainer and carpenter; I'm sure they can fashion you a new arm from leather and ash that will allow you to hold a shield.'

'That is very kind of you, my Lord King. If I am to serve you, I would like to be able to defend you and myself.'

'Of course; you will also be issued with new clothes, arms and armour and will have the pick of the stables for a mount. When we return to England, I will find some more land for you.'

'You are too kind, sire. I am humbled.'

'Not at all, I am in your debt. When I saw the Turc's lance, I thought the Devil had come for me.'

Marshal seized another chance to chide the King.

'Count your blessings. He'll come for us all soon enough, if you don't listen to those who know better.'

There was a sudden look of annoyance on the Lionheart's face. He stood up and placed his hand on Marshal's shoulder. Marshal was a giant of a man, but the King was just as tall.

'William, you're the only man in the world who I will allow to talk to me like that . . .'

He then paused. We waited, and a grin broke across his face.

'And I love you for it.'

The two men embraced.

'Marshal tells me that we have lost the good Abbot Alun and your men, trying to get the two Cypriot princesses to Constantinople. I'm sorry to hear that. Alun was one of the wisest men I have ever met; I would have given him Canterbury one day.'

I told the Lionheart the story of our fateful expedition, about which he was very sympathetic.

'I'm sad to hear the girls met such an awful fate. They were very beautiful.'

I was desperate to tell him just how beautiful they were, and how much I missed Anna. But my sense of honour persuaded me not to.

'I'm glad you came back. When I saw you again, I was reminded of the things that Earl Harold said to me at his estate in the Lot, when I asked him about my grandmother. I remember it well; he said that Father Alun would tell me all I needed to know when I became King. He said he would also tell me about England, and why it's so precious to all of us. Sadly, he never did.'

'He didn't think the Holy Land was the right place, sire. He also wanted to give you some precious items that you will cherish. All but one of them are in a casket in the Vatican Vaults.'

'And the other?'

'I have it, my Lord, but it does not mean anything without the casket.'

The Lionheart smiled.

'So, it will remain a mystery still? Are you going to adopt Alun's mantle as the mysterious sage?'

'If only I could. You should know, sire, that Alun was very badly hurt and in great pain. But he stayed alive by sheer willpower so that he could tell me what I needed to know. That's why I came back, so that his promise to Earl Harold and to England could be fulfilled.'

'Thank you for telling me. When we return to England, I will create a foundation in his name. But for now, get your new arm fitted. We leave for Ascalon soon.'

The King turned to leave. But before he had gone more than a couple of yards, he stopped and turned.

'Ranulf, I want you to know something about Acre. Those Muslim warriors died very honourably, like soldiers should. I was responsible for their deaths, a truth that bears down on me every day. Saladin also carries his share of responsibility. I hope he thinks about it as I do. I did what I had to do, as you did what you had to do. I respect you for that.'

He then left before I had time to respond.

*

Over the next week, I was given splendid new clothes, maille and weapons by the King's seamstress and armourer. I chose the new colours that I had promised myself for my pennon and shield – the legendary gules, sable and gold of Hereward of Bourne. However, the fitting of my new arm was painful.

The carpenter had carved a new lower arm for me. It had an iron hook instead of a hand and was attached to a cylinder of leather, like a heavy belt, which I could strap tightly to my forearm. Most importantly, he had made two dowelled joints with supporting straps that allowed me to fix my new arm to my new shield. Apart from the soreness it brought, it worked well.

When I joined the King's command, he and his lords were debating their next move. It was mid-October 1191, and the weather was becoming wetter and colder by the day. Saladin was still destroying Christian fortresses and eradicating anything of any value from the countryside. In turn, our sappers were rebuilding as fast as they could – especially Jaffa and Arsuf.

The Lionheart paced up and down, talking loudly.

'Do we wait until the spring to attack Jerusalem? I have sent messengers to Europe asking for more men and resources; they should be here by then. In the meantime, I propose we move south. We could occupy Ascalon and threaten Egypt; that would cause Saladin great unease.'

Baldwin of Bethune responded.

'My Lord King, the men are tired and our resources are thin.'

'I know, but we came here to liberate the Holy Land; we're not going home until that has been achieved. For the time being, let's leave a significant number of men here in Jaffa and move the main army to a forward position at Casal Maen, on the road to Jerusalem. It will test Saladin's mettle.'

Most nodded their assent, but spirits were low. Everyone had been away too long, and winter was looming.

The move forward was miserable. It rained almost every day, and sickness spread through the ranks. It said much for both the men's discipline and their regard for the King's resolve. In the simplest terms: wherever he went, they would go; whatever he did, they would do; whatever he demanded, they would supply. He never shirked a challenge, or avoided an adversity; he walked through knee-deep mud, just as his men did; and he bore every indignity and hardship with the rest of us.

The most difficult part of any army's journey is the transport of heavy equipment. Pushing and pulling the parts of our siege engines – especially the huge timber beams – became a nightmare. But the Lionheart was always in the thick of it, often stripped to his braies, just like his men, and happy to lend the power of his shoulder to the effort.

As we were too exposed to create field infirmaries, the sick travelled with us, but the King visited them every day. When he got a dose of diarrhoea – again, like the rest us – he used the side of the road as a latrine.

But the tactic worked, and Saladin withdrew his army closer to the Holy City, persuading the Lionheart to advance to Beit Nuba, only fifteen miles north of Jerusalem and not far from our encounter with the Turcomans of a few weeks earlier.

We made camp, but the conditions worsened and became no better than a winter in England. Morale plummeted, especially when high winds and snow created a blizzard, with drifts piled high against our tents. We could boil snow for water, but that was the only saving grace in dire circumstances. The cooks did the best they could, but our rations were reduced to a broth, which became thinner and thinner, supplemented by whatever bread could be baked from our diminishing supplies of flour. At least with very little to eat, the diarrhoea became easier to bear. I am sure any other army would have buckled under the burden, but with the Lionheart's fortitude to cling on to, the men held firm.

The King called a council of war and sought the advice of the Templars, the Hospitallers and the Palestine-born lords who knew the territory better than anybody. Their assessment was depressing to hear.

The biggest problem was the size of our army. We needed to keep a substantial number of men in Jaffa to protect our rear and our supply line to the sea. We also needed to deploy a large number to protect the road to the coast, which Saladin was already harrying relentlessly. We had ridden as close to Jerusalem as possible and the Lionheart had done detailed calculations with his siege engineers regarding the men and resources needed to surround the city and breach its walls. He knew what the arithmetic added up to.

'We are five thousand men short for an assault on Jerusalem; it's as simple as that. What say you all, gentlemen?'

Henry of Champagne nodded reluctantly, as did Hugh

of Burgundy. The masters of the military orders added their assent, as did the men of the Grand Quintet.

'Very well, we return to the coast for the winter. We will rebuild Ascalon, bide our time until the spring, and then launch our attack on Jerusalem when we have more men. I have written to the Abbot of Clairvaux asking that he issue a call to every Christian in Europe to come to our aid. Let us pray that the response is positive. In the mean time, we will also keep threatening to attack Egypt, and keep Saladin on his toes.'

We reached Ascalon on 12 January 1192. The army's sorry state had not improved. Our provisions were almost non-existent, the mud had become deeper and our horses, even without the weight of a man on their backs, found it hard to cope.

When we reached the coast, although our English contingent remained resolute, there were numerous desertions, especially from among the men of the French crusaders, whose King had long since left the Holy Land.

I was as tired as most. I had lost track of my age, but during my recovery in Jaffa – and especially when I felt how hard it was to regain my strength – my years caught up with me and I remembered that I was in my forty first year, an age when most knights would be hoping to retire. The King, at the age of thirty-five, was no longer the strident youth I had first met.

However, like the rest of the men, it was the Lionheart who lent me the fortitude to carry on. It was astonishing; every time my head dropped, or my shoulders drooped, and I looked to the King for encouragement, he was riding tall in his saddle, or striding forwards purposefully. He seemed only to have two moods: he was either smiling happily, cajoling us all to press on; or his jaw was set firmly, his eyes focused, demanding that we do the same. Never once did he look dejected or hesitant; we would have followed him to the fiery pit of Hades if he had asked us to.

I organized a roll call a few days later. It made for depressing reading for the Lionheart. Through death, sickness and desertion, we had lost almost 4,000 men, 280 knights and 400 horses.

When I presented the figures to the King, he made a very telling point.

'When King Philip and I left Vézelay, with the Emperor Frederick on his way down the Danube, our joint army was close to a hundred and fifty thousand men. Now, with Saladin at our mercy, we are not many more than fifteen thousand. Do you think God really wants the Holy Land back?'

22. Ascalon

We spent the rest of the winter rebuilding Ascalon. The Lionheart issued orders that every man had to work on the fortifications, including knights, lords and dukes. At least it kept us warm. He led by example and, wearing the simple clothes of an artisan, carried stone and mixed mortar like everyone else.

Thanks to so much labour, the citadel rose remarkably quickly, an achievement that pleased the Lionheart immeasurably. Modelled on castles he had rebuilt in Aquitaine, it was a fine fortification. He had a keen eye for military architecture and designed everything himself, down to the smallest detail.

As the King had said we would, we also made sorties to the south. We captured Darum and made a reconnaissance visit to Gaza, an ancient city on the road to Sinai and Egypt – a land we were sorely tempted to visit, if not to conquer. Again, on more than one occasion, the King put himself at risk by leading charges and getting involved in the thick of the fighting. So astounding were his exploits, the conviction became widespread, among friend and foe alike, that he was not a mortal man and that God's warrior angel, the Archangel Michael, sat on his shoulder. Some even believed that he *was* Michael, avenging the Muslims on God's behalf.

At dusk on the first evening after our arrival in Gaza,

the King asked Blondel and myself to walk with him along the beach. The sun was setting and, to its south, lay Egypt.

The Lionheart looked wistful.

'Great empires come and go. Over there, many years ago, there was one of the mightiest of them all. But, eventually, it fell – first to Alexander, then to Rome. In turn, they collapsed. My so-called Empire is only a generation old and my family have only been kings for four generations; my great-great-grandfather was a mere duke. Not much of a lineage compared to the pharaohs of Egypt, who ruled for thousands of years.'

Blondel started to hum his melodies. However, I felt compelled to answer.

'But, sire, your blood goes back many hundreds of years. Your English heritage goes back to Alfred the Great and beyond.'

'I suppose so, but I never think of myself as English. You remind me of Alun; I miss his words of wisdom, his everlasting patience and his love of England and its history.'

'There are many great warriors in your bloodline besides Alfred the Great. There is the Conqueror, and his Viking ancestors – and others you know, such as Charlemagne, and some you don't.'

'That sounds like another tempting yet mysterious morsel of the sort that Alun would offer.'

I came close to telling the Lionheart what I knew, but realized that it would all mean a lot more if I could tell him after I had been to Rome. So I changed the subject.

'Sire, did Alun tell you about Queen Bérengère's lineage?'

'That she is the grand-daughter of the Cid? Yes, he did.'

'What young warriors you two will produce.'

'I hope so, but she is not yet pregnant; not surprising, I suppose, as we are always apart.'

As the King was in a reflective mood, and I felt I had replaced Alun as his mentor, I tried to say something wise, just as my friend would have done.

'Sire, do you remember what Abbess Hildegard said in Rupertsberg? I think it was something like this: Your mind is much more powerful than your sword arm. That is why, when soldiers fight wars, they win land and riches. But when thinkers fight wars, they win men's minds. You can't change the world with land and wealth, but you can with men's minds.'

'I do remember, Ranulf. I often think of her words, and those of Alun and Earl Harold . . .'

He paused and turned to stare towards the north-west, in the direction of home.

'Come, let's eat and drink some wine; I think Blondel has a tune for us.'

We returned to Ascalon with thoughts of a glorious conquest of Egypt fuelling the King's imagination. But at Easter, the Lionheart's mood darkened as events in Palestine and at home in Europe brought depressing news. In the Holy Land, word came from Acre that rather than help fight for the Christian cause, Conrad of Montferrat, Marquis of Tyre, and Guy of Lusignan, ostensibly King of Jerusalem, were again squabbling over the Holy City's throne.

Not only that: Lusignan had recruited the Pisans to his

cause, while Montferrat had allied himself with the Genoese, thus splitting two of Richard's most important allies. The King was furious and sent Robert Thornham to Acre to point out to both of them that, until Saladin was removed from Jerusalem, there was no throne to fight over. It made no difference; neither man would compromise.

The news from England was also a cause for concern. It came from the Prior of Hereford, a trusted envoy sent by William Longchamp, the King's Lord Chancellor, who ruled England in his absence. His words made the Lionheart angry in a way that we had not seen happen in a while.

'My Lord King, the Lord Chancellor sends his affectionate greetings and his congratulations on your success here in the Holy Land. However, sire, I am the bearer of grave news from Westminster. Your brother John, Lord of Ireland and Count of Mortain, is acting as Regent and undermining the Chancellor's authority. The Chancellor has had to besiege Lincoln Castle because the Castellan, Gerard of Camville, swore allegiance to John and would not surrender the castle or allow himself to be replaced by Longchamp's nominee. In retaliation, John has taken the castles of Tickhill and Northampton. Your Chancellor fears John will take the throne, if you do not return soon.'

The Lionheart thanked the Prior and, exhibiting a more sanguine mood than I expected, asked William Marshal and Baldwin of Bethune to try to resolve the situation.

'Gentlemen, return to Poitou immediately. Seek the advice of my mother and, if she is well and thinks it advisable, ask her to accompany you to Westminster. Go via

Rouen and tell the Archbishop, William of Coutances, that he must accompany you. When you reach London, get John and Longchamp in the same room and, if necessary, bang their heads together on my behalf. John is a coward and will bide his time until he hears Saladin has put a lance through my heart; Longchamp is a good administrator, but he could not command authority over a flock of sheep. Tell them that if they are still squabbling when I get back, they will know my wrath.'

Although the King's 'wrath' at such a distance might have seemed like an empty threat, anyone who knew the Lionheart realized that it was far from hollow.

Confident that Marshal and Bethune would bring peace to England, the Lionheart then turned his attention to the dispute over the throne of Jerusalem. The quarrel was dividing the loyalties of his fellow crusaders and needed to be brought to an end. He called another council of his senior men and asked for their advice.

Their conclusions came quickly and were unambiguous. The King had to choose between Lusignan, a man who had a stronger claim, both legally and morally, and Montferrat, whose claim was weaker, but who would be a much stronger bulwark against future Muslim attacks. Their advice was clear: Give Jerusalem to Montferrat.

Of course, it was easy for them to be categorical, because they did not have to make the decision. But the Lionheart knew they were right and, although he felt a loyalty to Lusignan, he had little choice but to agree with the council's view.

As was becoming more and more apparent, the King was adding deepening wisdom to his military acumen and he dealt with his dilemma very adroitly. He sent Henry of Champagne to Acre to give Montferrat the good news, then asked Lusignan to come and see him in Ascalon. The excitable Poitevin must have known what the summons meant. When he arrived, he was very tense.

The Lionheart handled him with compassion.

'Guy, thank you for travelling such a distance. Champagne has journeyed the other way to give Montferrat the news I am about to give you. The lords of the Crusade and I have reached a decision about Jerusalem. It is to go to Montferrat, simply because he will be more able to hold it against Saladin. It is a decision based on expediency, not on just cause.'

Crestfallen, Lusignan's shoulders sank and his chin dropped on to his chest.

'Sire, kings rule by right, not by expediency.'

'If only that were true, my friend; sadly, it isn't. Listen, I think I have another expediency that may mean you will leave here with a much lighter heart. How much do you have in your treasury?'

'Am I to buy Jerusalem from Montferrat?'

'No, not a putative kingdom like Jerusalem, but a safe and secure realm.'

Intrigued, Lusignan's mood lightened.

'I can raise five thousand bezants, and twenty thousand in silver. But for where?'

'Cyprus.'

I looked at the others; we were all as surprised as Lusignan.

He started to smile.

'Is that possible?'

'It is, if I say so. I sold all rights and possessions to Cyprus to the Hospitallers when we left Cyprus last year. They have paid only the first instalment of forty thousand bezants, but they have created turmoil on the island by imposing heavy tithes to raise the balance of sixty thousand. And they're overdue on the payment. I will buy back the island for their first instalment and sell it to you for the same amount. If you give me what you have, you can pay me the rest from your income from the island's tithes over the next five years. But be kind to the Cypriots; if you are, you and your descendants could rule there until doomsday.'

'Sire, I don't know what to say.'

'Say yes, man; it's a choice between a kingdom that is currently in the hands of Saladin and to which no one supports your claim, or an idyllic domain secure in the Mediterranean where you would have no rivals.'

Lusignan looked around. He saw that we were all smiling, and his smile became a broad grin. He fell to his knees and, almost grovelling, thanked the King lavishly.

The Lionheart pulled him up by the arm.

'Go home and celebrate, find yourself a new wife and sire some heirs to the Kingdom of Cyprus . . .'

He then paused, before slapping Lusignan heartily on the back.

'But don't leave without emptying your treasury. I'll send Mercadier and a squadron to collect my geld.'

The Lionheart had been generous; the 60,000 still owed by the Hospitallers would have helped our cause enormously, but he had written it off for the sake of justice. Not only that: Lusignan's payment would only come in instalments. But the King had sympathy for his fellow-Poitevin and was grateful for his help on Cyprus. Although he had been foolhardy at the Battle of Hattin, he had been brave during the encounter and resolute while in captivity for over a year at the hands of Saladin.

A happy man, Lusignan made his way back to Acre to prepare for his reign over Cyprus.

Strangely, there was to be a twist in the tale of the Kingdom of Jerusalem. Two days after Conrad of Montferrat was given the good news about his succession to the throne, he was assassinated on the streets of Acre. Returning to the royal palace late at night after celebrating with his friend Philip, Bishop of Beauvais, he was asked for alms by two beggars. No doubt feeling generous, when he reached down from his horse to put a coin in the hand of one of them, he was pulled from his mount and had his throat cut.

It was thought that the perpetrators were the same Brotherhood of Assassins who had attacked the Lionheart outside Acre, but they had both escaped, so no one knew for sure. Guy of Lusignan was implicated by many, but as the attackers appeared to be Muslims, this seemed unlikely.

Henry of Champagne heard about Montferrat's death on the way back to us in Ascalon and immediately returned to Acre. To his apparent surprise, the local lords and the remnants of Philip of France's contingent asked him to succeed to the newly vacant throne. He demurred and asked for the Lionheart's view.

The King laughed out loud when he received Champagne's request, and scribbled his reply at the bottom of his letter.

Take it, boy; you are more than worthy. But marry Montferrat's widow, Isabella, otherwise she'll challenge you.

Your loving uncle,
Richard

It was a wise suggestion. Isabella had the blood claim to the throne, and the only way to deal with a potential threat from her, or any new husband she might acquire, was to marry her.

Only a week later, Henry of Champagne was duly married to Isabella of Jerusalem, who was heavily pregnant with Montferrat's child. The speed of events led many to suggest that it was Henry who had commissioned the Assassins to murder Montferrat.

When the Lionheart heard the rumours, he just smiled wryly.

'If he did, he's a cunning little bugger. I'll have to keep my eye on him.'

23. Consort for a Queen

Perhaps the marriage of Henry and Isabella and the unity it brought to the squabbles over the throne of Jerusalem, made the Lionheart think about the power of the bed-chamber in solving even the most intractable of problems.

One morning, over a good breakfast of fresh fruit and sweet wine, with the May sun rapidly warming the air, the King, who was in a particularly jovial mood, spoke of romance. But it was a suggestion for a coupling of a par-ticularly startling kind.

'My sister, Joan, is only twenty-seven, a widowed queen, handsome, broad of hip; she has borne a child already who, conveniently for my plan, died young. Saladin's brother, Saphadin, is, I am told, a handsome brute and the rock upon which Saladin builds his army.'

The King looked at us with a mischievous smirk on his face. Blondel, usually the quietest of the Grand Quintet, said what we were all thinking.

'Sire, apart from the fact that Saphadin must be nearly fifty, one of them would have to convert. And whichever one did would never be able to show their face again in their own community.'

'I know all that . . . but it would be a very elegant solu-tion, and could bring peace for generations.'

Robert Thornham responded laughingly.

'It's a pipe dream, sire; it would be like mating a dog and

a cat. God wouldn't tolerate it, quite apart from what Rome and Damascus would make of it. Can you imagine telling the archbishops at home?'

The Lionheart's bile was beginning to rise.

'There have been marriages between Muslims and Christians before – even between emirs and countesses.'

'But in this case you're talking about Saladin's brother and the sister of the King of England – a woman who also happens to be the Queen of a Christian realm.'

The Lionheart gave Robert one of those looks that meant the debate was at an end. But Robert could not resist one more comment.

'Well, I wouldn't like to be the one to ask Queen Joan!'

It was a quip he would regret.

'Really! Well, you've just won yourself that honour. You leave in the morning for Acre. You can ask her.'

Robert's expression turned from one of hilarity to a look of consternation, but he knew from the King's demeanour that there was no point in protesting. The Lionheart then turned to me.

'Who is the shrewdest Arabic speaker we have?'

'One of the senior Templars, Benoît of Geneva, can reach Saphadin's secretary, Abu Bekr. He speaks Greek and Latin and Norman.'

'Get a message to him. I will invite Saphadin to dine with me. I will take my tent out into the hinterland, to neutral ground; I will have only my personal retinue with me. See to it.'

I was shocked by the plan, as was everyone present; it was bold, to say the least, and may only have been a tactical move. But the Lionheart seemed serious.

*

Three days later, the rendezvous was arranged in an area of orchards and vineyards to the east of Ramla.

When he arrived, with an entourage of elegantly dressed stewards and qaadis, the Sultan's brother bore gifts of fruit, sweet drinks and Arab confectionery. He was indeed handsome. He was tall, with a long jet-black beard streaked with grey around his chin, and his lavishly embroidered satin coat in pale blue was in perfect balance with his midnight-blue turban. His rugged face was lined with the creases of a man of deep thought and wisdom.

Here was a man worthy of any queen.

The King was charm personified and they chatted amiably in Norman, although Saphadin stumbled from time to time and had to be helped by one of his qaadis and by Benoît of Geneva. One of Palestine's glorious sunsets heralded dinner, an excellent repast created specifically for an Arab guest. The centrepiece was a lamb Maqluba with fresh vegetables harvested that morning, which had been prepared by a local Arab from Jaffa. There was no alcohol in sight, but several sharbats of orange, lemon and pineapple were served from tall brass flasks that we had brought from the coast. Saphadin was impressed.

After dinner, the two men strolled through the groves together as if they had not a care in the world. The mutual respect was obvious.

Blondel went in front of us and sang as we walked; the two translators were on either side of Saphadin and the Lionheart, while his equerry and I held back at a respectable distance.

After a while, Saphadin stopped and spoke to me.

'Captain, I see you have lost your arm. Did we deprive you of it?'

'No, sire, it was the work of Armenians, in Ereğli.'

'Barbarians! You are lucky, few men leave an encounter with them alive.'

The Lionheart put his arm on my shoulder.

'Sir Ranulf is a fine warrior, my Lord Saphadin, and has become a good friend.'

'That is good; warriors should be friends, brothers in chivalry.'

Saphadin walked on, and his tone became more serious.

'You have treated me nobly, Melek-Ric, but let us talk as men. You have a proposition for me?'

'I do. There is a future for this troubled land that could bring peace without more bloodshed.'

'That is a prospect the Lord Saladin would treasure, as would I and men of all faiths.'

'We could agree a truce, part of which would allow access to the Holy Places to all men. Sultan Saladin would have sovereignty over all land from the high ground fifteen miles from the coast, and the Christian lords would rule along the coast to the west.'

'So we would rule in Jerusalem?'

'Yes, but it would be a free city, as would Jaffa. The road between the two would be free to all; you would have access to the sea and we to the Holy City.'

'But you have already made Henry and Isabella King and Queen of Jerusalem.'

'Yes, they would reside there, and you would reside in Jaffa as Lord of the Holy Land, with jurisdiction over both Muslim and Christian Palestine. In Europe, we call such a person an emperor, as in Byzantium and Germany, where an emperor rules over kings.'

'Indeed, we call such a man a Grand Caliph. But why would the Christian King of Jerusalem bow to a Muslim emperor?'

'Because he would be married to a Christian queen.'

Saphadin stopped and looked startled; even Blondel stumbled over the words of his chanson for a moment. The Lionheart had made his outrageous suggestion; it was a heart-stopping moment.

Saphadin looked bewildered, as if playing a game of chess and trying to work out what was hidden behind a clumsy feint.

'There has been nothing like this in history before, Melek-Ric.'

'Perhaps Antony and Cleopatra?'

Saphadin knew his history; it was not a good example to choose.

'Perhaps, but did they not lose in battle and commit suicide?'

The King was undaunted.

'But we could make it work.'

'And what of the small matter of who would be my queen?'

'My sister, Joan, a noble lady, a widowed queen in her own right and still young enough to bear you heirs.'

Saphadin walked on, still trying to think through the implications of what the Lionheart had proposed. The King let him go on alone. Blondel stopped singing and made a discreet exit back to the camp.

After a couple of minutes, Saphadin returned; he looked stern.

'Melek-Ric, I have two answers for you. The first is from one honourable man to another. This is what I, Malik al-Adil, the one you call Saphadin, say to you. You flatter me; I would be honoured to marry your noble sister and the prospect of becoming an emperor of this ancient land is very appealing to a humble servant of God. However, I have another answer for you. It is from me as a face of my people and of Islam, as an Emir of the Ayyubid Dynasty, answerable to the Sultan Saladin and the Grand Caliphs of Cairo and Damascus. Your suggestion is clever, but no more than that; it is preposterous in political terms. More than that, it is an insult to Islam, just as it is an insult to your faith. I am sorry.'

Saphadin then bowed deeply to his host, bid the King goodbye and was gone. The Lionheart turned to me.

'Well, my friend, I think I have upset my Muslim guest. At least he spoke his mind.'

'I don't think he is upset, my Lord. You proposed what he called a "clever" offer, one that would be perfectly acceptable in Europe; but not here, where faith makes men blind.'

'Well put, Ranulf. Your words remind me of Abbot Alun.'

'I wish he were here, sire.'

'So do I. Diplomacy is our only option; I need to find a compromise to offer Saladin that will satisfy both of us and keep our respective spiritual guardians happy. I relish fighting battles for the kingdoms of the earth, but not for the Kingdom of Heaven.'

'My Lord, you will find an answer. You and Saladin are both men of honour; between you, you will find a way.'

'Thank you, Ranulf, I am greatly comforted knowing that you are at my side.'

The subject was never mentioned again – especially when, a week later, Robert Thornham arrived back from Acre with an answer from Queen Joan.

Her response had been very similar to Saphadin's, but delivered in the harshest of terms – typical of the bluntness of siblings.

24. Jerusalem Beckons

After his daring plan for a future Holy Land fell on deaf ears, the Lionheart brooded for several weeks. His pride was hurt; he was certain it was a solution that would have brought lasting peace and could not understand why no one else saw it in the same way. Perhaps it was naive of him to think that the best way to end a conflict between mortal enemies was to bind them together in a shared future. It made perfect sense to him, but most other men were bound by convention and prejudice – two things that the Lionheart would hardly recognize, let alone be guided by.

I felt certain that the culmination of his torment would be a return to Europe, especially after he received a letter from his mother, Queen Eleanor, delivered by William Marshal and Baldwin of Bethune when they returned in the middle of May. The letter expressed her own concerns about the ambitions of her youngest son, John. Marshal and Bethune had extracted promises of good behaviour from both John and William Longchamp, but the situation in England remained volatile.

However, our prospects began to improve. At the beginning of June, the Lionheart summoned the Grand Quintet and myself to his new hall in Ascalon. Reports had reached us of reinforcements sailing from several ports in the Mediterranean. We heard that Henry of

Champagne had raised a formidable body of knights together with a large force of Turcopole mercenaries, both infantry and archers, to help him take control of his new kingdom and was on his way from Acre.

'Gentlemen, it seems that my attempts at grand diplomacy have failed. I have decided to revert to what I'm good at. We will attack Jerusalem. Summon the Templars and the Hospitallers and every Christian lord in the Holy Land. We will march as soon as the army is assembled. May has turned into June, and it's hot enough already. Robert, you will go to Jaffa. When the European reinforcements and Henry's contingent arrive from Acre, bring them on.'

We broke camp in Ascalon on 7 June 1192. It was a Sabbath and a mass was held for the entire army, celebrated by Hubert Walter, Bishop of Salisbury, and Rodolfo, Patriarch of Jerusalem, who had travelled from Acre in the hope of being reinstalled to his seat in Jerusalem's Church of the Holy Sepulchre.

Our mood was joyful; at long last, we all felt that Jerusalem was now within our grasp. The weather was warm, but not yet stifling. We were well provisioned, and progress was far quicker and much easier than our abortive attempt at the beginning of the year. Saladin sent skirmishers to hinder us all the time, but we repulsed them with ease, giving the King much sport, which he relished with his usual abandon. By 9 June we were camped beyond Latrun, and the next day advanced to Beit Nuba. We were now only a day's march away from our objective.

When news arrived that our reinforcements were assembling in Jaffa, the King issued the order to hold our ground and wait for the new arrivals. He was in fine spirits.

'Five thousand men and Jerusalem is ours. Let us ride to Montjoie, and take a look at it.'

Jerusalem was an incredible sight; its walls, towers and spires gleamed white in the distance through a shimmer of heat. The Dome of the Rock towered over the city, the orb of its golden roof glowing in the sunlight with almost the same intensity as the sun itself. To its right was Solomon's Temple, once the home of the Knights Templar, of which Earl Harold had been one of the nine, now legendary, founding members. I saw the Lionheart gulp, and there were tears in his eyes.

'So much effort and anguish, but there it is, the holiest place in the world. It is so beautiful, just as I imagined it would be, and far too precious for men to fight over. Would it not be easier for men to share it?'

'It would, my Lord. But men are not easily persuaded, except by greed and prejudice.'

'You sound more and more like Abbot Alun every day.'

'Well, he was a good teacher, sire.'

'Saphadin was right, sadly; my idea of a free empire for Palestine was preposterous. But it was worth asking, was it not?'

'It was, my Lord. Remember what Hildegard said about men's minds. Perhaps you have sown a seed that one day will flower.'

The King smiled; he seemed comforted by the thought.

'I shall hold dearly to that possibility.'

He turned back to gaze at the Holy City. The tears had gone from his eyes, replaced by a look of steely resolve.

'If the time is not yet here when we can achieve our objective by changing men's minds, let us do it with the power of our swords. If I must fight for the city, then that's what I'll do.'

He gave Fauvel a gentle kick and was away down Montjoie's slopes, no longer Richard the Philosopher, but once again the Lionheart.

On 21 June, three of our scouts appeared with news that would have troubled most generals, but not the King. A large army of Mamluk Muslim reinforcements, accompanied by a long baggage train of supplies, had been seen approaching from Egypt. The Lionheart was stirred by the information.

'Instead of kicking our heels, we have some sport! Ranulf, summon five hundred knights and muster a thousand cavalry. Ask Burgundy to join us with his French. The rest can stay here with William and Mercadier.'

It did not take long to reach the Mamluk column to Jerusalem's south-west. Their dust was obvious from several miles away, and the King ordered that we rest just beyond the settlement of Beit Jala. He gave instructions that the men should try to sleep during the evening; reveille was to be called at 3 a.m. While the men rested, the King, Robert, Baldwin and I dressed as Bedouin and made a reconnaissance of the Muslim camp. It was indeed a significant force. We estimated 3,000 assorted light cavalry, 6,000 infantry and a baggage train of carts too numerous to count in the fading light.

The King explained his tactics clearly and concisely, as usual.

'Blondel will take a squadron back to Marshal and Mercadier to tell them that we have engaged the Muslims. We will approach at a canter, downwind, which will deaden the sound of our approach. On the signal from my horns, we will attack at a gallop in four columns. Ranulf, you will stay close to me as I take the centre. Robert will take the left flank, Baldwin the right; we will give Burgundy all the fun by giving him the fourth column, formed up behind us as a second wave. Is that clear?'

It was.

But the night was not.

The moon was only three days old and so was of little help. But it was the time of the solstice, which meant that dawn was not far away. Even so, a massed cavalry charge in near darkness was a challenge for any army.

The King had developed a precise method for deploying his cavalry in darkness with the minimum of noise. The horses were saddled while still tethered and were kept occupied by the grooms feeding them where they stood. When all the mounts were ready, the captain of each conroi led his men to its assembly point by following a guide who had rehearsed the route several times. The men remained on foot, and the grooms continued to feed the horses to keep them calm. The assembly points for each conroi were marked by small fires, the light from which was shielded from the enemy by hurdles of brushwood.

Only when everybody was ready did the signal come to mount the horses, an order that passed from conroi to conroi by the rustle of men settling into their saddles. Then came a few moments of calm as the rustling ended, indicating that all was ready. It was a strange feeling; I could see a few men around me but knew that there were many more spread out in a formation that I could imagine, but could not see. I looked ahead, which was pointless. I might as well have been blindfolded, because ahead of me was just a black void. All cavalry charges were a test of courage, but to undertake one in total darkness was petrifying.

We advanced at a canter; fifteen hundred mounted men swept across the darkened landscape like a wave of avenging angels. Some horses tripped and fell, their riders trying to muffle their cries. But the only other noise was the steady rhythm of hooves, a pulsating sound that made my heart race.

When the horns sounded, we were at the crest of a ridge above the valley where the Mamluk column was encamped. Some of their fires were still burning – primarily the braziers of the perimeter guards – so we had something to aim for. By then, our approach had been heard and, as our gallop began, the fires were extinguished. We had no other guide except Fauvel, who carried the Lionheart five yards ahead of us. We may as well have closed our eyes as there was nothing to see except Fauvel's tail. It must have been much worse for the Duke of Burgundy and his men, who not only had to cope with the gloom but also to ride through a murk spiked with blinding dust.

Nevertheless, we soon breached the perimeter of the Muslim camp. Dawn's half-light now gave us shadows to aim for, all of which were scattering in different directions, desperate to find their horses and weapons, or a place to hide. It was carnage. Our cavalry consisted of disciplined phalanxes of men and horses, armed with swords and lances, formed up in compact multitudes, while the Mamluks were a haphazard rabble of largely unarmed men, easy targets for our experienced warriors.

As always, I stayed close to the King, watching his back as best I could. There was rarely a need as he slashed and chopped his way through our hapless opponents. The light was improving rapidly and as I looked around I could see the mass slaughter of a one-sided battle. Men on the ground running helplessly for their lives made easy targets for mounted warriors who were murderously adept at killing from horseback. Heads rolled, severed from necks with a single blow, and shoulders were cleaved down to men's ribcages. Lances impaled torsos, spilling innards over the ground, and blood splashed everywhere, covering men and horses until they were glistening in crimson.

The Lionheart never looked back. We knew that we were required to keep pace with him, and he knew that he could rely on us – such was the bond of trust between us. After what seemed like an eternity of death and destruction, we reached the end of the Muslim camp. The King reeled his horse round and led us on another rampage through the bedraggled remnants of our opponents. This was not a day to show mercy, and none was given.

The half-light offered some respite for the defenders, giving a few the opportunity to ride away, but for most, there was no escape. When we had finished our assault we regrouped to ride back and survey the results of our work. Bodies were strewn across a large area, almost all of them Mamluk. Many had been cut down by sword and lance, but many more had been killed or maimed under the hooves of our horses. At least half the Mamluk column appeared to have fallen.

But its baggage train was intact, as were most of its corrals of horses and camels. We acquired hundreds of each, and more than 150 carts of weapons, armour, tents, spices, herbs, clothing and medicines, as well as several surprisingly large chests of gold and silver. It was a major windfall, of which the Lionheart shared a more than generous proportion with Hugh of Burgundy and his French contingent.

When we returned to the bulk of the army there were celebrations in the camp at the news of the Mamluk gold and silver and the other booty, which usually meant a bonus for the men. The cooks began a feast of stewed lamb to make use of the bonanza of the requisitioned Muslim condiments.

We all felt that the fall of Jerusalem was now a foregone conclusion.

However, over the next few days, the mood changed.

The first setback was the news that, commanded by Saphadin, hundreds of Muslim reinforcements were on their way from east of the Euphrates and beyond. Then came a series of reports from our scouts which, added together, gave the King a logistical dilemma. Saladin had issued orders, over a wide arc around the Holy City, that every water cistern (most of which had been created by the sappers of previous Latin Kings of Jerusalem) be poisoned and every well filled in. Not only was this critical for the men, but also for the horses. It was a stark fact that made it even more pressing that we launch our attack on the city, as it contained our only available source of water, apart from the modest supply that we carried.

The Lionheart called for a tally of our stocks of water and then consulted his astrolabe. His calculations presented a clear picture.

'We must have the city in our hands and, most importantly, its wells available for our use by 30th June. Assuming that we can take the city within three days, this gives the men from Jaffa just two days to get here.'

The King jumped to his feet.

'Ranulf, send a squadron of hand-picked men to meet the column. They must tell Robert Thornham and Henry to come on with all speed.'

Early the next morning, while the King was enjoying breakfast, the squadron returned at a gallop, but with Robert Thornham at its head. He had ridden most of the night. The Lionheart was delighted, because it meant the column of reinforcements was nearby. The two men embraced, with the King beaming from ear to ear.

'Robert, tell me the good news. How many men?'

Thornham stepped away, looking forlorn.

'From Europe some Danes and Norse; men of the Low Countries; some Germans from various principalities; a few Iberians; and a large contingent from your realm.'

The King could sense bad news.

'How many?'

'Fifteen hundred knights, and three hundred sergeants and men-at-arms.'

'Burgundians? Franks?'

'A handful of each, against King Philip's wishes.'

'The scheming bastard! I wish I could get my hands on him. And Henry's men?'

'Not many; eighty or so knights, and two hundred men. There are some weapons and armour and some silver, but it's a meagre offering.'

The King cursed like a lowly soldier, a tirade that went on for a couple of minutes. The gist of it was his fury at the size of the European contingent. Thornham offered an explanation, but it did little for the Lionheart's humour.

'The English and Norman knights will tell you that both your brother, John, and King Philip Augustus are actively discouraging men from answering your call and that, indeed, they are openly plotting against you. The Germans and others are still committed, but since the death of Frederick Barbarossa they don't have a strong leader.'

'I can't believe Henry can only muster eighty knights to regain a kingdom! Is that all?'

'I'm afraid so, Richard. I'm sorry.'

'We can't take Jerusalem with two hundred and fifty knights, and five hundred men. I need twice that number of knights, and another five thousand men!'

The Lionheart then bellowed at his groom to get Fauvel saddled. Within minutes, he had ridden out of the camp, still in a fury.

I immediately summoned a squadron of his personal conroi and rode after him. It did not take long to find him; he was on Montjoie, staring out at Jerusalem.

I approached him with some trepidation, but he had become melancholy rather than angry.

'Take a last look, Ranulf. I doubt that we will ever see it again. Our time in Palestine is over, there is nothing more I can do. Even if we could take the city – and that would need a miracle from God – how could we hold it? If I stayed and imposed stability, where would our resources come from? John would seize England, and Philip Augustus would invade Normandy, Maine, Angers ... there would be no one to stop him.'

'Sire, you would have to leave the Holy Land to defend the Empire.'

'Of course I would. But how is Henry going to defend Jerusalem against Saladin? With only eighty knights!'

'There are the Templars and Hospitallers, my Lord.'

'Still not enough. Jerusalem has gone, we must accept that.'

'Sire, Saladin will not live for ever.'

'I know, but the notion of the invincibility of the Latin knight in the minds of the Muslims has gone. Others will follow Saladin. He's a great warrior and a chivalrous man, but there will be others.'

'But what of the rest of the Holy Land, my Lord?'

'The Christian lords can hold the coast. The land is fertile; if they have enough to pay the Pisans, Venetians and Genoese to supply them, they can prosper. Besides, those cities mean less to the Muslims, so there is a compromise to be struck with them.'

'What will you do, my Lord?'

'When we're sure the coast is secure, we go home. I fear there will be many battles to fight there. Will you help me?'

I gave my answer without hesitation.

'Always, sire.'

25. Battle of Jaffa

We began our withdrawal from Jerusalem on 4 July 1192. Our column was not harassed by Saladin's men, and we made rapid progress to the coast at Jaffa. By then, disappointment had turned to resignation within the ranks. Men started to think of home, and although there was bitter resentment at the attitude of King Philip and Prince John, the actions of fickle kings and princes had long since failed to surprise them.

Many of the men not directly loyal to the Lionheart started to disperse when we arrived in Jaffa, and he began to plan to send his own contingent home by sea from Acre. It took us less than three weeks to reach Acre, where we arrived on 22 July. The mood was sombre, both within our own ranks and among the citizens, but at least the Lionheart took some respite from his military responsibilities in being reunited with Bérengère and Queen Joan.

To add more misery to the Lionheart's gloom, urgent messages began to arrive in Acre within days. First came the news that Saladin's reinforcements had arrived in Jerusalem, numbering many thousands of eastern Muslims from Persia and the distant realms beyond it. This information did offer some comfort, in that it confirmed that the King had been right to withdraw from an attack on Jerusalem. But there was nothing positive in the despatch that followed.

On 28 July, a huge Muslim army had launched an attack on Jaffa, with siege engines and assault troops. Although the citadel had been newly rebuilt to the King's design and was formidable, the garrison was not large and would not be able to hold out for long. The King sprang into action; he summoned the Grand Quintet and the rest of the Christian commanders.

Once again, he was in his element, preparing and moving armies for war. And at his best, fighting them.

'Gentlemen, I will crowd as many men on to the ships at anchor here in Acre as I can, and I will lead them in an attack from the beach at Jaffa to try to stall the Muslim siege. We must not lose the city; it would cut our coastal kingdom in two, and give Saladin a route to the sea. I will take my lords: William, Robert and Baldwin, and Sir Ranulf. Henry of Jerusalem will lead the rest of the army along the coast with the Templars and Hospitallers. Mercadier and Blondel will stay here in Acre to stiffen our defences should Saladin mount an attack in the north.'

It was left to Robert de Sable, Master of the Templars, to query the obvious omission at our gathering.

'What of the Duke of Burgundy, and the French?'

'He came to see me last night. He has refused to join us and is returning home. He has been summoned to Paris by King Philip.'

William Marshal was puce with anger.

'But you gave him almost a third of the spoils from the Mamluks in the desert.'

The Lionheart smiled sardonically.

'That's the French for you. But worry not, I will have

my day with him, and with Philip Augustus. If not here, then in Europe.'

Despite adverse winds, our Pisan and Genoese ships transported us down the coast to Jaffa with remarkable speed. We had our first sight of the city at dawn on 1 August. It presented a worrying scene; there were numerous fires in the city and, as the light improved, we could see Muslim standards flying from the buildings. It seemed that we were too late.

The King ran to the prow of the boat and peered towards the shore.

'The citadel holds! There is no green flag on its pole, it flies the Three Lions. Prepare for a landing!'

Amidst the smoke from the many fires, it was difficult to see if the Lionheart was right, but few would dispute his notoriously keen eyesight. Then a courageous soul came into view. He was a Breton sergeant who had been lowered down the wall of the citadel, and had then swum out to us.

He was exhausted when we hauled him aboard, but he brought good news, if tinged with sadness. The Muslim catapults had breached the walls of the city, which had been burned and looted. Many inhabitants had been killed, but the citadel had held – just.

The King repeated his order to make a landing, and our captains turned our ships towards the shore. Our blood-red sails, the Lionheart's distinctive colour, billowed in a strong westerly wind from the far Mediterranean, and the ships lurched violently towards the shore. Once again, our arbalests were invaluable in covering our disembarkation and protecting our men against the Muslim archers. The ships could only approach to a point about fifty feet from the beach, for fear of running aground, which meant that we had to wade through deep water to make it to dry land.

The Lionheart shouted his commands as loudly as possible.

'Take off your maille; let's get ashore before the Muslims can form a line of defence.'

We helped one another pull off our hauberks and, within moments, the King was the first into the water, only pausing to help me get to my feet – something that was not easy with only one arm. He was also the first to put his feet on dry land. The rising sun from the east was in our faces and I could see him only in silhouette, running like a deer. The bright early-morning sun picked us out against the horizon, making us easy targets.

I looked around and saw men coming ashore in considerable numbers. William Marshal was nearby, with several Templars to my left and Hospitallers to my right. It was a comforting sight to see so many seasoned warriors, but our ranks were paying a heavy price from Muslim missiles – especially without our maille hauberks. As I watched the Lionheart ahead of me, oblivious to the arrows and javelins that flew all around him, I thought again of the Archangel Michael. Perhaps the lore was true; maybe he *was* God's warrior, immune from the weapons of mortal men.

Marshal and I called out to everyone to form a vanguard behind the King. By the time he reached the first Muslim defenders, we had formed a solid wedge of men behind him. Then the crash of clashing blades began, a sound that soon spread along the beach. The fighting was fierce – hand-to-hand at close quarters – but it was an exhilarating running battle, at a furious pace.

The Lionheart, with never any hint of fatigue, kept shouting to us and encouraging the men.

'Keep moving! . . . Don't let them form up! . . . Don't stop! . . . Keep them on the run!'

For the first time, my fabricated arm and modified shield were given a severe test, the worst part of which was the strain on my upper arm from repeated blows to my shield. I was under much more pressure than I had ever experienced before, and I found it difficult to keep up with the King. I missed Godric and the men; they would have got me through this.

Suddenly, I was confronted by three Muslim infantrymen, one of whom was a giant of a man. Their blows made me falter, then step backwards. I fell to my knees as the giant hit my shield with an almighty blow. The Lionheart saw me stumble and immediately came to my aid, bringing William Marshal with him. My attackers fled as soon as they saw our own pair of giants bearing down on them.

Marshal helped me to my feet, and the King shouted, 'Stay close, get in behind me!' before he tore off again into the fray.

It was, of course, paradoxical that I should need the King's help. Once I had been his guardian; now he was having to protect me.

After a few minutes, the tide of the encounter began to turn in our favour. Cutting through the melee, we could hear a repeated cry of alarm ahead of us.

'*Melek-Ric!*', '*Melek-Ric!*'

Even though our force was vastly outnumbered, the enemy were fleeing in front of us in droves, the panic spreading through them like a plague of fear. Once again, the Lionheart's valour and his legendary reputation had created havoc in the enemy ranks. The entire Muslim army began to retreat, granting us an opportunity to enter the streets of the burning city. We could see Saladin on his grey mount in the far distance, trying to turn his men, but to no avail. It was the only time we ever cast eyes on the revered Sultan.

The King called out to Marshal, 'Get the gates of the citadel open! Bring some pitch and plenty of flame; we must destroy the Muslim catapults.'

Baldwin and Robert had joined us. With a group of Templars, the King led us off to seize the Muslim ballista. There was little resistance, and Marshal arrived several minutes later with the materials needed to incinerate Saladin's siege towers and mangonels.

Against overwhelming odds, another remarkable victory had been achieved.

A triumphant procession into the citadel followed, where hundreds of citizens, packed in tightly with the garrison, had sought safety. People cheered from every vantage point and hollered in several languages, but they all meant the same thing.

'*Praise the Conquering Hero!*'

Some fell at the Lionheart's feet, and women rushed to kiss his hand. Children were held up high to see Richard, 'Coeur de Lion', who had rushed from Acre to save them – just as everyone had prayed he would.

He was a living Alexander, Arthur or Alfred. No one doubted it.

But there was still more to be done. Just as we began to relax and rest on our laurels, the King summoned us all together.

'Gentlemen, you remember what we achieved at Ascalon. Working parties are to be ready at first light tomorrow. We will begin repairing the city's walls; everyone works, no concessions. When the main army arrives, put them to work too.'

As ordered, work started on Jaffa's walls in earnest early next morning. As it did so, the Lionheart, already in the garb of an artisan, sent for me.

'Is Benoît of Geneva with us?'

'Yes, sire.'

'Tell him to contact Saphadin's man ... what is his name?'

'Abu Bekr.'

'Yes, tell him I would like to talk to Emir Saphadin about the situation at Jaffa.'

Two days later, a reply came back.

Please convey my warm regards to Melek-Ric. It is with regret that I cannot meet with you at the moment. The Sultan Saladin wishes to discuss Ascalon before we will discuss Jaffa.

The reasons for the refusal became clear on the evening of 4 August. Our groups repairing Jaffa's walls had just finished their day's work on walls that were far from secure. The Lionheart suddenly looked towards the east. I saw the alarm on his face, then I heard the distinctive rumble of massed horses. He barked his orders at me in quick succession.

'Form a defensive line ten yards from the wall, with pikes firmly anchored in the ground, shields raised and locked like the English! Tell William to deploy the arbalests and archers behind us. Robert is to organize secondary positions in the gaps on the walls, and Mercadier will form a third redoubt outside the citadel gates. Baldwin must get everything valuable and all civilians inside the citadel and close the gates. Only on my signal will we fall back to each defensive position, as required.'

The King had been presented with a sudden emergency and, as always, had responded with a military solution as elegant and sound as any great general of the past could have devised. Harold of England, who made the shield wall legendary, and Hereward of Bourne, who stood with him behind the mighty shield wall of the English housecarls at Senlac Ridge, would have been proud of him.

Within minutes, our bulwark of spears and shields was ready. Many men had not had the time to don their hauberks, but our wall was solid. It had the appearance of a giant hedgehog as the Muslim cavalry came into view.

They were a terrifying sight as they bore down on us. Closely packed with lances couched, it looked like they would overwhelm us. But at thirty yards, the King ordered the first volley of arrows and quarrels. They caused mayhem when they struck, bringing almost all of the front rank of horses crashing to the ground. The fallen bodies then disrupted the momentum of those behind. Significantly, the men and their mounts could see our bristling spears, adding more hesitation. As the first wave of riders tried to regain momentum, the ranks of cavalry behind began to career into them.

Eventually, some order returned and the attack resumed, but not with the same power or direction. Another volley of arrows did more damage. By the time the wave of horses reached us, few of them made any impact; several men and beasts just impaled themselves on our lances.

As soon as the Lionheart saw how weak their charge was, he ordered that we break our wall and strike out. He also had the horns sounded to call forward our other defensive lines to join our counter-attack. Inevitably, he led from the front, ruthlessly pulling a man from his rearing horse before running him through with his sword. He then jumped on to the mount, raised his sword and gave the crusaders' cry.

'*For St George!*'

By being the only Christian on a horse, and by loudly declaring his presence, the King had made himself the easiest target imaginable. But as the thrust of his sword reached its zenith, the setting sun caught the edge of his blade and cast a brilliant gleam into the eyes of the Muslim cavalry. Their reaction was astonishing; they must have thought they had seen a sign, a bolt of lightning from God, and they began to run like horses in a stampede. Some threw down their weapons, a few even fell to their knees and began to pray.

We all waited for the order to attack, but it did not come. Instead, the King dismounted, walked over to the

Muslims who were praying and raised them to their feet. Those fleeing saw what he was doing and stopped, looking back in awe. The Lionheart, half a head taller than the men around him and looking glorious in his resplendent mantle of the Three Lions, was twenty yards beyond our lines. He was alone among two dozen Muslims, with hundreds more only yards beyond them.

Several of our men, fearing for their King, began to move towards him. But I raised my sword arm to stop them.

The King was perfectly at ease and in control. Without a hint of apprehension, he slowly walked towards the men in the massed ranks of the Muslim army, who stood motionless as he approached them. When he had covered half the distance, he raised his sword, as if in a salute.

We heard the chants in response.

'*Melek-Ric!*', '*Melek-Ric!*', '*Melek-Ric!*'

Then, as calmly as he had walked towards them, the King turned and walked back towards us. As he did so, the Muslim army melted away in a hushed silence.

There was also silence in our ranks as the King walked past. No one who witnessed what happened that August day in 1192 outside the walls of Jaffa would ever forget it.

26. Campaign's End

Within hours of the end of the Battle of Jaffa, a message from the Muslim leadership arrived, not from Saphadin, but from his elder brother, the Sultan Saladin himself. He wanted to open negotiations.

I wondered whether the reaction of his army outside the walls of Jaffa had persuaded the Sultan that the King was unbeatable in battle, or at least that his army thought so. In any case, he wanted to parlay, but he laid down one overriding condition: he must control Ascalon, to give him access to the sea. This was a concession the King steadfastly refused to accept. It was a stalemate even before negotiations had begun.

Conditions in Jaffa were difficult. There were bodies to be cleared, sanitation had been disrupted, and it was vital to restore fresh water and food. When the land army arrived from the north, it only made matters worse by adding more mouths to feed. The King was exhausted, despite his protestations otherwise. He became ill with a severe fever and took to his bed. We were concerned for him; he lost weight by the day, and became grey and gaunt.

In the meantime, Saladin's position strengthened. I sent scouts to monitor his army. On 8 August, a large contingent of Kurdish light cavalry, Saladin's own people, arrived from Mosul on the Tigris. Two weeks later, more Mamluks came from Egypt. And just two days later the Sultan's nephew, al-Mansur, brought several hundred Yemeni desert cavalrymen and their dromedaries from the south.

The Muslims were tightening their grip around us.

I called a gathering of the Grand Quintet. We all agreed that if a compromise could be reached with Saladin, requiring the King to relinquish Ascalon, then we should persuade the Lionheart to do so. The Sultan had spies everywhere; if he found out that the King was ill, he would be surely tempted to attack Jaffa. If he did so, we might be able to hold the citadel for a while, but not the walls of the city. This would mean putting most of the citizenry and half the army at peril and entombing the rest inside the citadel's confined spaces.

William Marshal and I were designated to talk to the King, and Benoît of Geneva was asked to request that Saphadin meet with us in Jaffa.

Not the kind of man to cope well with the indolence of a sick bed, when we met with the King he had received news that had only added to his woes and made his temper worse. The revenge he had hoped to exact for the treachery of Hugh of Burgundy in refusing to participate further in the crusade had been thwarted by the man's death from illness in Acre.

William Marshal tried some words to soothe his anger.

'God will punish him, Richard, be thankful for that.'

'That gives me no satisfaction at all. God's vengeance is all very well, but what about mine!'

His outburst brought on a spasm of coughing that took some time to abate, leaving the King exhausted. We made our points regarding our current situation, and he listened carefully. At the end, he said little, merely asked that we summon his stewards to help him get washed and dressed.

As we left, he called after us.

'I will see Saphadin here, alone. What I know I have to agree to, I don't want anyone to hear pass my lips.'

Flanked by Christian knights in all their finery along every step of his way, Saphadin, dressed immaculately in his Arab coat and turban, walked into Jaffa alone on Tuesday 1 September 1192. Horns and trumpets sounded and drums beat. It was a momentous day for Christendom and for Islam. The King had tried manfully to make himself look fit and well and had ordered that those parts of the city that the Emir would see should look as clean and orderly as possible. What transpired between them was never revealed by either man. They talked for over two hours. As they did so, despite the fact that the heat of summer still held us in its fierce grip, the guard of honour remained in place and the entire population and the rest of the military stood in silence to await the outcome.

At last, the large oak door to the King's apartment opened and the Emir Saphadin walked out of Jaffa, just as he had walked in, dignified and expressionless. The silence continued until, a moment or two later, the Lionheart appeared.

Without his usual agility, he clambered on to a nearby wall to speak to the crowd.

'We have peace!'

A huge cheer echoed around Jaffa's walls. It carried across to the ships at anchor and followed Saphadin as he and his entourage rode away into the hinterland.

The Third Great Crusade was over.

The following day, a Muslim emissary appeared with the terms of the peace beautifully transcribed on vellum in Arabic and Latin. It was a complicated compromise, but one that saved face for both sides.

- Ascalon will be ceded to Muslim control, but its fortifications will be destroyed and not rebuilt until at least Easter 1196.
- The Christians will retain Jaffa and the coastal plain to the north as far as Acre and east as far as Ramla and Nazareth without let or hindrance.
- The principalities of Antioch and Tripoli will remain secure and unmolested.
- All fighting will cease forthwith and both sides will be allowed to travel and trade freely.
- Jerusalem will remain under Muslim control, but Christians and people of all faiths will be free to travel to the city, trade in the area and worship at the Church of the Holy Sepulchre.

It took some weeks for all the formalities to be agreed. Every Christian lord and Muslim emir had to signify their concurrence with their signature and seal. The Lionheart paid all his debts and used large parts of his dwindling treasury to pay the ransom on several hostages being held by the Muslims. Many Christian lords took the opportunity to visit the Holy City and pray at the Holy Sepulchre.

But the Lionheart's priorities lay to the north. He needed to retrieve his wife and sister from Acre, get his army home and confront the machinations at work in

Europe, wrought by a wily brother and a conniving King of France.

A still stricken King had to be transported to Acre on a cart. When we reached the city, a distraught Bérengère and Joan set about nursing him back to health. Blondel became a constant companion, singing the chansons the King loved so much and playing chess with him.

Slowly, his condition improved and he began the task of getting his army home. The mission was fraught with difficulties – some ubiquitous, some peculiar. The permanent obstacles were the Mediterranean winds, usually blowing against those going west, and the autumn weather in the Atlantic, which was already upon us and all but impossible to negotiate. To avoid those obstacles, the King ordered his captains to make landfall where they could, as far along the Mediterranean coast as possible. They were to abandon their vessels and return home on foot. Thus, most of the army departed over the next two weeks.

The particular problems of our return home came as a shock to us all. Although we knew that John was plotting against the Lionheart at home and had enlisted the support of the King of the French, we did not know the full extent of his scheming until reports reached us in Acre at the end of September. It had become a contagion throughout Europe. In order to save face in not being involved in the crucial battles in Palestine, the rulers of the Holy Roman Empire and the French Kingdom had spread stories of Richard's intransigence, bullying and brutality – especially his execution of his prisoners at Acre.

All the French and German allies had been recruited to

the cause. The Count of Toulouse, the kingdoms and principalities of Italy – and even Pope Celestine – were all involved in a war of hateful words designed to destroy the King's reputation.

Philip of Dreux, Bishop of Beauvais, who had been a close friend of Conrad of Montferrat, toured Europe, railing against the Lionheart. Some of his words reached us in a letter from Queen Eleanor to Bérengère.

The King of England betrayed our Lords, Philip of the French and Henry of the Germans, by negotiating with the heathen Saladin behind their backs. He conspired with murderers to have the throat cut of the noble Lord, Conrad of Montferrat, the rightful heir to the Kingdom of Jerusalem, and he had the estimable knight Hugh, Duke of Burgundy, poisoned in his own hall. He is a savage man, capable of great cruelty and wicked deceit. Worst of all, he gave away the keys of the Holy City to the infidel.

Rather than reacting with justifiable anger, the King smiled when he heard the Bishop's words read to him. However, his calm demeanour belied the fact that our route home was beset by difficulties and would have to pass through hostile territory. These were lands stirred up by a hysteria that claimed Richard the Lionheart was not the hero of a valiant war against a mortal enemy in the Holy Land – a war conducted largely on his own when his major allies returned home – but was an evil demagogue who had betrayed Christianity to Saladin, the Devil incarnate.

The King called us all together on Sunday 28 September, and we celebrated mass. Afterwards, he summoned what was, to all intents and purposes, a council of war.

'Under the care of William, my beloved Bérengère and dearest Joan will depart with their households and my personal conrois on Tuesday. My other devoted friends – my Grand Quintet, as Sir Ranulf has dubbed them – will make their own way home by whatever method they think fit. Divided between them, they will carry home what is left of my treasury and belongings. As for myself, I will delay a while. It seems I am a wanted man across Europe and so I will travel home as a devout Knight Templar, Anselm of Poitiers, with only a sergeant and two men-at-arms. We will all rendezvous in Caen, at Christmas at the latest, for a celebratory feast together.'

There were handshakes and embraces all round, and everybody made their final preparations to leave. As I had not been mentioned in the King's list of departers, I sought clarification from him.

'Sire, what would you have me do?'

'How old are you, Ranulf?'

'I am forty-one, sire.'

'Do you not want to retire to your estates in England and find a wife? I intend to extend your land when we return.'

'You are very kind, sire, but I would prefer to serve you a little longer – and certainly until you return to your realm. As for a wife, I have known two remarkable women; I lost one to God and the other to the Devil. I doubt I will ever meet their like again.'

'Another mystery for me! But I think I remember the

one you lost to God. She was the sultry Basque beauty you took to Rupertsberg?'

'Yes, my Lord; her name was Negu. But she decided to become a bride of Christ instead.'

'That is indeed a shame, she was very beguiling. And the other . . . the one taken by the Devil?'

'I'd rather not say, sire.'

'I think I know. She was killed by the Devil's agents, am I right? The Princess Anna, who was killed in Anatolia with Abbot Alun and your men.'

'It was the worst moment of my life.'

'I know, Ranulf. You were a different man when you came back.'

'Sire, please keep that confidence to yourself; it is very important to me.'

'Of course. I am only too aware of the sorrow of unfulfilled hopes. In my case, sweet Bérengère is still not with child. I hope she is not barren; if she is, I'll have to put her aside and go to the Pope for a new wife . . .'

He paused, thinking about the implications of what he had just said. Then he returned to the subject at hand.

'Now, what about the things in the Vatican we talked about; is it not time to retrieve them before I return home?'

'It makes sense, sire.'

'I intend to sail up the Adriatic Sea to Venice. I will put you off at Brindisi or Bari, and you can make your way to Rome from there.'

'Are you sure, my Lord? That will leave you very exposed, accompanied by just three men.'

'But they are good men; I will be fine, and I think I am

capable of looking after myself. Besides, you're not much use to me with a hook for an arm!'

Although the King was teasing me, in essence it was true. I was only of marginal use in a fight. The King then embraced me warmly.

'I will miss you, Ranulf. But we will see one another in Caen, at Christmas, when I hope you will be able to show me all those mysterious things I need to see.'

'I will miss you too, sire.'

We finally left Acre ten days later. Neither of us would ever see the Holy Land again.

The King was adamant that one day he would return. He knew that Saladin was in his mid-fifties and might not live much longer. He also knew that his peace with Saphadin had a finite life of no more than three or four years. He made it clear to Henry of Champagne, the putative King of the Holy City and its patriarch-in-waiting, that he intended to return and lead a new crusade once he had brought stability to his Empire at home.

Although it broke his heart to do so, as a symbol of his intent, he left his beloved Fauvel with Henry, asking him to look after the mighty steed until his return.

Sadly, it never came to pass.

27. A King's Ransom

It was a lonely voyage across a wild and windy Mediterranean. We were just four poor Soldiers of Christ and the small Genoese crew of a modest trading ship who, thinking us no more than fee-paying cargo, paid us little attention.

When the time came, it was difficult to leave the King. We had been almost constant companions for over fifteen years. Little did I know that our time apart would be far longer than either of us anticipated.

My journey to Rome was uneventful, but enjoyable. I was hailed wherever I went as an heroic crusader – and one with a severe injury to prove my valour. Monks fed me and gave me shelter; families took me in and invited their friends to come and hear my stories; people all along my route gave me food and gifts. I was asked to kiss babies, and some mothers even said they would name their sons after me.

When I reached the Vatican, I asked to speak to Monsignor Claudio, the Master of the Archives, a tall, gaunt man from Padua. He was very suspicious of my intentions and took me into a small garden at the side of the ancient cathedral before sitting me down and summoning a young English-speaking priest.

I used Alun's name and told him the story of Earl Harold's scribe, Gilbert Foliot, and of Thibaud of Vermandois, Cardinal Bishop of Ostia, the recipient of the casket.

Although he acknowledged all the names I mentioned, he remained stony-faced and said nothing. A nonchalant shrug of the shoulders was his only response.

I then unwrapped the Talisman of Truth, the strange relic that I had kept with me since Alun, in his death throes, had hidden it under the tree in Anatolia. Alun had suggested that I should wear it, but I never felt comfortable with the thought and had always kept it firmly hidden from view. I handed the amulet to Claudio; his eyes widened, and his face softened for the first time.

'I remember Father Alun. He was a clever man and a holy one.' He then returned the talisman to me. 'But this is the work of the Devil. We have many other of his works here; this amulet belongs with them.'

'Monsignor, I am only a messenger. Alun asked me to deliver the Talisman of Truth and the casket you hold to the King of England.'

The Master looked at me, clearly reluctant to let anything leave his archives. At length, he relented.

'As you wish; the Cardinal left precise instructions that when an emissary came, I was to release the casket.'

He then stood and gestured to me to follow him. Accompanied by the young priest, we passed two heavily armed Papal Guards, who looked more like north Europeans than Italians. We entered the old church at the back of the nave, emerging through a small doorway. After nodding at two more Guards, who stood alert on either side of a second narrow doorway, Claudio led us down a long flight of tight spiral stairs into the crypt.

It was an unnerving, oppressive place, full of eerie echoes, with only two small oil lanterns giving an indistinct glow to its broad arches and vaulted ceilings. The young priest then told me that I must wait with him while Monsignor Claudio went to retrieve the casket.

His footsteps receded as he disappeared into the murk, followed by the ever fainter sounds of heavy doors being opened and closed. After a while, there was a silence so still I could hear myself breathe.

I was disappointed; I had hoped that I would be able to enter the vaults and see their ancient tombs and mysterious relics. Legend said these included objects as old as Rome itself, and treasures that would astonish the world. My father had told me that all the Popes were buried in the vaults, including St Peter himself. I had harboured hopes of seeing all their mausoleums laid out in neat rows. But all I could see were shadowy columns and dark voids.

It was a smaller crypt than I had thought it would be. But the young priest assured me, in a hushed tone, that there was a labyrinth of vaults extending deep underground and for many yards beyond the walls of the nave. Some of the most secretive chambers could only be entered by Monsignor Claudio and the Pope himself, and many had not been opened for decades. He hinted at some of the contents, shaking his head and muttering about 'precious relics of Jesus', 'revelations known only to the Holy Father' and 'abominations too awful ever to be revealed'. My appetite was whetted, but I could get nothing more out of him.

After what seemed like an age, Monsignor Claudio returned with the casket, an impressive piece of craftsmanship with a heavy bronze clasp. He placed it gently on a small oak table in front of me. As I moved to look inside

– to be sure it contained all the manuscripts Alun had mentioned – I found that it was heavier than I thought it would be, and securely locked.

The Master handed me a small key. But before I opened the casket, he put his hand on mine and blessed its contents.

'There are remarkable stories in those pages; guard them well.'

Everything was in the casket, bound in immaculate sheaves of vellum, just as Alun had said it would be. I added the Talisman of Truth and closed the lid.

I was required to sign and seal a document to confirm that I had taken the artefact from the vault, then I was led back up into the basilica. As I walked across the nave, Monsignor Claudio called after me.

'If you would like to return the casket one day, please do so. We will happily take it back. The talisman you carry is not a charm; it is the Devil's Amulet, and it belongs here.'

I spent a few days wandering the ancient ruins and modern splendours of Rome. It was difficult to imagine what the city had been like in its pomp, because most of the land beyond the Vatican's precincts was made up of hillocks of debris where cows and goats grazed amidst glimpses of fallen columns the size of trees and blocks of stone as big as a cart.

Occasionally, a piece of a shattered and long-forgotten statue could be seen – a hand, or perhaps a limb, or a disfigured face. The ground was like a midden of the past, where every step I took meant treading on fragments of the once mighty Roman Empire. In certain places, huge buildings were still intact and some were still being used.

One in particular, a great circular colossus, bigger than three cathedrals, had towering arches that contained churches, shops and artisans' workshops. I was told it was once a place for festivals and circuses, where men would fight in front of huge crowds and where early Christians were tortured and killed for their beliefs.

It occurred to me that nothing much had changed over the hundreds of years since.

Autumn was beginning to bite, and I was tempted to stay in the south until the spring. But I knew that our Christmas rendezvous in Normandy beckoned, so I began to travel north. I also wanted to find a quiet place to read the contents of the precious casket. I needed to find a monastery, and a priest whose English or Norman was good enough to help me read the Latin text.

I eventually found the help I needed at the remote Benedictine Abbey of Sant'Antimo, near Siena. I paid a generous price for my lodgings and, in return, two young monks, one from Rouen and one from Gisors, helped me read the manuscripts.

It was an enthralling experience. Surrounded by wooded hillsides and the tranquillity of monastic life amidst the abbey's vineyards and meadows, we chose a different location each morning and afternoon. I tried to follow the Latin script, but eventually I realized it was simpler just to sit back and listen to the captivating stories of England's recent kings and to the remarkable exploits of Hereward of Bourne and his descendants. I felt highly privileged – especially having known Earl Harold, the man who united the two dynasties.

I had been a proud Englishman before I heard the

accounts, but was even more fiercely so when I finished hearing them. I now felt emboldened to place the Talisman of Truth around the neck of the man who was its rightful recipient: Richard, King of England, the Lionheart, a man who Hereward and Torfida would have been proud to call their King.

When we had finished, I thanked my Benedictine hosts, who knew little of England's history and cared less for its intrigues. Even so, I swore them to secrecy before making my way north once more.

I arrived in Caen well before the Christmas activities. However, to my horror, there was no sign of the Lionheart. Indeed, nothing had been heard of him since we had left Palestine. Queens Bérengère and Joan were there, as was the Grand Quintet, and Queen Eleanor was on the way from Poitiers. A great celebration had been planned; everyone had returned safely from the Great Crusade and, despite Prince John's malicious endeavours and those of the Count of Toulouse, the Empire was still intact.

But the feast's host was nowhere to be seen.

Nor did he appear in the New Year.

Anxious for news, Queen Eleanor returned home. Seeking solace, a distraught Bérengère went to the nuns at Beauvais. The Grand Quintet sent out messengers in search of information about the whereabouts of the Lionheart. A flurry of responses came in the middle of January; they brought news that would create a sudden sharp turn in my life's journey and that of my King.

On his way back from the Holy Land, word that the King was travelling through the eastern Alps had reached

Leopold, Duke of Austria. He immediately issued orders for the King's arrest and despatched hundreds of men throughout his domain to hunt him down. The Lionheart escaped from several ambushes and made it as far as a village close to Vienna, by which time he had lost his men in various skirmishes. He had become exhausted and ill with a fever, and sought refuge at a roadside inn. While delirious and unable to rise from his bed, he was arrested by a posse of the Duke's men.

Stripped of all his weapons, armour and possessions, he had been imprisoned in less than comfortable circumstances in Durnstein Castle, on the Danube. Duke Leopold had allied himself with Henry, the Holy Roman Emperor, and with Philip Augustus, King of the French. They meant to humble the Lionheart and bring his Empire to its knees. Prince John, ever eager for the Plantagenet throne, was their acolyte. Only Bérengère's family in Iberia and William the Lion, King of the Scots – who remembered the King's generosity in the Quitclaim of Canterbury – refused to join the conspiracy.

Lesser men, jealous of the Lionheart's prowess and reputation, had him in their grasp and were going to exact a high price for his release. In geld, their price was 150,000 Cologne Silver Marks – £100,000 sterling – almost more bullion than anyone had ever counted before. But more than that: they required that the King pay homage to them in all his lands and domains.

The demands were unprecedented and created uproar across Europe among fair-minded people – not that this made any difference to the King's plight. Pope Celestine excommunicated Duke Leopold for the crime of imprisoning a brave crusader, and all chivalrous knights – including French and German men of honour – were appalled. But Europe's most powerful men were playing for stakes that allowed no respect for chivalry.

All my instincts cried out to me to rush to the Danube to be with the King, but it made no sense. He was being held deep inside the German Empire, behind the walls of a formidable fortress; it would take an army to free him, or all the silver in Europe.

Within two weeks, Queen Eleanor had pulled the Empire together and called a Great Council of England at Oxford to begin the process of raising the immense ransom. When she addressed the great men of the land, they gasped at the size of the ransom. As the Archbishop of Canterbury said, it was at least four times the revenue that the King would expect to raise from the entire realm in a year. It would impoverish everyone, from the highest to the lowest, and at a time when the country had not yet recovered from the huge burden it had to carry in order to pay the Saladin Tithe, to fund the Great Crusade to the Holy Land.

Even so, the process began.

Every knight had to pay one pound of silver, every lay person had to give a quarter of his income, and every church had to deliver all its chalices and plate in gold and silver. Every lord was required to make a personal contribution proportionate to his wealth, and all the merchants of the wealthy burghs – especially the Jewish brokers and financiers – were asked to do the same. William the Lion of Scotland sent 5,000 pounds, and the Jews of London raised over 30,000 between them, while those of York sent 15,000.

The silver was melted into ingots and carried to St Paul's in London, where it was stored in large chests in the crypt under the guard of an elite corps of warriors from the King's retinue. It soon became the largest treasury England had ever assembled.

When Queen Eleanor was sure that it was possible to raise the geld, she summoned me to see her at Westminster.

Although the Queen was seventy years of age, she still looked like a woman in the prime of middle age. She also retained her uniquely intimidating aura, which had only been enhanced by age. As I walked across Westminster's Great Hall, she was standing at a table with several of her entourage, staring intently at plans for what appeared to be a new wharf by the Thames.

I stood and waited for my summons to approach her. I could hear her asking clear and concise questions and issuing precise instructions. There was no doubting who was ruling England in the Lionheart's absence.

I looked around, admiring the beautiful tapestries that almost covered every inch of the hall's cold stone walls. There were no hunting dogs by the fire and no straw on the floor to collect the detritus of man and his animals; this was the hall of an elegant Queen, not an earthy King. Eleanor's floor was covered by ornately woven carpets that she had brought back from Palestine. Instead of dogs sprawling on them, young men lounged, playing music for the ladies of the court, who hovered around them, smiling in appreciation.

The men-at-arms who stood sentry at the doors, although large and imposing, were much more handsome and far younger than the usual garrison soldiers. They were also dressed more like courtiers than warriors, and wore bright-blue capes and tunics braided with cloth of gold. I smiled to myself, wondering how I would look in such an outfit.

Queen Eleanor finally noticed that I had arrived, and turned to look at me. She was remarkably slim and attractive in an immaculate pale-blue kirtle and matching wimple. I bowed and she nodded in response, with just the hint of a warm smile.

'Sir Ranulf, I want you to go to the Germans. The King knows you and trusts you. Keep your Hospitaller's black mantle and cape; they will ease your passage. You will travel with two Cistercians, the Abbots of Boxley and Robertsbridge. Both are Lotharingians; they are clever and speak German, but are totally loyal to me. Both are also physicians, in case the King is in need of care.'

The Queen was at her impressive best. She had thought of everything and, although she was a mother in distress at the fate of her son, she spoke with authority and clarity.

'Tell the King that all is well with the Empire and that the ransom will soon be ready. Prince John is under control, and Philip Augustus will not make a move as long as I'm alive.'

'Very well, ma'am. What of Queen Bérengère? He is certain to ask.'

'Do you mean, has she produced an heir?'

'Well, ma'am, we all know he is anxious about the succession.'

'She miscarried shortly after she returned from Palestine; it is the third time. I fear she may not be able to carry a child to full term. However, the King does not know about the earlier miscarriages.'

'Should I tell him?'

'Yes, he needs to know that at least she's fertile. I don't want him to put her aside just yet. There's still hope. And, in any event, until he returns, it makes no difference.'

I bowed and prepared to make my exit.

Queen Eleanor walked towards me and lowered her voice. In so doing, she became the mother who had been disguised by the Queen.

'Sir Ranulf, give him my love when you see him and bring him home safely.'

'Of course, ma'am.'

I bent down on one knee and kissed the ring on her left hand. As I did so, she gently rested her right hand on my head. It was a gesture meant for her son, a humbling moment I would never forget.

Before I left, I was given letters from both Queens, gifts from the Grand Quintet and many others, scrolls of vellum concerning matters of state, and two chests of books, clothes and keepsakes of various kinds. I left my precious casket in the crypt of St Paul's.

I met my two companions at Rochester, and we were soon beyond Antwerp and sailing down the Rhine. The spring of 1193 was in the air and the journey, despite my two somewhat dour ecclesiastical companions, was pleasant enough.

When we got close to Abbess Hildegard's monastery at Rupertsberg, I could not resist the impulse to pay a visit to find out what had become of the beautiful Negu. It had been almost fifteen years since we had travelled here together, but my memory of her was still vivid.

To my great disappointment, although Negu was still at

Rupertsberg, she was visiting another foundation down-stream on the Rhine, a monastery we had passed early the previous day. I was intrigued to discover that Negu had developed a beautiful singing voice and had become one of the most learned nuns at Rupertsberg. She was even being talked of as a future Mother Superior.

Although I was not able to see Negu, I did pay my respects at Hildegard's grave. A simple affair with just her name, carved in her own alphabet, on a plain stone slab, it was set in the open fields of the monastery, not far from the main gate. She had said she wanted to be buried on productive land so that her remains would enrich the earth, rather than have them fester in a churchyard. I smiled when I heard the story and remembered fondly her warmth and humour. Perhaps Negu had become like her?

When we reached Nuremberg, we heard that the King had been moved to a new place of captivity. Leopold of Austria had bartered the Lionheart, like a rich man's con-cubine, to Henry, the Holy Roman Emperor, who had imprisoned him in Trifels Castle in Swabia, an enormous edifice on the Queich River, a tributary of the Rhine. Infuriatingly, we had to retrace our steps.

When we finally reached Trifels, it was the middle of April. The King had been in captivity for over three months, and I was concerned for his welfare. He was the most restless and impatient man I had ever met; I was worried about his health and his state of mind.

28. Trial at Speyer

My anxieties about the Lionheart deepened when I saw the Castle of Trifels. The Emperor could not have chosen a worse place. It sat on a thin crest of rock high above the river valley, surrounded by thick forests. It was as if the castle walls were an extension of the rock itself; they were so high, with so little level ground around them, as to make them impossible to besiege. The nearest village was two hours away, on the valley floor, and was no more than a small hamlet.

I said a silent prayer to thank God that it was spring, because it must have been even more depressing in the depths of winter.

The villagers confirmed that Trifels did, indeed, hold an important foreign king. But they warned us that the Castellan was a brute of a man. They also said that his garrison was an unpleasant crew of thugs, who caused trouble in the surrounding area whenever they ventured out in search of amusement.

After negotiating the steep and rutted track to the castle's barbican — so steep that our pack horses found the ascent exhausting — we found the drawbridge up and the portcullis closed. There were no sentries to be seen on duty. We had no option other than to shout loudly to announce our arrival.

We got no response for almost an hour, after which

time a sergeant appeared at one of the barbican's arrow slits and told us, in no uncertain terms, to go away. Despite our protestations, he just walked away without any further comment.

The hour was late and there was little point in going back down to the village, so we found a comfortable place in the nearby forest and made camp for the night.

We were woken early the next morning by the sound of the drawbridge being lowered and the portcullis being raised. Shortly afterwards, half a dozen men rode out to confront us. At their head was a very large man, who looked like he had once been a formidable warrior, now gone to fat. His manners matched his unwholesome appearance.

'What business brings you to Trifels?'

'I am Ranulf of Lancaster, and my companions are Clovis, Abbot of Boxley, and Charles, Abbot of Robertsbridge. We are from England, the realm of King Richard, and are sent by his mother, Eleanor, Dowager Queen of England, Duchess of Aquitaine, Countess of Poitiers.'

'That is an impressive list of titles, but they mean nothing here. I am Rudolph of Landau, Castellan of Trifels. This is the domain of Henry, Emperor of the Germans, and his brother, my Lord, Conrad, Duke of Swabia. Be gone with you, Hospitaller.'

'We are emissaries from a mother to her son. She would like to know if he is well.'

'He is well.'

'We would like to see him.'

'This is the Emperor's repository for his coronation regalia and his crown jewels; no visitors are allowed.'

'We pose no threat. I am a one-armed man, and my companions are men of God.'

He circled me on his mount, a prodigious black stallion big enough to carry a man of his significant proportions.

'Listen, my friend, you would not be a threat if you were three of the greatest warriors in Christendom; this fortress is impregnable, its garrison a match for anyone. Leave, before you are taken inside to join your King.'

'I will not leave; I'm sure your Emperor would not be happy if he knew you had denied access to an emissary of a Dowager Queen, sent to ascertain the well-being of her son.'

I could see the Castellan vacillate at the mention of the Emperor's name, but his hesitation did not last long.

'This is your last warning. Your King is kept in our largest chamber, almost as big as mine, but there are real dungeons at lower levels. They will become your resting place if you don't leave now.'

I had a decision to make and, with few options available to me, I made it quickly. I grabbed the bridle of the Castellan's horse and yanked it hard, making the stallion rear wildly. The move caught the big Swabian by surprise and he tumbled out of his saddle, hitting the ground hard. I seized the moment, put my foot on his chest and my sword to his throat.

'My companions are going back to the village and will wait for word from me. You can lock me away with my King, but let these men of God go, so that they can take words of comfort back to his mother.'

Rudolph of Landau squirmed and grimaced, but he knew that the tip of my sword was pressed hard against his Adam's apple. He hissed at me.

'You're a dead man, either now or very soon.'

I hissed back.

'I don't think so; if you kill me as an emissary from a queen to a king held for ransom, your Emperor will not have a friend in Europe. He will have you skinned alive.'

The Castellan knew I had a point. After a moment's thought, and a deep breath, he relented.

'Agreed. The monks can go to the village – but no further, until I hear from my Lord, the Duke. You must surrender yourself to me.'

I gestured to the two abbots to make a hasty return down the hill, handed my sword to one of the Castellan's henchmen and began to walk across the drawbridge. Rudolph of Landau was helped to his feet, which he managed with some difficulty, and then followed me into the castle.

As the portcullis fell and the drawbridge rose, I stood in the centre of the bailey and feared the worst. My dread reminded me of my tribulations at Wolvesey at the hands of Earl Harold's chilling inquisitor, Máedóc.

I was right to make the comparison. Within the blink of an eye, I felt a sickening blow to the back of my neck, and then – nothing.

The next sensation I felt was the chill of the unyielding surface of a cold, dank stone floor. My neck was so sore and stiff, I could not move it; my hook and arm had been removed, as had my cape, mantle, weapons and armour. I was left wearing just my chemise and braies and was chilled to the bone. My head throbbed, as it had done at Wolvesey, and I felt the same sense of desperation. In many ways, my situation was worse; I was considerably older and had only one good arm with which to defend myself.

Several days passed, during which my only contact with the outside world was a daily bowl of thin stew that was passed through a small door at the top of my cell and placed on a high ledge. There was no light, and it was impossible to see even a glimmer of anything around me, but my good hand soon calculated the dimensions of my space. It was a tall, thin rectangle, the length of a man and a little wider than the span of a pair of shoulders. In height, the shelf was about as far as I could reach; I guessed the door in the ceiling to be a little higher.

I counted my blessings; at least I could lie down, and it was possible to turn round. But that was the best of it. Moments of panic came often and were hard to suppress; to all intents and purposes, I was in a tomb.

It was also totally silent, the air putrid, mainly from the stench of my own waste, and the walls and floor dank. The fact that I could not feel mortar joints between the stones of a man-made oubliette, led me to assume that I was entombed deep in the bowels of the castle in a chamber carved from solid rock. My nightmarish ordeal at the hands of Máedóc at Wolvesey, almost twenty years ago, had come back to haunt me.

The worst parts of my torment were the bitter cold – even though it was spring outside, the icy rock knew nothing of the seasons – and the sense of total isolation.

This was particularly hard to deal with, so severe that it seemed like Hell on earth. At Wolvesey, at least, I had known that I was being put to the test and could cling to that knowledge to help save my sanity. This time, I was at the mercy of a brute just like Máedóc, but one who had no particular reason to keep me alive.

I lost track of the days; I was in a state of utter terror most of the time, not far short of losing my mind. I think I had been there for about ten days, but it could have been more, when relief finally came.

The small door above me suddenly opened, which allowed in an unbearable shaft of light. A ladder was lowered, on to which I was able to clamber, and I was helped to a room much higher up in the castle. It was hardly a lord's chamber, but at least it had a window and a bed. A half-butt of warm water was produced, in which I could cleanse myself, and my clothes, weapons and armour were returned to me, as were my hook and arm. I felt whole again. I was given reasonable food and my chamber even had a garde-robe, so that I no longer had to live with my own shit.

Gradually, a sense of normality returned and my terrors began to subside.

About a week later, Rudolph the Castellan appeared, looking just as menacing as he had before. He was accompanied by my erstwhile companions, the Abbots Clovis and Charles.

'You are a fortunate man, Ranulf of Lancaster. The Emperor has summoned the King to his court on the Rhine. You and the two abbots are to accompany him. An escort has been arranged for early tomorrow morning. Be ready at dawn.'

He then turned and left, slamming the door behind him. As the two abbots began to examine me for any ill effects from my confinement, I shot questions at them.

'Have you seen the King?'

Clovis did most of the talking.

'Yes, this morning; we were escorted up from the village.'

'How is he?'

'Thin, pale and melancholy. He has not been harmed, and he is not being held in a dungeon. But his room is small and the food is barely enough to keep a child alive, let alone a man of his proportions. He sends his greetings.'

'When can I see him?'

'In the morning; the Castellan won't allow us to see him again until we leave.'

'Where are the things we brought from England?'

'Either confiscated or destroyed.'

'Even the letters from Eleanor and Bérengère?'

'Even those.'

'That Castellan is an evil bastard. How long have I been here?'

'Thirteen days in the oubliette, and eight days in here. You're a little thin; but otherwise you seem to be in good condition, given what you've been through, and for a man of your age.'

The Abbot's supplementary point gave me a jolt; I was forty-two years old, and time was moving on. It made me think.

With an escort of two dozen men, we left the godforsaken castle of Trifels just after dawn the next day. It was impossible to speak to the Lionheart, although I did catch a brief glimpse of him; he was confined in a covered cart, which was like a cell on wheels, and we were kept well away from him. One of his wrists was manacled to the cart and he was dressed like a peasant. He could have been a common criminal being taken to the gallows.

Clovis had been right; he was thin and pale, and the appetite for life had gone from his face. I turned to the Abbot.

'Is he tied all the time?'

'Only when he's being moved. Apparently, he escaped three times on the way from Vienna, so they chained him. His right wrist is very raw, but I've persuaded them to chain his other hand.'

Our destination was the City of Spires, Speyer on the Rhine, only a few miles north of Trifels, where the Emperor was to hold his Easter Court. It was here that I was eventually allowed to talk to the King.

The Lionheart was given rooms in the royal apartments in Speyer Palace, while the abbots and I were billeted with the Emperor's garrison. I was taken aback when I saw him.

His once distinctive mane of hair had thinned and was streaked with grey. He looked drawn to the point of frailty, and he had lost a considerable amount of weight. More disconcertingly, the notorious fire that used to burn so brightly in his eyes was no longer there. He was slumped in a chair when I arrived; when I greeted him, he barely lifted his head to acknowledge me.

'Welcome to my new abode, Ranulf.'

'A royal apartment, sire, and one fit for a King.'

'Indeed, a considerable improvement on that hole at Trifels. But I fear I may be sent back there after this little tête-à-tête with Henry.'

'My Lord, I'm sure the abbots have told you, the ransom is being collected. It will soon be complete, and then you can go home.'

'This is not about a ransom; it is about vengeance and humiliation. They mean to make me grovel. The price is set so high in order to punish me. It's not intended to make them rich; they're rich already.'

'My Lord, we will get you home, worry not.'

'Ranulf, I will only be released when they have had their revenge.'

Two days later, on Palm Sunday, Richard, King of England, was brought before Henry VI, Holy Roman Emperor, Lord of the Germans, in the nave of St Mary's, the huge Cathedral of Speyer.

The Lionheart was dressed neatly and cleanly, but only in the plain mantle and cloak of a lowly knight. He was denied any weapons or regalia, despite the fact that he was the legitimate ruler of a realm at least on a par with Henry's domain.

In contrast with the Lionheart's drab brown cloak, the cathedral was a blaze of colour. Its bright red sandstone columns provided a perfect canvas for the gleaming silks and rich furs of the guests. Henry had summoned his aristocratic and ecclesiastical nobility from far and wide. They were so many that they filled the floor of the entire nave in serried ranks of bejewelled necks, ermine-clad shoulders and coroneted heads. The cathedral rang with the cacophony of thousands of voices, in many different languages, their volume rising as they competed with one another to be heard.

Only a few paces from Henry's imperial dais, a clear space had been left for the King to stand in. As if in a Roman arena, he resembled an exotic animal, captured and put on display for the amusement of the crowd.

The Emperor's Chamberlain rose and the entire gathering fell silent within moments, leaving just distant echoes reverberating around the walls.

It was soon obvious that this was not an audience with the Emperor; it was a public trial in front of the entire Holy Roman Empire. Indeed, if the Lionheart's judgement had been accurate, it was to be a public humiliation.

Henry looked imperious, as was his right; the crowd of princes, dukes, lords and their ladies looked contemptuous, as was not their right; the King, the only man on his feet, stood in the centre of the only open space in the vast cathedral, looking forlorn. I wanted to rush to his side, but we were ten yards away and under guard.

The Chamberlain's voice rose.

'Richard, King of the English, you are brought here to St Mary's, the Cathedral of Speyer, in the presence of his Imperial Highness, Henry, Emperor of the Romans, to answer to God for the sins you have committed in His name . . .'

He paused to look at the Emperor, who nodded, impatient for his Chamberlain to continue.

'You are required to answer to the following heinous crimes. First: that you betrayed the trust and confidence of Henry's vassal, Leopold, Duke of Austria, and disgraced him by tearing down his Imperial Standard from the walls of Acre in the Holy Land. Second: that you connived and plotted in the brutal murder of the noble Lord, Conrad of Montferrat, King of Jerusalem. Third: that you dishonoured Christ our Redeemer and the whole of Christendom, by failing in your duty to reclaim the Holy City, and that you did compound this by then treating with the heathen Saladin and granting him sovereignty of God's Holy Places.

'The Emperor has asked Henry of Maastricht, Archbishop of Worms, to preside over a conclave of the Bishops of the Empire to pass judgement on these charges. What say you to these charges?'

With a smug expression on his face, the Chamberlain then sat down.

The King, who had kept his head bowed as the indictments were read, was impassive, his chin on his chest, his shoulders stooped. He looked like a broken man, unable to respond.

But then he raised his chin and began to look around. He fixed his eyes on sections of his audience and stared at them intently. If his lonely isolation at Trifels had cowed him, this huge crowd awakened him. I could see anger rise in him; the fire began to glow in his eyes once more. The Emperor had made a mistake by making a public declaration of the King's so-called 'crimes' and had compounded his error by taunting the wounded beast.

The Lionheart took a stride forwards, towards the Emperor; his prodigious height was suddenly more apparent, his warrior's frame more intimidating. Dignified once again, he looked towards the Chamberlain and smiled at him.

'My Lord Chamberlain, I am grateful to you for explaining to me why I have been held in captivity these last months. It is one thing to be held for a crime; it is quite another to be held without reason or charge. So now I know; I am grateful to you. You say that I am held on three counts, so let me respond to them.'

The Emperor looked ill at ease. He had clearly calculated that the highlight of his Easter Court would be the public humbling of a broken man. But the Lionheart's sudden transformation was not part of the plan. The King turned his back on the Emperor and looked at men in the audience who appeared to have fought many a battle.

'First of all, the taking of Acre. I make no apology that my standard was raised on the Citadel of Acre, and mine alone. The city had been besieged for many months by Leopold of Austria and Conrad of Montferrat, but my strategy and my army won the day and made the city ours. What man among you would not raise his standard in those circumstances?'

He paused to let his question sink in.

'Duke Leopold had fought with me, and he shared a portion of the spoils to reflect the size of his contingent. But it was my victory.'

He turned, fixing his stare at another group of Teutonic warrior lords.

'As every man here knows, a flag of victory is but one symbol of the courage of many, and so it was at Acre. The King of France's standard flew on one of the towers of the city walls, over an area that became the French Quarter, as did the gonfalon of the King of Jerusalem.'

Then he smiled; he had the audience in his thrall now,

like a Greek orator in the Agora of Athens. He turned to the Emperor and lowered his voice to add emphasis.

'We raised the Imperial Standard of the Holy Roman Empire above the barbican of Acre. But Leopold was not happy with that. He wanted it on the Citadel. We met together to discuss his claim, all four of us: Leopold and Conrad; Philip Augustus, King of the French; and myself. All three of us rejected Leopold's request – it was not my decision alone – and agreed that the status quo should remain. Leopold was annoyed and withdrew his forces from the city, so I had his Imperial Standard removed and returned to him.'

The Archbishop of Worms then stood and bowed to the Emperor before addressing the Lionheart.

'My Lord King, can you verify your account?'

'Of course, ask any man who was there. I see some in this nave. The Imperial Standard was not torn down, it was removed respectfully, with full military ceremony, and sent to the Duke's camp, where he was preparing to leave for Europe.'

Amidst very audible mutterings, the Archbishop sat down and cast a questioning glance at the Emperor. The King continued his response.

'The death of Conrad of Montferrat was a tragedy. He was by far the best man to succeed as King of Jerusalem and it was my emissary, Henry of Champagne, who took him the good news. He was killed shortly afterwards by the Assassins, a lethal bunch of Muslims led by a fanatic called Hassan-i Sabbah . . .'

He paused again, seeking out another group of fearsome-looking magnates in the audience.

'Needless to say, Sabbah does not accept commissions from Christians.'

The Lionheart's caustic ending produced peals of laughter that rang around the nave and gave rise to even more discomfort for the Emperor. The King was warming to his task, and now went on the offensive.

'The final accusation, my Lord Chamberlain, is the most hurtful. Unlike your Lord, the Emperor Henry, who did not take the cross, and Philip Augustus, King of the French, who did, but then returned home, I and my fellow crusaders fought with all our might to free the Holy City. But after the tragic loss of the Emperor Frederick Barbarossa, and the return to Europe of most of his mighty army, our task was all but doomed from the outset.'

He glared at the warriors in the room. Many of them must have been with Barbarossa's army when it returned. Some of them must have been with Leopold at Acre and would have left long before the army of the Great Crusade approached Jerusalem.

'Despite being heavily outnumbered, we defeated Saladin's army at Arsuf and came close to taking Jerusalem. Indeed, I had the privilege of seeing it from less than ten miles away. But we did not have the men to take the city. More importantly, had we succeeded, who would have defended it? It is a long way from the Christian coast and isolated in a sea of Muslims.'

The Chamberlain rose, attempting to bring the Lionheart's tirade to an end. But the King glowered at him.

'I am almost finished; this assembly must hear me out.'
He raised his voice so that it reverberated around the

sandstone walls of St Mary's and across every realm in Europe.

'I did not abandon hope. We stalked the Holy City; we threatened Egypt itself. I sent a clarion call to Europe asking for more men. So did the Sultan Saladin. But his call for reinforcements was answered in droves from all over Islam. I waited and waited, but when the reinforcements arrived from Europe, they came as a noble few, rather than the mighty host we needed.'

Then he came to the climax of his tour de force.

'And I have to say to you, my Teutonic friends, when I stood and stared at the walls of Jerusalem for the last time, knowing that I could not breach them, other than a few of your countrymen in the heroic ranks of the Templars and the Hospitallers, there were very few German faces beside me!'

His audience was stunned and uncomfortable.

The King delivered his coup de grâce. He had recognized a face in the audience, a Hospitaller, distinctive with his white cross and black mantle.

'Lothar, Lord of Schwerin, you were with us outside Jerusalem. Tell this noble gathering if anything I have said today is untrue.'

Lothar stood and spoke in a strong voice.

'It was as you described it, my Lord King.'

The reverse of what the Emperor had intended had happened. He was the one who was embarrassed, not the King.

But the Lionheart was still not finished.

'So I say to you all, what was I to do? Saladin is not an evil being, a creature to frighten children; he is an honourable man and a great warrior. He has a different faith, a belief that is a mystery to us – indeed, it is alien to us – and for that, he will, one day, have to answer to the one true God. However, because of the treaty we now have with Saladin, Jerusalem is an open city. Christians come and go under safe passage guaranteed by the Sultan. They are free to trade and, most importantly, are free to pray at the Church of the Holy Sepulchre.'

The King then turned towards the Archbishop and his fellow ecclesiasts and spoke to them directly. He lowered his voice and became conciliatory in tone.

'My Lords, esteemed Bishops, I think you will agree it is a far better outcome than many thought possible after the sad loss of Barbarossa.'

The gathering burst into spontaneous, animated conversation. They were shocked at what they had heard. The Lionheart's eloquence had not only made a compelling case in his defence, but he had also concluded with a telling reminder that, if 100,000 Holy Roman men had not returned home after the death of their Emperor, the story of the Third Great Crusade might have been very different.

Emperor Henry's face had become thunderous. He looked around, as if in search of the culprits who had given him false accounts of what had happened in Palestine. Fortunately for his future well-being, Leopold of Austria was not there to answer the obvious questions about his version of events. Almost in a state of panic, Henry beckoned to his Chamberlain to speak.

'The Archbishop and his conclave will now deliberate on the indictments and report back to the Emperor tomorrow. A feast has been prepared in the cathedral cloisters; the stewards will assist you. Please leave in an orderly fashion, the cathedral is very full.'

I looked at the Lionheart. He was twice the man he had been an hour ago. Many of the gathering paid their respects to him before the Emperor's men escorted him away. He had won a great victory, perhaps the most important of his life, and he had achieved it not with his sword but with his words. The Abbess Hildegard would have heartily approved.

Accounts of his defence would soon spread around Europe like a fire across a field of stubble. His bravura had not made him a free man, but the intended humbling of a great King had been thwarted.

29. Purgatory

After the King was taken away from the nave of St Mary's, I did not see him again for several days. It was a very fraught interlude. Although it seemed unlikely that the Emperor would harm him after what had happened in the cathedral, the King was a long way from home and in the grip of a very angry and humiliated man.

Perhaps an 'accident' would be arranged, or a sudden 'illness'. Neither Charles nor Clovis could get anyone to divulge anything regarding the Lionheart's whereabouts; we were restricted to our billet and closely watched. My anxiety grew with every day that passed.

Then, early on the fourth morning, our door was thrown open and, accompanied by a posse of warriors, a sergeant ordered us to be ready to leave within the half-hour. To my horror, by the end of that day, we were back in the castellated ossuary of Trifels. This time, I was spared the oubliette that I had suffered before, but was instead given the comparative luxury of a small room high up in the north-west tower. At least it had a garderobe, a window and a palliasse to sleep on. Clovis and Charles were nearby, but the Lionheart was nowhere to be seen.

I wrestled with the conundrum. Did our return to Trifels mean the King was safe, or doomed? I decided that it must be good news. If he had come to an unfortunate end, there would be no reason to keep us alive, so he must still be amongst the living. However, as soon as I had come to a positive conclusion, I changed my mind. If they had murdered the King, it would look much more suspicious if we also died. Thus, we would be spared to add credibility to his 'accidental' death. Perhaps the deed would be done at Trifels at the hands of the odious Castellan.

My mind spun with the possibilities.

Two days later, all three of us were taken to a higher level in the tower.

In a simple room, but one that was a little more refined than mine, looking quite relaxed and humming a tune, was the King. This time, his greeting was reminiscent of the Lionheart I remembered. He jumped to his feet and embraced me warmly.

'Good to see you, Ranulf, if not in the most auspicious of circumstances.'

'It is good to see you, sire.'

'What did you think about Speyer; wasn't it splendid?'

'Indeed it was, my Lord. How did the Emperor get himself off the hook you put him on with your performance?'

'Very cleverly. The next day, the Archbishop gave his judgement; but the Emperor would not allow it to be announced in public. I was exonerated of all charges.'

'So, does that mean you are free to go, sire?'

The King smiled, and I realized immediately how naive my question had been.

'My dear Ranulf, you have been around the halls of power long enough to know nothing is as simple as that. The Emperor summoned me to see him in private. Only his Chamberlain and the Archbishop of Worms were there. He was furious with me, but took great satisfaction in outlining his devilish scheme.'

The King turned to the two abbots.

'You are to return to England tomorrow; listen well, you must take this news to Queen Eleanor. The Emperor is now saying that, as the charges against me have been repudiated and Leopold of Austria is now the villain of the piece, he has done the noble thing by acting as guarantor of the ransom demanded by Leopold.'

Abbot Charles saw through the ruse straight away.

'But, sire, that's tantamount to the same position as before.'

'Of course, but it gets the Emperor off the charge of being my cruel jailor and passes the opprobrium to Leopold.'

'So, my Lord, if Henry is guaranteeing the ransom, then you can go?'

'I'm afraid it's much more diabolical than that, good Abbot. The Emperor is also saying that Leopold will only accept his guarantee when the geld is delivered. And as no one other than Queen Eleanor can produce such a sum in the immediate future, I have to stay in Germany until she has arrived with a convoy of cartloads carrying enough ingots to cover Henry's pledge.'

We all looked bewildered.

'Yes, it's a semantic trick. My plight is exactly as it was before, and any man with the intelligence of a stoat can see through it. But, on the surface, it saves the Emperor's face. It's stunningly clever in its simplicity.'

The King strode to his window and looked out across the valley below and, beyond it, to the Rhine.

'So, gentlemen, make haste to Westminster and tell the Queen to stoke the furnaces and melt barrels of coins into silver ingots as fast as the smiths can toil. In the meantime, Ranulf and I will play chess and watch the summer bloom in Swabia.'

I looked at the King; all my anxieties for his future returned. Trifels was a purgatory for him and would not be eased when he discovered that I had never played chess.

As the two abbots rose to leave, the King stopped them.

'I have a scroll for you. It is for Blondel; it's a new chanson I have written for him. Songs help me with the loneliness. A few weeks ago, I heard of the treachery of two companions who were with us in the Holy Land, Geoffrey of Perche and William of Caïeux. Their lands are on the border with King Philip's French realm, and they have declared for him. This brute of a Castellan here made sure I was given the news when it arrived from Paris. So, I have written a little lament; it's rather melancholy, I'm afraid, but it reflected my mood at the time and comforted me. It's called "No Man Who's Jailed".'

He then sat in his chair and started to sing in a melodious voice with a timbre as fine as any troubadour.

Feeble the words and faltering the tongue
Wherewith a prisoner moans his doleful plight;
Yet for his comfort he may make a song.
Friends have I many, but their gifts are slight;
Shame to them if unransomed I, poor wight,
My winters languish here.

English and Normans, men of Aquitaine,
Well know they all who owe homage to me

405

That not my lowliest comrade in campaign
Should pine thus, had I gold to set him free;
To none of them would I reproachful be
Yet – I am a prisoner here!

This have I learned, here thus unransomed left,
That he whom death or prison hides from sight,
Of kinsmen and of friends is clean bereft;
Woe's me! But greater woe on these will light,
Yes, sad and full of shame will be their plight
If long I languish here.

No marvel is it that my heart is sore
While my lord tramples down the land I trow;
Were he but mindful of the oath he swore
Each to the other, surely I do know
That thus in duress I should long ago
Have ceased to languish here.

My comrades whom I loved and still do love
The lords of Perche and of Caïeux
Strange tales have reached me that are hard to prove;
I ne'er was false to them; for evermore
Vile would men count them, if their arms they bore
'Gainst me, a prisoner here.

And they, my knights of Anjou and Touraine
Well know they, who now sit at home at ease,
That I, their lord, in far-off Allemaine
Am captive. They should help to my release;
But now their swords are sheathed and rust in peace,
While I am prisoner here.

There were tears in my eyes by the time the King had finished, as there were in his. I knew that Blondel would sing it beautifully and it would soon be heard in every hall and village in the Lionheart's Empire.

Later, as the two abbots carried the King's lyrics with them to England, I wondered whether the noble Lionheart would not only be remembered as a great warrior, but also as one who could charm a hostile audience with the power of his rhetoric and write songs of great charm and poignancy.

The King had been right, his release did not come quickly. Summer blossomed, which at least brought the modest comfort of warm air to temper the frigid stone walls of Trifels, but then its fruits perished with the nip of autumn. I was allowed to visit the King every afternoon, from twelve until the beginning of the Dog Watch, at four. We were also allowed to walk around Trifels' keep every morning for an hour, the only exercise we were granted. We were closely watched by several guards, who maintained their surly demeanour week after week.

Our food was plain but had improved from our first visit, and the King regained some weight and colour. After much patient tutoring from the King, I did learn to play chess. We carved the pieces ourselves from fallen twigs we found in the bailey and scratched a board into the King's table. We gave names to all the pieces from the King's family and entourage; he took particular pride in naming his king William the Conqueror, while I named mine Harold of England. Perhaps that is why I always lost.

Eventually, the game proved to be a source of frustration rather than comfort, because I was never able to offer a serious challenge. If I took my time to try to find the right move, the Lionheart became impatient. And if I moved without sufficient thought, it led to a stupid mistake, which made him even more irritated.

We rarely saw Rudolph the Castellan, who seemed content to stay on the top floor of the keep, getting fatter and fatter. Once a week, a girl – and sometimes more than one – was brought from the local village so that he could indulge himself. These visits made our plight even more unbearable – especially when we could hear his grunting and the girls' squeals of pleasure, no matter how contrived they might have been. We sometimes played a little game in which we vied to decide whether their yelps were genuine or not. Either way, the thought of the fat Swabian pleasuring the local girls for a couple of pieces of silver was an image that did little for our peace of mind.

Eventually, the King did ask about Bérengère and whether she had become pregnant after their time together in Acre. He had hesitated to pose the question, fearing that he already knew the answer.

'I suppose you would have given me the news when you arrived, had the Queen produced a child?'

'I would have, of course, sire. Queen Eleanor thought that you should know that the Queen Bérengère miscarried the child she had conceived in the Holy Land.'

The Lionheart immediately turned and walked to the window to hide his distress. He leaned his head on its wooden jamb and stared northwards.

'Will I ever have an heir? It has been too long.'

'But she's not barren, my Lord; many women miscarry with their first child.'

I decided not to tell him about the other miscarriages; his mood was dark enough as it was.

'If we never get out of here, that imbecile of a brother will inherit the throne! I must get back to England.'

'We will be home soon, sire. The smiths are melting silver every day, and your mother is in charge; you know it will be done. We will be home by Christmas, I'm sure.'

'You know nothing about it! Don't patronize me, I'm not a bloody fool. We could rot in here until the end of my days. I would not be the first.'

Flashes of anger like that became more and more frequent as autumn's onset bit hard. Confinement was the one thing that could tame the lion in him, and he became more and more morose.

He tried to compose new chansons, but without much success, until it became another source of frustration. Eventually, he abandoned them all and just dwelt on his one chanson for Blondel, which he began to call his 'Song of Despair'. It was a thing of great charm and, although it had always been a lament, he had sung it with a sense of hope. But now he started to sing it with despair in his voice, until it became unbearable to listen to.

Once again, he became the broken man I had found at Trifels.

He began to bellow challenges to the guards and the Castellan, driving himself into incoherent rages. My daily visits offered little comfort. Although they began politely, with the usual pleasantries, they soon descended into tirades during which he would vent his spleen at me.

It became hard to bear, and I began to dread my visits.

The King's appearance deteriorated. He stopped trimming his beard and washing himself; he began to throw his food around his room and out of his window.

I feared he was losing his mind.

The grim circumstances came to a head in early September 1193. The winds and rain of autumn had brought more misery and there was still no word of the ransom being paid. I was woken in the early hours of a Wednesday morning by the King shouting insults and threats, which he had begun to do at all hours of the day and night.

I did not realize it at the time but the day was significant. It was 8 September, his birthday. He was thirty-six years old and, despite being the ruler of a vast empire and the greatest warrior in Christendom, he was alone and in despair.

It was a still night and his anguished voice rang around the valley of the River Queich like a howl from Hell. The Castellan's temper must have snapped. Doors banged, the sound of many footsteps reverberated and there was much shouting, until it became frighteningly obvious that the King was being beaten. The assault went on for some time; I heard sickening blow after sickening blow.

I banged on my door and shouted at them to stop. Eventually, I wailed, begging them to cease, but to no avail. After what seemed like an eternity, the dreadful noise from the beating ended. I heard the sound of running footsteps, and doors being slammed shut.

Then it was my turn; but I am sure my pounding did not last as long as the King's. After a few minutes, I lost consciousness and was spared more pain.

It was difficult to know whether I came round the next morning or several days later, but it was certainly early in the day. A woman who claimed to be a physician, although she more closely resembled a witch, was tending my bruises with a poultice. I only saw her that once and, ominously, she refused to tell me how the King had fared – or even whether she had seen him.

With a certainty worthy of the highest physician in the land, she told me I had several broken ribs and probably a crack in my jaw; eating and, indeed, any movement at all would be painful. Needless to say, I needed little confirmation of my injuries.

My recovery took several weeks, during which time I heard not a whisper from the Lionheart's room above mine – not even footsteps, or a door being opened. I assumed he must be dead, but then I wondered. If that were the case, why on earth was I still alive?

My apprehension about the Lionheart's welfare was salved in late October, when he reappeared at Trifels. I had recovered sufficiently to be able to take a morning walk around the keep. As I did so one cold day, with the threat of winter in the air, the portcullis was raised and a squadron of men rode in at the head of a cart. To my immense relief, the King was sitting at the back of the dray. He was manacled, but was sitting upright and looked much better than the last time I had seen him. He looked well manicured and in reasonable health, although he still seemed sullen and withdrawn.

At least he nodded at me in recognition as he was taken to his room.

*

Three days later, to my relief, I was allowed to see the King. He was calm and cogent.

'They took me to the monks at Heidelberg. They have the finest physicians in Germany there. They had nearly killed me; I spat blood for a week. On the second night, they gave me Extreme Unction. I was resigned to my death.'

'Well, sire, I can assure you that you are still here; I am delighted to see you looking so well.'

'Do you know what kept me alive? The thought of what I'm going to do to that fat bastard upstairs. He'll taste the sweetness of my revenge soon enough.'

Then he smiled at me; it was something he had not done in a long time.

'Ranulf, I am sorry that I behaved so badly, but being kept like a rat in a barrel is a torture I cannot bear.'

'I understand, sire. You were not made for confined spaces and days of idleness.'

'How were you treated?'

'Not as badly as you, just a couple of broken ribs. A witch came to see me to tend my wounds.'

The King greeted my words with another smile, this time a mischievous one, like the old days.

'Was she pretty?'

'No, sire. She was old, with a face like a gargoyle!'

'Shame.'

'Did you hear any news from the monks at Heidelberg, sire?'

'Yes, my mother has raised the ransom; she has amassed dozens of cartloads of silver. They are calling it the greatest treasure in history. Most of it has come from England. I'm growing fonder of your homeland by the day.'

These words were followed by a third smile; the lion in the man had been revived.

But our tribulations were far from over. Christmas loomed and word arrived of yet another twist in our tale.

The Castellan brought us the news, salivating as he did so.

'I have disappointing news for you. Your brother, Prince John, has been conspiring with Philip, King of the French, to extend your stay with us. Indeed, you will be delighted to hear that it is such a lucrative offer, it may give us the pleasure of your company on a permanent basis.'

His smirk was so infuriating that the King could not constrain himself from flying at the Swabian and grabbing him by the throat. It was a futile gesture. The man was a giant; with the help of four of his men, he was easily able to cast the King off. As he did so, he struck the Lionheart a vicious blow across the face.

'You should be careful, my tame lion, I may be your guardian for life. I could make your existence very unpleasant.'

The King wasn't cowed by the big man. He spat blood from his mouth and then spat out his answer at him.

'You are the one who should be careful. One day we will meet on equal terms. And when we do, I'll kill you like the fat pig that you are.'

I thought the Castellan would be provoked into yet more violence, but he had additional information, which was much more hurtful.

'Prince John has agreed a treaty with Philip of France. He has ceded the whole of eastern Normandy beyond Rouen to the French, as well as all the castles and fortifications in the border area.'

The Lionheart winced; it was the vital territory that his

Norman ancestors had fought so hard to win for over two hundred years. He had spent a fortune in recent decades fortifying and defending it. Now his brother had given it away in the blink of an eye.

'As part of their treaty, they have written to my Emperor and offered him sixty thousand pounds if he will detain you until the end of next year. Or a hundred thousand if he will hand you over to them. Your brother must be very fond of you!'

'He's a coward, just like you!'

Still not rising to the King's bait, the Castellan just turned and walked out. But as he did so, he barked an order at his guards.

'Isolate them for a week, confined to their rooms! Only one meal a day, half a ration each, and one jug of water.'

It was a difficult week, but at least it was only a week.

By the time it was over, Christmas and New Year had come and gone. I was beginning to wonder whether our stay in Trifels would, indeed, become permanent and whether the King and I would see out our days in that wretched place.

When I next saw the King, he was still in a fury about the news he had been given.

'Is there no hope we can escape from here? I must get home before that fool of a brother of mine gives away the Empire.'

'I've thought about escape every day, sire, but I think it would be easier to break into the castle than to get out. But I don't doubt the Queen; I know she will deliver the English silver soon.'

'I don't doubt my mother, either. But John will have won many friends by making big promises to them. The geld he has offered in exchange for my continued captivity is the same amount as my ransom; I fear he may have gained control of it.'

'I doubt the English will let him have it; they are so fond of you.'

'You have such faith in your English people.'

'I do, sire, but they are your people as well.'

'I suppose they are ... which reminds me. Did you retrieve what you wanted to find in Rome, the things that you said would make me fall in love with the English?'

'Yes, I did, sire.'

'Well?'

'I have read the manuscripts, and they are truly remarkable.'

'So, what do they say?'

'They tell such a long story of two families, it is hard for me to remember the details, my Lord.'

'I don't want the details, just the heart of it.'

'But, sire, it's the details that make the story. Please wait until you can hear the full account. It will be worth it, I promise.'

'Oh, very well, I've learned to trust you, as I trusted Alun. And I suppose it can't be more important than the need to get out of this place.'

Our salvation came soon afterwards in the form of a squadron of Henry's Imperial Guard which, according to its Captain, had been sent to escort us to Mainz, to appear before the Emperor once more. This time, the meeting would be held in the presence of several dignitaries from the Lionheart's Empire, including his redoubtable mother, Eleanor of Aquitaine.

Our weapons and armour were returned to us, and we were given good horses. As soon as we were ready to leave, the Lionheart turned to the Captain of the Guard.

'Am I still a prisoner?'

'Yes, sire.'

'May an imprisoned King issue a chivalrous challenge?'

The Captain hesitated a little, but then answered clearly.

'I don't see why not, my Lord.'

The King rode over to where the Castellan was standing and looked him in the eye.

'I told you that you would feel my wrath.'

He then turned back to the Captain.

'Captain, you are my witness. I challenge Rudolph of Landau to meet me in combat at Mainz; Sir Ranulf of Lancaster will be my second.'

The Captain looked at the Castellan, who was distinctly perturbed. But after composing himself, he nodded his agreement.

I was concerned that it was reckless of the Lionheart to issue a challenge to a man of little consequence – especially as he was still far from strong and healthy. But it was typical of him, and a sign that the fire had returned to his belly.

Never one to pass up the opportunity to right a wrong, or avenge a slight, the King meant to have his revenge.

30. Debauchery and Decadence

The gathering at Mainz, at the beginning of February 1194, was held in a red sandstone cathedral as imposing as its twin at Speyer, and with a similarly impressive guest list. But this time there were some significant differences.

The King was not asked to stand in front of the Emperor like a common criminal, and he looked much healthier than he had done before. He was dressed in his royal regalia, which had been brought from Westminster, and stood proudly with a large contingent from his Plantagenet Empire, the most important of whom was Eleanor, the Dowager Queen. Despite now being over seventy years of age, she was the most striking woman there.

She had personally escorted a caravan of silver bullion so large that it took a fleet of ships to get it across the Channel and an army 2,000 strong to escort it from its landfall in Antwerp. With her were many of the great and good of the land. England's Chancellor, William Longchamp, who had been battling with Prince John for years to keep him at bay and had helped Eleanor raise the ransom, was on her right. On her left stood Walter of Coutances, Archbishop of Rouen, and Savaric of Bohun, Bishop of Bath. Flanking them in their finery were all five of the Grand Quintet, the finest soldiers in Christendom, beaming at the King from ear to ear.

Perhaps the most heart-warming presence for me was the dozen members of the King's personal conroi, from Westminster. Men from my own corps, they were Englishmen to a man; all were over six feet tall and looked immaculate in their red mantles. They stood as a guard of honour behind the Queen who, as usual, wore a dazzling, pure-white kirtle and cape.

To the King's great satisfaction, facing him on the opposite side of the Emperor Henry were not only the same nobles who had heard his stirring speech at Speyer, but also his nemesis, Leopold, Duke of Austria. The King made sure to catch his eye whenever he could, and on each occasion he smiled broadly at him, rubbing salt into the wounds of his liberation and his public shaming of Leopold at Speyer.

There was little drama in the formal proceedings at Mainz, other than the flamboyant kiss of peace delivered by the Emperor to the Lionheart as he handed a Plantagenet son back to the bosom of the dynasty's grand matriarch. It was an egregious act the King later called the most expensive kiss in history.

Eleanor said nothing; her serenity and dignity spoke volumes, as did her fortitude in making the recovery of her son her personal crusade. Her great resilience was not lost on her German audience.

There was also a moment of mocking humour from the Lionheart when Henry gave the King a copy of the letter he had received from his brother, Prince John, and King Philip, offering a huge inducement to detain the Lionheart in Germany. The King laughed out loud as he read it, and exclaimed at the end.

'I must applaud my brother's assessment of my worth. All the silver in England; what a compliment he pays me! I will be sure to thank him when I see him.'

There was just one more issue to resolve for the Lionheart before we left the Holy Roman Empire. He dealt with it early the next morning, on Mainz's Champ de Mars. The King had told few people about his challenge to Rudolph of Landau and there were no more than a dozen people present.

The Lionheart did not want any public accolades, just vengeance. A duel with swords and shields was agreed.

Just before the men came to blows, a priest from the cathedral appeared, an emissary from the Emperor.

'Sire, the Emperor asks that you show mercy to the Castellan; he was only doing what was asked of him.'

The King was blunt in his response.

'Tell the Emperor that I hope the Castellan was doing far more than was required of him. Even so, he should be comforted in knowing that I will show the man the same mercy he offered me and that I will return to him in equal measure the courtesies he extended to me.'

Rudolph of Landau looked terrified. He knew he had little chance against the legendary warrior, and that he would be given no quarter. But he had no choice; the challenge had been made in front of one of the Emperor's captains and could not have been declined.

No words were exchanged between them. The King had said all that needed to be said at Trifels.

The Castellan carried a huge longsword, longer and heavier than any I had ever seen. It made no difference.

Even though the King was debilitated by over a year of harsh treatment, he parried his opponent's wild swings with ease. The Lionheart was far nimbler than the Swabian – especially in coordinating his blade and his shield – and he was soon able to get under the arc of the man's attempted blows. The King's deadly thrust came quickly, as he bent one knee and plunged his blade deep into the ample gut of the German.

The big man fell to his knees, mortally wounded.

The Lionheart removed his blade as the Castellan looked at him with the woeful eyes of a dying stag. His plaintive expression did not incline the King to hesitate; he took a mighty swing, which almost severed his adversary's head.

The Lionheart had already turned, and had taken a stride, by the time Rudolph of Landau hit the ground with a heavy thud.

The King did not look back.

Preparations were soon made for our long procession up the Rhine. The King wanted to thank his old friend, Adolf, Bishop of Cologne, who had helped Queen Eleanor in her negotiations with the Emperor, and so planned to spend a few days with him. When I heard that, I asked the King for permission to travel to Rupertsberg to see Negu.

He was effusive in his response.

'Of course, my friend. If the flame still burns brightly between you, bring her back to England. I promised you a future when we return; there is one for both of you, if you wish. She can have a nuns' foundation in parallel with the one I intend to create for Abbot Alun. It is the least I can do.'

'Thank you, sire. Let's see if an ageing, one-armed knight appeals to her as much as I did when I was a young man.'

'Worry not, Ranulf, you're a hero of the Great Crusade, of England and of the Empire. Besides, when we return home, you will be a rich man; that is usually a key to unlocking a woman's heart. I have some favours to call in while I am in the Low Countries, and intend to sail for England from Antwerp in the second week of March. Meet me there.'

My life, and that of the King, had suddenly taken a dramatic turn for the better – especially in contrast with the black days we had just been through.

The journey to Rupertsberg gave me time to reflect. I was weary of travel in distant lands and of the toils of war. The thought of rekindling my passion for Negu suddenly became very appealing. It would need to be a clandestine arrangement if she wanted to continue as a nun. But if the Lionheart was true to his promise, and would create a foundation for her within my lands in the north of England, we could control our own destiny. Although they had turned sixty and would now be in their dotage, my mother and father were still alive, as far as I knew. I was desperate to see them before they died and make them part of my peaceful future within the King's Empire. I wanted to tell them about my adventures and see them take pride in what I had done.

My life with the Lionheart had been an astonishing journey for me. There had been much hardship and not a little pain, but what I had gained in return was worth almost any price. The loss of Alun and my absence from my parents were my only real regrets, but I had become reconciled to both. Losing Negu was also a blow, although it had been her choice and one that was, under the circumstances, inevitable. Perhaps, now that things had changed—

But then I pinched myself; a new beginning with Negu was an unlikely prospect. I had not seen her for years, and much had happened to both of us in the meantime.

I was full of nerves when I reached Hildegard's famous foundation at Rupertsberg, especially when I announced myself at the gates and asked for Sister Negu. I had washed and cleaned the Hospitaller's mantle and cape I still wore, and had trimmed my hair and beard. The young novitiates on duty scurried inside, giggling as they went, making me feel like a young knight paying his first call at the household of the young maiden he wished to court.

I was asked to wait in the cloisters, where I sat and watched the nuns quietly at prayer. I was the subject of a few stares and whispers – and, no doubt, much speculation about my hook for a hand.

'I am told a mighty crusader is here to see me.'

The voice came from behind and startled me.

'They said you look like you have fought many battles . . . and that you only have one arm.'

Negu had hardly aged. I could only see her face, framed tightly by her wimple, but it had almost no wrinkles. Her eyes shone brightly, her figure seemed trim and she had the self-confident bearing of a mature woman of the Church.

'I see I find you well; you have obviously flourished here at Rupertsberg.'

'I have, indeed. I see that you have also prospered, if with a few scars to prove it.'

'They are a price worth paying; I have had my share of adventures.'

She took my good arm.

'Come, let's walk. We'll find a quiet place in the garden. The gossip will be halfway round the women already that Sister Negu's lover has returned.'

We walked and talked for over an hour. We shared a restrained embrace and exchanged fifteen years' worth of stories. She laughed at my escapades; I smiled at her achievements.

That evening, she arranged for us to eat together in private in one of the small chapels of the monastery.

'I will always be grateful that you brought me here. Otherwise, I would have been a rich man's whore – until I was thrown in the midden as too old – or dead from the pox.'

'Will you stay here?'

'Why do you ask?'

'I'm just curious.'

'What about you?'

'King Richard has given me some land in the north of England, near my childhood home. He's promised me some more when we return. I want to see my parents; as far as I know, they are still alive.'

'No wife to take home with you, then?'

'No, there has been no time for women in my life.'

'I find that hard to believe.'

'Well, a few local girls to calm the beast from time to time.'

'Of course! But no serious romances?'

'Just one, a princess . . . but only a single tryst. She was murdered when I was supposed to be protecting her. It took me a long time to get over it.'

'It sounds like her memory still haunts you.'

Negu was right, of course, but I changed the subject. It was my turn to question her.

'And how have you coped with celibacy?'

Negu's expression suddenly changed. Her animated demeanour became very serious.

'I'd like you to do something for me.'

'What would you like me to do?'

'Go away and leave me in peace.'

I was mortified.

'Don't look so worried, it's just for a day; I need time for reflection. Come back tomorrow evening, and I will arrange for us to eat here again.'

'But I've only just arrived—'

'I know, but you've suddenly walked back into my life after fifteen years. There is so much to think about. I suppose I should say that I need to pray. But whatever it is, I need time to do it.'

'Negu, you are the one who took the decision to stay here.'

'I know, Ranulf, but please do as I ask. We can talk again tomorrow.'

A little bewildered, I nevertheless did as she asked and found a room in the village.

After a sleepless night, I spent the next day wandering

the banks of the Rhine, my mind in a turmoil, wondering what conclusions Negu was coming to.

When I arrived back at the monastery gates, I was even more anxious than I had been before. Negu also seemed tense when we met, and our dinner together began awkwardly. I feared the worst.

She had poured several cups of Rupertsberg's famed kirsch before she began to relax. Then she took a deep breath and I sensed that our reunion was destined to be short and platonic.

'Last night you asked me how I had coped with celibacy.'

'I did, and I'm sorry if I upset you. I was thinking like the young lovers we once were.'

'So was I. And I was enjoying it; I felt like a woman again. That's why I asked you to go. I'm third in the hierarchy here, I'm not supposed to feel aroused by crusaders who come calling.'

'I'm sorry.'

'Don't be; you haven't taken a vow of celibacy. And I'm flattered that you think I'm still attractive.'

She smiled sweetly and rather uncertainly, then stared into her almost empty cup of kirsch before filling it to the brim and quaffing a deep draught of it.

'So . . . you asked me about celibacy last night.'

'It doesn't matter, it was wrong of me to ask.'

'It does matter. The truth is, I don't deal with it at all well. There was a young monk a few years ago. He was sweet and very handsome, but I had to stop it; it became too dangerous. Then there was Philip of Heinsberg,

Archbishop of Cologne, one of Barbarossa's favourite warriors, a Prince Bishop who owned half of Germany. He died last year, but four years ago he started inviting me to his Palace for "meditation". I was flattered and eventually gave in. He treated me well, but I soon realized I was just his harlot – one of many. Since then, there have been others, but I've managed to slowly rid myself of male suitors over the past two years.'

'And now you are content?'

'No, my feelings are locked away, dormant.'

She smiled again, this time holding my gaze without embarrassment. I was beginning to feel aroused, in a profound way that I had not experienced for a long time, and, to my delight, knew that the old fire still burned in both of us.

'When I heard that I had missed you, after you called last year, my heart missed several beats. I'm very pleased you came back.'

'So am I.'

'How long can you stay?'

'I have to meet the King at Antwerp. We sail for England in the second week of March.'

'Will you stay until then?'

'Of course.'

'Tell me, besides your left hand, have you lost any other parts of your anatomy?'

It felt like we had been playing a teasing game of sexual chess, and I had just been put into checkmate.

It was a good game to lose.

Over the next few days we consummated our reborn passion many times; it was gloriously debauched and decadent. It was as if the years had not passed and we were in Aquitaine again.

Although Negu broke her vows in every way imaginable, she was very adamant about the morality of it. For her, being a nun was about the good deeds done by the nuns of Hildegard's foundation, about the beauty of the music they sang and about the knowledge and wisdom she had acquired at Rupertsberg. Chastity was a nonsensical rigour imposed by the Church. Negu had no doubt that Hildegard would have approved.

As for my part, I was simply happy to have fallen in love again – and with a woman with whom I wanted to spend the rest of my life.

Although we were discreet, rumours abounded within the community and Negu was summoned to see the Abbess. It was the ideal moment for me to reveal the future that the King had promised to make available to us in England.

Negu had, of course, remembered Alun. I explained to her how he had become a close friend and adviser to the King, and I described the tragedy of his death. When I told her that the Lionheart had promised to create a foundation in his honour, and that she could be part of it, she leapt with joy at the prospect.

'We follow the rule of St Augustine of Hippo here. I have reached the rank of Conventual Prioress, one level below an abbess, so I can govern a priory of nuns in my own right.'

'Whose permission do you need?'

'I don't need anyone's sanction – except God's, of course – but I do need the funds to buy the land, and some women to come with me.'

'Well, if you can bring the nuns, the King will provide the geld.'

'There are fifty women here who will follow me to the ends of the earth. Finding some monks, and an abbot to lead them, should be easy along the Rhine; there are dozens of monasteries, most of them overcrowded.'

'In that case, what are you waiting for?'

'Nothing, my love. The conversation with the Abbess should be fairly straightforward. When she starts asking difficult questions, I'll be able to tell her I'm leaving.'

'How long will it take you to be ready to leave with your monks and nuns?'

'About three months.'

'That will give me enough time to make good the offer from the King. I will send three ships to Antwerp to collect you, at the beginning of June; I'll give full instructions to the Master of the Harbour before I leave.'

As I made my way north from Rupertsberg, I reflected on the strange paradoxes of life. Had the Lionheart not been captured in Austria and imprisoned on the Rhine, I would never have seen Negu again.

Fate plays its hand in strange ways.

31. Return of the King

The Lionheart spent his remaining time in Germany and the Low Countries building on the friendships he had won by his performance at Speyer. Many in Europe now realized that his deeds in the Holy Land had been misrepresented by those with an axe to grind. Word travelled to realms far and wide that, in truth, he had been the only Christian leader to act with courage and tenacity against Saladin.

We sailed from Antwerp on 11 March, aboard a ceremonial fleet sent by Queen Eleanor. After a pause to wait for the winds and tide on the coast, we arrived at Sandwich, in Kent, on the morning of 13 March 1194, an auspicious day for all of us. It was the Sabbath, and we rode to Canterbury to give thanks for our safe arrival.

News spread quickly that the King had landed. At Ash, close to Sandwich, people rushed out to wave as we rode through. Astute as ever, the Queen made sure that heralds rode ahead of us to announce the King's return. From Wingham onwards, especially at Littlebourne and Canterbury itself, the scenes were reminiscent of his coronation five years before; every hamlet, village and burgh gave us a rapturous welcome.

The Lionheart was overjoyed, and turned to me with a broad grin on his face.

'I have just cost these people a quarter of their livelihood!'

'I told you they loved you, sire.'

It was true; he was the Lionheart, their King, a man who shared their blood. If only they knew just how much.

When we reached Westminster, where the people lined the route cheering wildly, we were greeted with heartening news. Prince John had hidden himself away in Normandy on hearing the news of his brother's release, leaving his supporters in England isolated. As a result, all those who had plotted with him against the King had capitulated and declared their loyalty to the Lionheart; all save one. The garrison at Nottingham refused to believe that the King had returned.

Itching for a fight against any traitors he could find, the Lionheart acted quickly.

'Mobilize my cavalry! Bring the sappers and the Greek fire, we have work to do.'

The siege did not last long. Initially, the defenders refused to surrender, claiming that the man wearing the Three Lions on his mantle was an imposter, sent to trick them. The King was furious and, as he had done all his life, led us in an attack on the barbican.

After the sappers destroyed the heavy oak doors of the barbican with a huge battering ram, the Lionheart pulled down his helmet and charged forwards. He had lost little of his speed and agility and, as usual, it was difficult to keep pace with him.

As he reached the arch of the barbican roof, he suddenly gave the signal to crouch down and, in that moment, a volley of crossbow bolts passed over our heads from the platoon of arbalests he had positioned behind us. A bolt from a crossbow at close quarters is a fearsome weapon and several defenders were taken clean off their feet from the impact, while several others ran for cover.

Then the Lionheart resumed his charge. I could see the look of horror on the faces of the defenders when they realized that the man wearing the Three Lions was indeed their King.

The fighting was ferocious, but brief. The Lionheart made a beeline for a huge sergeant, who took an almighty swing at him as he approached. This was a fatal move against a swordsman as skilled as the King. He simply ducked under the arc of the blade and thrust his own sword deep into the man's ribs, just below his right arm. The blood spewed across the courtyard and the big man let out a squeal like a stuck pig.

The fight seemed to go out of our opponents at that point, and they began to surrender. There were a dozen or so bodies at our feet, and several injured men. Among the dead was William of Wendenal, High Sheriff of Nottingham and the Royal Forests, a long-time supporter of Prince John.

Frustratingly, despite the loss of their barbican, the defenders within the castle still refused to surrender, and the main castle gate remained closed.

The King turned to me, smiling.

'More sport tomorrow.'

Then he gave instructions for the bodies of the fallen – men who, despite their traitorous allegiance to Prince John, were still his subjects – to be removed with due ceremony and respect, before ordering his men to set up camp for the night.

The next day, when we began to build one of the huge siege engines used in the Holy Land and to prepare the Greek fire, the castle gates opened. Leading out the garrison were the last two rebels who had allied themselves to Prince John's cause: Robert Brito and Hugh of Nonant. They were both lords of little consequence who, like many others, had gambled that the King would not return from his captivity.

They fell to their knees and begged the Lionheart for forgiveness, which he duly granted. Not only that: he stepped forward and lifted both of them from the ground.

'Go to Prince John in Normandy; tell him that he has nothing to fear from his brother, who loves him dearly. Reassure him that, for the future of England and the Empire, he will be treated with magnanimity, as I have treated you.'

After the breaking of the siege, the King called a Great Council of the realm to gather at Nottingham and then, while the preparations were being made, we went hunting in the Forest of Sherwood. Propitiously, the land was owned by Earl Harold. I learned that it had been a gift from the Lionheart's great-grandfather, a grateful King Henry Beauclerc, while the Earl was in his service.

Two days later, when we were deep in the forest and relaxing by a camp fire, the King handed me a sealed scroll.

'These are the deeds to Earl Harold's estates. He holds much of this forest, but also land at Barnsdale and Loxley

Chase. These estates are yours now; he had no heirs, so it is only right that they should go to you.'

I was shocked and delighted.

'I am so grateful, my Lord. You are more than generous.'

'Not at all, you deserve it. The income will give you a life of comfort; after what you have been through on my behalf, that's the least you should expect. I must also make good my promise to establish a foundation for Abbot Alun. Will you help me with that?'

'I will, indeed, sire. In fact, may I offer you an ideal solution?'

He looked at me inquisitively.

'Do I sense that you have hatched a plot, and that it may involve the beautiful Negu?'

'I have and it does, my Lord. My rendezvous with Negu at Rupertsberg exceeded my wildest dreams. In fact, with your agreement, we would like to establish a foundation in memory of Alun. She holds the status of Prioress in the Rule of St Augustine and can easily recruit a prior, monks and nuns from the Rhine to begin a new community.'

'A cunning scheme, my friend.'

The Lionheart laughed heartily, and put his arm around my shoulder.

'And if this foundation happened to be near your lands in the north, where you and Negu could enjoy communion together on a regular basis, that would be, as you put it, "an ideal solution"?'

'Something like that, my Lord.'

He then laughed again, with even more gusto.

'Let me speak with Roger de Lacy, Lord of Bowland; he's a good man and owns most of the lands north of the Ribble. I'm sure he can find you a place where a community can flourish.'

We hunted well in the ancient Forest of Sherwood, and it was a time of unbounded happiness for me. I had brought the King home safely, he had regained control of England, and it looked like Negu and I would have a life together.

I had only one more task to perform, which was to complete my undertaking to Earl Harold and pass on his casket to the King.

But for that, I had to wait for the right moment.

At the Council of Nottingham, which began on 30 March 1194, the King made secure the resumption of his authority over England. He appointed nineteen new men to be sheriffs of the domain's twenty-eight shires, all of which produced substantial income for the Exchequer. He also accepted a large number of pleas and requests from plaintiffs and made numerous other appointments. They were mostly petitions that had not been pursued while Prince John held sway – because men did not trust him – and they brought more new income. At the end of the Council, William Longchamp, the King's Chancellor, announced that Winchester's treasury held 25,292 pounds in gold and silver, a large increase over the previous year's amount.

As the Council closed and the King thanked everybody for their attendance and loyalty, he raised his sword and proclaimed loudly.

'Now to Normandy, to deal with the lamentable King of the French!'

He called me over a little later, still beaming about the geld he held at Winchester.

'You were right, my friend, this is a land of good and loyal people. Not only that, it is rich and pays its taxes. I have a sufficient war chest to meet Philip Augustus head on and win back what John has given away. I have mobilized the army and called out the Grand Quintet. I am seeing William the Lion at Southwell Minster next week, to make sure he and his Scottish lords still support me, and then I will sail to Normandy. A fleet of a hundred ships is gathering at Portsmouth – a new port I am creating in the west – ready for the crossing to Barfleur.'

'Very well, sire, I will be ready.'

'No, Ranulf, not this time. Get Negu established in the north first. She will need your help; it is a lawless part of the world, but one that you know well. You are to take a two-year sabbatical, then you can join me.'

'But, sire, your campaign could be over by then.'

'I doubt it; the border with the French is not like England. Loyalty means nothing there. With Philip's meddling and John's duplicity, it will take me years to bring them to heel.'

'I hope this does not mean the end of my service to you?'

'Of course not, I will always be in need of your wisdom and your friendship.'

The King put his hands on my shoulders and embraced me warmly.

'Come, I want you to meet Roger de Lacy; he has some news for you.'

The Lord of Bowland was a direct descendant of one of William the Conqueror's warriors at Senlac Ridge and the epitome of the formidable Norman warlord of the past.

'Ah, Sir Ranulf, the King has told me about you. I would be honoured to have you as a tenant.'

'The honour would be all mine, my Lord.'

'The King tells me that you want to bring to the north a prioress from the community of Hildegard of Bingen?'

'Indeed, my Lord.'

'And that she is not only a woman of similar worth to the good Abbess Hildegard, but is also very beautiful?'

'She is, and a very devout woman of high repute.'

'So I hear.'

He cast a mischievous glance at the King.

'Well, I have the ideal place for you. It's in the valley of the Wharfe, at Bolton, just north of Skipton. The land is held by Hawise, Countess of Aumale, daughter of my cousin Alice of Romille, my vassal at Skipton Castle. She has just married again and is so rich from her holdings in Normandy, she can spare a small estate in the distant north. It has enough arable land along the valley for a reasonable community to thrive, and there is grazing for sheep that extends high on to the moors above. Will that do?'

'It will, my Lord; I am most grateful.'

'Very well, my steward will draw up the documents. The King has told me that you saved his life more than once and went through the purgatory of prison with him. That being so, you will have the tenancy at two-thirds of the price.'

'Thank you, my Lord.'

We shook hands and the King placed his gauntlet over them.

'Be good to one another and honour all your deeds and duties.'

That evening, at the feast to close the Council of Nottingham, Blondel sang the chansons of the troubadours. They included the 'Ballad of Robyn of Hode', which had become a favourite with the army. I smiled nostalgically, because I now knew from reading Earl Harold's story that it had been composed by his faithful companion, Eadmer, and that the deeds described in the ballad were those of the Earl himself.

Blondel also sang the King's lament, 'No Man Who's Jailed', which he performed beautifully and captivated the audience. I looked at the King, and saw the pain of those many months in captivity pass fleetingly across his face; our memories of Trifels were still raw.

On 17 April 1194, the Sunday after Easter, in the presence of his mother, Dowager Queen Eleanor, and William the Lion, King of the Scots, the Lionheart had his coronation reaffirmed at Winchester. All the prelates, earls, barons and knights of the realm came to pay homage to the greatest warrior in Europe.

Flanked by the Grand Quintet and led, with his sword held high, by William the Lion, the King wore the royal crown and full regalia as he walked from his royal chamber in St Swithun's Priory into the cathedral to be blessed by Godfrey, Bishop of Winchester. Prayers were said for his campaign against Philip and the French, after which a splendid feast was held in the cathedral cloisters.

The mood was jubilant, a celebration for the return of a King they thought they had lost.

It was a heartwarming moment for me too, and so reminiscent of the Lionheart's original coronation on that wonderful September day in 1189. The occasion was not as grand, but much more poignant.

So much had happened in the intervening years. I looked at the King's imposing but elegant frame and watched as the guests stared at him, in awe of his presence. Many had tears in their eyes; so did I.

Following the coronation celebrations, while the Lionheart made his way to Portsmouth to assemble his fleet, I obtained his permission to travel to St Paul's to retrieve Earl Harold's casket.

I wanted him to read its contents before he left for France and, if he could be persuaded, to wear the Talisman of Truth during his campaign against Philip.

I arrived back in Portsmouth on May Day with the burgh in the midst of the ancient festival. The King was enjoying lunch with Queen Eleanor when I arrived; I was honoured that she spoke to me directly.

'Sir Ranulf, I have heard how important you were to the King in Germany. I owe you as much as he does, which is a great deal.'

'Ma'am, it is a privilege to serve you and the King.'

'I hear that you are taking some time away from his retinue to begin a foundation in the north. Perhaps I could visit it one day. I have never been beyond the Welsh Marches, but the King tells me the weather can be unkind.'

'Not to someone with your constitution, ma'am.'

The Lionheart smiled at my fawning over his mother.

'So, you have finally brought the casket?'

'Yes, sire. I left it with your steward.'

'I will look forward to reading it.'

I knew that the King's Latin was excellent, so I waited expectantly for several days in the hope that he had begun. I saw him daily as he busied himself, in his typically meticulous way, with every detail of the preparation of the fleet, but nothing was mentioned.

He and his quartermasters counted every component of his siege engines. All the reams of quarrels and arrows were accounted for and loaded and every horse, soldier and sailor was placed on a roll call which was read every morning. I decided he was far too busy to spend hours reading two manuscripts of vellum as thick as a man's thigh.

But then, on 10 May, just two days before his embarkation, he summoned me to join him for dinner at the new hall he had had built at Portsmouth Harbour. To my surprise, the Dowager Queen was with him.

'Ranulf, welcome; sit and eat with us.'

Until the stewards cleared away the dishes, leaving us with just wine and cheese, normal conviviality ruled during the meal. Then his senior steward brought in the casket, placed it next to the King and opened its lid.

'Well, my friend, I started these reluctantly; there are so many pages. It was only out of respect for Alun that I persevered. But, eventually, they became compelling.'

'I know, sire; my Latin is not as good as yours, so I struggled to grasp the details.'

'But you knew what they contained from Alun?'

'Yes, but he was only able to impart the barest outline as he lay dying.'

'I now understand why you and he drew such inspiration from these stories. They are remarkable.'

'That is why I wanted you to read them before we went our separate ways.'

'I have told the Queen the gist of what these pages contain.'

She looked at me sternly.

'Sir Ranulf, who else knows what is in the manuscripts?'

I decided not to mention the two young Tuscan monks sworn to secrecy at the monastery of Sant'Antimo.

'Just the three of us, ma'am.'

'Well, that is how it must remain.'

I felt the strength in her that overpowered everyone who met her. Her next question was typically shrewd.

'Can we be sure the contents are a true account?'

'I believe so, ma'am, there are too many worthy scribes involved for them to be false.'

'I want the casket and its contents burned, but the King is prevailing upon me not to do so. He says they are too important to be destroyed.'

The King was quick to offer reassurance.

'Of course they are, mother. Earl Harold is my grandfather and I am a direct descendant of Hereward of Bourne, the bravest man this island has ever produced. We should be proud; apart from his courage here in England fighting the Conqueror, he fought with the Normans of Sicily, was Captain of the Emperor of Byzantium's Varangian Guard and was a friend of El Cid.'

'Yes, yes, Richard, but the stories in those manuscripts must never be told.'

'Why not? Sweyn of Bourne, Earl Harold's father and my great-grandfather, was one of the heroes of the First Crusade; he took the lance intended for Robert Curthose at the Battle of Tinchebrai!'

'Yes, so you told me, but he conceived Earl Harold in the desert with Hereward's daughter, Estrith, who was an Abbess of the Norman Church!'

'Well?'

'That makes him the bastard child of a nun and a peasant boy from Lincolnshire! Not only that: this account says that all three of Empress Matilda's children were sired by Earl Harold, not by Geoffrey of Anjou.'

The Queen's point suddenly hit home with the King, whose judgement had become dulled by the excitement of his newly found lineage. He looked saddened.

'Perhaps we should burn them, after all.'

The Queen slammed closed the lid of the casket.

'Of course we should. Not only was your grandfather a bastard, whose own grandfather's English Brotherhood fought Norman rule until their dying breaths, but he cuckolded Geoffrey of Anjou and fathered Empress Matilda's three sons, all of them bastards! One of whom was my husband and your father!'

She was livid, furious that the purity of her noble blood had been sullied.

'Our family is full of peasants and rebels! What's worse, I've been tupped by one of them and have borne him eight children!'

She drew a deep breath and calmed herself down. Then she looked the Lionheart in the eye.

'Bastards don't become kings any more; your legitimacy as ruler of this Empire could be challenged by all and sundry, if these pages were ever to be revealed.'

The King looked forlorn.

'I suppose you're right. It appears that our great Plantagenet Empire is not even Plantagenet.'

'Exactly.'

My head was spinning by the time the King turned to me.

'What do you think, my old friend? You've carried these secrets for long enough.'

'It is difficult to answer, sire. England's story means so much to me, and I am proud of what has been done by the men and women in those manuscripts.'

The Queen flashed a mien of anger that was fierce enough to make a flower wilt.

'It's got nothing to do with Sir Ranulf. If I had my way, his head would come off and the secret would die with him!'

The King stared into his goblet of wine and looked at his mother.

'Worry not, Ranulf, the Queen doesn't mean it. You are an old and trusted friend. I will think about it overnight. Come back tomorrow morning.'

Although I was reassured by the King, I had no doubts that the Dowager Queen had meant exactly what she had said.

I saw the King early the next day. He was already dashing around the harbour issuing orders with a dozen scribes, sappers and stewards in his wake.

He took me to one side.

'Ranulf, I need your trust in this. I have told the Queen that I have done the sensible thing and that the casket and its contents have been destroyed. However, I cannot bring myself to do it. It is my story and I care not a jot for my legitimacy as King or otherwise; let any man try to take this Empire from me. After all, there was no greater bastard than William the Conqueror. I want the manuscripts preserved so that one day, perhaps, the real story can be told.'

'Sire, tell me what you want me to do and it will be done.'

'My Senior Steward has wrapped the casket in plain sackcloth and put it on a good sumpter. Take it with you and when you lay the slab of your new altar at Negu's priory, protect it well in lead and bury it deep in the ground. It matters not if it isn't found for a thousand years, but one day the deeds of Hereward's Brotherhood and Edgar's Brethren will finally be revealed to all.'

'Your third cousin would be thrilled to know of your decision.'

'Is that my relation to Alun?'

'Yes, your great-great-grandparents were brother and sister; Edgar the Aethling on Alun's side and Margaret of Scotland on your side.'

'Astonishing! You always said I would fall in love with England.'

'Go safely, sire.'

'Thank you. I go first to Bérengère; I'm afraid she is not well, and I fear she may not be able to give me an heir.'

'I am sorry to hear that, my Lord.'

'My mother says I should divorce her, but I am too fond of her for that.'

'I will pray that all may be well.'

'Thank you, we all pray for that.'

'There is one more thing, sire.'

I took out the leather pouch containing the Talisman of Truth.

'I hoped you would wear this?'

'I will, at all times and with great pride, my friend.'

It was a moment of mixed emotions for me. I was elated and relieved that I had finally completed my mission for Earl Harold, but I was also saddened to think that my astonishing adventures at the right hand of the most noble and courageous man in Christendom were at an end.

I also thought of Alun, at rest in what I hoped had become a place of beauty for him in Anatolia, cleansed of the horrors of his death. He would be so proud of the Lionheart, and so proud of England under his new reign.

32. Bolton Priory

I met Negu and her little band of brothers and sisters at Sandwich in early June 1194. She had brought Magnus, a very austere-looking prior who seemed to take his devotions very seriously, and in their wake, like a badelynge of ducklings, walked thirteen tonsured monks and nine wimpled nuns. All were under thirty years old and – other than the prior – were a good-humoured bunch.

Negu was in good spirits and, thankfully, England was at its best for our journey, with long June days and warm sunshine, so I did not have to make excuses for the weather in the north. That would have to come later.

The Lord of Bowland's land by the Wharfe was a paradise. The river was wide and full of trout, and the meadows by its banks were flat and fertile. Its high ground extended on to wild moorland but was perfect for hardy upland sheep. Skipton, only five miles away, was a small, remote burgh, but it had a good market and a robust garrison to keep us safe from the occasional raiders who still roamed the wastes of the far north.

We chose our ground for the priory's buildings, and after employing local carpenters to build us temporary wooden buildings we began the process of buying stone and hiring masons. Good masons were not difficult to find, because many of the cathedrals and castles begun by the Normans two and three generations ago had now been finished, or were nearing completion.

Negu brought a nest egg of geld from Germany, most of it given to her by local bishops who prized her charms. I had inherited a significant sum derived from the income of Earl Harold's lands in Nottinghamshire. Roger de Lacy's generosity continued, and he gave us a hundred pounds, while the Countess of Aumale donated thirty pounds and Hugh, the Castellan of Skipton, a further twenty pounds. By late October, the footings had been dug and the foundation level of local millstone grit was in place. It was a sight to behold, and we were very proud of it.

The community of young Germans were happy in their new surroundings; they soon made themselves popular with the locals by bringing much-needed work and trade, and by offering vital succour for the sick and needy.

I began the construction of a hall for myself on higher ground, to the north of the priory. But until it was ready, Negu and I enjoyed our trysts together in the seclusion of the nearby woods, or hidden in the gorse of the desolate moors. Our excuse was the search for medicinal herbs, but I was aware that this arrangement caused Negu some anguish, and she often reminded me that the subterfuge could not continue indefinitely.

When the hall was completed, Negu felt that she could finally relinquish her obligation to her mentor, Hildegard, and to her order of nuns. She gave up her habit and renounced her vows in a solemn gathering of her Bolton community. Her companions understood her reasons, and there was only support and understanding from them.

Freed from her obligations, we were able to rekindle the passion we had shared at our reunion in Rupertsberg. Becoming intimate again proved a delight; our couplings were not quite as frenetic as in the early months, but they were just as fulfilling.

When we had first met, as young lovers, we were both finding our way in the world, using whatever gifts we had been granted to better ourselves, and our love was an all-consuming passion. Now, we had both achieved so much in life, and our rediscovered love was much more mature – still passionate, but based on the wisdom that comes with a lifetime of experience.

Winter came and went, and the building work on the priory made rapid progress. The walls of the nave had risen to a height of almost four yards, and the community's refectory and accommodation were nearing completion.

In the summer of 1195, Geoffrey Plantagenet, Archbishop of York, the Lionheart's illegitimate half-brother, came to bless the foundation stone of our altar.

Before he arrived, Negu and I made our preparations to put Earl Harold's precious casket to rest. Two nights before the service, we stayed up late, drank some wine, and then made our way to the place where the altar slab would be laid. I had borrowed one of the masons' spades and, while Negu held a lantern, I dug a deep hole for the lead box and its casket and placed it in the earth.

I covered it with a piece of linen and then a heavy shroud of sackcloth, and began to replace the soil and rubble. It was an emotional moment, tinged with a strong sense of melancholy. It marked the end of a long saga for

Hereward and his family. Their legacy lived on, of course, embodied in the King himself, but it felt as if their personal journey was now over. They had fulfilled everything England could have expected of them, and they could now rest in peace.

I assumed that one day, perhaps many generations hence, the casket would be found. I smiled to myself, imagining the look of astonishment on the faces of those who would then read its contents.

Negu knelt down beside me and held my hand.

'I am very proud of you, Ranulf. You have served your King as well as any man could have done. You have also done a great service to Earl Harold and his family, and to your country. I am lucky to have met you, and even more fortunate that you came back to find me.'

'Thank you, my darling. I am the lucky one. What a life I have had! And now I have even more to look forward to, with you.'

On the day of the ceremony, Roger de Lacy and several local knights and burgesses accompanied the Archbishop of York. He placed a clay ampoule of holy water and a cross in the earth before the stone slab was laid, and then consecrated the ground so that mass could be said.

As the mass came to an end, and the Archbishop gave his final blessing, Negu and I gripped each other's hands tightly. We were both smiling broadly; the rest of the gathering were also smiling, in celebration of a special moment, as a new abbey became sanctified.

But we had even more reason to celebrate. Hereward and his descendants were all at rest, and now their story had been enshrined in a holy place.

It was a fitting location. The mighty Einar, one of Hereward's loyal companions who died during the Siege of Ely, had been born only a few miles away, at Skipton. Not only that: Hereward would have passed by this very spot on his journeys to and from York during his campaigns against the Conqueror, in 1069.

We could not have chosen a better place.

Our life of bliss continued into 1196 when, in May of that year, a squadron of the King's Guard at Westminster rode up from Skipton. They looked splendid in their royal finery and immediately stirred in me fond memories of my time with the King.

'Sir Ranulf, greetings; I am Thomas, Captain of the King's Second Conroi at Westminster.'

'Welcome to Bolton Priory, Captain. You are an Englishman?'

'I am, and proud of it. The King is encouraging Englishmen to join his Guard, thanks – if I may say so – to you, Sir Ranulf.'

'Well, I'm gratified to hear that. But how can I help you?'

'The King has sent word from Rouen. He requests that you join him there before Midsummer's Day. He has a commission for you.'

'I hope it is not a crisis?'

'No, indeed, his campaign against the French is going well. I believe he wants you to help him with a new fortification.'

'Then tell him that I will be with him directly and will be honoured to serve him again.'

449

'We are to wait and be your escort; we are billeted at Skipton.'

'Very well, I'll need two days to organize a few things here and to clean my weapons and armour.'

'We will wait for you at Skipton, but there is no need to prepare your old weapons. The King has sent you new arms and a fine bay destrier.'

The Lionheart had been generous, my new weapons and armour were of the finest quality – even William Marshal or Mercadier would have been proud to own them. He had also been thoughtful – he had remembered that my colours were those of the redoubtable Hereward – and had sent me a new shield and pennon in the gules, sable and gold of legend. He had even made sure that the back of the shield had a cross-member to which I could peg my false arm and hook.

Negu had been at the nearby village of Giggleswick when my summons arrived, and I had mixed feelings about telling her of the King's command. I was torn between my duty to the King I revered and my desire to remain in the paradise that was Bolton and Negu.

But she saw the situation much more clearly and was adamant about what I should do.

'The King gave you two years; he's been true to his word. If he has sent for you, he needs you. You lose nothing. I will still be here, and so will the Priory – hopefully a little bigger than it is now.'

'But the campaign may go on for years. And if he wants me to help build his fortifications, I could be there until doomsday!'

'Well, that would not be ideal. But you are his sworn

retainer; you have little choice. If needs be, I will come out and join you.'

'But what about Bolton?'

'Magnus is more than capable of taking care of the priory on his own. Why don't we give it two years? And then, if you're still there, I will join you.'

'Are you sure?'

'Of course! I survived for fifteen years without you, so I can surely manage two more. If there is no change at the turn of the century, when you will be approaching fifty years of age, I'm sure the King would let you go and allow you to return to Bolton.'

Despite Negu's reassurances and the clarity of her pragmatism, it was difficult to leave Bolton. I had to remind myself of my duty to the King. I also remembered my promise to Alun when he was dying, and my original mission from Earl Harold.

Throughout my journey to Portsmouth, I was haunted by the contrast in my emotions between my current summons to serve King Richard and my first journey to Westminster, as a young recruit, to join the service of his father. As a callow youth, every step was a stride into an exciting new world and I feared nothing: now, every step took me further away from Negu and I had far too much to lose to countenance fearless bravado.

It was only when we had passed Rouen and reached a huge loop in the Seine at Thuit, twenty-five miles to the south-west, that I saw what the Lionheart had in mind for me. On the far side of the bend, on the eastern bank, hundreds of artisans and peasant labourers were constructing a burgh of some size. Above the bustle, on a limestone precipice 300 feet above the valley, another large group of men were hewing rock to level the top of the crag. I knew immediately that this was going to become my obsession for some time to come.

When I saw the King, he was the epitome of health and vigour.

'Ranulf, my dear friend, I am so pleased to see you. How is Negu? And how is the foundation?'

'She is blooming, my Lord, and the priory is growing by the day.'

'You don't mean she's pregnant?'

'No, sire, that would make life rather difficult for us—'

'Neither is Bérengère. Sadly, there have been no more pregnancies. But let us dwell on easier matters; I will tell you about my plans here.'

He took me to his campaign tent which – unlike the headquarters for a battle, full of commanders and lieutenants – was heaving with master masons and sappers.

'I have been able to win back Normandy's heartland from Philip. But before I push on to secure the Vexin, I must make Rouen safe from attack.'

He strode over to a large table, on which lay a broad sheet of vellum and an assortment of rules, set squares and compasses.

'I've looked at ground in the border area between Normandy and France. It's no wonder the Norman dukes found it so difficult to keep their south-east border secure; the Seine cuts through it like a knife through butter. I intend to build a monolith on the river so resilient that it will blunt any knife, no matter how formidable. Come, let's take a look at it.'

With his entire team in our wake, he pulled me outside like a child excited by a new toy.

'Isn't it magnificent? It reminds me of Earl Harold's home at St Cirq Lapopie. On it, I'm going to build the Castle of the Rock, the mightiest fortification in Christendom.'

Becoming even more animated, he then pulled me back inside the tent.

'I am the master mason. Look at the drawing, it's stupendous, even if I do say so myself! The main bailey's outer walls have fifteen round towers, protected by a ditch forty feet deep. After that, there is a massive inner wall, surrounded by another ditch, plus a drawbridge and a portcullis. Then, in the middle of the inner bailey, there is a third and final redoubt, the keep. All the walls will be eighteen feet thick.'

I was amazed.

'Eighteen feet, my Lord? No castle has ever had walls that size.'

'This one will! But that is only the half of it. There will be two wells, which will be dug down to river level, three hundred feet deep. But the most important part is the high middle wall.'

He leaned over the drawing and began to outline his design.

'Not only will it have walls of great depth, but they will be constructed to a new design. Having watched for years as straight walls crumble under the impact of huge stone missiles, I've realized that defensive walls shouldn't be straight. The walls of my middle bastion are nineteen concentric arcs. Look: missiles will slide off, rather than punch holes in the outside. Also, the circular shape means that the arrow slits have a much wider arc for shooting – so, no blind spots!'

I had never seen anything like it. His arced walls were a series of curves, like half towers, and as soon as I saw them I realized how effective they could be.

'My Lord, this talent is in your blood. Hereward's wife, Torfida – you will have read about her – understood the formulae and skills of the master masons, and worked on the great cathedrals. Her daughter, Estrith, Earl Harold's mother, was one of the churchwrights of Norwich.'

'I know; they have been my inspiration.'

I peered at the plans and drawings and soon saw another feature that was not familiar.

'Sire, all the towers have overhanging structures at their top. What are they?'

'Another of my rather clever ideas. I call them "machicolations"; it comes from an old form of my Occitan language, from "macher". In English it means something like "neck crusher". Each of the towers will have stone corbels at the top, so that I can build an overhang of about a foot. There will be holes in the overhang, so that—'

He had devised another idea that was so simple, yet so clever, that as soon as he described it, I was able to finish his sentence.

'—so that the defenders can drop missiles on their attackers and "machicolate" them!'

'Exactly, using incendiaries, or hot oil.'

'It's very clever, sire.'

'To tell the truth, they are not entirely my original idea, I saw them on the barbican at Darum – a very clever Muslim engineer must have dreamed them up – but I'm happy to take the credit.'

I looked at the dimensions on the plan and worked out its scale.

'Sire, it's a colossus; it will take years to build.'

'No, fifteen months; these men are going to build it for me, and you're going to make sure they do it on time.'

'Fifteen months is surely not possible, sire.'

'We have done the calculations. I have recruited every mason in the Empire, and many more from elsewhere. They will have hundreds of carpenters and labourers to support them. By the end of September, you will have an army of six thousand men here. Your budget is twenty thousand pounds, and your completion date is January 1198 – eighteen months from now. Any questions?'

Further questions were futile. Although not a stone had been laid, and most of the workforce had not yet arrived, six thousand men was a mighty host – and twenty thousand pounds was an enormous budget. I remembered back to the King's Council at Nottingham, when the Chancellor had announced that the King's annual income from the entire English realm was just over twenty-five thousand pounds.

I was required to meet a near impossible challenge, but I had been given the resources to make the Lionheart's dream come true. I set to work with two incentives: first, to pick up the King's gauntlet; and second, to return home to Negu as soon as possible.

33. Castle of the Rock

The King left Les Andelys in the autumn of 1196 to resume his war against the French. Subtle diplomacy was as vital to his new campaign as his ability on the battlefield. Indeed, his skills in the political arena were becoming as formidable as his military prowess.

His strategy was impressive. His new Castle of the Rock on the Seine would be his fulcrum for an attack on the Vexin. But at the same time, he would use diplomacy to persuade some of King Philip's vital allies to change their allegiance. He had two main targets – the old nemeses of his dynasty – the Counts of Toulouse, and the immensely rich and powerful Counts of Flanders. They were his most important neighbours and, for France, their allegiance was critical.

The year had brought a stroke of luck for the Lionheart, one which opened a door of opportunity to strike a deal with the Toulousains. The old count, Raymond V, an irascible old war horse who had no time for his old rivals from Aquitaine, had died, to be succeeded by his son, Raymond VI, who was a much more pliable man.

In October, the King met with the Count in nearby Rouen, a meeting that I was asked to attend, where he forged an agreement that significantly changed the course of his war with Philip.

The Lionheart renounced the Plantagenet claim to Toulouse, granted Raymond the lordships of Cahors and Agen and gave him the hand in marriage of his sister, Joan. It was not the first time he had been prepared to use his sister's charms as the mortar to solidify an alliance. This time, the bond worked.

Then, another death opened the other doorway to a kingdom that was central to the King's plans. Baldwin IX succeeded his father as Count of Flanders; the Lionheart seized the moment.

He invited Baldwin, a dashing young prince that the Lionheart grew to like immensely, to Rouen. He wined and dined him, making available as many of the city's most attractive young girls as the prince could ravish. The young man was in awe of the Lionheart. When he was offered generous trading terms in his most important markets, in England, and a goodwill payment of four thousand pounds, a new pact was formed.

With his allies secured diplomatically, the King went on a military offensive. He split his forces, giving the Grand Quintet freedom to mount their own assaults. William Marshal captured the fortress of Milly in the Loire, in May 1197, and Mercadier pulled off an even bigger coup by capturing King Philip's cousin, Philip of Dreux, the Bishop of Beauvais. This was perhaps the man the Lionheart despised more than any other; he had spread the poisonous rumour that the King had been behind the assassination of Conrad of Montferrat on the streets of Acre. He had the Bishop imprisoned and told his jailor to throw away the key.

The King himself took Dangu, a castle in the Vexin

only four miles from Gisors. The tide of the war began to turn in his favour and many more strongholds fell to him in Berry and the Auvergne. By September 1197, satisfied that he had won the first phase of the war, the King sent for Count Baldwin and together they sent an envoy to King Philip, calling for a truce.

The three men met in a meadow close to the Castle of the Rock on the Seine, a spot chosen deliberately by the Lionheart, so that Philip could see the huge bulwark rising above him. The meeting was not amicable. There was too much bitterness from years of conflict between them – especially from their animosities in the Holy Land – and Philip's plotting and scheming afterwards. Neither Richard nor Philip spoke; all the negotiations were conducted by intermediaries, while the two just stared at each other, their mutual contempt plain for all to see.

The Lionheart showed admirable restraint; as a younger man, he would not have been able to contain himself, and would have provoked a flaming row or worse.

Eventually, a truce was agreed for a year; trade would be resumed and prisoners exchanged. But there was not even a handshake to seal it. The two kings just rode away, without either of them ever acknowledging the other's presence. Nevertheless, the pact was signed and the deed done.

Once again, the King had used his head rather than his muscle. He needed to refill his coffers, re-equip his army and rest his men. He also wanted to oversee my work during the completion of the Castle of the Rock.

While the Lionheart had been fighting the French, I had been fighting the hourglass and the sundial. My arithmetic improved dramatically as I used the master masons to help me calculate the rate of progress of the walls against the passing of the days. The arrival of the autumn of 1197 slowed things down, but I paid the stonecutters and the masons a daily bonus in bad weather to keep them working. Once we got the flow right from the quarry to the masons' yard, and from there to the building platforms on the walls, the rate of daily progress became consistent.

I enjoyed the challenge, but as sleep became a luxury, fatigue became overwhelming. Even when I did fall asleep, my dreams – which were mainly nightmarish in content – involved the incessant rhythm of the mason's mallet and endless miles of limestone walls that, more often than not, tumbled down on top of me.

By the middle of October, I had the Lionheart's company at Les Andelys on a full-time basis once more. His energy was as relentless as usual.

'You have done a remarkable job, Ranulf, and you're on schedule. Do you have a firm completion date for me?'

'I do, sire, the middle of January.'

'Good, let's say the Feast of the Epiphany.'

'But, my Lord, that's the sixth!'

'I know, but it would be ideal to raise the Three Lions on the Castle of the Rock on such an auspicious day.'

In early December, I offered the men extra shifts. They were already earning small fortunes, but most of them grabbed with both hands the opportunity to earn even more. We took no rest, except for half a day on Christmas morning so that mass could be said.

By Tuesday 6 January 1198, we were ready.

It was like a coronation. Queen Eleanor came, and the Grand Quintet were there; most of the dignitaries from the Empire south of the Channel attended, as did several from England. Drums, horns and trumpets heralded the raising of the Lionheart's standard, while the 6,000 men who had built the goliath, and the thousands more in the local area who had supported them, threw up a roar that rolled down the valley of the Seine and must have been heard in Paris.

Even though it was January, after some early-morning mist in the valley had cleared, the sky was deep blue and the sun shone brightly to welcome the King's masterpiece. It was an astonishing sight; its limestone walls were almost pure white and its gleaming towers looked like giant sentinels, each with their pointed helmet of bright-red tiles.

The castle had been completed exactly to the King's original plan. It was a brilliant piece of design that the senior mason later confessed to me he thought could never be built. Even though the interiors were bare, and there was no provision for cooking or sleeping, the King insisted on a feast for the dignitaries in the main hall of the keep. He also decided that he would spend the night on its floor, with only a large fire in the hearth and a simple palliasse to sleep on.

Later that evening, after eating well and consuming vast quantities of his favourite wine from Aquitaine, the King thanked me for everything I had achieved.

'I have signed over a significant bonus for you at Winchester; you must build a house for yourself in England that is an appropriate reward for what you have done here.'

'Thank you, sire. I have enjoyed the challenge. I had serious doubts when I began. But where there's a will, there's a way.'

'You must be missing Negu and your northern shires.'

'I am, my Lord. As it will take several months to finish the interiors, I had thought I would send for Negu so that she could stay until everything is completed.'

'Excellent idea! I will organize an escort for her first thing in the morning.'

His expression then changed; he looked troubled.

'Bérengère is ill, in mind and body. She is frail and her mind wanders. I have spoken to my mother; we are going to take good care of her. But when I have Philip where I want him, hopefully at the end of this year, there will have to be a divorce. Mother has several candidates in mind, including Yolanda, the sister of Baldwin of Flanders. She is twenty-three, but is still intact, or so they say. Her father refused to let her marry until he found the right suitor, but now that he's dead and the young count thinks the world of me, the time is right. I must have an heir soon, or we will be back where we were when my great-grandfather died, with dynastic war breaking out.'

'What is she like?'

'I spoke with her twice in Bruges, when I was with her brother. She has the body of a goddess and makes my sap rise just by being in the same room as her. She'll give me a nursery of heirs, I'm sure of it.'

'Is the match made?'

'My mother assures me it is all but agreed.'

*

To my delight, Negu appeared at Les Andelys in April 1198, by which time I was, in effect, the Castellan of the Castle of the Rock.

The King would make frequent appearances in between military sorties and diplomatic excursions, but even when he was here, he would usually go hunting, leaving me to run the castle, complete with my own garrison.

So when I greeted Negu, it was as a lord of his own domain. It was a source of great amusement for her.

'Well, my Lord, I am honoured to be admitted to your mighty "Castle on the Rock"; it is so big!'

She had a mischievous grin on her face and, as always, I enjoyed her playful teasing. It was good to see her again.

'How is the priory?'

'You will be pleased to know, it will be finished soon.'

'Well, we can start building again. The King has given me a gratuity to build a new hall, just for the two of us.'

'Oh, Ranulf, the King is so generous. Let's make a start as soon as we're back. In England everyone talks about him all the time. They say he's like the Kings of England before the Conquest – brave and strong. They all love him. If only they knew what we know!'

'Perhaps they do. People have strong instincts, and perhaps they sense his pedigree.'

'How much longer do you have to stay?'

'Probably until the autumn. Will you stay with me?'

'And enjoy the delights of your huge edifice on the rock? Of course!'

The truce between the King and the French did not hold beyond the spring, and 1198 became another year of war, with the Lionheart inexorably wearing down the King of France. The climax came at the end of September when the King mustered a large force and crossed the River Epte at Dangu and began to encircle the French stronghold at Gisors.

Philip responded with an army of 300 knights and over 2,000 infantry. The French advance was seen by the Lionheart's patrols and, with his usual gusto and even though the contingents of William Marshal and Mercadier were some distance away, he immediately led a cavalry charge into the heart of the French ranks.

Philip was caught by surprise; his cavalry was still coming on in a thin column. The vanguard of the Lionheart's attack cut the column in two, causing panic. Unable to form up into a phalanx, the French crumbled under the weight of the Lionheart's assault. Within minutes, Philip's force took flight.

Three dozen French knights were drowned in the Epte when too many tried to cross a narrow bridge. King Philip himself was dragged from the water, only moments away from drowning. The infantry scattered in all directions, many of them running headlong into the cavalry of Marshal and Mercadier, which cut them down in droves. They also detained over 100 of Philip's knights as they tried to escape across open ground.

When the arithmetic was done later, it was calculated that the King had routed the French force with just 130 men, 30 knights and 4 conrois of cavalry. Most importantly of all, the knights killed in the skirmish, and those captured later, were the cream of King Philip's army, a grievous loss.

Badly wounded by these losses and with winter about to bite, Philip asked for a truce until the turn of the year, when the two protagonists would meet to discuss a long-term peace agreement. Although this represented excellent news for the King's cause, it did delay the departure Negu and I had planned, pushing it forward into 1199. That was not a disaster in itself, but I was rapidly approaching my fiftieth year. My bones were beginning to ache – especially when exposed to the cold winds that wrapped themselves around the Castle of the Rock, turning its eighteen-feet-thick walls into an ice house.

We spent the winter emptying the surrounding forests to pile their timbers on to our fires, but the heat produced by the hefty logs never seemed to extend beyond the air a few feet away from the hearth. At night, our bed warmers made very little difference, no matter how hot the embers we put into them. I thanked God that I had Negu's body to comfort me – a source of heat that did not seem to need too much fuel to make it glow.

On 13 January 1199, in the depths of what was a particularly harsh winter, the two men who had been close friends for years and had embarked on the Third Great Crusade together, but who had since become mortal enemies, met once more. Such was the depth of their animosity, Philip remained on horseback, while the Lionheart stayed on board the galley that had brought him up the Seine. Ten yards apart, the two men shouted their terms at one another. Philip agreed to accept the position as it stood in September 1198; he thus conceded the Vexin, which the Lionheart had managed to wrestle from him. Most significantly, for Negu and myself, the peace agreement was extended for five years.

The Lionheart returned to the Castle of the Rock in triumph. He had restored the Plantagenet Empire to where it had been before he left for the Holy Land.

He was jubilant.

'Ranulf, take your lady home with you; your work is done.'

34. Pierre Basil

Negu and I were close to leaving the Castle of the Rock, at the beginning of February 1199, when the Lionheart came to our chamber with a mix of fury and despair in his eyes.

'The beautiful Yolanda has just got married! I had no idea, my mother told me that an agreement had been made. They must have deceived her. There has been a plot hatched here, I swear it; it is either Philip or his allies.'

Negu took the King's arm and led him to a chair.

'I'm so sorry, sire. Can we help?'

'When are you leaving?'

'We were going to leave next week.'

'Come south with me. Mercadier is having some local problems in the Limousin. I can't fight here, because of the truce. But I can find a battle or two down there. It will give me time to think about where I'm going to find a bride!'

We consoled the King for over an hour and sent for wine to ease the process. I then tried to persuade him to travel in the opposite direction.

'Come home to England, my Lord. We'll help you find an English rose, and she can produce sturdy sons for you to add more English blood to your noble pedigree.'

He smiled and looked at Negu.

'What do you think? You're a Basque; don't you think we need some warmer blood in our lineage?'

Negu looked at me with a mischievous grin on her face.

'Perhaps, sire. But in my experience, the English can be quite warm!'

At Negu's teasing words, the King's disposition became much sunnier.

'When is England at its best?'

'In June, my Lord.'

'Then let's have a concordat. You come with me to the Limousin until the spring, and I will come to your priory in June, where I will make your man the Earl of Lancaster and you can find me an English bride.'

Spending a few months in the Limousin with the noblest man in Europe was hardly an imposition – especially as my reward would be an earldom. If it came to pass, I would be the first Englishman to receive an earldom since the days of King Harold of Wessex, over 130 years before.

Negu, who had developed the same indomitable audacity as her mentor, Hildegard, linked her arm through the King's.

'We will keep company with you in the south; it will be a privilege. If you're to wed a fair English rose, you had better have your fill of the dark maids of the south beforehand.'

We mustered a modest force and left for the south in the middle of March. Mercadier was at odds with the Counts of Angoulême and Limoges, both of whom were supporters of Philip of France, and was besieging the castle of Chalus-Chabrol. It was not far from Poitiers, and the King felt comfortable in the land of his youth.

When Mercadier showed the Lionheart the disposition of the castle and its tall tower, he issued his orders with typical speed and decisiveness.

'Bring up the arbalests to keep the defenders' heads down. The sappers need a solid canopy to work under, from where they can dig under the walls. Let's make a start!'

Compared to the sort of challenge he had faced in the past, Chalus was like swatting a fly. There were no more than forty people within its walls, including women and children. Within two days, the King was fidgety with boredom.

On the evening of 26 March, we had eaten an early supper and the King was pacing the floor of his tent. We had eaten a roast of boar and the Lionheart had drunk more than his usual share of the rich Claret wine of Graves, his favourite. Not even the emollient charms of the local girls could calm his restless mood.

'Sire, there are two very pretty young fillies outside the tent. Would you like me to bring them in?'

'You can tell the girls to wait, Ranulf.'

He was still agitated and needed the joy he derived from combat much more than the delight he obtained from female flesh.

'Ask my sergeant to bring my arbalest and some quivers of quarrels. Let's see if I can pick off a few marksmen on their battlements.'

'I will, my Lord, but I'll also get your page to bring your maille.'

'I don't need armour. It's almost dark; they won't be able to see me, let alone hit me.'

Obduracy was one of the King's hallmarks, and no amount of persuasion would convince him to wear his hauberk. Despite his obstinacy, I made sure his Sergeant-at-arms and two of his men brought their shields as protection, should any of the local arbalests manage to get a quarrel close to the Lionheart's large frame.

He took a flask of wine with him. When we reached the walls of Chalus, he began to loose his quarrels at the battlements, even though there were no defenders to be seen. It was almost dark and the night air was beginning to chill us. So, reluctantly, the King gave up the futile exercise of trying to hit targets that would not present themselves.

'Let's go back; it's getting cold. I think I might warm myself with one of your young ladies. I hope they will be an easier target for my trusty quarrel.'

The Lionheart handed his arbalest to his sergeant and turned to walk back to his tent. As he did so, a thin but strident voice cried from the battlements above us.

'*Bâtard!*'

Other than the cry, none of us saw or heard anything in the gloom. But as the King turned to see where the voice came from, he recoiled backwards sharply. He only gave a muffled moan, as if he had stubbed his toe, but when he hit the ground I could see that a quarrel had embedded itself in the top of the Lionheart's left shoulder. At first, I thought the injury was superficial.

The King seemed calm and still.

'How is it?'

'Not too bad, sire. We need to get the bodkin out, but it doesn't look too bad.'

Then the King winced. I called for a lantern and looked more closely at the wound. It was worse than I feared. His collarbone was shattered; his jerkin had a wide gash in it and was already soaked in blood.

I tried not to sound alarmed and quietly asked the Sergeant to call for the physician and to find Mercadier. As I did so, the Lionheart stirred and began to get to his feet, even though I tried to stop him.

'I don't want to keep the girls waiting; give me your good arm.'

We managed to make it to the tent. But as soon as we crossed the threshold, the King staggered and we both collapsed to the floor.

I shouted for Negu, who rushed to help us.

The Sergeant then appeared with worrying news.

'Sir, the Lord Mercadier has been hunting and is not back yet. And we can't find the physician anywhere; he may be with a local woman.'

'Well, find him! Turn out every bed in the area.'

The King's shoulders were nestled in Negu's lap, who was crouched behind him and sitting on her haunches. Blood was flowing freely from the wound, and I could see the pain on his face.

But the King remained calm.

'This bodkin needs to come out; I'm bleeding like a stuck pig, we need to staunch it.'

I looked at Negu; she nodded.

'I'll do it.'

The King grasped her hand.

'Have you treated wounds before?'

'We didn't have to remove many arrowheads at Rupertsberg, but I've tended many an injury from scythes and ploughs.'

'That's good enough for me. Let's get on with it.'

I called over the King's Steward and two of his guards, and between us we held him firmly. Negu began to clean the area around the wound with wine, which made the Lionheart wince. She then tugged a little on the shaft of the arrow, before stopping with a look of alarm on her face.

'The shaft has been deeply scored just below the bodkin. It has been gouged so that it will break off when someone tries to remove it.'

It was an old archer's ruse, but it took time to do and was only used for a one-off shot, of the sort used by a hired killer.

The King forced a smile.

'It seems someone who dislikes me wants me dead. Let's make sure he doesn't get his way. You'll have to dig the bodkin out.'

Negu took a breath and nodded to us to hold her patient tightly. Then, with some speed and dexterity, she snapped off the shaft and grasped the tang of the bodkin.

'My Lord, are you ready?'

'No, but don't hesitate. Use all your—'

Negu did the deed before the Lionheart finished his sentence. She had to twist the tang sharply to get it free. When she did so, a considerable amount of flesh and bone came out with it. The King cried out in agony. But such was the pain and shock that he fell back, unconscious.

Negu sighed deeply and then took control again.

'Heat a blade; I need to seal the wound.'

As the blade was being made hot, Negu packed cotton into the wound to stem the bleeding. She held up the arrowhead to show me. It was the worst kind, not a simple bodkin, but a swallowtail broadhead, with barbs almost an inch long to inflict the maximum damage. It was an expensive arrow, not one for use in bulk in battle, but one intended to kill a man in a single strike.

Negu looked at me; she was in tears.

'I don't think he'll ever use his left arm again . . . I think he's lost all feeling in it.'

The Lionheart jolted back to consciousness when Negu applied the blade to his wound. The searing had to be extensive as the wound was so big. The smoke and stench were overwhelming, and the King's cries difficult to bear.

But it was done.

Negu bound the shoulder as firmly as she could before she collapsed in spasms of anguish and exhaustion.

We sat with the King all night; he hardly slept, and neither did we.

By dawn, the Lionheart had become feverish and agitated.

'I must get up; I need to finish the siege.'

He tried several times to get to his feet, but he was too weak. He began to drift between moments of clarity and long periods of delirium. The pain seemed unrelenting.

Later that day, Mercadier appeared, by which time the King's colour had drained away and the fever had taken a firmer hold. He took one look at the Lionheart and immediatcly sent messengers to summon Bérengère, Queen Eleanor and the rest of the Grand Quintet.

He feared what Negu and I feared; the injury was severe, and the bleeding beneath the surface may not have stopped.

'I will send for Jean de Veyrac, Bishop of Limoges, he's the nearest high prelate.'

Negu, thinking she may have hastened the Lionheart's demise, was distraught.

'We should also find the King's physician.'

'He's a dead man; he will be executed as soon as he's found. They can bring someone from Limoges with the Bishop, but I fear his skills may be redundant.'

The next morning, when we cleaned and dressed the wound, it looked angry. The skin was fiercely hot to the touch, and the King was very edgy. Negu had prepared a poultice and a medicinal broth, both based on cures devised by Hildegard.

'We must get his fever down.'

As Negu was applying the poultice, Mercadier noticed the talisman around the King's neck.

'What in God's name is that?'

'It is the Talisman of Truth, something very precious to him.'

Mercadier grasped the chain to remove it.

'It is an amulet of the occult; it has no place around the King's neck.'

'Leave it! It belongs to the King.'

Few men ever crossed Mercadier, or spoke to him as I did, but he knew that my resolve was unshakeable. He backed off and walked away.

'I'm going to finish the siege; I want the man who did this.'

Negu's poultices and broth began to work, and the fever appeared to relent a little.

But on the fourth day, she summoned me as she was dressing the wound. What I saw turned my stomach, and I had to leave.

Negu joined me outside the tent when she had finished.

'The wound is putrefying; it's gangrene.'

'What can we do?'

'We could try canker maggots, but the infection is very deep. The King knows; I think he accepts the inevitable.'

I went inside to see him.

'Sire, is there anything I can do to make you more comfortable?'

'Whatever happened to those two maidens?'

'I can send for them, sire.'

'Good, I'll see them tonight. I will have my strength back by then. Organize a feast with the best Graves.'

There were tears in his eyes; he knew he was dying. I put my good hand on his chest, and he rested his strong right hand on it.

'We have been through a lot together, my friend. Will you stay with me until the end?'

'Of course, sire.'

My eyes filled with tears, and they began to roll down my face.

'No tears, Ranulf. Not when I'm gone, either. I'm afraid there is nothing to stop John taking the throne now. If I try to prevent it, war will follow and it will tear the Empire apart. My mother is the only hope to steady the ship. She will need you and the Grand Quintet to help her. If she calls on you, please go to her and do all you can.'

'I will, until my dying day.'

'Let's hope that day is much further away than mine!'

The King closed his eyes, but then they sprang open again.

'You should take the talisman. If my mother sees it, she will suspect that I did not destroy the manuscripts. Besides, I think my time with it is over and that I should return it to its guardian.'

I lifted it off his neck as gently as I could and put it into its leather pouch.

'How will you find its next recipient?'

'I don't know, sire. Perhaps I should bury it with the casket and let it find its own inheritor. I suspect it's been buried before and has always been found. Maybe it's time for it to be dormant again.'

'Knowing who has worn it before me, I have been proud to wear it. It would comfort me to think that I may be the last of its heirs in its current life. Perhaps you should go back to St Cirq Lapopie and lay it to rest with my grandfather. It would be good to know it was in the soil of Aquitaine. He grew to love my homeland, as I grew to love his. I'm glad England has found peace after so many years of violence and anguish. Thanks to you, I now know it is my home too and that I share the blood of its people. When you return, give them my love; walk through its fair meadows and by its sweet streams, and think of me.'

The King gripped my hand; he closed his eyes once

more and fell into a sleep that, for the first time in days, seemed restful.

The siege of Chalus-Chabrol was ended by Mercadier two days later. The sappers had dug deep under a corner of the castle walls and had managed to bring it down into a heap of rubble. It did not take Mercadier long to find the culprit who had shot the King, and he dragged him before us in chains. He had been badly beaten.

The Lionheart was slowly slipping away, but he was still conscious for short periods.

Mercadier roused him.

'Sire, I have brought the man who shot you. I can't get him to say much.'

The King peered at the man and asked to be lifted so that he could see him better.

'You are no more than a boy. How old are you?'

The young man, who was little more than eighteen, looked at the King with a sneer of contempt and answered defiantly.

'Old enough to kill you.'

Mercadier kicked the boy in the groin, sending him sprawling.

'Hold, Mercadier! The boy has the heart of a lion and the eye of a hawk. I don't want him hurt. Ranulf, help him up.'

He adopted a gentle tone with his assailant.

'What is your name?'

'Pierre Basil, a son of the Limousin.'

'Where did you learn to use an arbalest as accurately as that?'

'My grandfather taught me, as he had my father and my brother. He also showed me how to make the swallowtail quarrel and how to dip it in leopard's bane and pig shit to make sure it killed its target.'

'Then he is a wonderful teacher.'

'Was! He's dead now, as are my father and brother.'

'How did they die?'

'My grandfather died two weeks ago; he was old. But *you* killed my father and brother!'

'Where?'

'In a skirmish near Pacy-sur-Eure in Normandy, late last year. You cut my father down with your sword, and my brother was trampled to death by your horse.'

The Lionheart looked at the boy. His eyes were moist, but there was also a look of admiration on his face.

'They would be very proud of you; you have avenged them.'

He then turned to Mercadier.

'Set the boy free, and give him a hundred shillings.'

Mercadier was furious. But out of respect for the King's wishes, he took the boy out of the tent much more gently than he had brought him in.

The boy's confession that he had used poison and pig shit to make his missile more lethal explained why the Lionheart now faced his maker.

By Sunday 3 April, the King was still alive, but fading fast. Queen Eleanor and the Grand Quintet had arrived, but not Bérengère, who was not well enough to travel.

A vigil was organized around the King's bed. His tent had become a shrine, where members of his army came every day to pray for him. The Bishop of Limoges gave him Extreme Unction and we all awaited his death as calmly as we could, knowing that that was what he would have demanded.

The words the King had spoken to Mercadier about the boy were his last. He lost consciousness permanently, his great strength the only thing keeping him alive, but Queen Eleanor said that when she took his hand, she could feel him tighten his grip on her.

Richard I of England, known to the world as the Lionheart, the name he had earned when only a boy, died in the early evening of 6 April 1199.

There were no tears from those gathered around him, just an enormous sense of desolation, a void created by the loss of the finest man any of us had ever known. We drew strength from his presence in our lives; the tears would wait until the months and years to come.

His body was laid out under the awning of his tent so that his army could file past and show their respects. They were not short of tears; grizzled campaigners wept openly, and many fell to their knees to touch the hem of the Lionheart's cape. Some left flowers and the bulbs of spring, others left pieces of silver, or little tokens they had carved for him.

They had followed him to the far reaches of the earth and were immensely proud of it.

According to his wishes, and in his family's tradition, his heart was taken to Rouen by the Grand Quintet. His mother took his body to the Abbey of Fontevraud, in the Loire, so that he could be buried next to his father.

Negu and I went south, to St Cirq Lapopie, where we

completed our obligations to the Lionheart, and also to Earl Harold and Abbot Alun. We met the local families to which Harold had left the estate – a charming group of simple Quercynoise folk – and they left us alone to pay our respects at Earl Harold's grave.

It was a beautiful spring day, with nature beginning to bloom in Quercy's forests. I had bought a small silver box in Brive as a home for the talisman and, as the Lionheart had suggested, I used my seax to dig a deep hole at the base of Earl Harold's headstone as a resting place for the ancient amulet.

At sunset, on an evening to lift the soul, Negu sat and stared across the beautiful valley of the Lot, as I sat by Earl Harold's grave and fulfilled my promise to tell him the story of his grandson's life and deeds.

I am sure he was as proud to hear it as I was to tell it.

We were sad to leave the paradise that was St Cirq Lapopie, but knew that we had our own utopia waiting for us in England.

Negu and I made our way back to Bolton Priory. It was a subdued journey home. We were both full of reflections and memories, and lingered in several places: in Poitiers, with Queen Eleanor; at the Lionheart's new tomb in Fontevraud; at Rouen and at Westminster. We finally reached Bolton Priory in time to enjoy the best of a beautiful English summer.

The priory was all but complete and Negu and I began to adjust to a tranquil future together in our haven in the valley of the Wharfe. In the midst of that splendid summer, I often thought about the resting places of those whose stories I had come to know so well. Some like Hereward of Bourne, Sweyn of Bourne and Earl Harold of Hereford were at peace on foreign soil. Others like Torfida and her father, the Old Man of the Wildwood, were at rest in English soil in the wildwoods they cherished so much.

When Negu and I took our daily walk in Strid Wood by the Wharfe, our own piece of ancient woodland, through which the Pennine River hurried like a torrent, I always thought about the Wodewose, our Green Man of English legend. Was he watching over us, as King Richard's ancestors Torfida and her father believed? Did the Wodewose approve of what had been done by them, and by those who followed them, in England's name?

I derived great satisfaction from being sure that he did.

As for our memories of the Lionheart, we thought of him every time we strolled by the Wharfe, as he had asked us to, and as we sat by the fire in my hall – especially during the long winter nights. We reflected on the happy times, and sometimes on those that had been less than pleasant. We tried not to bury the sad memories; they had been as much a part of our journey as the happy times, and they were good for the soul. We remembered the astonishing effect the Lionheart had on those around him; his companionship and humour; his strength and courage; his fearsome temper and indomitable spirit. We knew we would never meet his like again, but felt honoured that we had known him so well.

In the autumn of 1203, Roger de Lacy came to stay with us. He was about to depart for the Limousin, to become Castellan of the Lionheart's Castle of the Rock.

He had become a good friend and wanted to say farewell. He brought a poem with him, which had been circulating in England for a while. It had been written by Geoffrey of Vinsauf, a Norman poet and a monk at St Frideswide's Priory in Oxford.

When Lord Roger read it to us, we wept openly. It said everything that could be said about our friend, the noble Lionheart.

Oh death! Do you realize who you snatched from us?
   To our eyes he was light; to our ears melody; to our minds amazement.
He was the lord of warriors, the glory of kings, the delight of the world.
In life he inspired with such terror that he is still feared now he is dead.
By this lesson you have made us know how brief is the laughter of the earth, how long are its tears.

Epilogue

John Lackland, the fifth son of Henry Plantagenet, was crowned King of England at Westminster on 27 May 1199. His reign was not a happy one. He presided over the loss of Normandy to Philip of France and the decline of the Plantagenet Empire beyond the Channel.

He was vain and vindictive, and was disliked by his senior magnates and by his subjects. His relationships with the Celtic kings and princes of Ireland, Scotland and Wales suffered greatly, leading him to trust no one and to harbour petty jealousies.

In the year 1212, his inability to inspire affection, as well as the huge taxes he had to levy to pay for his campaigns against the French, led to a revolt by his senior lords, which flung England into chaos.

By then, our good friend, Roger de Lacy, had died. But his son, John de Lacy, the Eighth Earl, had become very close to us; we thought of him as our grandson. Although he was still just twenty years old, he was one of England's most respected young lords and a leader of the revolt against King John.

Three years later, the rebels had brought the King to his knees and he agreed to settle with them on their terms. Although I was sixty-four years old, when John de Lacy asked me to travel with him to witness the ceremonial confirmation of the agreement between the King and his lords,

I was honoured to do so. It was especially appealing as young John was one of the twenty-five lords charged with making sure the King kept to the terms of the settlement.

The deed was signed in the presence of all the magnates of England in a water meadow next to the Thames, at Runnymede, close to William the Conqueror's fortress at Windsor. It was called the Great Charter of the Liberties of England.

When its terms were read, my heart swelled with pride.

Much of what Hereward and his rebels had fought for at Ely 140 years before, as well as the hopes of his Brotherhood and the dreams of his daughter's Brethren, had come to pass.

Its principles were based on the Charter of Liberties that Edgar the Atheling had been instrumental in creating for the coronation of Henry I, in 1101.

In the Great Charter, King John agreed to accept that, like any man, he was subject to the law of the land and that all men had the protection of the law, even against a king, if that king's actions were judged by the law to be cruel or oppressive.

As King John affixed his seal to the Great Charter, I looked at John de Lacy. He was a handsome young warrior. I thought of Hereward at the same age, of Earl Harold and all the others. They would now be content in their resting places; their journey was over, their ambitions fulfilled.

I made my way back to the north to bring the news to Negu. Our journey would also come to an end soon, but we would face it with joy in our hearts.

Acknowledgements

To all those who have made this possible – dear friends, loving family, dedicated professionals – I will always be grateful.

With much love and grateful thanks.

Dramatis Personae

(Entries are listed alphabetically according to the name most often used in the novel.)

Ayyubid Dynasty

The Ayyubid dynasty was a Muslim dynasty founded by Saladin. It ruled much of the Middle East during the twelfth and thirteenth centuries.

After the death of Saladin, his sons contested control over the sultanate, but Saladin's brother, Saphadin, eventually established himself as Sultan, in 1200.

Baldwin of Bethune

Through the stormy years of King John's reign, Baldwin occupied himself with running both his extensive estates in England. He died in October 1212 at Burstwick in Yorkshire, and was buried in the chapter house at Meaux Abbey, of which nothing now remains.

Bérengère

Bérengère never visited England during King Richard's lifetime, but she probably did so following his death. She also sent envoys to England to enquire about the pension she was due as Richard's widow, which King John failed to pay. Although Queen Eleanor of Aquitaine intervened and Pope Innocent III threatened John with an interdict if he did not pay, King John still owed her more than £4,000 when he died. However, during the reign of his son, Henry III of England, her payments were made.

Bérengère eventually settled in Le Mans and became a benefactress of the abbey of L'Épau in Le Mans. She died, in 1230, at the age of sixty-five. Her skeleton was rediscovered during the restoration of the abbey, in 1960. The remains are preserved beneath the stone effigy of the Queen, to be found in the chapter house of the abbey.

Blondel de Nesle

Little is known of his whereabouts or his circumstances after the Third Crusade. In fact, his role with King Richard and exact identity are subject to much debate. Today, his name is attributed to twenty-five songs of the twelfth century.

Eleanor of Aquitaine

When war broke out between King John and Philip of France, in 1201, Eleanor declared her support for John, her son. She set out from Fontevraud to her capital, Poitiers, to prevent her grandson, Arthur I, Duke of Brittany, John's enemy, from taking control. Arthur learned of her whereabouts and besieged her in the castle of Mirabeau. As soon as John heard of this, he marched south, overcame the besiegers and captured Arthur. Eleanor then returned to Fontevraud, where she took the veil as a nun. Eleanor died, in 1204, at the age of eighty-two. She was buried in Fontevraud Abbey next to her husband Henry and her son Richard. By the time of her death she had outlived all of her children except for King John of England and Queen Eleanor of Castile.

Guy of Lusignan

Guy of Lusignan died in 1194, without surviving issue. He was succeeded by his brother Amalric, who received the royal crown from Henry VI, Holy Roman Emperor. Descendants of the Lusignans continued to rule the Kingdom of Cyprus until 1489. He was buried at the Church of the Templars in Nicosia.

Henry II of Champagne

Henry died, in 1197, after falling from a window at his palace in Acre in what was almost certainly an accident. Suggestions that he was behind the assassination of Conrad of Montferrat are still current. His widow, Queen Isabella, remarried soon after his death, to her fourth (and last) husband, Amalric of Lusignan, who became King of Cyprus after the death of his brother, Guy of Lusignan. She died, in 1205, at the age of thirty-two.

Henry VI, Holy Roman Emperor

When Henry added the Kingdom of Sicily to his personal and imperial domain, in December 1194, he became the most powerful monarch in the Mediterranean and Europe. He died of malaria in Messina, on 28 September 1197, although many believed he was poisoned.

Hugh III, Duke of Burgundy

The most loyal of all the French lords after the departure of his King, Philip of France, he stayed with the Lionheart until the summer of 1192. He died on 25 August 1192, but there is no record of the cause of his death. King Richard was accused of being behind it by Philip, Bishop of Beauvais, a close friend of Conrad of Montferrat. According to the chronicler Richard of Devizes, the Bishop of

Beauvais said that Richard 'had ordered Marquis Montferrat's throat cut, that he poisoned the Duke of Burgundy; that he was an extraordinarily savage man and as hard as iron'.

Joan of Sicily

Joan was married in October 1196, at Rouen, as the third wife of Raymond VI of Toulouse. She was the mother of his successor, Raymond VII of Toulouse, and had a daughter, Mary, born in 1198. Raymond treated Joan badly, and she was afraid of him. In 1199, while pregnant with a third child, Joan travelled northwards, hoping for the protection of her brother, Richard the Lionheart, but he had just died. She then fled to her mother, Queen Eleanor, at her court at Rouen, where she was offered refuge and care. She died in childbirth and was buried at Fontevraud Abbey.

John, King of England

When John became King, in 1199, war with France was renewed. By 1206, John had lost Normandy, Anjou, Maine and parts of Poitou. He became increasingly unpopular as taxes rose dramatically to pay for his campaigns and his rule was more and more ruthless. His barons became ever more belligerent until civil war broke out, in May 1215. When the rebels seized London, John was compelled to negotiate and, on 19 June, at Runnymede on the River Thames, he accepted the baronial terms embodied in the Magna Carta, which limited royal power, ensured feudal rights and restated English law. It was the first formal document stating that the monarch was as much under the rule of law as his people, and that the rights of individuals were to be upheld even against the wishes of the sovereign.

Leopold V, Duke of Austria

Leopold's share of Richard the Lionheart's vast ransom, said to be twenty-three tons of silver, is thought to have formed the foundation for the Austrian mint, and was used to build new city walls for Vienna, as well as to found the towns of Wiener Neustadt and Friedberg in Styria. However, the Duke was excommunicated by Pope Celestine III for having taken prisoner a fellow crusader. In 1194, Leopold's foot was crushed when his horse fell on him at a tournament in Graz and he subsequently died of gangrene. He was buried at Heiligenkreuz Abbey near Vienna.

Mercadier

After the death of King Richard, Mercadier entered the service of John, his successor. On Easter Monday, 10 April 1200, he was assassinated while on a visit to Bordeaux to pay his respects to Eleanor of Aquitaine. His murderer was a man-at-arms employed by Brandin, a rival mercenary captain in the service of King John.

Philip Augustus, King of France

When John became King in 1199, Philip invaded John's French domains, forcing him to surrender Normandy, Brittany, Anjou, Maine and Touraine. Philip later conquered Poitou. In 1214, at Bouvines, the French defeated the allied forces of King John, the Holy Roman Emperor Otto IV and those of the Count of Flanders. The victory established France as a major European power. Philip continued the construction of Notre-Dame Cathedral in Paris, built the first Louvre, paved the main streets and walled the city. He died on 14 July 1223 and was buried in the Cathedral Basilica of Saint Denis.

Philip of Cognac

Although thought to be King Richard's illegitimate son, little is known of him. Philip had reached adulthood by the end of the 1190s, when his father married him to his ward, Amelia, the heiress of Cognac in Charente. However, she died without issue. It is thought he died early in the 1200s.

Pierre Basil

Despite the pardon Pierre Basil received from Richard the Lionheart, a vengeful Mercadier would have none of it. Shortly after the Lionheart's death, he had the boy dragged into the bailey of Castle Chalus-Chabrol where, in front of a large crowd, he was flayed alive. Mercadier justified his action by saying that although the King might have forgiven him, he had not.

Robert Thornham

After King Richard's death, Robert Thornham allied himself to King John. He was appointed Seneschal of Anjou and of Gascony, in 1201. In 1205 he was made High Sheriff of Surrey before returning to France as Seneschal of Poitou. He died on 26 April 1211.

Saladin

Salah al-Din Yusuf ibn Ayyub was born in Tikrit, Iraq, a Muslim of Kurdish origins. Despite being Christendom's most formidable opponent, his achievements, nobility and chivalry won him universal respect among Christians as well as Muslims.

Saladin died of a fever on 4 March 1193 in Damascus, not long after King Richard left the Holy Land. At the time of his death, he possessed one gold piece and a handful of silver. He had given away his immense wealth to the poor. He was buried in a mausoleum in the garden outside the Umayyad Mosque in Damascus.

Saphadin

Al-Adil (Saphadin to the crusaders), the younger brother of Saladin, was born in June 1145 in Damascus. Following Saladin's death, he played the role of kingmaker during the succession dispute between Saladin's sons and became governor of Damascus. He was later proclaimed Sultan and ruled wisely over both Egypt and Syria for nearly two decades until 1217. He encouraged trade and good relations with the crusader states, but took up arms again on hearing news of the Fifth Crusade, despite being over seventy years old. He fell ill and died while on campaign, in August 1218, and was succeeded by his son Malik al-Kamil.

William Marshal

William Marshal supported King John after Richard's death and did so to the end of his reign. John created him the First Earl of Pembroke. After John's death, William became regent for the young King Henry III. Fulfilling a vow he had made while on crusade, he was invested into the order of the Knights Templar on his deathbed. He died on 14 May 1219, at Caversham, and was buried in the Temple Church in London, where his tomb can still be seen. The title 'Earl Marshal of England', an honour now held by the Dukes of Norfolk, originates from his name.

Glossary

Alaunt

A now extinct breed of dog, thought to be the ancestor of large modern breeds, such as mastiffs. They were used to hunt large animals, including bears and boar, and as guard dogs.

Amalfi cross

The Maltese cross, also known as the Amalfi cross, is the symbol associated with the Knights Hospitaller (the Knights of Malta) and with the island of Malta.

Angevin

The House of Anjou, usually referred to simply as the Angevins, was a noble family of Frankish origin that emerged as the rulers of the Kingdom of Jerusalem and the Kingdom of England in the twelfth century.

Through the marriage of Geoffrey of Anjou to the Empress Matilda, the family achieved control of England and Normandy, and the marriage of Geoffrey's son Henry II (Curtmantle) to Eleanor of Aquitaine expanded the family's holdings into what was later termed the Angevin Empire.

After King John lost the Angevins' continental territory, along with Anjou itself, to the Capetians (Kings of France), in 1204, the family became known as the House of Plantagenet, adopting Geoffrey's nickname, and ruled England until the reign of Richard II, after which the succession was disputed by two cadet branches, the House of Lancaster and the House of York.

Although Richard the Lionheart's army in the Third Crusade is usually referred to as the 'English' army, it was in fact an Angevin army and would have contained many more from south of the Channel than from north of it.

Antioch, Siege of

The capture of the great fortress of Antioch was vital to the success of the First Crusade – without control of Antioch, the crusaders could not have moved on to Jerusalem. The siege lasted for seven and a half months, and conditions for the crusaders were often worse than for those inside the city. Located in the valley of the Orontes, in mountainous country, the city itself was on the valley floor, with the almost impregnable citadel high in the mountains above. Antioch finally fell on 9 February 1098.

Apoplexy

Apoplexy was the word used for centuries to describe sudden loss of consciousness and death. Strokes and heart attacks would often have been described as apoplexy in the past.

Arbalest

An arbalest (or arbelist) is one who shoots a crossbow. The term can also be applied to the bow itself. An arbalest was much larger than earlier crossbows and had greater tensile strength, giving it a greater force. The strongest windlass-pulled arbalests could be accurate up to 300 yards. A skilled arbalest could shoot two bolts per minute. Arbalest is a medieval French corruption from the Roman name *arc ballista*.

Artuqid

The Artuqid dynasty was a Turcoman dynasty that ruled in Eastern Anatolia, Northern Syria and Northern Iraq in the eleventh and twelfth centuries.

Assassins

The origins of the Order of Assassins can be traced back to around 1080. The order's first Grandmaster, Hassan-i Sabbah, was a passionate devotee of Isma'ili beliefs. Because of the unrest in the Holy Land caused by the Crusades, Hassan-i Sabbah found himself not only fighting other Muslims, but also the invading Christian forces.

The name 'Assassins' may have come from the Arabic *hashishi*, meaning 'hashish users'. It could also have derived from the Egyptian Arabic word *hashasheen*, meaning 'noisy people' or 'trouble-makers'.

Astrolabe

An astrolabe, from the Greek *astrolabos*, meaning 'star-taker', is an elaborate measuring device historically used by astronomers, navigators and astrologers. It was used to locate and predict the positions of the sun, moon, planets and stars, to determine local time and latitude and for surveying and triangulation.

Atabeg

Atabeg, Atabek or Atabey, the equivalent of a prince, is an hereditary title of nobility of Turkic origin, indicating the lord of a region or province, usually subordinate to a monarch.

Atheling

The Anglo-Saxon name for the heir to the throne. Interestingly, the name 'Clito' – as in William Clito, the son of Robert, Duke of Normandy, and claimant to the English throne – was a Latin version of the same thing. The Germanic form was 'Adelin' – as in William Adelin, the son of King Henry I (Beauclerc) and heir to the throne, who drowned in 1120.

Attar of roses

Attar of roses, or rose oil, is a fragrant oil distilled from fresh petals of the rose family. Rose oils are a valuable ingredient of fine perfumes, liqueurs, scenting ointments and toilet preparations.

Bailey

See 'motte and bailey'.

'Ballad of Robyn of Hode'

The earliest printed version of 'The Ballad of Robyn of Hode' appeared sometime after 1492, called a 'Gest of Robyn Hode', a printed version of an old ballad which told of the bravado of heroic outlaws who fought for the oppressed and downtrodden. The earliest handwritten version is called 'Robin Hood and the Monk'. It is preserved in manuscript form at Cambridge University. Written around 1450, it contains many of the elements still associated with the legend. Several historians argue that at least part of the folklore associated with the story of Robin Hood may have been inspired by the deeds of Hereward of Bourne (also known as 'The Wake').

Bezant

A gold coin from the Byzantine Empire.

Blackletter

Blackletter, also known as Gothic script or Gothic minuscule, was a script used throughout western Europe from approximately 1100 until well into the seventeenth century. Blackletter is sometimes called Old English.

Bloody flux

Bloody flux is the old name for dysentery, an inflammatory disorder of the intestine. It results in severe diarrhoea containing mucus and/or blood in the faeces, with fever and abdominal pain. If left untreated, dysentery is often fatal.

Bodkin

A bodkin is a type of arrowhead, a squared metal spike used extensively during the Middle Ages. The name comes from the Old English word *bodkin* (or *bodekin*), a type of sharp, pointed dagger.

Bolton Priory (now Abbey)

Bolton Priory flourished until the early fourteenth century, when Scottish raiders caused serious structural damage to the priory, resulting in the temporary abandonment of the site. Building work was still going on when the Dissolution of the Monasteries resulted in the termination of the priory in 1539. The east end remains in ruins. The nave of the abbey church was in use as a parish church from about 1170 onwards. It survived the Dissolution of the Monasteries and is still used to this day.

Braies

Braies are a type of pantaloon worn in the Middle Ages. In the later Middle Ages they were used exclusively as undergarments. Braies generally hung to the knees or mid-calf, resembling what are today called shorts. They were made of cotton or linen.

Bucentaur

The Bucentaur was the state galley of the Doges of Venice. It was used every year on Ascension Day up to 1798 to take the Doge out to the Adriatic Sea to perform the 'Marriage of the Sea' – a ceremony that symbolically wedded Venice to the sea.

Burgh

The Saxon name for a town or city.

Butescarl

The seaborne equivalent of a housecarl, the medieval equivalent of a modern-day marine.

Capetians

The House of Capet ruled the Kingdom of France from 987 to 1328 after succeeding the Carolingian dynasty. The name derives from Hugh Capet, the first Capetian King, who was a descendant of the Carolingians. The direct House of Capet came to an end in 1328, when the three sons of Philip IV all failed to produce surviving male heirs to the French throne.

Cappa robe

A long-sleeved, ankle-length ecclesiastical robe, tied at the waist by a corded belt. Usually made from cotton or wool, for Templars it would have had a slit at the front and rear so that it could be worn on horseback. In battle, the cappa would have been worn over a full-body hauberk of chain mail.

Carucate

The carucate was a unit of assessment for tax used in most Danelaw counties of England, and is found in the Domesday Book. The carucate was based on the area a plough team of eight oxen could till in a single annual season. It was subdivided into oxgangs, or 'bovates', based on the area a single ox might till in the same period, which thus represented one eighth of a carucate.

Castellan

A castellan was the governor, constable or captain of a castle. The word stems from the Latin *castellanus*, derived from *castellum* (castle).

Castle of the Rock

The castle is now called Château Gaillard and is regarded as the finest fortification of the Middle Ages. Henry IV of France ordered the demolition of Château Gaillard in 1599. Today, its ruins are listed as an historical monument by the French Ministry of Culture and are open to visitors.

Catapult

Castles, fortresses and fortified walled cities were the main form of defence in the Middle Ages and a variety of catapult devices were used against them. As well as attempting to breach the walls, missiles and incendiaries could be hurled inside, or early forms of biological warfare deployed, such as diseased carcasses, putrid garbage or excrement. The most widely used catapults were the following:

Ballista

Similar to a giant crossbow and designed to work through torsion. Giant arrows were used as the ammunition, made from wood with an iron tip.

Mangonel

These machines were designed to throw heavy projectiles from a bowl-shaped bucket at the end of an arm. With a range of up to 1,300 feet they were relatively simple to construct, and wheels were added to increase mobility.

Onager

Mangonels are sometimes referred to as 'onagers'. Onager catapults initially launched projectiles from a sling, which was later changed to a bowl-shaped bucket.

Springald

The springald's design was similar to that of the ballista, effectively a crossbow propelled by tension. The springald's frame was more compact, allowing for use inside tighter confines, such as the inside of a castle or tower.

Trebuchet

Trebuchets were probably the most powerful catapult employed in the Middle Ages. The most commonly used ammunition was stones, but the most effective involved fire, such as firebrands and the infamous 'Greek fire'. Trebuchets came in two different designs: traction, which were powered by people; or counterpoise, where the people were replaced with a weight on the short end of an arm. A simplified trebuchet was known as a 'couillard', where the trebuchet's single counterweight was split, swinging on either side of a central support post.

Cerdic/Cerdician

The dynastic name of the Kings of Wessex, who ultimately became Kings of England, from Egbert, King of Wessex in 820, to Edward the Confessor's death in 1066. The only exceptions were the three Danish kings, Cnut and his sons Harold Harefoot and Harthacnut, between 1016 and 1042. The name reputedly derives from Cerdic, a prince of the West Saxons from circa 600, who was an ancestor of Egbert, the first King of England.

Chanson de geste

See 'Song of Roland'.

Chemise

A simple garment worn next to the skin to protect clothing from sweat and body oils, the precursor to the modern shirt. The chemise seems to have developed from the Roman *tunica* and first became popular in Europe in the Middle Ages. Women wore a shift or chemise under their gown or robe. Men wore a chemise with their trousers or braies, and covered the chemise with garments such as a doublet or robe.

Chignon

A female hairstyle that can be traced back to antiquity, where the hair is swept back from a central parting and tied in a loosely folded bun at the back of the head.

Chrism

Chrism is a Greek word literally meaning 'an anointing'; it is also known as myrrh, holy anointing oil or consecrated oil. It is an oil used in the administration of certain sacraments and ecclesiastical functions in Christian churches.

Christian Holy Land

Following defeat by Saladin's forces in 1187 (after which most of Palestine was controlled by the Ayyubids), a rump crusader state in the northern coastal cities survived for another century. However, despite seven further crusades, the crusaders were no longer a significant power in the region.

Churchwright

A church builder or architect.

Cilician Gates

The Cilician Gates, or Gülek Pass, is a pass through the Taurus Mountains connecting the low plains of Cilicia to the Anatolian Plateau, by way of the narrow gorge of the Gökoluk River. The southern end of the Cilician Gates is about thirty miles north of Tarsus, and the northern end leads to Cappadocia.

Cloth of gold

Cloth of gold is a fabric woven with a gold-wrapped or spun weft. In most cases, the core yarn is silk wrapped with a band or strip of high-content gold. The Ancient Greek reference to the Golden Fleece is thought to be a reference to gold cloth. Cloth of gold has been popular for ecclesiastical use for many centuries.

Coif

See 'hauberk'.

Conroi

A squadron, twenty-five strong, of cavalry.

Constable

Historically, the title comes from the Latin *comes stabuli* (count of the stables) and originated from the Eastern Roman Empire. Originally, the constable was the officer responsible for keeping the horses of a lord or monarch. The title was imported to the monarchies of medieval Europe, and in many countries developed into a high military rank and great officer of state, for example, the Constable of France.

Conventual prioress

A conventual prioress, or prior, is the independent superior of a monastery that is not an abbey and is therefore called a priory.

Cordwainer

A cordwainer is a shoemaker/cobbler who makes fine soft leather shoes and boots. The word is derived from *cordwain*, or *cordovan*, the leather produced in Cordoba, Spain. Historically, there was a distinction between a cordwainer, who made shoes and boots out of the finest leathers, and a cobbler, who repaired them.

Corselet (corselette)

Now an item of female underwear, the corselet was originally a piece of armour, covering the torso, made of leather or mail – chain or lamellar. The origin of the English word comes from *cors*, an Old French word meaning 'bodice'.

Crumhorn

The crumhorn is a musical instrument of the woodwind family, most commonly used during the Renaissance period. The name derives from the German *krumhorn* meaning 'bent horn'. This relates to the Old English *crump* meaning 'curve', surviving in modern English in 'crumpled' and 'crumpet' (a curved cake).

Cuspidor

A spittoon, from the Latin *conspuere*, from *spuere* (to spit).

Danegeld

The Danegeld (or 'Danish tax', literally 'Dane money') was a tax raised to pay tribute to Viking raiders and save a land from being ravaged. It was called the 'geld' or 'gafol' in eleventh-century sources; the term Danegeld did not appear until the early twelfth century. It was characteristic of royal policy in England during the ninth to the eleventh centuries, collected both as tributary – to buy off the attackers – and as stipendiary, to pay the defensive forces.

Danelaw

The Danelaw is an historical name given to the part of England in which the laws of the Danes held sway and dominated those of the Anglo-Saxons (in contrast with 'West Saxon law' and 'Mercian law'). The areas that comprised the Danelaw are in northern and eastern England. The origins of the Danelaw arose from the Viking expansion of the ninth century, although the term was not used to describe a geographic area until the eleventh century.

Destrier

A Norman warhorse, often called the Great Horse. Modern shire breeds like the Percheron and Suffolk Punch may descend from destriers, but they may not have been as large as today's shire horses. In fact, a destrier was probably not a breed, just the name for a horse bred and trained for war.

Donjon

See 'motte and bailey'.

Dorylaeum, Battle of

A major battle of the First Crusade (the Great Crusade) fought between the Christian army of the Latin Princes and the Seljuk Turks. It was fought on 1 July 1097, in the north-west of Anatolia, as the crusaders began their long march to Palestine.

Dwale

Dwale was a medieval anaesthetic. There were many versions, but most contained bile, opium, lettuce, bryony, mandrake and hemlock. There are records of dwale in numerous literary sources, including Shakespeare's *Hamlet*, and John Keats's poem 'Ode to a Nightingale'.

Ely, Siege of

The Siege of Ely was the last redoubt of the English Revolt against Norman rule, in 1069. By 1071 only a small number of survivors, led by Hereward of Bourne, who later became better known as Hereward the Wake, remained besieged by King William at Ely, at that time an island in the shallow waters of the fens. William's siege was successful in the autumn of 1071. Most of the defenders were killed, while a few survivors are thought to have escaped into the fens or the wildwood; all became legends.

Eunuch

A eunuch was a person who had been castrated early enough in life for it to have major hormonal consequences. Castration was carried out so that he might perform specific social functions. The practice was well established in Europe among the Greeks and Romans. In the late Roman Empire, the Emperors Diocletian and Constantine were surrounded by eunuchs for activities like bathing, hair cutting, dressing, and many bureaucratic functions. Eunuchs were thought to be loyal and indispensable and enjoyed great influence at court. At the Byzantine imperial court, there were a great number of eunuchs employed in domestic and administrative functions and they had their own hierarchy.

Euskara

The Basque name for the Basque language of south-western France and north-eastern Spain.

Excalibur

Excalibur is the legendary sword of King Arthur, sometimes attributed with magical powers or associated with the rightful sovereignty of Great Britain. The sword has long been associated with the Arthurian legend. In Welsh, the sword is called Caledfwlch. In Geoffrey of Monmouth's *History of the Kings of Britain*, he says the sword was forged in Avalon and Latinizes the name 'Caledfwlch' as Caliburnus. When Monmouth's work was interpreted in Europe, writers altered the name further until it finally took on the popular form Excalibur.

In *Perceval* by Chrétien de Troyes (late twelfth century), Gawain carries Excalibur: 'for at his belt hung Excalibur, the finest sword that there was, which sliced through iron as through wood'. If the story of Richard the Lionheart's gift of Excalibur to King Tancred of Sicily is to be believed, its whereabouts remain a mystery. Tancred died in 1194. When the Holy Roman Emperor, Henry VI, invaded the island later that year, he ordered Tancred's reliquary and tomb to be opened and their treasures removed. Twenty packhorses of gold and silver, jewels and silks, tapestries and carpets were found and sent to Trifels Castle, in Germany. The treasure included the Sicilian coronation robes, which were used in the ensuing centuries by the Holy Roman Emperors and are now on display in Vienna. Excalibur was not mentioned among the treasure, and to this day Sicilians still believe that it is buried in a secret location somewhere on the island.

Extreme Unction

The anointing of the sick or dying carried out in extremis as part of the Last Rite of passage. The Last Rites traditionally include three elements: penance, unction (anointing) and receiving the Eucharist (Christ's Sacrament) in order to prepare the dying person for the next life.

Faris

A Muslim/Arab cavalryman, usually carrying a status similar to the European knight.

Fitz

A prefix to patronymic surnames of Anglo-Norman origin. This usage derives from the Norman *fiz* or *filz* (son of) which was coupled with the name of the father (for example, FitzGilbert, meaning 'son of Gilbert'), as in the Scandinavian tradition of adding *-son* behind the father's name, and the Gaelic traditions 'Mac' and 'O'.

Fletcher

A fletcher is a maker of arrows. The word is, via Old French, related to the French word *flèche*, meaning 'arrow'; the ultimate root is the Frankish *fliukka*.

Fontevraud Abbey

The abbey was originally the site of the graves of King Henry II of England, his wife Eleanor of Aquitaine, their son King Richard I of England, their daughter Joan, their grandson Raymond VII of Toulouse, and Isabella of Angoulême, wife of Henry and Eleanor's son King John. However, it is thought that there is no longer a corporal presence of Henry, Eleanor, Richard or the others on the site. Their remains were probably destroyed during the French Revolution, but their tombs and effigies remain.

Futuwwa

An Arabic term that has similarities with chivalry and virtue. It was also a name of ethical urban organizations or 'guilds' in medieval

Muslim realms that emphasized honesty, peacefulness, gentleness, generosity, hospitality and avoidance of complaint in life. In modern-day dialects of Arabic (for example, in Egypt) the term is sometimes used for youths who do quasi-chivalrous acts such as helping others resist intimidation by rival groups.

Garderobe

The term garderobe describes a place where clothes and other items are stored, and also a medieval toilet. In European public places, a garderobe denotes the cloakroom, wardrobe, alcove or an armoire. In a medieval castle or other building, a garderobe was usually a simple hole discharging to the outside leading to a cesspit or into the moat, depending on the structure of the building. Such toilets were often placed inside a small chamber, leading by association to the use of the term garderobe to describe them.

Geld

Another word for money in Dutch and German (*gelt* in Yiddish), in medieval England it meant tax, tribute or a ransom – as in Danegeld.

Gold Ampulla

An ampulla was, in Ancient Rome, a 'small nearly globular flask or bottle, with two handles'. The word is used in archaeology for flasks, often handle-less and much flatter, containing holy water or holy oil in the Middle Ages, often bought as souvenirs of pilgrimages. Materials include glass, ceramics and metal. The glass Holy Ampulla was part of the French coronation regalia and believed to have divine origins. Similar is the Gold Ampulla in the British Crown Jewels, a hollow, eagle-shaped gold vessel from which the anointing oil is poured by the Archbishop of Canterbury at the anointing of a new British sovereign during their coronation.

Golden Horn

The Golden Horn is an inlet of the Bosphorus to the east of the city of Constantinople (Istanbul) forming a natural harbour that has sheltered ships for thousands of years. It is a scimitar-shaped estuary that joins the Bosphorus just at the point where that strait enters the Sea of Marmara, thus forming a peninsula, the tip of which is 'Old Istanbul' (ancient Constantinople).

Gonfalon

A small tailed flag or banner, flown from the top of a lance or pole to indicate lordly status, common throughout Europe. It would carry the colours, crest or heraldry of its owner.

Grand Domestic

The title of *Megas Domestikos*, or the Grand Domestic in English, was given to the commander-in-chief of the Byzantine land army.

Greek fire

The secret weapon of the Byzantine emperors. A sort of ancient napalm, it was invented by a Syrian engineer, a refugee from Baalbek, in the Egyptian city of Heliopolis in 673. The mix of ingredients, a closely guarded secret, was reputedly handed down from emperor to emperor. It has remained a secret to this day, but was thought to be a combination of pitch, sulphur, tree resin, quicklime and bitumen. The key ingredient may well have been magnesium, which would explain why the 'fire' would burn under water. Varieties of it began to be used by other navies, most using pitch. The 'fire' was often poured into wooden barrels or clay pots before being lit and hurled at the enemy.

Guige

A guige is a long strap, typically made of leather, used to hang a shield on the shoulder or neck. This technique was primarily employed when the shield was not in use. Nevertheless, soldiers also wore the strap in this fashion in combat: it allowed for two-armed combat, with the soldier handling a second weapon. The guige also allowed the shield to be worn on the back while using a two-handed sword, or enabled soldiers to work on siege machines without discarding the shield. It gave the shield extra support in intense hand-to-hand combat. Guiges usually had buckles to adjust their length. Most information about the use of guiges comes from various medieval works of art, such as the Bayeux Tapestry.

Hattin, Battle of

The Battle of Hattin took place on Saturday 4 July 1187, between the crusader Kingdom of Jerusalem and the forces of the Ayyubid dynasty under the command of the Sultan Saladin. The Muslim armies under Saladin captured or killed the vast majority of the crusader forces, removing their capability to wage war. As a direct result of the battle, Islamic forces once again became the major military power in the Holy Land, soon re-conquering Jerusalem and several other crusader-held cities. These Christian defeats prompted the Third Crusade, which began two years after the Battle of Hattin.

Hauberk

A maille (chain-mail) 'coat', worn like a long pullover down below the groin. Hauberks for the infantry were slightly shorter so that the men could run in them, and were only split at the sides. Cavalry hauberks extended to the knee and were split front and back. Hauberks were often worn with 'chausses' (maille leggings, worn like trousers). The maille could extend into a hood (coif) like a balaclava, but had a flap (ventail), in front of the throat and chin that could be dropped for comfort when not in the midst of battle. Three kinds of maille were used and were progressively more expensive: ordinary ring maille, scale maille and lamellar maille (when overlapping individual plates were fastened together by leather thongs).

Hearthtroop

The elite bodyguard of kings, princes and lords of the ninth, tenth and eleventh centuries.

Heraldic terms

Azure: blue

Bend: diagonal stripe like a sash

Field: background of a shield, usually consisting of colours or metals (tinctures) or symbolic vair

Gold (or): yellow

Gules: red

Passant: a 'lion passant' is walking, with the right forepaw raised and all others on the ground

Roundel: sphere

Sable: black

Tierce: a third part of a shield (background), usually a band down the left-hand side

Vair: variegated furs (ermine, squirrel, etc.)

Housecarl

The elite troops of the Anglo-Saxon kings, following their establishment by King Cnut in 1016, in the Danish tradition. Cnut brought his own personal troops to supplement the English fyrd (citizen army) when he succeeded to the throne following the death of Edmund Ironside.

Jerusalem

After the city of Jerusalem fell to Saladin in 1187, a period of huge investment began in the construction of houses, markets, public baths and pilgrim hostels, as well as the establishment of religious endowments. However, for most of the thirteenth century, Jerusalem declined to the status of a village – a result of the city's fall in strategic value and the Ayyubid internecine struggles. In 1244, Jerusalem was sacked by the Khwarezmian Tartars, who suppressed the city's Christian population and drove out the Jews. The Khwarezmian Tartars were driven out by the Ayyubids, in 1247. From 1250 to 1517, Jerusalem was ruled by the Mamluks. During this period many clashes occurred between the Mamluks on one side and the crusaders and the Mongols on the other. In 1517, Jerusalem fell to the Ottoman Turks, who remained in control until 1917.

Jihad

Jihad is a religious duty of Muslims. In Arabic, the word translates as a noun meaning 'struggle'. A person engaged in jihad is called a mujahid; the plural is mujahideen. Jihad is an important religious duty for Muslims. A minority among the Sunni scholars sometimes refer to this duty as the sixth pillar of Islam, though it occupies no such official status. In Shi'a Islam, however, jihad is one of the Ten Practices of the Religion. In western societies the term jihad is often translated by non-Muslims as 'holy war'. Muslim authors tend to reject such an approach, stressing non-militant connotations of the word.

Keep

See 'motte and bailey'.

Khanjar

The khanjar is the traditional dagger of Oman. It is similar to the Yemeni jambiya. The khanjar is curved and sharpened on both edges. It is carried in a sheath decorated in silver, on a belt similarly decorated in silver filigree. A khanjar appears on the flag of Oman, as part of the national emblem of Oman. There are many uses of the khanjar. It is a symbolic weapon, worn by men after puberty. Nowadays, it is used as a type of formal dress item and for stylistic purposes. Drawing the khanjar from its sheath was a social taboo before the 1970s, and men would only do that if they sought revenge or for assassination.

Kilij

A kilij, from the Turkish *kiliç* (a sword), is a type of one-handed, single-edged and moderately curved sabre used by the Turks and related to cultures throughout history.

Kipchak bow

A recurve-style bow used throughout Asia Minor in the Middle Ages. Like a Turkish bow, it got its name from the Kipchak tribe who, as the Golden Horde, ruled the western part of the Mongol Empire until the thirteenth century.

Kirtle

A kirtle is a long tunic-like dress worn by women in the Middle Ages into the baroque period. The kirtle was typically worn over a chemise or smock and under a formal outer garment or gown.

Knights Hospitaller

The Knights Hospitaller, also known as the Knights of St John, Order of St John (and currently The Sovereign Military Hospitaller Order of St John of Jerusalem of Rhodes and of Malta), were among the most famous of the Western Christian military orders during the Middle Ages. The Hospitallers arose as a group of individuals associated with an Amalfitan hospital in the Muristan district of Jerusalem, which was dedicated to St John the Baptist and was founded around 1023 by Blessed Gerard Thom to provide care for poor, sick or injured pilgrims to the Holy Land.

Knights Templar

The Poor Fellow-Soldiers of Christ and of the Temple of Solomon, commonly known as the Knights Templar, were among the most famous of the Western Christian military orders of the Middle Ages and existed for nearly two centuries. Founded by Christian zealot Hugh de Payens and eight associates in 1119, it was officially endorsed by the Catholic Church around 1129. The Order became a favoured charity throughout Christendom and grew rapidly in membership and power. Knights Templar, in their distinctive white mantles with a red cross, were among the most skilled fighting units of the Crusades. Non-combatant members of the Order managed a large economic infrastructure throughout Europe, introducing financial techniques that were an early form of banking, and building fortifications across Europe and the Holy Land.

The Templars' existence was tied closely to the Crusades; when the Holy Land was lost, support for the Order faded. Rumours about the Templars' secret initiation ceremony created mistrust and King Philip IV of France, deeply in debt to the Order, took advantage of the situation. In 1307, many of the Order's members in France were arrested, tortured into giving false confessions, and then burned at the stake. Under pressure from King Philip, Pope Clement V disbanded the Order in 1312. The abrupt disappearance of a major part of the European infrastructure gave rise to speculation and legends, which have kept the 'Templar' name alive into the modern day.

Lateen sail

A lateen (from the French *latine*, meaning 'Latin'), or latin-rig, is a triangular sail set on a long yard mounted at an angle on the mast, and running in a fore-and-aft direction. Dating back to Roman navigation, the lateen became the favourite sail of the Age of Discovery.

Latt

An ancient Arabic mace, usually with a heavy bronze or lead head, sitting atop a thick wooden shaft of ash.

Leine

The leine is a unisex smock of Celtic peoples, not unlike a Roman toga. The word means 'shirt' and early descriptions from the fifth to the twelfth centuries talk of a long smock-like linen garment, ankle-length or knee-length, either sleeveless or with straight sleeves.

Leopard's bane

Derived from aconite, a genus of over 250 species of flowering plants belonging to the family *Ranunculaceae*. Known as 'the queen of poisons', it is also known as monkshood, wolf's bane, women's bane, devil's helmet or blue rocket. It has been used as a poison all over the world for centuries.

Locutory

A room in a monastery for conversation, also a place where monks or nuns might meet with people from the outside world.

Lodestone

A lodestone is a naturally magnetized piece of the mineral magnetite. Ancient people first discovered the property of magnetism in lodestone. Pieces of lodestone, suspended so they could turn, were the first magnetic compasses and their importance to early navigation is indicated by their name, which in Middle English means 'course stone' or 'leading stone'.

Lute

A lute can refer to any string instrument having the strings running in a plane parallel to the sound table, more specifically to any plucked string instrument with a neck (either fretted or unfretted) and a deep round back. The player of a lute is called a lutenist, lutanist or lutist, and a maker of lutes (or any string instrument) is referred to as a luthier.

Lyam hound

A lyam hound or lime-hound (also known as limer or lymer) was a scent hound, used on a leash in medieval times to find large game before it was hunted down by the pack. The term originates from the Middle English *lyam*, meaning 'leash'.

Machicolations

A machicolation is a floor opening between the supporting corbels of a battlement, through which stones, or other objects, could be dropped on attackers at the base of a defensive wall. The design was adopted in the Middle Ages in Europe when Norman crusaders returned from the Holy Land. A machicolated battlement projects outwards from the supporting wall in order to facilitate this. The word derives from the Old French word *macher*, 'to crush', and *col*, meaning 'neck'.

Maille

See 'hauberk'.

Manticore

A Persian legendary creature similar to the Egyptian sphinx (which is female). It has the body of a (male) red or golden lion, a human head with three rows of sharp teeth and a trumpet-like voice. Other aspects of the creature vary from story to story. It may be horned, winged, or both. The tail is that of either a dragon or a scorpion, and it may shoot poisonous spines or arrows. Sometimes it is portrayed as a hunter armed with a bow. It may have come into European mythology in Roman times or as a result of the First Crusade.

Mantle

A mantle (from *mantellum*, the Latin term for a cloak) is a long, loose cape-like cloak for outdoor protection worn by men and women from the twelfth to the sixteenth century.

Maqluba

Maqluba, sometimes pronounced as Maaluba or Magluba, is a traditional dish of the Arab Levant and Palestine. The dish includes meat, rice and fried vegetables placed in a pot, which is then flipped upside down when served, hence the name, which translates literally as 'upside down'.

Mark

In the twelfth and thirteenth centuries German silver marks were equivalent to two-thirds of a pound of sterling silver.

Mead

Mead, also called honey wine, is an alcoholic beverage that is produced by brewing a solution of honey and water. It may also be produced by brewing a solution of water and honey with grain mash, which is strained after fermentation. Depending on local traditions and specific recipes, it may be flavoured with spices, fruit or hops (which produce a bitter, beer-like flavour). It may be still, carbonated or naturally sparkling, and it may be dry, semi-sweet or sweet.

The tradition of mead-making as a by-product of beekeeping still continues, a well-known example being at Lindisfarne, where mead continues to be made to this day, albeit not in the monastery itself.

Melek-Ric

The Arab name for King Richard, literally 'King Richard'. Such was his reputation that for generations Arab children were warned that if they did not behave, 'Melek-Ric will come to get you!'

Midden

A domestic waste and sewage dump for a village or burgh. A word of Scandinavian origin, it is still in use in Scotland and the English Pennines.

Millstone grit

Millstone grit is the name given to a number of coarse-grained carboniferous sandstones which occur in northern England. The name derives from its use in earlier times as a source of millstones for use principally in watermills. It is found in the Peak District, Pennines and neighbouring areas of northern England.

Miniver

Miniver is an unspotted white fur derived from the stoat, and with particular use in the robes of peers.

Mos Militum

A code of knightly ethics, loosely based on the ancient noble tradition of the Roman aristocracy and the influence of Islamic ethics, such as those of the Futuwwa, which appeared in the late eleventh century and formed the basis of the values of the Age of Chivalry.

Motte and bailey

A motte-and-bailey castle is a fortification with a wooden or stone keep (or donjon) situated on a raised earthwork called a motte, accompanied by an enclosed courtyard, or bailey, surrounded by a protective ditch and palisade. Relatively easy to build with unskilled, often forced labour, but still militarily formidable, these castles were built across northern Europe from the tenth century onwards, spreading from Normandy and Anjou in France, into the Holy Roman Empire in the eleventh century. The Normans introduced the design into England and Wales following their invasion in 1066.

Nobilissimus

From the Latin *nobilissimus* (most noble). Originally a title given to close relatives of the Emperor, during the Comneni period, the title was awarded to officials and foreign dignitaries.

Occitan

Also known as Lenga d'òc by its native speakers, Occitan is a Romance language spoken in southern France, Italy's Occitan Valleys, Monaco and Catalonia's Val d'Aran (the regions sometimes known unofficially as Occitania). It is also spoken in the linguistic enclave of Guardia Piemontese (Calabria, Italy). Occitan is a descendant of the spoken Latin language of the Roman Empire. It is an official language in Catalonia, known as Aranese in Val d'Aran. Occitan's closest relative is Catalan.

Ostmen

The Ostmen were the Norse-Gaels, a people who dominated much of the Irish Sea region, including the Isle of Man and western Scotland, for most of the Middle Ages. They were of Gaelic and Scandinavian (Viking) origin. Other terms used include Scoto-Norse, Hiberno-Norse, Irish-Norse and Foreign Gaels.

Oubliette

From the French, meaning 'forgotten place', this was a form of dungeon which was accessible only from a hole in a high ceiling. The word comes from the same root as the French *oublier* (to forget), as it was used to hold those prisoners that captors wished to forget.

Outremer

Outremer, French (*outre-mer*) for 'overseas', was a generic name given to the Crusader States established after the First Crusade: the County of Edessa, the Principality of Antioch, the County of Tripoli and especially the Kingdom of Jerusalem. The name equates to the 'Levant' of the Renaissance. The term was, in general, used to refer to any land 'overseas'; for example, Louis IV of France was called 'Louis d'Outremer' as he was raised in England. The modern term *outre-mer* (spelled with a hyphen) is used for the overseas departments and territories of France (*Départements d'outre-mer*).

Palliasse

A thin mattress of linen, wool or cotton, filled with animal hair, straw, wool or even sawdust.

Pectoral cross

A pectoral cross or pectorale, from the Latin *pectoralis* (of the chest), is a cross that is worn on the chest, usually suspended from the neck by a cord or chain. In ancient times pectoral crosses were worn by both clergy and laity, but during the Middle Ages the pectoral cross came to be indicative of high ecclesiastical status and was only worn by bishops and abbots.

Pennon

A small streamer-like flag, flown at the top of a knight's lance to signify his status. It would have a combination of one, two or three colours to identify him, his origins or the lord he served.

Pennyroyal

Pennyroyal is a plant in the mint family *Lamiaceae*. The leaves of the European pennyroyal exhibit a very strong fragrance similar to spearmint when crushed. Pennyroyal is a traditional culinary herb, folk remedy and abortifacient (a substance that induces abortion).

Phrygian cap

The Phrygian cap is a soft conical cap with the top pulled forward, associated in antiquity with the inhabitants of Phrygia, a region of central Anatolia. In the Roman Empire, it came to signify freedom and the pursuit of liberty, probably through a confusion with the pileus, the felt cap of emancipated slaves of ancient Rome. The Phrygian cap is sometimes called a liberty cap.

Pike

A pike is a pole weapon. It is a long, sometimes very long (even up to sixteen feet and beyond) thrusting spear used extensively by infantry. Unlike many similar weapons, the pike is not intended to be thrown, but is a defensive weapon, especially against cavalry. Pikes were used by the armies of Philip of Macedon and Alexander the Great and regularly in European warfare from the early Middle Ages until around 1700, wielded by foot soldiers deployed in close order. They were also common in the armies of Asia.

Pipe Rolls

Sometimes called the Great Rolls, they are a collection of financial records maintained by the English Exchequer, or Treasury. The earliest date from the twelfth century, and the series extends, mostly complete, from then until 1833. They form the oldest continuous series of records kept by the English government, covering a span of about 700 years.

Plenary indulgence

In Catholic theology, an indulgence is the full (plenary) or partial remission of temporal punishment due for sins. The indulgence is granted by the Church after the sinner has confessed and received absolution. They are granted for specific good works and prayers. Abuses in selling and granting indulgences were a major point of contention when Martin Luther initiated the Protestant Reformation, in 1517.

Postern

A postern is a secondary door or gate, particularly in a fortification like a city wall or castle curtain wall. Posterns were often located in a concealed location, allowing the occupants to come and go inconspicuously. In the event of a siege, a postern could act as a sally port, allowing defenders to make a sortie on the besiegers.

Pugio

Shorter than the gladius (the standard heavy, stocky sword of the Roman army), the pugio was a side-arm, a weapon of last resort, a tool of assassination and often a highly decorated status symbol for senior army officers and members of the equestrian class.

Purple

The colour of the robes of the emperors of Byzantium and, before them, the emperors of Rome and the early bishops of the Church. 'The Purple' has become synonymous with imperial rule, piety and tradition and purple is still regarded as the colour of power and authority.

Putrid fever

One of the many names for epidemic typhus. The name comes from the Greek *typhos* (hazy), describing the state of mind of those affected. Symptoms include severe headache, high fever, severe muscle pain, falling blood pressure, stupor, sensitivity to light and delirium.

Pyx

A pyx or pix, from the Latin *pyxis* (box-wood receptacle), is a small round container used in the Catholic, Old Catholic and Anglican Churches to carry the consecrated Host (Eucharist) to the sick or those otherwise unable to come to a church in order to receive Holy Communion.

Qaadi

A qaadi is a judge ruling in accordance with Islamic religious law (sharia) appointed by the ruler of a Muslim country. Because Islam makes no distinction between religious and secular domains, qaadis traditionally have jurisdiction over all legal matters involving Muslims.

Quarrel

A quarrel, or bolt, is the term for the ammunition used in a crossbow. The name is derived from the French *carré* (square), referring to the fact that they typically have square heads. Although their length varies, they are shorter than longbow arrows.

Routiers

Routiers were bands of mercenary soldiers, mainly infantry, dating from the mid-twelfth century. They were usually seen in France,

Aquitaine and Occitan but also in Normandy, England and the lands of the Holy Roman Emperor. They were noted for their lawlessness and ruthlessness. King John's use of mercenaries in his civil wars led to the condemnation and banishment of mercenaries in the Magna Carta, in 1215.

Sable

The sable is a species of marten which inhabits forest environments. Its range in the wild originally extended through European Russia to Poland and Scandinavia. It has historically been harvested for its highly valued dark-brown fur, which remains a luxury good to this day.

Sanctus bell

In the Roman Catholic Church and in some Lutheran, Anglican and Methodist churches, the sanctus bell, a small hand bell or set of bells, is rung shortly before the consecration of the bread and wine into the Body and Blood of Christ, and again when the consecrated elements are shown to the people.

Scapular

The monastic scapular dates from as early as the seventh century in the Order of Saint Benedict. It is a large length of cloth suspended both front and back from the shoulders of the wearer, often reaching to the knees. It may vary in shape, colour, size and style. Monastic scapulars originated as aprons worn by medieval monks and now form part of the habit of monks and nuns in many Christian orders.

Seax

A short, stabbing sword, sometimes as short as a dagger. Seax is an Old English term for 'knife'.

Senlac Ridge (or Hill)

The original name for the site of what is now known as the Battle of Hastings in 1066 between the Norman army of William, Duke of Normandy, and the English army of Harold, King of England. Victory for William led to a Norman dynasty on the English throne and a dramatic new course for English and British history. A few miles north of Hastings on England's south coast, it was originally known in English as Santlache (Sandy Stream), which the Normans changed into Sanguelac (Blood Lake) and which was then shortened to Senlac. Senlac Hill was approximately 275 feet (84 metres) above sea level, before the top of the ridge was levelled off to create Battle Abbey.

Shamshir

A shamshir is a type of sabre with a curve of five to fifteen degrees from hilt to tip. The name is derived from the Persian *shamshir*, which means 'sword'.

Sharbat

Sharbat (or sherbet) is a popular West and South Asian drink that is prepared from fruits or flower petals. It is sweet and served chilled. Popular sharbats are made of one or more of the following: rose, sandalwood, lemon, orange, mango or pineapple. The word 'sharbat' is from Persian and 'sherbet' is from Turkish, both of which in turn come from the Arabic *sharba* (a drink). The word is related to 'syrup' in English, *sorbet* in French and *sorbetto* in Italian.

'Song of Roland'

The 'Song of Roland' (in French *'La Chanson de Roland'*) is an heroic poem based on the Battle of Roncesvalles, in 778, during the reign of Charlemagne. It is the oldest surviving major work of French literature.

Succubae

In folklore traced back to medieval legend, a succubus (plural, succubae or succubi) is a female demon or supernatural being appearing in dreams who takes the form of a human woman in order to seduce men, usually through sexual intercourse. The male counterpart is the incubus.

Tabor

Tabor refers to a portable snare drum played with one hand. The word 'tabor' is an English variant of a Latin-derived word (*thabor*) meaning 'drum'. It has been used in the military as a marching instrument since antiquity, and also as accompaniment in parades and processions

Talwar

The talwar is a type of curved sword or sabre from the Indian sub-continent which was used in the Arab world throughout the Middle Ages and is still found in the modern countries of India, Pakistan, Bangladesh and Afghanistan.

'Te Deum'

The 'Te Deum' is an Ambrosian Hymn or A Song of the Church, an early Christian hymn of praise. The title is taken from its opening Latin words: *Te Deum laudamus* ('Thee, O God, we praise'). Saint Ambrose was Archbishop of Milan and became one of the most influential ecclesiastical figures of the fourth century. The Ambrosian Chant was named in his honour because of his contributions to the music of the Church.

Thegn

A local village chieftain of Anglo-Saxon England. Not a great land-owner or a titled aristocrat but the head of a village. Thus, thegns formed the backbone to the organization of Anglo-Saxon life. While serving with the army, usually as part of their service to the earl of their province, they formed a large part of the king's elite fighting force, the housecarls.

Theme

The Byzantine Empire was organized into military districts or themes, which reflected different nationalities within the Empire. Themes were responsible for generating their own regiments for the Emperor's army. In turn, retired soldiers were granted lands in the military theme from which they served. By the end of the eleventh century, there were thirty-eight themes in the Byzantine Empire, each composed of between 4,000 and 6,000 men, giving a standing army of approximately 200,000 men.

Tinchebrai, Battle of

The Battle of Tinchebrai was fought on 28 September 1106, in Normandy, between an invading force led by Henry I of England, and his older brother Robert Curthose, the Duke of Normandy. Henry's knights won a decisive victory, capturing Robert and imprisoning him in England and then Wales until Robert's death in Cardiff Castle. The battle itself only lasted an hour. Most of Robert's army was captured or killed. Besides Robert, those captured included Edgar the Atheling and William, Count of Mortain. Most of the prisoners were released, but Robert Curthose and William of Mortain were to spend the rest of their lives in captivity.

Trireme

Originally an Ancient Greek galley with three rows of oars, each above the other. It was a vessel of war and the oarsmen's strength could produce a ramming speed of significant impact.

True Cross

The legend of the True Cross first appeared in the fourth century. Supposedly either fragments of the cross, or the whole cross, on which Christ was crucified at Calvary, these were said to be housed in the Basilica of the Holy Sepulchre in Jerusalem. Around 1009, Christians in Jerusalem hid part of the cross and it remained hidden until the city was taken by the European knights of the First Crusade. Arnulf of Chocques, the first Latin Patriarch of Jerusalem, had the Greek Orthodox priests who were in possession of the cross tortured in order to reveal its position. The relic that Arnulf discovered was a small fragment of wood embedded in a golden cross, and it became the most sacred relic of the Crusader Kingdom of Jerusalem. It was housed in the Church of the Holy Sepulchre under the protection of the Latin Patriarch, who marched with it ahead of the army before every battle.

It was captured by Saladin during the Battle of Hattin, in 1187. While some Christian rulers, including Richard the Lionheart, the Byzantine Emperor Isaac II Angelus and Tamar, Queen of Georgia, sought to ransom it from Saladin, the cross was not returned and subsequently disappeared from historical records. However, several fragments of the cross are claimed to be genuine in many Christian places of worship – so much so that, at the end of the Middle Ages, the radical theologian John Calvin said that if all the pieces of the True Cross were to be added together, a ship could be made from the timber.

Turcopoles

From the Greek, meaning 'sons of Turks', they were locally recruited mounted archers employed by the Christian states of the Eastern Mediterranean. The crusaders first encountered Turcopoles in the Byzantine army during the First Crusade. These auxiliaries were the children of mixed Greek and Turkish parentage and were at least nominally Christian, although some may have been practising Muslims. The Turcopoles served as light cavalry providing skirmishers, scouts and mounted archers, and sometimes rode as a second line in a charge, to back up the Frankish knights and sergeants.

Umayyad Caliphate

The Umayyad Caliphate was the second of the four major Islamic caliphates established after the death of Muhammad. The caliphate was based on the Umayyad dynasty, hailing from Mecca.

Varangian Guard

The elite bodyguard of the emperors of Byzantium for several hundred years. They were well-paid mercenaries who also shared in the booty of the Emperor's victories, thus the Guard could attract the finest warriors. Most were drawn from Scandinavia and were often referred to as the 'Axemen of the North'. Their loyalty was legendary, as was their ferocity. It is thought many of Harold of England's surviving housecarls joined the Guard after the Battle of Senlac Ridge, in 1066.

Vellum

Vellum is derived from the Latin word *vitulinum*, meaning 'made from calf', leading to the Old French *vélin* (calfskin). Vellum is mammal skin prepared for writing or printing, to produce single pages, scrolls, codices or books. It is a near-synonym of the word 'parchment', but 'vellum' tends to be the term used for finer-quality parchment.

Ventail

See 'hauberk'.

Villein

Villein was a term used in the feudal era to denote a peasant (tenant farmer) who was legally tied to a lord of the manor. Villeins thus occupied the social space between a free peasant (freeman) and a slave. The majority of medieval European peasants were villeins. An alternative term is 'serf', from the Latin *servus* (slave). A villein could not leave the land without the landowner's consent. The term derives from Late Latin *villanus*, meaning a man employed at a Roman villa or large agricultural estate

Wimple

A wimple is a garment worn around the neck and chin, which usually covers the head. Its use developed among women in early medieval Europe. At many stages of medieval culture it was thought to be unseemly for a married woman to show her hair. A wimple might be elaborately starched, creased and folded in prescribed ways, or supported on a wire or wicker frame (cornette).

Genealogies

The English Monarchy from the House of Wessex to the
Plantagenets

The Eleventh- and Twelfth-Century Emperors of Byzantium

The Twelfth-Century Princes of Antioch

The Twelfth-Century Kings of Jerusalem

The Late-Twelfth-Century Popes

The Twelfth-Century Kings of France

The Twelfth-Century Holy Roman Emperors

The Twelfth-Century Kings of Navarre

The Twelfth-Century Kings of Sicily

The Twelfth-Century Rulers of Cyprus

The Twelfth-Century Grand Masters of the Knights Templar

The Twelfth-Century Grand Masters of the Knights Hospitaller

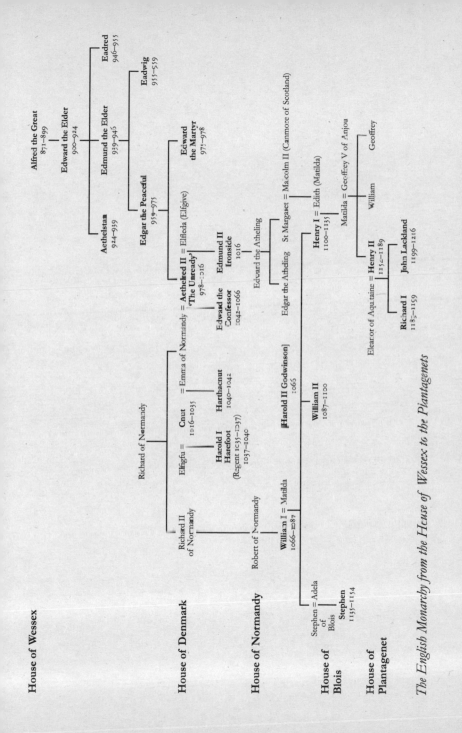

The English Monarchy from the House of Wessex to the Plantagenets

The Eleventh- and Twelfth-Century Emperors of Byzantium

Comnenian Dynasty

1081–1118	Alexius I Comnenus
1118–1143	John II Comnenus (the Beautiful)
1143–1180	Manuel I Comnenus (the Great)
1180–1183	Alexius II Comnenus
1183–1185	Andronicus I Comnenus

Angelus Dynasty

1185–1195	Isaac II Angelus
1195–1203	Alexius III

The Twelfth-Century Princes of Antioch

1098–1111	Bohemond I (Tancred, Prince of Galilee, regent, 1100–1103; 1105–1112)
1111–1130	Bohemond II (Roger of Salerno, regent, 1112–1119) (Baldwin II of Jerusalem, regent, 1119–1126; 1130–1131)
1130–1136	Constance (Fulk of Jerusalem, regent, 1131–1136)
1136–1149	Raymond of Poitiers (by marriage)
1153–1160	Raynald of Châtillon (by marriage)
1163–1201	Bohemond III (Raymond of Tripoli, regent, 1193–1194)

The Twelfth-Century Kings of Jerusalem

1099–1100	Godfrey (Protector of the Holy Sepulchre)
1100–1118	Baldwin I
1118–1131	Baldwin II
1131–1153	Melisende (with Fulk of Anjou until 1143; with Baldwin III from 1143)
1131–1143	Fulk of Anjou (with Melisende)
1143–1162	Baldwin III (with Melisende until 1153)
1162–1174	Amalric I
1174–1185	Baldwin IV the Leprous (with Baldwin V from 1183)
1183–1186	Baldwin V (with Baldwin IV until 1185)
1186–1190	Sybilla (with Guy of Lusignan)
1190–1192	Conrad I of Montferrat (disputed)
1192–1197	Henry I (II of Champagne) (with Isabella, half-sister of Sybilla)
1197–1205	Amalric of Lusignan (fourth husband of Isabella)

The Late-Twelfth-Century Popes

Number of Succession	Dates	Regional Name
171	1 September 1181–25 November 1185	Lucius III
172	25 November 1185–19 October 1187	Urban III
173	21 October 1187–17 December 1187	Gregory VIII
174	19 December 1187–20 March 1191	Clement III
175	21 March 1191–8 January 1198	Celestine III
176	8 January 1198–16 July 1216	Innocent III

The Twelfth-Century Kings of France

1108–1137	Louis VI (the Fat) (son of Philip I)
1137–1180	Louis VII (the Young) (son of Louis VI)
1180–1223	Philip II Augustus (son of Louis VII)
1223–1226	Louis VIII (the Lion) (son of Philip II Augustus)

The Twelfth-Century Holy Roman Emperors

Salian Dynasty

1086–1125   Henry V
             (elected 1099)

Supplinburger Dynasty

1075–1137   Lothair II
             (elected 1125)

Hohenstaufen Dynasty

1093–1152   Conrad III
             (elected 1138)
1122–1190   Frederick I (Barbarossa)
             (elected 1152)
1165–1197   Henry VI
             (elected 1191)
1176–1208   Philip of Swabia
             (elected 1198)

Welf Dynasty

1176–1218   Otto IV
             (elected 1198, as rival to Philip of Swabia;
             elected 1209 as sole Emperor)

The Twelfth-Century Kings of Navarre

1134–1150	García Ramírez (the Restorer) (son of Ramiro Sánchez of Monzón and Cristina Rodríguez Díaz de Vivar, daughter of El Cid)
1150–1194	Sancho VI (the Wise) (father of Bérengère)
1194–1234	Sancho (the Strong) (brother of Bérengère)

The Twelfth-Century Kings of Sicily

House of Hauteville

1105–1154	Roger II (the Great)
1154–1166	William I (the Bad)
1166–1190	William II (the Good)
1190–1194	Tancred of Lecce
1192–1194	Roger III (son of Tancred, co-regent)
1194	William III (brother of Roger, deposed)

House of Hohenstaufen

1194–1197	Henry I of Sicily (Holy Roman Emperor, elected 1190; married Constance, daughter of Roger II)
1197–1250	Frederick I of Sicily (Holy Roman Emperor, elected 1212)

Prior to 1184, Cyprus had been part of the Byzantine Empire since the division of the eastern and western parts of the Roman Empire, in 395. It remained Byzantine despite frequent Arab and Muslim raids and incursions, which caused great destruction and major loss of life.

In 1185, Isaac Comnenus, the great-grandson of John II Comnenus, Emperor of Byzantium from 1118 to 1143, inveigled his way into position as the island's ruler, declaring himself Emperor in 1189.

House of Comneni

1189–1191   Isaac (Emperor)

House of Lusignan

1192–1194   Guy
1194–1205   Amalric
             (The Lusignans ruled Cyprus until 1489)

1118–1136	Hugh de Payens (Founder and First Master)
1136–1147	Robert de Craon
1147–1151	Everard des Barres
1151–1153	Bernard de Tremelay
1153–1156	André de Montbard
1156–1169	Bertrand de Blanchefort
1169–1171	Philip of Milly
1171–1179	Odo de St Amand
1181–1184	Arnold of Torroja
1185–1189	Gerard de Ridefort
1191–1193	Robert de Sablé
1193–1200	Gilbert Horal
1201–1208	Phillipe de Plessis

The Twelfth-Century Grand Masters of the Knights Hospitaller

1099–1120	The Blessed Gerard (Founder and First Master)
1120–1160	Raymond du Puy de Provence
1160–1163	Auger de Balben
1162–1163	Arnaud de Comps
1163–1170	Gilbert d'Aissailly
1170–1172	Gastone de Murols
1172–1177	Jobert of Syria
1177–1187	Roger de Moulins
1187–1190	Armengol de Aspa
1190–1192	Garnier de Nablus
1193–1202	Geoffrey de Donjon

Maps

N

100 miles

100 km

Dunfermline

Durham • Monkwearmouth
✳
Ashgyll Force

York

Chester • Lincoln

Bourne • Norwich

Ely

Abergavenny • Oxford • Wivenhoe

Cardiff • Cirencester • London

Glastonbury • Canterbury

Salisbury • Winchester • Dover

English Channel

England in the Twelfth Century

Europe in the Twelfth Century

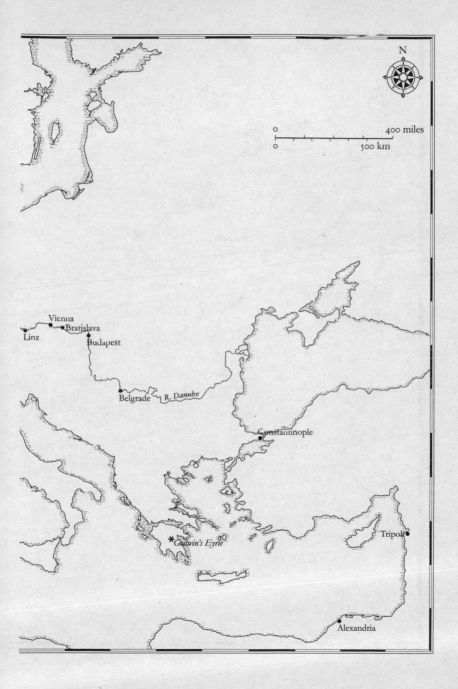

N

Genoa

Venice

Senj

Zadar

Vis

Rome

Messene

200 miles

200 km

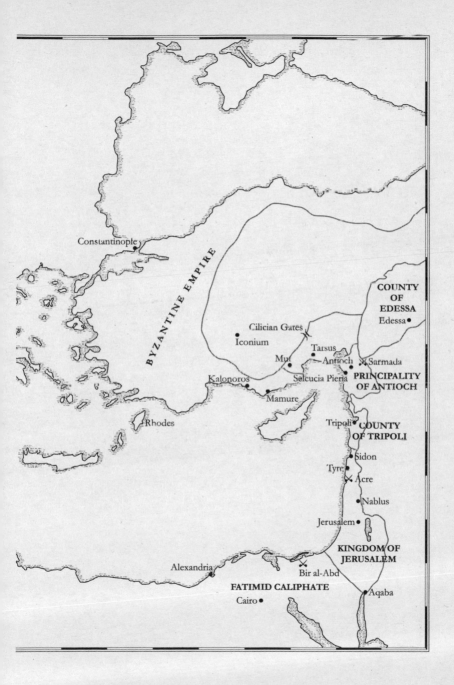

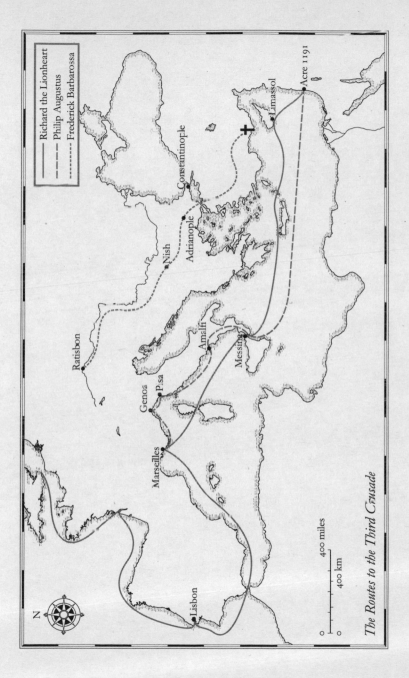

The Routes to the Third Crusade

N

Richard the Lionheart
Philip Augustus
Frederick Barbarossa

Acre 1191
Limassol
Constantinople
Nish
Adrianople
Ratisbon
Amalfi
Messina
Genoa
Pisa
Marseilles
Lisbon

0   400 miles
0   400 km

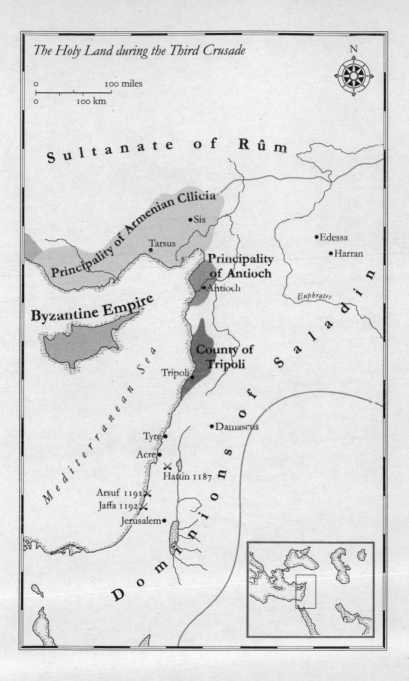

The Holy Land during the Third Crusade

N

0 — 100 miles
0 — 100 km

Sultanate of Rûm

Principality of Armenian Cilicia

• Sis

Tarsus •

Principality
of Antioch

• Antioch

• Edessa
• Harran

Euphrates

Byzantine Empire

County of
Tripoli

Tripoli •

Dominions of Saladin

Mediterranean Sea

• Damascus

Tyre •

Acre •

✕
Hattin 1187

Arsuf 1191 ✕
Jaffa 1192 ✕

Jerusalem •

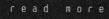

STEWART BINNS

CONQUEST

1066 – Senlac Ridge, England. William the Bastard, Duke of Normandy, defeats Harold Godwinson, King Harold II of England in what will become known as the Battle of Hastings.

The battle is hard fought and bloody; thousands of lives are spent, including that of King Harold. But England will not be conquered easily – the Anglo-Saxons will not submit meekly to Norman rule.

Although his heroic deeds will nearly be lost to legend, one man unites the resistance. His name is Hereward of Bourne, the champion of the English. His honour, bravery and skill at arms will change the future of England. His is the legacy of the noble outlaw.

This is his story.

'Stewart Binns has produced a real page-turner, a truly stunning adventure story'
Alastair Campbell

STEWART BINNS

CRUSADE

1072 – England is firmly under the heel of its new Norman rulers. The few survivors of the English resistance look to Edgar the Atheling, the rightful heir to the English throne, to overthrow William the Conqueror. Years of intrigue and vicious civil war follow: brother against brother, family against family, friend against friend.

In the face of chaos and death, Edgar and his allies form a secret brotherhood, pledging to fight for justice and freedom wherever they are denied. But soon they are called to fight for an even greater cause: the plight of the Holy Land.

Embarking on the epic First Crusade to recapture Jerusalem, together they will participate in some of the cruellest battles the world has ever known, the savage siege of Antioch and the brutal Fall of Jerusalem, and together they will fight to the death.

'A fascinating mix of fact, legend and fiction … this is storytelling at its best' *Daily Mail*